ALAMO HEIGHTS

Alamo Heights

a novel by Scott Zesch

Library of Congress Cataloging-in-Publication Data

Zesch, Scott.
    Alamo Heights : a novel / by Scott Zesch
cm.
    ISBN 0-87565-194-1 (alk. paper)
Alamo   Heights   (Tex.)—History—Fiction.   2.   Hispanic
Americans—Texas—San Antonio—Fiction. 3. Alamo (San Antonio,
Tex.)—History—Fiction. I. Title
PS3576.E765A46   1999
  813'.54—dc21   98-41219
                                                          CIP

Illustration and book design by Barbara Mathews Whitehead

ACKNOWLEDGMENTS

I never got tired of researching this story, and I'm indebted to many people at the following research centers who made my work more enjoyable: the libraries of the University of Texas at Austin, especially the Center for American History, the Harry Ransom Humanities Research Center, and the Nettie Lee Benson Latin American Collection; the San Antonio Public Library; the San Antonio Museum Association, particularly the Witte Museum, Bill Green, and Karen Branson; the Daughters of the Republic of Texas Library at the Alamo; the M. Beven Eckert Memorial Library in Mason, Texas; and the New York Public Library. In addition, L. Robert Ables' excellent article "The Second Battle for the Alamo," published in the January 1967 issue of *Southwestern Historical Quarterly*, pointed me in the right direction numerous times.

Laura Austin, my former teacher and favorite critic, scribbled comments on the original manuscript that were funny, insightful, and enormously useful. I'm also grateful to many others who read my drafts at various stages and offered their suggestions: Steve Adams; Jay Brandon; Marc Castle; Chan Chandler; Jane Dentinger; David Dreyfus; James Ward Lee; Norman Weiss; Gene Zesch; and Lucinda Zesch. Myrna Wallace and Sara Puig Laas helped me with the Spanish. Special thanks to Will and Melissa Reardon, who kept me informed of recent controversies involving the Alamo.

Most of all, I thank my editor, Judy Alter, and my agent, Victoria Sanders, for their counsel and encouragement, and for all their efforts on my behalf; and TCU Press, for giving me this opportunity.

For my Parents

I'll meet you at Alamo mission
We can say our prayers
And the Holy Ghost and the Virgin Mother will heal us
As we kneel there in the moonlight in the midnight

—Peter Rowan

The International Club of San Antonio
requests the honor of your presence
at a Reception and Banquet
in honor of

The Honorable Elihu Root
Secretary of State of the
United States of America

on Saturday, September 28, 1907
at Seven O'Clock in the Evening

The Colonial Room
Menger Hotel

R.S.V.P.   *Black Tie*

Antonio Herrera, Esq.
Secretary

Before daybreak on the morning of the accident, a 1904 Peerless tourer raced the length of River Avenue, missing mud puddles by inches and easily overtaking everything in its way. Fired by a four-cylinder, twenty-four-horsepower engine, the Peerless was built to run. And the driver—her auburn hair spilling out from beneath a veiled picture hat, her crimson motoring scarf trailing in the wind—was out to prove its prowess.

The narrow lanes of downtown San Antonio twisted and veered unexpectedly. She took those turns without braking.

A Mexican hay vendor pulled his wagon aside and stared. Passengers on the streetcar pointed. Two liverymen sneered. A horse started, nearly throwing a young cowboy spent from late-night carousing.

The driver ignored them all. Her name was Rose De León Herrera, and she was the first woman in San Antonio to drive her own motorcar. Her white Peerless was no commonplace machine; it was luxuriantly fitted with four brass headlamps, padded leather upholstery, and an ivy-green extension top. The vehicle rounded the corner at Commerce Street and headed toward the railroad station.

Outside the International and Great Northern depot, four members of the Ladies' Reception Committee, all sporting oversized coiffures, waited anxiously. Mrs. Herrera sped up beside them, sounding the Gabriel exhaust horn, and brought the automobile to a lurching halt. She grinned. Her front teeth were a bit large for her dainty mouth; but that only made her smile more disarming.

"Buenos días, ladies."

Edna Duvalier, a tall, frosty woman with no bosom, stepped forward and announced: "You're late."

"So is the train," replied Rose, unconcerned. She climbed down and brushed off her maroon linen duster. The other women started decorating the Peerless, draping it with chartreuse ribbons and miniature yellow roses.

The station platform had been transformed for the occasion into a jungle of palm sprays and trellises laced with honeysuckle. It was packed with dignitaries and well-wishers waving American flags. All this fuss was in honor of Elihu Root, who was passing through San Antonio on a diplomatic mission to Mexico.

Mrs. Herrera worked her way through the crowd. In the dawn's light the delicate blush of her fair complexion was just starting to bloom. She found her husband, Antonio, who had just come from breakfast with the Mexican envoys. Socially, this was a pivotal day for him.

"Did you check the Prest-O-Lite?" he asked her.

Silently she counted: uno, dos, tres . . . . They had discussed the motorcar's acetylene level four times since the night before. "Antonio. I won't be driving our guests in the dark. Why are you worried about the headlamps?"

"Because I don't want *anything* to go wrong."

She made a chipmunk face at him and pinched his cheek.

"Don't," he scolded. "Not here." But he could barely keep from beaming: *his* wife had been chosen from all the ladies of San Antonio to escort Mrs. Elihu Root on a tour of the city.

One person, however, had not wanted Rose Herrera to drive. Edna Duvalier resented her fellow clubwoman's influence in civic affairs. She located the Herreras on the platform. "Rose. Don't even think about taking Mrs. Root out to San José. We won't have time."

Mrs. Herrera turned to face her. Edna Duvalier had dark, heavy eyebrows that she arched threateningly whenever she sounded a battle cry. "Relax, Edna," said Rose. "If we're running late, we can skip the drive through Alamo Heights."

Mrs. Duvalier responded with a single bark of a laugh. "I think not." Her own house was on that part of the tour.

She had more to say, but just then the Ninth Infantry Band burst into rousing strains of Sousa. A mammoth locomotive eased its way into the station, its machinery churning and hissing as it inched to a halt. Moments later the Root party emerged from their private Pullman. The secretary of state, his wife and daughter, and their entourage of bureaucrats, aides and reporters negotiated the narrow iron steps with care, waving and trying to conceal their travel-weariness. The spectators cheered eagerly.

Mr. Root and his men boarded a Pierce Great Arrow bound for City Hall. The crowd surrounded the women as they prepared to leave on their tour. The Peerless was in line to take the lead. Up front with Rose Herrera sat Clara Root, an elegant woman with large doe-eyes. Edna Duvalier clambered into the tonneau, scowling and fanning herself impatiently. The second vehicle was a Ford Model C owned by a burly German brewer with a handlebar moustache. He was driving Miss Edith Root, along with Mrs. Root's private secretary and a reporter for the *San Antonio Journal*.

Mrs. Duvalier was still simmering. "Our driver is awfully determined, Mrs. Root," she remarked with a brittle laugh. "Wild horses couldn't drag me out to some old heap of rocks from 1776."

"1720," Rose corrected. "Mrs. Root, after we've seen Mission San José—"

"A ruin," mumbled Mrs. Duvalier.

"—we'll go look at some lovely new houses in the *suburbs*." Mrs. Herrera tightened her grip on the gearshift.

Clara Root studied the controls. "Isn't the Peerless a racing marque?" she asked.

"Why yes," answered the driver, surprised and delighted. She hadn't expected her guest to show an interest in motoring.

Mrs. Duvalier sighed. "Well, let's get ready for six miles of rough roads and dust and shantytowns."

Mrs. Root replied, "That's quite all right. I'm hardy."

"¡Bueno! So is my car," said Rose, with a triumphant wink at her guest. The Peerless took off with a jolt.

It was a cloudless and brilliantly sunlit morning. Within minutes the tenements of the city had dwindled to a few tumbledown adobe jacals and irrigated farms. The two motorcars passed through lustrous green fields of alfalfa and cotton, flourishing in the South Texas warmth and bordered by clusters of radiant yellow sunflowers. Bees, butterflies, grasshoppers all swarmed around the blossoms. The early autumn air was thick with the scents of mountain laurel and tilled earth, mingling with pungent traces of burnt motor oil.

Rose kept up an enthusiastic commentary while she dodged rocks and straddled boggy holes. "San José was the largest of the Franciscan missions here," she explained. Preserving the city's Spanish heritage was her passion, even more so than motoring.

The Peerless struck a bump. "For the love of Moses," hissed Mrs. Duvalier.

The driver ignored her. "It was known for its statues of the saints—until the cavalry started using them for target practice!" Impulsively she reached across and touched Mrs. Root's shoulder. "Most of the missions here have fallen into terrible disrepair."

"So of course we *must* see them," sniffed Mrs. Duvalier. "And use up an hour getting out there."

Rose glanced behind her. "An hour, Edna?"

The road had leveled enough for her to slip the Peerless into high gear. The automobile accelerated. Its engine rose in a steady crescendo.

Mrs. Duvalier panicked. "Rose—what's that noise? What are you doing?"

"Just keeping us on schedule, Edna."

"Rose, for God's sake—look out! Do you hear me?"

She did, but with a blast of the Gabriel horn, Mrs. Duvalier was silenced. Clara Root grabbed her seat.

The Ford was no match for the Peerless. The German driver waved his cap frantically, imploring Mrs. Herrera to slow down. She was about to do so when Mrs. Root shouted over the engine's roar: "Can you make it go faster?"

Rose beamed. She threw the transmission into final drive. Seconds later the meter registered forty, nearly forty-five miles per hour. The Model C's reflection in her side mirror grew smaller. Wind whipped through the open carriage. Edna Duvalier shrieked and held on to her hat, her crepe de chine veils encircling her arms like tentacles. But the two women up front ignored her, rapt in the heady sensation of wide-open speed.

Before long the ragged outline of Mission San José y San Miguel de Aguayo came into view. Rose pointed it out. Mrs. Root was hardly interested. "Faster, if you can!" she cried. "Go on!"

"If we hit fifty," yelled Rose, "it will be—"

She broke off suddenly, as if struck by a blow, and cut the throttle. "My God."

Clara Root strained to see what had startled the driver so. They had come upon a crew of Mexican men repairing the low wall that fronted Mission San José. The Peerless was losing momentum. Mrs. Herrera stared and groaned, "Oh God no. . . ."

"What is it?" asked Mrs. Root.

"Look! Concrete!"

It was true. That ancient wall, built of yellow stones carefully selected by long-gone Spaniards and perfectly stacked to maintain their balance—stones that were hand-chiseled, positioned and mortared under an artist's care—had been entirely concealed, encased in a faceless slab of cold gray concrete.

Then, from the back seat: "Rose, look out!"

"Oh!"

The Peerless stopped short with a smack. The impact jerked the women back and forth like three puppets. The engine coughed once, revived briefly, and died. Everything was still. Then steam started spewing from the radiator.

Rose crossed herself. "Oh God! Are you—is anyone—"

Stunned, the others said nothing. Then the two women in the front seat scurried down to inspect the damage: Mrs. Root checked the fender for scratches, and Mrs. Herrera kicked the ruined stone wall. Edna Duvalier remained in the back seat, clutching her collar, her eyebrows frozen at a severe angle.

The car had veered off the road and into a ditch. Its front tire had struck a low stack of cement sacks, ripping open the top one. Cement dust mixed with mist from the radiator, drifting across the shiny white hood.

The foreman of the work crew rushed toward them. He was a large-bellied Mexican man with a club foot.

"Never mind!" Rose shouted, waving him back. "Todo está bien. Everyone's all right."

But he wasn't concerned about their welfare. "¿Cómo? Look what you've done! That was a full sack of cement. Now you've spoiled it."

She bristled. "I certainly hope so."

He disregarded her. As the spray from the radiator subsided, the man examined the front wheels with grave deliberation. "You've got your wheel completely stuck in this ditch," was his verdict.

"Yes, I was born with eyes," she muttered.

The foreman motioned to a couple of the young Mexican laborers, who put aside their trowels and hurried over.

"Señora, qué buen chofer. How did you do this?"

"¡Cállese! Por favor. And why in the name of God is this wall covered in concrete?"

The man looked at her as if she were a lunatic. Then he and his two helpers threw their weight against the front grating and tried to rock the Peerless. It was stuck. The foreman looked up at Edna Duvalier and said, "Lady, you might want to step down."

"But you see, I don't," came the icy reply.

Rose assailed the man again: "Señor. Tell me why this wall is covered in concrete."

He was straining against the car and didn't answer at once. "Uh! Why do you think? To hold it up."

"And it's already set? You can't scrape it off?"

He didn't respond. She felt sick. She picked up a shovel and tried to knock some of the concrete off the rock wall. But the damage was already done.

"Look!" she exploded. "I'm Mrs. Herrera. I got this project started, and this wall was supposed to be—"

"¿Qué? I know who you are." The man was sweating and breathing hard. "But I take my orders from the city. You ladies wanted the rocks to show, but the council voted you down. That's what they call democracy."

Rose called it patronage. A local business magnate had recently opened a cement plant in San Antonio. His cronies on the city council were bending over backwards to oblige him with public contracts. She fumed.

"Besides," the foreman grunted, "what's wrong with concrete?"

"It's ugly."

"Well, it's modern, isn't it?"

"It's certainly not Spanish," replied Rose.

A rejoinder came from on high: "Nor is San Antonio — any more." It was Edna Duvalier, from her regal perch, finally avenged.

Rose glared at the foreman. "Pícaro! You should be ashamed. Now your grandchildren will never see what their ancestors built."

"Maybe not," said the man, grinning, "but they'll see what *I* built."

"And that's the pity."

Clara Root had kept her distance during this tiff. Now she was looking back down the road at the Ford Model C, gradually getting larger in the distance.

Mrs. Duvalier turned and saw it too. She snapped: "This is a fine mess, Rose. Now the *Journal* will really have something to report."

The wheel finally came clear of the ditch, and the automobile shifted back. The young men muttered in relief. But they were too late: the group in the Ford would certainly catch up and see that Rose Herrera had run off the road while driving Mrs. Elihu Root. It was an unspeakable calamity for the Ladies' Reception Committee and for all of San Antonio.

The women climbed back aboard. Then the foreman cranked the engine for them. It sprang to life.

Rose glanced meekly at her guest. "Mrs. Root, I'd never had a mishap. . . ."

The statesman's wife smiled to reassure her. "Rose, believe me, I'll always treasure this ride with you. Next time we'll break fifty."

The Ford pulled up beside them. Agog, the *Journal* reporter was already leaping to conclusions. The German driver leaned over and yelled, "Everything all right, ma'am?"

"We were just waiting for you," replied Rose. But the tire tracks, the ripped cement sack and Edna Duvalier's stormy countenance belied her.

Rose looked back at the foreman and sulked. "Gracias, señor. I suppose I'm indebted to you."

"No, but you owe the city for this sack of cement."

"Ssss!"

"Just don't expect me to be there the next time you wreck this thing," he grumbled. The reporter took note.

"Oh! You ought to get a medal," she scoffed.

"You ought to get a horse and buggy," he replied. "And a driver."

But she had already slipped the Peerless into gear and moved on.

Concrete. *Concrete!* She was still trembling, cursing the treachery of the city council under her breath. There would be hell to pay for this. And soon.

"Well," huffed Mrs. Duvalier, "what an adventure. Now we've all had our excitement for the day."

Mrs. Root grinned privately at the driver. Rose rolled her eyes in reply. They both knew that *that* was a foolish thing to say. It was ten o'clock and the day had just begun.

2

That evening should have been a triumph, the most extraordinary event yet in Antonio Herrera's burgeoning legal career—for he was finally *in.* Perhaps not entirely in: but as secretary of the International Club, he was in charge of the great banquet, the culmination of the festivities honoring Elihu Root. He had finally arrived at the portal of San Antonio society. During the previous weeks he had devoted himself fanatically to the banquet, agonizing over every detail. It seemed that, in one way or another, he had spent a good many of his forty years preparing for this event.

In months to come, his resentment still festering, he would wonder how his own wife could have robbed him of *his* evening so unexpectedly. He got the first devastating report from his law partner, Horatio Franck. Who had heard the news from his wife, Augusta. Who had attended the ladies' luncheon, where it was relayed from ear to disbelieving ear in unmuffled titters. The blow was so crippling that Mr. Herrera had left the Root reception at City Hall feeling queasy.

It was inexcusable. God damn it—inconceivable! His wife was the undisputed master of the motorcar. Of all days for an accident!

That night at the Menger Hotel he looked for her. The balconied rotunda hummed with the small talk of elegantly attired men and women. They drifted around marble columns and decorative Queen Anne screens, as the last rays of the gloaming filtered through the stained-glass skylight and cast tinted shadows across their faces. These were powerful people, every one.

Then he saw her: a pillar of burgundy silk across the room, standing alone by the potted palms. As he approached, she looked up and smiled warmly. Her nonchalance infuriated him.

"How did it happen?" He interrogated her in a low tone to avoid attention.

Her face fell, and she took his arm. "Antonio, I'm sick about it. They've covered the whole wall at San José. With concrete! From the west corner—"

"I don't care about the wall. How in the hell did you run off the road?"

"How do you think! I took one look at that concrete."

"For God's sake! What about Mrs. Root?"

"Clara? She's fine. It was nothing." Avoiding his glare, she moved ahead into the crowd, her rage over the wall renewed. She was aching to lash out at any city councilman present.

He pursued her closely. "Damn it, Rose. It wasn't *nothing*. And you can't keep something like that quiet."

But this was no time for a spat. Elihu Root was being escorted from the refreshment pavilion to the stately dining room.

Mr. Herrera took his wife's elbow. "Come." He led her toward the procession.

This was it. The Root banquet—Antonio Herrera's rite of passage into the circle of the elite—would proceed as planned, automobile accident or not.

3

The last guest to arrive at the banquet was Wilton Peck of Philadelphia. Hurrying across the empty rotunda, he tore off his hat and hurled it toward an attendant. At a long mirror he paused to straighten the part in his graying hair. Then he slipped into the banquet hall, glancing around nervously. The consommé was already on the tables.

"Damn it," he muttered.

Mr. Peck was a newcomer to San Antonio. He was late for the banquet because of an artist. That fact was especially galling to him. Artists made him uncomfortable, and he didn't mix with them as a rule.

But on this occasion he'd had no choice. His employer, the Willingham Hotel Company of Philadelphia, had sent him out alone to handle every particular of its new hotel project here, including artwork.

San Antonio didn't agree with Wilton Peck. He found it rough-edged and isolated. Beneath its facade of modern brick buildings were latent traces of its frontier past, suddenly surfacing in the form of a drunken fandango or knife fight. The town had too many cowboys and Mexicans. And the women here were unusually forward, which unnerved him.

However, success in the Alamo City meant promotion back home. So, uncomplainingly, Wilton Peck had set out for the hinterlands. His first purchase in San Antonio had been a pair of Lucchese Brothers cowboy boots that he absolutely despised. But he was determined to fit in. By God, he was going to tough it out in Texas until the Willingham Palace made headlines, and his own comfortable niche in Philadelphia was secure.

Peck was a man of modest stature and a trim frame, in an era when physical mass was a measure of a man's significance. He was also afflicted with a nervous tic: whenever he got flustered, he let out a single loud hiccup, produced by a sharp intake of breath. Aware of his shortcomings, he knew he would have to work especially hard to make his presence felt. And so he did. A cunning operator in the private offices of City Hall, he called on the local officials, plying them with gifts of cigars and whiskey. At the Business Men's Club he glad-handed the mayor. And late one evening in Brackenridge Park, he let himself be violated in a buggy by a councilman's boorish daughter.

But Wilton Peck's most important task, not yet finished, was securing a site for the new hotel. He was on the verge of buying a lot that would give the Willinghams the best location in the city: next door to the Alamo. Someday, he hoped, the Willingham Palace could incorporate the Alamo itself as a tourist mecca, complete with a gift shop, and charge admission.

For the hotel's lobby, Peck had decided to commission a sculpture by Mathilda Guenther, a German artist who had built her reputation in Europe and now made her home in San Antonio. Like many artists, Madame Guenther lived across the river in the Bohemian neighborhood of La Villita, which, to Mr. Peck's way of thinking, was nothing but a den of European hedonists. He wandered among the plain, tidy cottages until he located her house, a large block of yellow brick with columned galleries attached to both stories. The first floor was her studio, the second her apartment. He climbed the steps and rang the bell. Eventually the door was opened by an ancient black man with a formal, cross demeanor.

"Wilton Peck to see Madame Guenther. Please." The hotel man produced his card.

The doorkeeper took the card reluctantly. "Madame is in the process of creation," he sniffed, "and cannot be disturbed."

Peck had been warned beforehand that the eccentric artist admitted only those callers who interested her. This snub made him mad. "I've come about the hotel commission. She must have received my message."

The doorkeeper said nothing but turned and vanished into the unlit hall. Peck was left standing on the gallery for an insultingly long time, while a German baker next door repeatedly played the same polka on a concertina. When the black man finally returned, he simply motioned for Peck to follow.

Mathilda Guenther's studio was a huge, cluttered room with a bare concrete floor. The air seemed unnaturally cool, and Peck imagined himself in a mausoleum. The half-formed clay figures, with their odd shapes and missing limbs, made him shiver. Somber busts stared at him, reminding him of death masks.

In the intense glare of a factory lamp sat the artist, a bulky woman in a peculiar black frock that extended only slightly below her knees, her lower limbs covered with buttoned black leggings. Her hair was pulled back in a severe knot. She was older than he had expected: sixty, sixty-five perhaps. He recalled that her art had been dormant for several years while she set up a utopian colony in East Texas, from which had come rumors of experimental herbs, radical Negroes, and free love.

Madame Guenther was modeling a life-sized figure of a powerful man in a reclining position. Her hands and forearms were caked in white clay. She didn't look up at him.

"Come in, Mr. Peck." Her voice was authoritative, with a distinct German accent.

He moved closer. "Madame Guenther, I don't believe I've had the honor—"

He stopped short. Out leapt one of his loud hiccups. On the other side of the artist, stretched out on a pallet in casual repose, was a young man of tremendous proportion—completely naked. And what was it about the man's posture? Was he—surely not. Peck couldn't help but look. Good God! The man's wrists and ankles were strapped to the pallet with leather bands. He wondered what incredible sort of perversion . . . .

The naked oaf looked up indifferently at Peck, who hiccuped again. Madame Guenther stopped working as she became aware of her visitor's unease. "On the floor there—that is my Prometheus. Known to the plebeian world as Mickey Dye. And you met my man Silas Toombs on your way in." She turned to her model. "Strain," she commanded quietly, breaking off into coughs. The man on the floor half-heartedly pushed against the leather bands to give her a pose of struggle.

Madame Guenther resumed shaping the clay figure's torso. "You've come about the hotel piece."

Peck tried to collect himself. "Yes, the new Willingham Palace, downtown. We're hoping to build it next to the Alamo. Where the Hugo & Schmeltzer warehouse is, uh, is now. After it's torn down, of course."

The room became uncomfortably quiet. "Umm."

"This will be—"

Prometheus shifted and yawned, carelessly exposing his member. Peck winced but stifled another hiccup.

"Madame Guenther, this will be a first-class hotel, like nothing this part of the country has ever seen."

"Umm." She stopped her work and coughed again. "Mr. Dye. You can unbind yourself."

The model tore free of the leather straps, stood upright a full six feet, scratched his thigh uncouthly, and, to Wilton Peck's relief, put on a robe.

The sculptor turned her full attention to her caller. "So what do you have in mind?"

Peck came aglow, illustrating his thoughts with his arms. "An Alamo scene, Madame Guenther. You're the only artist who could do this. A whole panorama of the battle of the Alamo, stretching across an entire wall. Maybe across the whole lobby."

The artist watched him intently. Her eyes were blue ice.

"Colonel Travis, Jim Bowie, Kit Carson—was he there?—no, Davy Crockett, I think it was. With Santa Anna's army climbing over the walls by the thousands. The last stand."

Madame Guenther raised her eyebrows, mocking. "All these figures, Mr. Peck?"

"Not a free-standing sculpture, of course. We won't have room for
that. The kind where the figures are—you know, posed against the
wall, like a mural. What do you call it?"

"Bas-relief," the woman answered coolly.

"That's it. Bas-relief."

"Umm." Madame Guenther deliberated for a long time. When
she finally spoke, it was without emotion. "Mr. Peck, in my experience, bas-relief sculpture is appropriate for only one thing. And that
is to decorate a tombstone."

Peck flushed in indignation. "Madame, this piece will put your
name in the limelight. It'll take up an entire wall."

The woman suddenly pounded her fist on the table, sending clay
flying. "You are stuck on this idea—an entire wall! You confuse
breadth with art. What you are describing is—how would one say
it?—*art by the square yard.*"

Peck was taken aback. "Madame."

"I know the kind of monument you speak of. Filled with clichés!
Something that will be an ornament to the room."

"Absolutely not."

She went back to work with a dismissive wave. "Mr. Peck, you say
I am the only artist who could do this. Well, I am sure you can find
any number of tombstone cutters who can do this—this *thing* you
want. You don't need an artist."

By now the corporate chameleon had lost all coloring of civility.
He was shaking. "Madame, the Willingham Palace will be the finest
hotel in the Southwest. And we have the money to hire the finest
artist. I don't have to consort with—with anarchists and—crackpots
who keep naked men—" He hiccupped.

Madame Guenther breathed deeply to dispel her anger. Then she
coughed. "Mr. Dye." Prometheus extinguished his cigarette and let
his robe fall.

The artist turned to her visitor. "What you see here, Mr. Peck, is
titled 'Prometheus Bound.' At first my client wanted something not
so conflicted. But I convinced her that the Titan rebel must show us

15

both struggle and repose. Perhaps, in time, you will come around and see that I am right. When you change your mind, and your attitude, I might reconsider your proposal."

He was astounded. "Madame, whatever gave you the impression I would offer you a second chance at this job?"

She looked at him with no trace of ill will. "If you want first-rate sculpture in Texas, Mr. Peck, you have no other choice."

She was right, and that made him even madder. "I'm sorry I've wasted your time and mine," he snarled. The housekeeper Toombs already had his hat waiting for him.

"I will send you my answer tomorrow, Mr. Peck," the woman called after him. But he was already out the front door.

The whole incident—the naked man, the insolent artist, the sullen Negro—had so flustered Peck that he had lost track of time. When he left the artist's lair, he was unable to get a carriage or a streetcar to Alamo Plaza; he had to huff all the way from La Villita to the Menger Hotel on foot. He had missed the pre-dinner reception altogether: a valuable opportunity to ingratiate himself with the city's prime movers.

Art by the square yard!

Never again, Peck vowed. Never again would he deal directly with artists. Madame Guenther had given him his first defeat in San Antonio, and by God it was going to be his last. He brooded through all the banquet courses, even well into coffee.

Two hundred Texans and their guests from Washington and Mexico City had been treated to a procession of lobster canapes, caviar and black bread, consommé julienne, soft-shell crabs, asparagus aspic, filet mignon with béarnaise sauce, grouse with truffles, salad jardiniere, celery, olives, hard rolls, cheeses, and raspberry glacé, each entree accompanied by a complementary wine. When coffee was served Antonio Herrera finally relaxed. The accident in the Peerless was forgotten, the equilibrium restored. His evening was a triumph after all.

His wife was entertaining a young man across the table with tales of the early Spanish friars, punctuated with digs at the city council for neglecting the missions. Although it was her habit to observe the rules of propriety and gracious behavior, Rose Herrera wasn't at all shy. Old-timers said she had inherited the excitable spirit and panache of her De León ancestors.

With the evening under control, Mr. Herrera gazed at his wife with pride. He had married into royalty. Both her parents descended from the oldest stock in San Antonio, the Canary Islanders of 1731. Those first Spanish settlers had been a brave but contrary lot, constantly locking horns with the viceroys and mission priests in land disputes. In every generation since then, Mrs. Herrera's forebears had thrown themselves into some kind of public strife. Her grandfather, Francisco De León, had died fighting at the Alamo in 1836; that single act of valor redeemed a multitude of her own father's less noble scrapes.

Her next birthday would be her thirty-eighth, and her arms and waist tended toward fullness now. But her face, her delicate hands were still smooth. Her auburn hair was piled in an elegant bouffant dome, a single rebellious strand dangling down the nape of her neck.

She turned. In profile her bosom was ample; occasionally the peaks of her breasts showed through her corset. Antonio could still picture that form, unclad and pale and young, against the brazen orchid sheets she once had favored. It had been a long time ago. Her arms were slender then, her hair long and unpinned, falling across her rounded shoulders in great billowy folds. In his mind he traced the curves of her breasts, the contours pressed in his memory like faded floral tokens; he recalled the way he had stared, a callow young man, fascinated by the prominence of the nipples—Good God! he tried not to think of that, not now—how those nipples, the same rouge color as her lips, had slipped through his fingers and brushed warm against his bare chest. He remembered the scent of lavender on her, and the fragrance of honeysuckle blossoms that drifted across their bed on light summer wafts as she cried out in tiny sharp breaths. Back then she had loved him without restraint, banishing any false modesty from their private life.

Suddenly he realized he was aroused. Blushing, he drew himself close to the table and leaned forward.

The program began. Rose ended her conversation. She took his hand, and he clasped hers.

The toastmaster was Senator H. B. "Hobo" Pratt of Laredo. He welcomed the guests, recognizing the dignitaries present.

The Washington delegation: cheers!

The envoys of President Díaz: salud!

Governor Campbell, Mayor Callaghan: to your health!

The ladies: Mrs. Clara Root, Miss Edith Root.

Several others, including a local historian—

"—who for years has worked like the dickens to preserve our state's Spanish landmarks: Mrs. Rose De León Herrera. Y'all give this little lady a big hand."

That toast came as a surprise. At the head table Clara Root

applauded warmly. Perhaps this was her doing. Across the room Edna Duvalier told her companions: "You'd think he'd have enough horse sense not to mention *her*, after this morning."

Antonio released his wife's hand to applaud. He was proud, of course; but it also gnawed at him. This wasn't her evening.

Then, in horrified disbelief, he watched everything come undone, as his perfectly planned banquet disintegrated into a nightmare. His wife should have acknowledged her accolades with a modest nod. A smile at most. Nothing, *nothing* in the senator's toast had given her any further license. But amidst the applause, she stood up to respond.

"Senator Pratt, Secretary and Mrs. Root, emissaries of President Díaz, ladies and gentlemen, you are much too kind to recognize me when there are far more distinguished guests present. Pardon me for reminding you: if we San Antonians sing the praises of our heritage to our visitors, then let our city council conceal that heritage with concrete—*concrete*, mind you—our words are just noisy gongs and clanging cymbals. Shame on us! I urge you all to go out and see what the city has done to the wall around San José. Then join me in fighting this type of mindless commercialism. Thank you."

There was a stunned silence. Most people's glasses were still suspended midair. Even the loquacious Senator Pratt didn't know what to say. Mrs. Duvalier, embarrassed for the Ladies' Reception Committee and for all of Texas, made a production of hiding her face in her hands.

Then, quickly, Clara Root broke out in vigorous applause. A few of Mrs. Herrera's club sisters joined her. The response from the other guests was barely polite.

Rose sat down. Suddenly weak, she stared into her coffee cup. Her husband said nothing as he turned away. But the pressure of his stony silence became so intense that, before the next speaker was through, her composure was shattered. At the first break in the program, she got up.

Without looking at her, Antonio whispered, "If you dare move as much as an eyebrow—"

"Please, I need some air." She took advantage of a full round of applause welcoming the secretary of state, winding her way through the long white tables and out of the dining hall.

Two men watched her go. One was her husband. The other, in the rear of the big room, stared perplexed at the figure with the auburn bouffant hair. Wilton Peck wondered what to make of this Mexican lady who had caused such a stir. Whoever she was, he certainly wouldn't want her as an enemy. In fact, his run-in with Madame Guenther had reminded him that he couldn't afford to make any enemies until he had safely acquired the lot by the Alamo. And this Herrera woman might even be a useful ally. Early next week he would make it his business to win her confidence.

5

B y that time the sky was black and heavy with clouds. The Menger patio, sheltered within the hotel's wings, was lit only by a few gas globes. She followed the flagstone walkway, overgrown with an abundance of bougainvillea and elephant ears. Near the fountain she sat on a wrought-iron bench. Several parakeets were fussing in the palms and pomegranate trees.

Through the tiny lattice panes of the bay window, she could barely make out the figures of the guests in the Colonial Room. She wondered how Antonio was holding up. Ten minutes had gone by since she left the banquet, and he hadn't come to retrieve her.

She was certain he would never completely forgive her for that tirade. In all honesty, she couldn't blame him. It had been a rash, impulsive act: the De León in her. She hadn't considered the consequences. What's more, lashing out at the city council hadn't given her the satisfaction she wanted. She had only drawn attention to her own failure to prevent their shameful action.

She prayed that her speech wouldn't be mentioned in the paper the next morning. Antonio would accuse her of splashing her name across the *Journal* once more.

"My club work is good for your career," was her usual response. They both knew that wasn't entirely true. He was a real-estate attorney. And she was gaining a reputation as a foe to developers, as she became increasingly embroiled in the public squabbles for which San Antonio, the cradle of revolution in Texas, was famous.

She was sorry she had mortified Antonio with her speech, before he'd even had time to recover from the automobile incident. Truly she did want her husband to succeed, if only because he craved approval so badly. But she wasn't able to maintain the course he desired of her. For a time, to placate him, she had kept Tuesday as her at-home day for receiving callers. It was no use. Each Tuesday some civic skirmish inevitably flared up at City Hall—another landmark threatened with desecration—taking her away from home.

Her husband fretted over any break with convention, and she understood why. The son of a mail carrier from the West Side, he still felt like an imposter. Having climbed to a respectable position through good luck and hard work, he was desperate to secure his footing, terrified that one small misstep would land him back in obscurity. Antonio Herrera had few confidants. Only rarely did he visit his family or boyhood friends. Nor did he enjoy social functions in Alamo Heights, which he approached with all the apprehension of a final examination. Herrera kept to himself and his work and his orchard, which had come to occupy his time at home.

She had first met her husband at the Mexican Social Club's Christmas ball in 1889. At nineteen, Rose De León was thought to be on the road to spinsterhood. That didn't bother her nearly as much as it did her family. An honors graduate of Ursuline Convent, she was prepared to support herself by teaching and writing popular histories.

Antonio had just finished his law studies in Mexico City. When he returned to San Antonio, the old Tejano elite had taken the impoverished young man under their wing. He was intelligent, honest and eager to please. Dressed in a tawdry black suit that fit him like a burlap sack, he seemed overwhelmed at the ball. His attempts at social protocol amused her at first, then garnered her sympathy as the evening went on. He tried so hard.

For an hour he studied the other dancers as the brass band played sentimental favorites. Then he invited her to join him in a waltz. They were an ungainly couple on the floor. He kept running over her feet and blushing. A little rusty herself—she hadn't danced in the four years since her father died—she was unable to cover for him.

"Please forgive me, Señorita De León," he would murmur each time, very formally and in English.

She struggled not to laugh but eventually gave in. "Counselor, if you would stop reminding my ears," she teased him, "my feet wouldn't notice half so much."

She was afraid she had hurt his feelings. But after a moment he smiled too. Later he took her elbow and led her outside. In the December chill, they stood contented beneath the yellow glow from the windows. Moments later his arm stretched gently around her waist. She placed her hand on his lapel. His breast felt reassuring. The Antonio she fell in love with was endearingly naive and entirely genuine.

At San Fernando Cathedral they took their vows in the summer of 1890. At first they had known great happiness together. But before they had lost their youth they would bury two children. Gradually he gave himself to his work, she to hers. Her preservation fights—and more recently her motoring—had rejuvenated her. But the more laurels Antonio gained in his law practice, the more his spirit receded, replaced by an excess of caution.

Relations in the Herrera household had become strained. The couple went their separate ways and talked past each other at the dinner table. Recently their son had started slipping out of his room late at night, not to return until daybreak.

Her husband blamed her for that. "You let him run wild. Why can't a woman with your abilities keep track of only one child and two servants?"

What hurt her, even after all these years, was his reference to only one child. "Enrique is sixteen years old," she would retort. "And he *is* part De León; he has to breathe a little. What am I supposed to do, hire a nanny?"

But the boy's absences worried her, too. All that day she hadn't seen him, and she feared he had run off again. She hadn't told her husband.

Rose sighed, a slow sigh of surrender. Then she stood up and circled the quiet, deserted patio before she went back into the rotunda. It was nearly time for Mr. Root's address. She would need to take her seat quickly. Antonio would probably sue her for divorce if she made her entrance while the secretary of state was speaking.

Of course, by this time Antonio would have made all the necessary excuses for her absence. He was no longer awkward in society, the shy, earnest law student from the West Side stepping on schoolgirls' toes and murmuring apologies. Now his manners, like his clothes, were perfect.

Oh, Antonio, she thought. *Antonio.*

She peered through the doors of the dining hall. The sight of the guests sickened her. Seated in that room, belching and sweating from overeating, were the fat, self-important men who were reaping huge profits from encasing her city's heritage in concrete.

She stood there for a moment, deliberating. Then she turned and walked quickly in the opposite direction, through the hotel lobby, brightly lit and bustling with bellhops, past the mahogany reception desk and potted palms and out the front door. Antonio's powerful people could go to hell. She needed to visit her grandfather.

6

The solitary figure in burgundy silk passed by the open windows of the billiards room, strolling alongside the queue of carriages and automobiles on Alamo Plaza. Little of Mexico, even less of Spain, was still visible in the plaza. Soon the old San Antonio of hand-carved stones and bright decorative tiles would look like every other city in America. Often the Chamber of Commerce lauded the city's Mexican charm and color. But privately, the new merchants saw no profit in charm and were wary of too much color. Their shops were built of workaday brick.

Rose Herrera kept walking into the darkness, past the transfer company, the stable, the undertaker's parlor: then across Crockett Street and along the row of dingy boarding houses and saloons. At the north end of Alamo Plaza she stopped directly in front of its namesake. The chalk-stone chapel of the Alamo, tarnished by time and neglect, looked lonely at night. Set back from the street lamps, its chiseled columns and bell-shaped parapet were almost hidden in the long shadows.

The modern downtown had all but swallowed up the old Spanish mission compound of San Antonio de Valero, popularly known as El Alamo. Only two of its many buildings still stood. One was the well-known chapel of 1757. The other was the adjacent convent, later used as a barracks by the military. It was in the small rooms of the convent that many of the Texas rebels had perished in hand-to-hand fighting during the war for independence from Mexico.

But over the decades the Alamo convent had suffered much more neglect and degradation than the chapel. It currently served as the Hugo & Schmeltzer grocery company's warehouse. An astonishingly tacky wooden shell completely disguised the original stone walls. Topping it was a crenellated rim and an octagonal sentry tower with protruding toy cannons. Rose shook her head in dismay. Although the design of the warehouse facade had been intended to reflect the revolutionary history of the plaza, the result looked less like a fortress than an amusement park arcade.

Rose had a key to the Alamo chapel. The state owned the property, but, as president of the San Antonio Chapter of the Daughters of the Republic of Texas, she was the official custodian. That morning she had given Clara Root a tour of the premises. Now she was going to have a private look. She approached the massive arched doorway and fumbled at the lock.

"You there. Who's that?"

She glanced over her shoulder. A policeman was approaching from the plaza.

"You can't go in there," he said.

"It's all right, Poppy."

The slender gray-haired man drew closer and squinted. "Oh— Mrs. Herrera. I couldn't see who it was."

"No, of course not." She glanced down politely when she saw the tobacco spittle running along his chin.

"I beg your pardon, ma'am."

She was at a loss to explain. "I was over at the Menger. I just thought I'd check on a few things. From this morning."

"Certainly, ma'am. Can I help you with the lock there?"

"Gracias, no—I've got it."

The door swung open before her. Inside, the cavernous stone sanctuary was dark and empty.

"Here. You'll need a torch," he offered.

"No, I'll manage. The shutters aren't fastened."

"Aren't you scared to be going in there alone?"

She smiled at him. "I enjoy the quiet."

He raised his eyebrows. "Whatever you say, ma'am. Have a pleasant evening." He went back to walking his beat.

She liked the Alamo chapel at night. Her father once told her an old legend that had frightened her as a child: when General Andrade's men tried to destroy what was left of the Alamo after the battle of 1836, they were warded off by spirits with flaming swords. The legend no longer frightened Rose. In fact, she was comforted by the idea of being surrounded by supernatural protectors. There were spirits here, she felt; but somehow they seemed rueful now, not vengeful.

The windows high overhead provided just enough light for her to navigate through the sanctuary. On either side of her were gaping doorways leading into small dark chambers. The one she entered was the sacristy, where Mrs. Dickinson and the Mexican women had huddled during the two-hour battle. From there, Rose passed through a low door into the adjacent Hugo & Schmeltzer warehouse. It was not part of the state property. But to her, although the building was now used as a grocer's storeroom, it was still the convent of the Alamo. She claimed a right as official custodian to enter it.

The long stone corridor was lined with whiskey crates and smelled of mildew. She felt her way to the main warehouse, where cracks in the shutters admitted thin shafts of light from the plaza. Something scurried out of her path: a mouse, or maybe a lizard. She kept moving. Her gown was collecting dust at the hem; but she didn't plan to go back to the banquet. Her object was just ahead: the musty compartment on the southwest corner.

She pushed open the heavy wooden door. Then she took a deep breath and waited for her eyes to adjust. This was what she had come for. It was the room where her grandfather died.

There was no rational reason why, after so many visits to this room, it still overwhelmed her. Just standing on this site of so much sudden and violent death made her tremble. Leaning into the wall, she concentrated on etching every angle and crevice into her memory again.

Here the De León family had set its course. Had her grandfather been more politic, Rose Herrera might have become the señora of a large hacienda in Mexico. Francisco De León had once been a close confidant of General Santa Anna. But when the Mexican president placed his own will above the restraining hand of the law, her grandfather broke ranks. Like his fellow loyal Tejanos—Captain Juan Seguin, Francisco Ruiz, José Antonio Navarro—Francisco De León had cast his lot with the Texas rebels against their Mexican rulers. Sometimes she suspected her grandfather was just looking for a good fight.

If he was, he had found it.

This room had been his final refuge. Here Francisco De León—federalist, gentleman, and scholar—fought alongside American yahoos who couldn't even write their names. His six-year-old son, Fermin, hid in the sacristy next door with Mrs. Dickinson and the women. Whatever thoughts De León was able to muster at the end, any revelations he might have had as he faced the consequences of his bravado, came to him within these walls.

They didn't shelter him long. Soon he took the muzzle shot and the bayonet. One by one, the last of his rebel comrades howled and raged and sank into the rubble. Then all was still.

That day heralded the dawn of the new independent Republic of Texas. It was also the beginning of the end for the De Leóns and others like them. The American yahoos, who remembered the Alamo with a vengeance, didn't remember the Mexicans kindly, no matter which side they had taken during the fight against Santa Anna. News of recriminatory raids at Victoria and La Bahía caused many Tejanos to abandon their homes and flee. Like it or not, Rose De León Herrera was an heir to all that had come out of the Alamo. It had claimed her as one of its own.

Fortune did not take pity on the rebels who survived the battle. The Alamo would continue to exact its price for the rest of their lives. Mrs. Dickinson and her daughter had drifted into unhappy marriages, penury and harlotry. Travis' slave Joe, who fought at the colonel's side, was returned to a life of bondage and hunted down when he tried to escape.

Mrs. Herrera's own father, Fermin De León, gradually lost everything he held dear. When Francisco De León died in glory, he left a legacy of land, influence and nobility. At the time of his son's death, just after he'd lost Tres Piedras Ranch, the De Leóns were clinging to what was left of their nobility.

And so Rose Herrera remembered the Alamo in her own way. It was a monument to an ideal her grandfather was willing to forfeit his life for. His hazy dream of a democratic republic had been derailed by unscrupulous adventurers. But to her, the Alamo was a reminder that she must never surrender the things that mattered: not to the profiteers and philistines storming the walls, nor to city councilmen covering those walls with concrete.

Suddenly Mrs. Herrera whirled around. Someone had coughed just outside the room.

7

She remembered: she had left the chapel door open.

In a panic, she retraced her steps through the main warehouse and along the connecting corridor. Good God! If the chapel were vandalized by prowlers because of her carelessness, she would never live down the shame. She rushed through the sacristy, then back into the Alamo sanctuary.

The big room was empty. She checked the baptistry, the powder store, the rooms on the south side. No one was there.

She heard another cough. It came from outside. Not from the plaza out front: from the vacant lot behind the chapel and the warehouse.

She unfastened a shuttered window and squinted. At first she saw only a pile of discarded lumber and wire coils. Then, as the moon broke through the clouds, she noticed a slight movement. Beneath a sprawling live oak tree stood a large, dark form.

Mrs. Herrera unbolted the rear door and stepped outside. "Who's there? ¿Quién está ahí?"

The figure turned. It was a woman.

Rose advanced into the moonlight. "Who is it? What are you doing here?"

The other woman came out from the shadows of the branches. "I am Mathilda Guenther," she announced defiantly, as if defending her territory.

Rose relaxed. She started picking her way through the weeds and debris toward the woman. "Thank God. I mistook you for a vandal."

The German woman mocked her without smiling. "And if I had been? What were you going to do?"

"I don't know. Probably hit you with one of these boards. You're lucky I asked first. I'm Mrs. Herrera." She extended her hand. The other woman took it guardedly.

"I've heard that name, yes."

"You don't say! It's such an uncommon one in San Antonio. Shall I call you Miss or Mrs.?"

"Madame is what I prefer."

"I've admired you for some time, Madame Guenther."

The artist scoffed. "Ach! You've admired *me*? That's silly. You've admired my work. What do you know about *me*?"

Rose laughed. "Only what people say." She was amused by the artist's dogged directness, her seeming determination to offend.

"Of course, fools must talk. And what are people saying these days? Be completely truthful with me. I want to know."

"Well, they say that you're a perfectionist. Blunt. Unusual in your personal habits. Free in your private relations. A socialist, perhaps even an anarchist. An advocate of rights for women and Negroes. Hard to know. And hell to be around."

The older woman smiled in spite of herself. "And you believe all that?"

"No, but I'd like to. And so would you, I think. I called on you at home once. But you wouldn't admit me."

"I thought you were one of those clubwomen."

"I am."

"There. You see."

That made Mrs. Herrera bristle. "Madame Guenther, you should see what we're doing nowadays—"

"I'm not interested—"

"Clubs are means of power. Or did you think we clubwomen just sat around gossiping and exchanging recipes?"

The other woman peered at her and chuckled. "I remember now. You wrote that letter in the *Journal.* I even clipped it."

"Which one? I must have written hundreds."

"About how women should not squander their time on trivial things. And that sewing societies are hallmarks of the old century—like bloomers. Hah! Marvelous rhetoric! I liked that one very much. You also drive that automobile?"

Rose grinned. "The Peerless?"

"I thought so. I want you to take me motoring."

"If you're stout of heart, I will. Madame Guenther, I expected to meet you some day. But not here—at least, not at this hour."

"I don't keep regular hours, Mrs. Herrera."

"So what are you doing at the Alamo?" Rose pressed.

Madame Guenther was evasive. "I was working and needed some air. I could ask the same of you. What are you doing here?"

"I'm the custodian of the Alamo."

"Oh. Then I suppose you could sue me for trespassing."

"I'd never sue an artist. They have no money, right?"

"Exactly . . . ." The woman trailed off into a coughing fit.

"Is it too cool for you out here?" Rose tried to pull the woman's shawl closer around her bosom.

The artist drew back, fending off any assistance. "No. It's congestion. The dust in my studio." She coughed again.

"I'm sorry."

Madame Guenther shrugged. "I sleep in a chair these days. I have trouble lying down. But no, the air is not too cool."

"We should go inside anyway. Before we step on a snake."

"Don't worry," said Madame Guenther. "I carry a pistol."

"My God. Now I *am* worried."

They started toward the chapel. "You have the markings of education, even intellect," said the artist, as if surprised.

This time Rose wasn't sure if she was more offended or amused. "How kind, Madame Guenther. And me being merely a simple clubwoman."

For the first time the other woman seemed embarrassed. "Mrs. Herrera, you can see that I am not kind. Neither am I intentionally cruel. I just don't take time to disguise my thoughts in stupid pleasantries. I still have much work to do, and I'm running out of years. That is all it is."

Rose couldn't recall ever meeting anyone who seemed so contemptuous of the social graces, or so distant and cool, as this woman. She wondered how a person could ever grow close to someone so determined to hold the world at arm's length.

They entered the chapel. Rose bolted the rear door and fastened the window. The artist was at her side, studying her. "So. I am not satisfied. Does the custodian of the Alamo ordinarily come here at this time of night?"

Rose stared at the woman. "Tell me. Do you believe in the communion of the saints?"

Madame Guenther brushed aside the question with a wave of her hand. "I gave up the church long ago."

"That's not what I meant. I'm a Catholic myself, but you might say I come to the Alamo to commune with my ancestors. That's the pagan in me. My grandfather died here."

"In this building?"

"No, in the convent next door. It's the warehouse, now. Come, let me show you around. Not many people get to see the Alamo in the moonlight." Then she gave the sculptor a full tour, recounting the battle of 1836 and the events leading up to it. She pointed out the room where Bowie died, and the sacristy where Mrs. Dickinson hid with Fermin De León and others.

"I am an admirer of your Texas revolution," said Madame Guenther. "I see it as a great beginning."

"Well," sighed Rose, "I've never known just what to make of it myself."

They were standing in the center of the sanctuary. "Mrs. Herrera," said the artist. "I have kept something from you. I did not come here tonight by chance. I wanted to view this site. You see, I have been asked to do a sculpture for the new hotel next door."

"Next door?" She didn't bother to conceal her alarm.

"You have not heard of this?"

"I don't know what you're talking about."

Madame Guenther shrugged. "The Willingham Palace, I think it is to be called. Some silly name."

"Where?"

"In this lot outside. Where we were before."

Rose was aghast. "You don't mean—no! Surely they don't plan to build a hotel next to the convent?"

"Which one is the convent?"

"The warehouse. The Hugo & Schmeltzer building."

"Oh—that. No, they plan to tear that down and build the hotel over it."

It was fortunate that some Daughter of the Republic had left a swivel chair in the middle of the sanctuary that morning. Rose suddenly had need of it. It took her a moment to reply. "You must be mistaken."

"No. I am getting on in years, but my comprehension is fine. This Mr. Wilton Peck from Philadelphia came to me, just this evening."

Rose sat silently, hunched over. She took several deep breaths.

A hotel. Impossible.

A big concrete atrocity on top of the Alamo.

The chamber where her grandfather and many others made their last stand for their vision of what was just, where they were felled in terrified agony by rifles and bayonets—that room, that sacred site, leveled and forgotten and covered with—with what?

A piano lounge?

A hairdressing salon?

Good God Almighty! Suddenly the desecration of the wall at San José seemed minor in comparison.

The sculptor was perplexed. "Mrs. Herrera, this warehouse is a travesty."

"No! You don't understand," said Rose, greatly agitated. "That building next door is the Alamo convent. The long barracks. Where the rebels died."

Madame Guenther was skeptical. "That wooden building? It is too modern."

"The wood is new. But the walls underneath are original. My father showed me."

"Hunh."

They must have passed a full minute in silence. Madame Guenther awkwardly shifted her weight from one foot to the other. Rose felt as if she might suffocate. She grabbed the German woman's hand and pressed it hard. "Madame Guenther, how am I going to stop this?"

The sculptor raised her eyebrows. "Well, I don't know that this hotel company has even purchased the lot yet."

"The owners promised me . . . ." She was too distraught to finish.

Madame Guenther, not used to open displays of emotion, felt uncomfortable. "Hunh."

Rose pressed her hand again. "Will you help me? At least lend your name to my cause? You must have a great deal of influence."

The other woman was incredulous. "Me? You've said yourself: people think I am a lunatic, a heretic, an anarchist, a floozy   "

"I don't care. I think you're a genius."

Madame Guenther gently worked her hand loose. "Besides, I am well past sixty. I have no energy for other people's causes."

"Help me think, then. I'm at a loss. But I'll do whatever it takes."

The artist looked at her with a mix of irritation and pity. "Do you realize how much stamina is required to do battle with these capitalists? They will crush your spirit and leave you bleeding. How can this mean that much to you?"

"You have no idea. This is my life—my legacy. You don't know what I've had to go through already just to keep the missions from falling to pieces or being torn down for scrap."

The older woman smiled. "All right, then. I suppose you know what lies ahead of you."

They thought for a minute.

"Madame Guenther—I hope you didn't accept the commission."

"I have not yet decided." Despite her renown, the artist wasn't in a financial position to decline commissions lightly.

The policeman appeared in the doorway. "Everything all right, ma'am?"

Rose looked up. "Yes, Poppy," she said weakly. "We're going now."

He looked at the artist suspiciously. Then he nodded and left.

Rose stood up slowly. The initial feeling of panic had passed, and her fighting spirit had already taken its place. They walked toward the front doors in silence. As they stepped out, Madame Guenther handed her a card.

"Call on me next week. Thursday is a good day. Early. We can talk more about what you should do. This is not my concern, of course, but I feel some sympathy for you."

Rose managed a smile. "How do I know you'll admit me when I call?"

"You are not like the other clubwomen. I know you will not waste my time."

They were outside on the plaza. "Then I *will* call on you, Madame Guenther."

She slammed the heavy wooden door behind them and locked it.

"But I won't give this Wilton Peck and his hotel company four days' head start. My God no! By Thursday I'll already have a plan in action."

They stood before the Alamo chapel and gazed at its pale stone walls in the lamplight. Then Rose turned to the Hugo & Schmeltzer building and pointed to the southwest corner. "That room. Right there."

The artist nodded.

"Madame Guenther, do what you think best about the commission. But believe me, Mr. Wilton Peck will have to get his wrecking crane over my dead body before he builds his hotel. He's going to come face to face with hell and brimstone before this is over. Anyway, I'm grateful to you for telling me."

"I think you would have learned about it, soon enough."

"It might have been too late. I just hope it's not already."

They took one last look at the chapel. Then Rose took the artist's arm. This time the older woman didn't resist.

"Come," Rose said. "I'll walk with you as far as the Menger."

The plaza was quiet now, except for the saloons. The two women had the sidewalk to themselves. They were heading for their respective work: one to sketch a battle, the other to wage one. In the darkness behind them, the Alamo stood deserted, a silent sentinel.

MENGER HOTEL

SAN ANTONIO, TEXAS

September 28, 1907

My dear Mrs. Herrera:

Your brave and spirited defense of your city's heritage tonight did honor to your Alamo ancestor. I intend to keep abreast of your future endeavors.

Cordially,
Clara Root

8

The doorman handed Rose the note when she entered the hotel lobby. Clara Root's praise gave her a lift. The automobile accident and the wall at San José were out of mind now. Like iron shackles, the Willingham Palace held her attention captive that night, overshadowing her other problems: Antonio, her speech at the banquet, their wayward son.

The carriage ride home seemed endless. Antonio had refused to take the Peerless to the Menger, where gossipmongers could look for scratches and relive the morning's disaster. Instead, the Herreras took their black rockaway. Antonio preferred the horse-drawn carriage. He was proud of his horses. Furthermore, the motorcar scared him, and he resented his wife's mastery of it.

But the rockaway made for a rough trip. Every time the wheels struck a rut, the carriage lurched. Santos, the coachman, broke into drunken song, urging the horses on. Both passengers were edgy.

Antonio had nothing to say. He raised the jalousie and stared out the window. His wife fidgeted with her gloves. "You did an excellent job organizing things, Antonio."

She drew no response and expected none. But it was a start.

She regretted her speech at the banquet. Of course the city council deserved it; but she had done three things to try Antonio's patience that day: wrecking the Peerless, speaking her mind uninvited, and losing track of their son. And he would need all the patience he had once she launched her attack on Wilton Peck and the new Willingham hotel.

Soon her name would be in the papers again. Antonio would seethe and lecture and finally—well, she didn't really know. She had never pushed him to his breaking point.

It wasn't a good time to broach the subject, but eventually her agitation got the better of her. "Do you know anything about a sale of the Hugo & Schmeltzer building?"

He shook his head without looking at her.

"I heard there's a man from Philadelphia trying to buy it," she continued. "For the Willingham Hotel Company. Wilton Peck?"

"I don't know." He seemed to recall the name from the guest list. However, he was in no mood to talk to her.

Rose longed to take her husband's hand, but she didn't dare. Instead she studied him in profile. Antonio Herrera was not a particularly handsome man. Of medium build, he had an aquiline nose and rough, pockmarked cheeks. But his thick black hair and moustache and the intelligent expression behind his dewy eyes offset his deficits nicely. He hadn't gone to seed, like most men his age.

She tried once again. "Have you heard if the Hugo & Schmeltzer is on the market?"

"No. You're the one always in the middle of things. You'll probably hear before I do."

Stung, she said no more. He was determined to sulk. She was just as determined to receive his absolution and put the banquet and the accident behind them.

They got home at midnight. Antonio helped his wife onto the asphalt driveway. Then he rode to the garage to supervise Santos and the horses. Rose climbed the broad granite steps to the porch and went in the front door alone.

The Herreras occupied a smart, golden-brick house, notable for its twin Oriental canopies extending over the second-floor sun deck, separated by a single attic dormer. It was Antonio who had insisted that they build the big house in Alamo Heights. He thought the move was necessary for appearances. He also needed space for his fruit trees and modest pecan orchard.

Rose still mourned their move from downtown to the Heights. She found the suburbs dull and insular, insensitive to the pulse of the contentious city. The Peerless and the club meeting halls had become her substitute homes.

The front rooms were dark when she entered, except for the hurricane lamp in the vestibule. Rose hurried up the oak stairs to Enrique's bedroom. She saw a light underneath the door and heard his guitar.

Thank God. He was home. One of her sins was forgiven.

She tapped lightly and entered. The boy looked up at her without expression. She smiled. "Buenos noches."

He returned her greeting somberly.

"How was your evening?"

He shrugged. It had become hard to get words out of him.

"Have you been here?"

He nodded.

"All night?"

He stopped playing. Then he asked quietly, with a trace of resentment: "How was my father's banquet?"

She paused. "Eventful." She sat on his bed and changed the subject. "What is this song you were playing?"

"It was . . . it was nothing."

"Let me hear the Bach piece, please." He was working on a Tarrega arrangement of one of her favorite sonatas.

The boy looked away. "It's very late."

"Por favor."

Avoiding eye contact, he granted her request. His taut hands worked the guitar frets in sure clenches.

Enrique was dark-complexioned, like his father, with alert brown eyes and a handsome but inscrutable face. Rose knew that her husband was preparing their son for greatness: Franck, Herrera & Herrera, perhaps, or maybe local politics. But Enrique was only interested in his guitar. Music was his passion, just as history was his mother's.

Their son was a good boy, quiet-spoken, an honors student at St. Mary's Academy. But she seldom saw him smile any more. His bouts of melancholy worried her. For fifteen years he had been a good-natured charmer, occasionally erupting in a fit of De León rage. But once he turned sixteen he became a mystery to them. Silently he withdrew. His mother blamed herself: maybe she had spent too much time on her clubs. The harder she tried to stay close to him, the more he pulled away.

Several times over the past few weeks, Enrique had stolen out of his window at night, leaving his lamp lit as a decoy, and not returned for many hours. They had no idea where he went. Perhaps it was a girl. Possibly he had discovered the bawdy houses on Produce Row. But his mother sensed something else was troubling him. Antonio was ready to send him to a military school, but Rose convinced him they should wait. The restlessness might run its course.

Midway through the Bach piece Enrique stopped, angry with himself. "It's no good. I still can't get through the adagio."

His mother stood up and walked over to his chair. She smoothed his black hair. "Enrique. Atención un momento."

He tensed.

She paused, uncertain. "Always remember who you are."

He glanced up at her blankly.

His look made her smile at her own obscureness. "Your ancestors. We De Leóns are a noble and spirited people. But sometimes we let ourselves get carried away. Be careful."

He nodded. His mother knew she hadn't broken through. But she decided not to press any further. She had no proof that he had been doing anything untoward during his night journeys.

She left his bedroom and walked down the dark-paneled hallway to her own. The Herreras had decided against separate bedrooms when they built their house; sometimes Rose wondered why. Antonio was disengaging his collar studs when she entered. He stared at her in his mirror as she passed by.

He wasn't going to confront her, she realized. Instead he would torment her with his practiced hurt glances and angry silences. He was waiting for guilt to get the better of her. And it would, soon enough; they both knew that.

In her boudoir she took off her gown and hung it in the wardrobe. As she removed the pins from her bouffant dome, her hair fell in bunches around her pale shoulders. Then she brushed it in long, luxuriant strokes. She knew she was stalling.

It bothered Antonio that beneath the stylish gowns he furnished for her, she still wore her old-fashioned Mexican undergarments. Several times she had baited him: "Are you afraid I'll have an accident in the Peerless and be taken to the hospital, and the doctors will remove my gown and say, 'Herrera has deceived us; we didn't know his wife was a Mexican'?" He had ignored the question. Now that she'd actually had an automobile accident, she wouldn't pose it again.

The layers of lace were constricting; she peeled them off with relief. Rose had started to feel helpless against the force of gravity, as if her body had determined of its own volition what shape it would take. She hissed at the mirror and turned away.

A hotel on top of the Alamo.

She told herself to stop thinking about it. There was nothing she could do until morning.

She still heard Enrique's guitar through the open window, faintly now: an old Mexican ballad. Maybe he would stay home that night. She dampened a cloth and wiped the perspiration from her face and neck, then her arms and legs. Squeezing the cloth against her throat, she let the water drip down her bare breasts in winding rivulets. Finally she splashed herself with lavender and put on a loose night-gown. Then she went back into the bedroom to make peace.

The ceiling fan was circulating leisurely. The only light came from the lamp on her nightstand. Antonio was already in bed, facing the far wall, his back brown and smooth against the white linens. The weather was still too warm for him to wear pajamas.

She slid into the bed and arranged the sheets. He didn't respond.

She leaned over. His eyes were open. "How are you feeling?" she whispered.

Without looking at her, he said in a hoarse, deliberate tone: "How in God's name do you think I'm feeling?"

She fought back tears. "Antonio, please."

"You know what tonight meant to me."

She touched his neck. It still felt tight. His arm twitched.

"Antonio, you know I—I didn' t mean to."

He grunted.

"I'm sorry if I embarrassed you—"

"For Christ's sake—"

"It was just a reaction. I had to—"

"Just another reaction. Why in the hell can't you think before you act, Rose? For your son's sake, if not for mine."

"Antonio—"

Impulsively, she threw her arms across him, her bosom pressed hard against his back. Through her nightgown his shoulders felt feverish. She could smell traces of his nervous sweat. Unable to speak, she let her fingers run the length of his upper arm repeatedly. He didn't move. She held him closely for a long while, her face buried in his hair, then his neck, choking back any sound. Finally he reached for her forearm and stroked her wrist. Still he didn't look at her.

"I'm so sorry," she whispered.

He nodded. She looked at him again and kissed his rough cheek. There was no more she could do. She sighed and released him and extinguished the lamp.

He turned. "Is Enrique—"

"Shh. Yes. Tomorrow."

It was done. She settled into their bed for what was left of the night. She needed rest for the battle ahead.

But it was several hours before she slept. Every time she thought about the Alamo and the Willingham hotel, her heart started pounding again. Wilton Peck: she couldn't put a face on him, but already the name taunted her. She pictured one tormenting scene after another. *Too late,* she thought. Concrete and steel covered the Alamo. Chorus girls strutted across the place where her grandfather fell. Her imagination grew darker throughout the night and the early morning hours, as she lost her grip on her consciousness and drifted into the domain of wild, irrational terrors.

Across town, beneath a bright factory light, the artist, still at work, sketched the fall of the Alamo again and again without satisfaction. Finally she crumpled the paper and tossed it aside. She went to her office.

GUENTHER STUDIO
502 Villita Street
San Antonio, Texas

September 28, 1907

Hand Delivered by Silas Toombs

Mr. Wilton Peck
Clifford Building
Commerce Street Bridge
City

Dear Mr. Peck:

This is to inform you that I have decided to decline your commission, for personal reasons.

For the bas-relief sculpture you have in mind, might I recommend the services of Bexar Mortuary Stonemasons.

In utmost sincerity,
Mathilda Guenther

O n Sunday morning Rose was fully dressed at dawn. She let her husband sleep. She roused Enrique with great energetic shakes. He scowled at her and mumbled.

"Get dressed. Hurry."

"What time—"

"Never mind. I'll be waiting at the garage."

She drove her son to the earliest mass at San Fernando Cathedral instead of their usual midday service. He was still half asleep. During the Agnus Dei, she caught his eyes wandering around the chalky limestone walls of the sanctuary, with their crudely carved stations of the cross, and up to the high vaulted ceiling.

"Pay attention," she whispered.

"I don't understand Latin."

"Try."

He listened. "¡Auxilio! ¡Socorro! What's he saying now?"

"Shh. Be quiet."

Entirely by accident, she made him grin. "You don't know either," he teased.

"Más respeto," she chided.

She scanned the congregation as she nervously fingered her rosary, looking for anyone who might be able to tell her about the Hugo & Schmeltzer sale and the hotel. There was no one. She sighed impatiently.

Immediately after the eucharist, she motioned to Enrique to follow her down the side aisle, while the priest chanted on. The boy could hardly keep up with her pace. She didn't even stop to light a candle at the shrine to the Alamo rebels.

Outside on Main Plaza Enrique cranked the Peerless. His mother tore off her black veil and pulled her motoring hat over her hair. He was barely in his seat before she took off. As they headed up Avenue C, she asked him, "Will you be home this afternoon?"

He seemed uncomfortable. "I don't know."

"I may need you to run an errand."

He looked away and stared at the pristine lawns flying past.

When they got home, Antonio was having a leisurely breakfast as he plowed through the *Journal*. He seemed content. The glowing report of the previous day's events must have raised his spirits. Apparently, it didn't mention his wife—either her mishap or her speech. And he would be pleased that she took Enrique to mass: it was part of the boy's grooming, to see and be seen. She kissed his forehead as she hurried by. He wiped his moustache, greeting her.

Then she stuck her head in the kitchen. "Eloisa. I'll take coffee at my desk today."

"¿Qué?"

"En seguida, por favor."

The cramped rectangular chamber off the dining room had been intended as a sewing nook. She had turned it into her library and study. There she sequestered herself for the rest of the day—and went to war.

First she typed a letter on stencil to all the local Daughters of the Republic of Texas. She sent Enrique downtown to his father's office to duplicate it on the mimeograph.

Next she telephoned as many DRT members as she could reach at home.

When Enrique finally returned with the letters, she scribbled personal messages on them and addressed all the envelopes. Then she summoned her coachman Santos to deliver them around town on his bicycle.

SAN ANTONIO CHAPTER
Daughters of the Republic of Texas
"Texas, One and Indivisible"

Rose De León Herrera, President
1211 Townsend Avenue
San Antonio, Texas

September 29, 1907

My dear fellow Daughters:

Gird yourselves for battle.

While we have been sleeping, the Alamo has fallen under its most dire threat since General Santa Anna unfurled the red banner of no quarter and sounded the degüello in 1836.

The Willingham Hotel Company of Philadelphia is trying to purchase the Hugo & Schmeltzer property—which contains the original walls of the Alamo convent—and raze those walls to erect a hotel.

Tear down the Alamo! Why, even school children would know better, and would rise up against the perpetrators of such a sacrilegious act.

Some of you may recall that many years ago, I obtained a verbal promise from the owner, Mr. Hugo, not to sell the property to anyone else without first giving us an opportunity to acquire it. We must hold him to that promise.

There is no time to lose. Daughters, I am convening an emergency meeting of the San Antonio Chapter. Please come to my home at 10:00 a.m. tomorrow morning. I implore you—cancel your luncheons, your fittings, any social obligations of lesser consequence. The fate of the Alamo is at stake. I am counting on all of you.

Your sister,
Rose De León Herrera

By Sunday evening she was still roused to fight. But there was no more she could do until the next morning. For no apparent reason, she rearranged all the books on her shelves. Dissatisfied, she put them all back where they were before.

Finally, her energy dissipated, she sat down to read the Sunday *Journal* cover to cover, searching without success for any mention of the Hugo & Schmeltzer property or Wilton Peck. She even checked the society column. It was no use. The sly rat from Philadelphia wasn't ready to tip his hand to the press just yet. Frustrated, she threw her pen across the desk.

Then one of the names she noticed in the society column made her shudder. Quickly she flipped the page.

THE SAN ANTONIO JOURNAL

Sunday, September 29, 1907

Tales & Tattlers

Isn't she the lucky girl? Miss Alva Carson, that ravishing, restless redhead and heiress to the Tres Piedras Ranch near Laredo, became Mrs. Robert Keane at St. Patrick's Cathedral in New York last July. The successful suitor is no Johnny-come-lately; his grandfather founded the United American Press Association.

The happy, handsome couple then embarked on a honeymoon cruise to India and the Orient, returning to their home at New York's Ansonia Hotel last week just in time for the debut of Miss Carson's—whoa! we mean Mrs. Keane's—fabulous first novel, *Angelina, Sweetheart of the Chaparral.* Whew! This is one young socialite who allows no grass to grow under her feet!

Her novel tells the heroic, heart-rending story of Angelina Del Rio, a brave girl from the wild Texas prairie who sacrifices her life to save her true love, a Yankee financier. However, this stirring story is not altogether a tragedy, for in it the author recounts some amusing and thrilling anecdotes from her own girlhood on a South Texas ranch. We have not yet received a copy, but our sources tell us: *Angelina* is G-O-O-D!

Mrs. Keane will arrive in San Antonio in a few days and will be at the Carolina Tea Room from 2:00 p.m. on Thursday to autograph copies of her new book. To what formidable feat will this fearless and talented young lady next devote her energies? We'll keep our ears to the ground!

A nyone who had ever tangled with Alva Carson Keane knew
there was nothing she wanted that she couldn't get. That
included an apartment at the Ansonia Hotel. Laced with layers of beaux-arts trim and topped with frothy rounded turrets, the
Ansonia was touted as New York's most luxurious residential hotel. It
was the address of choice for writers, musicians and show people.
Toscanini stayed there, as did Caruso and Ziegfeld.

Mrs. Keane and her new husband needed a suitable flat until
they finished building their manse in New Rochelle. For the young
author of *Angelina, Sweetheart of the Chaparral*, the Ansonia was the
only choice. The manager warned her that her prospects were bleak.
But Mrs. Keane got her publisher and lawyers on the scene, and they
convinced the manager that this Texas ranch heiress was an up-and-
comer in the literary world.

And so Alva Carson Keane got her Ansonia apartment: nine spa-
cious rooms on the twelfth floor, with distant views of Central Park
and walls thick enough to silence Toscanini. Mrs. Keane had determination. And she had a *lot* of money.

On Sundays Alva lunched downstairs in the Ansonia's elegant
Fountain Room, while her husband golfed in Westport. Like most
wealthy women, she was never at a loss for company when she
wanted it. This Sunday's companion was Max Rosenthal, her publisher and most trusted advisor, next to her daddy. Mr. Rosenthal was
expending great efforts to promote *Angelina, Sweetheart of the
Chaparral*. His work had paid off. Alva was still scanning her menu

when he broke in, unable to contain his news any longer.

"Did you read in the *Times* about the Mencken brothers buying the New Amsterdam Theatre?"

Alva didn't look up. She wasn't interested. "Max, you know I don't read the business section. Keane's the financial writer. I'm the romantic."

"They're planning to open a big show there in January. So a few weeks ago, I sent the Menckens an advance copy of *Angelina*. No response. Then yesterday, B. J. calls, all excited. He thinks it would make a terrific show. All of a sudden he's talking about closing a deal fast. A few hours later, I get a formal note from Paul. They want it. They've *got* to have it. The Mencken brothers are going to buy the rights."

His news didn't provoke the reaction he had expected. "I don't know, Max. I can't see *Angelina* as a play."

Rosenthal was crushed. "Why not?"

"It's too outdoorsy. It . . . sprawls."

"So? It'll be a big show. Besides, anything goes these days. Look at the stuff on Broadway. You could do a show about dancing kangaroos if you wanted to."

"Why would I want to?"

"Of course, I told them you'd insist on writing the script yourself—"

"When did you say they want to open it?" she interrupted.

"In January."

She burst out with an involuntary laugh. "That's three, three and a half months—Max, that's ridiculous. I couldn't possibly write a script by the time they'd need it."

"Sure you could. The Menckens always get a show up fast."

"But aren't their shows always musicals? *Loud* ones?"

"No, they do straight plays, too." Rosenthal tugged nervously on his beard. He wasn't sure why he was always a little obeisant in Alva Keane's presence.

She gave him a coy pout. "Max, you rascal. What am I going to do with you? Last week you told me to get busy on a new novel."

Rosenthal laughed warily. "Alva, this is Broadway. Do you know what this means? The exposure? It'll sell thousands of copies of *Angelina*. Help sell the next book, too."

Finally the author let go; her arms flew as she took full control of the conversation. "All right. But it's got to be a quality production, understand? Not a spectacle. No flying scenery. No magic tricks. And I see real actors in this. None of these vaudeville clowns."

"Of course—"

"High drama, Max. No silly business. And I see a real Mexican playing Angelina."

"The Mencken brothers mentioned Maggie McPherson—in a dark wig, of course—"

"I don't want Maggie McPherson in a dark wig."

"Fine. I'll tell them."

"When would they need to see a draft?"

"You'll find out soon. What time does your train leave for Texas tomorrow?"

"I don't remember. Mid-afternoon, two or three."

"Good. You have a meeting set up with Paul Mencken tomorrow morning at ten, in his office."

She cackled. "Max!"

"B. J. won't be there. He and Paul hate each other, hardly ever go to the same meetings. But Paul's the better one to talk to; he's not so high-strung. A little cold, maybe, but you can charm him."

They were both leaning forward intently. "I don't want them to change the story," she insisted.

"You're the writer."

"I know, but I've heard the Menckens are tough."

"You're no pushover yourself."

"Just look after my interests, Max."

"Absolutely." For an instant it occurred to Rosenthal that he was willingly placing himself between the Mencken brothers—the meanest producers working on Broadway—and the equally head-strong Alva Carson Keane. He was destined to become a human sacrifice. He tried not to think of that now.

She was sorting through things. "I still don't see when I'm going to write this. I've got a full plate in Texas. There' s the autograph parties. And I was hoping to do a little riding and shooting at the ranch."

"You can write it—on the train, on your horse, branding cattle, whatever it is you do down there. Just take a little pad. Now listen. Mencken's office is at Fortieth and Broadway. Be on time; Paul Mencken always is. It'll take about an hour. No, exactly an hour, if Paul's running the meeting."

Alva wasn't listening. Her thoughts were racing far ahead into her theatrical future. "I wonder which of the Barrymores would make a better Farnsworth—Lionel or John?"

"Mencken's secretary, some little snip, told me, 'He's giving Mrs. Keane a full hour of his time, and he doesn't do that for just anybody.' I said, 'Yes, well, neither does she.'"

"Max, you'll be at our party tonight, won't you?"

"Of course."

"Get there early. Coach me on how to handle Paul Mencken."

"All right, I'll—"

"But not too early. I'm going out to Flushing to do some target shooting this afternoon."

"Again? If you get any better, they'll put you in the Follies."

"Max, I'm going home to Tres Piedras. And I have a reputation to uphold." She looked around. "I think this calls for champagne—Jesus, where is that waiter?"

Everyone at Tres Piedras Ranch, from Oscar Carson down to his youngest vaquero, was handy with a rifle. A person had to be, to take out coyotes. But Carson's daughter Alva had the distinction of being unusually accurate with a pistol as well. Her daddy attributed it to her ability to remain cool and steady in any situation. Alva liked to prove herself. She never carried a rifle on her saddle, as her daddy told her to, but instead rode the range with a Colt .45 Peacemaker, popping rattlesnakes and knocking off prickly pear leaves with shots that some of the cowboys couldn't have made with a Winchester.

When she was fourteen, Alva Carson became a local legend around Laredo because of what happened on one of her daddy' s cattle drives. Alva was between boarding schools at the time and was spending a year on the ranch. It was the first time her daddy had let his only daughter make the long trip from Tres Piedras to the stockyards of San Antonio. Whenever Oscar Carson told the story, it all started the morning he learned the thirty head were missing. But Alva's role in the incident really began the night before.

The sky was fiery orange and streaked with gray-purple clouds by the time the drovers stopped that first evening. They set up camp twenty miles northeast of Laredo on the dry chaparral near Webb. Alva loved the outdoors. She unsaddled Badger, her bay gelding, then hobbled him and sent him off to graze. All afternoon the girl had taken cat's-claw and mesquite thorns in her arms as stoically as any cowboy. Only now did she take time to inspect the scratches.

Her daddy rode by. "Alva, don't let your horse wander out of sight. You and Domingo will have the first watch tonight." He spurred his chestnut mare and took off to supervise the men. Out on the range, it was hard to distinguish Oscar Carson from one of his hands. He had gotten his start as a low-wage cowpuncher from Tennessee, albeit an unusually ambitious one. By the time he was thirty the other cowboys called him "Sir" to his face. Behind his back he was already known as "The Old Man." Piece by piece Carson had acquired 263,000 acres of Spanish land grants along the Rio Grande, bearing old Texas names—Gutiérrez, García, De León.

That night, after a supper of beans, bacon, tortillas and coffee, Alva and Domingo Cantú mounted their horses for the first watch. Domingo was a slender, nimble wrangler of eighteen. Every few minutes the girl rode past him as they circled the herd. Once he stopped to roll her a cigarette. While he was lighting it, she thought she heard horses' hooves in the darkness. They listened. The herd seemed a little restless. But they didn't see anything, so they thought no more about it.

When their watch was over, Alva and Domingo sipped whiskey by the fire until deep into the night. Alva identified the constellations. She confided in the wrangler that she was home because she'd been kicked out of school in New York. Domingo taught her some old songs in Spanish. She didn't want that night to end.

The next morning she woke to hear her daddy shouting at one of the hands: "God damn it, I heard you the first time! But thirty head don't just disappear overnight. Look again!"

Three of the vaqueros got on their horses and made another round in the thornbush. The missing steers weren't there. Some of the men thought they'd heard the cattle stirring the night before. Oscar Carson suspected rustlers. Alva knew what that meant. They'd never see those thirty steers again. However, when they got back from San Antonio, her daddy would take his men across the Rio Grande one night and come back with compensation from some Mexican herd.

Alva's brother Tom rode up to their daddy. "The hands think it must have happened during Alva's watch." Tom was two years her senior and thought his sister was much too young to be put on watch during a cattle drive.

Carson grimaced. "Daughter, did you notice anything unusual last night?"

"No, sir," she lied.

He didn't believe her. His face turned red. "Alva, someday you and Tom will run Tres Piedras and all our other ranches. You have to learn to take charge and pay attention to what you're doing. Now go saddle up. You and Domingo are going to look for those strays."

Alva felt as if a horse had kicked her in the stomach. Several of the vaqueros were listening; they must have thought it was her fault. And her daddy knew those steers were probably across the border by now. He was just doing this to teach her a lesson. She saddled Badger while the men kicked dirt over the fire and packed up what was left of the gear. The cowboys started circling the herd, gathering the drift cattle.

The Old Man gave her instructions. "I want you and Domingo to ride south, back toward the ranch. If you find those strays in a couple of hours, you'll be able to catch up with us. If they're more than two hours away, just push them on back to the ranch, and we'll sell them next time. But whatever you do, keep going till you find them."

"All of them," her brother Tom added. "I reckon they're scattered from here to Corpus Christi by now."

The girl was near tears. Her first cattle drive was as good as over. Badger whinnied in distress as Alva headed him in the direction opposite the herd and the other horses.

She and Domingo rode together for half an hour; then they split up so they could cover more ground. It was barely eight o'clock, and the day was already hot. By noon the sun had sapped all her energy. There was still no sign of the strays, and she knew there wouldn't be. Alva stopped when she got to a rounded earthen knoll above a dry ravine: she had reached the northernmost section of Tres Piedras. She slid off Badger and pulled a canteen out of her saddlebag.

By then Alva hated her daddy. She didn't think it was fair of him to punish her this way. All morning she had plotted her revenge. She would ride into Laredo, to Dos Amigos Cantina, where she would become the town's youngest barmaid. She would wear low-cut scarlet dresses—even though she had no cleavage—and swear in Spanish and drink whiskey. She might flirt with saddle tramps, even Mexicans. The Old Man would—

What was that? She smelled smoke.

Then she saw it, billowing out of the ravine. A grass fire! Alva started running down the slope as fast as she could in her boots and spurs. She had no idea how she was going to put it out.

Then she happened to think: the ravine was barren, filled with sand. How could the fire have started? There was nothing to burn.

She stopped and listened. There were voices coming from down there. They were loud, but not angry; in fact, it sounded like a fiesta. She couldn't see anyone, but she realized what was going on: amidst the shouts and laughter, she heard cattle lowing.

Now she was scared. She looked all around for Domingo. They hadn't crossed paths in over an hour. And her Peacemaker was up in her saddlebag. Alva started scrambling back toward the oak tree where she'd tied Badger.

"¡Muchacha!"

She froze and looked around. A bandido was waving at her from across the ravine. He grinned. Even from a distance she could see the cartridge belt strapped across his chest. Timidly, she waved back.

"¡Venga para acá!" he ordered, still grinning. His compadres emerged to take a look at their visitor. They were five in all. Alva was within the men's rifle range, so she had no choice but to amble toward them. She'd heard of white women being ravished by bandidos as far upcountry as Cotulla. She wasn't sure what "ravished" meant, but instinctively she tightened her chaps.

In the bottom of the ravine, the bandidos had the cattle bunched up in a makeshift brush pen. There were a lot more than thirty head: they must have visited several ranches along the way. The bandidos had slaughtered one of the calves. They were roasting big hunks of beef over the fire, using mesquite branches for spits. One of them handed her a portion.

"Gracias," she replied, trying to play along with the men's high spirits. She wasn't sure how she was going to get out of this, but she knew it was best not to interrupt their feast.

Another bandido handed her a bottle of mescal. It burned her throat, but she pretended to like it. "¡Muy bueno!" she told them. The bandidos laughed loudly.

She wondered why they were treating her so hospitably. Was it just so they could laugh harder when they turned the tables and knifed her? Or were they fortifying her because they planned to take her hostage? She tried to concentrate on the meat, which was charred. But she was hungry, and it tasted good. For a moment she lost some of her fear.

"¿Tienen tortillas?" she asked.

The bandidos laughed, but less jovially this time. Alva knew enough Spanish to make out their jeering remarks about the gringa who had to have tortillas with her meat. The girl was almost certain she saw one of them make a slashing motion across his throat and grin.

"No, señorita," another bandido said in mock apology. "Perdón."

"I have some tortillas on my horse," she offered in her broken Spanish. They laughed again, seemingly pleased. To her surprise, one of them told her to go get the tortillas.

Alva never looked behind her as she climbed the embankment. She was sure they were about to shoot her in the back. But they didn't. She wondered if maybe they weren't planning to harm her after all.

When she reached Badger, she knew it was her last chance to flee. The bandidos couldn't see her.

But her daddy was counting on her to bring his steers home. She reached in her saddlebag and pulled out her Peacemaker and some extra cartridges. Then she crept back down the slope to the edge of the ravine. There she took cover behind an agarita bush.

Crack! Her first shot hit an oak tree just above one bandido's head. The next nipped at another's heels. She aimed in different directions, hoping they would think there were several men shooting at them. The cattle stirred and bawled.

The bandidos were still trying to reach their rifles by the time Alva emptied her revolver. In their confusion they only fired a few wild shots. By the time she'd reloaded, four of the men were climbing on their horses. The fifth, who wasn't much older than Alva, was trying to open the brush pen and free the cattle. Alva fired in his direction. He jerked back and yelled. Then he stumbled toward his horse.

Once Alva had emptied her six-shooter a second time, the bandidos were out of sight. The ravine was quiet and empty, except for the smoldering fire and the cattle.

A week later Oscar Carson returned to Tres Piedras from San Antonio. His daughter was waiting for him on the front porch of the ranch house. "Go take a look in the horse trap, Daddy," she said.

Alva could barely keep from grinning when he returned a few minutes later from the small pasture behind the house. Oddly enough, he didn't look happy. All he said was, "Alva, that trap isn't big enough to hold all those steers. Can't you see how they've eaten all the grass down?"

Later he would learn how his fourteen-year-old daughter had rescued his steers and those of his neighbors by chasing off five Mexican cutthroats, a story he would tell many times during his life. But Alva never forgot his first reaction.

That was only one of the reasons Alva didn't much like to tell this story. She also remembered how those Mexican cutthroats, as her daddy called them, had given her food and drink and then set her free. And that wasn't all. Alva suspected she'd unintentionally shot the young Mexican who had tried to free the cattle. At the time she had felt too sick to check the ground for blood. Later she wondered if the boy had ever made it back across the border with his companions, or if he'd bled to death somewhere out on Tres Piedras. Every time she returned to the ranch, she took a few target shots at that ravine to convince herself she was too good to have made that kind of mistake.

Still, she felt obliged to use the most famous episode of her ranch days in her novel. The night before she left for Texas, Alva's husband Robert gave her a small farewell party at their Ansonia apartment. One of the guests asked her to read from *Angelina, Sweetheart of the Chaparral*. The author selected the chapter about a cattle drive, in which Angelina bravely rescued the herd from bandidos who surely would have slit her throat had she not taken up a pistol and started firing on them.

At that same hour but many miles away at a very different party on the West Side of San Antonio, another writer had captured the guests' attention with a fiery rendition of his new work, which, although it featured no bandidos or cattle drives or gunplay, also celebrated a heroic act.

JESUS AT THE CHILI STAND

A Mariachi Ballad
Decrying the Bourgeoisie Cultural Oppression
That Has Infiltrated the San Antonio of Today

Words and Music by Rafael Menchaca

Every day at the hour of noontide
At the Plaza de Armas on the green,
All the ladies and gents of distinction
Come to sample Tejano cuisine.

My good friend Jesus is a vendor
Of chili beyond all compare—
So dark it can make you suspicious,
So hot it can make you sprout hair.

Now Jesus tries to lure all the gringos;
He entreats every Jimmy and Jack.
But alas, our Jesus speaks no English
Except "Thank you, please pay now, come back."

So Jesus came to ask me a favor:
"Rafael, won't you make me a sign?
Something catchy, inspired and in English
That will get people standing in line."

So I thought half the night for a slogan.
Then I painted these words bold and red:
"IF YOU HUNGER FOR HEAVENLY CHILI,
COME TO JESUS, YOU SINNERS, BE FED."

The next day the line was miraculous;
Five thousand were fed, people swore.
If Jesus had walked out on the water,
It couldn't have startled us more.

All at once rose a frightful commotion;
All the demons of hell were set loose.
Some young devil was spewing and hissing,
Set to crucify poor old Jesus.

He was red in the face from his tirade.
He was sporting a tail, so they say.
He was cloaked in a hideous garment
That said "Bexar County Y.M.C.A."

He was shouting, "You heathen, how dare you
Use our savior's dear name in this way?"
While Jesus, who could fathom no English,
Stammered, "Thank you, come back now, please pay."

The young devil knocked bowls off the table
When Jesus offered something to eat.
Then he picked up the sign that offended
And threw it clear out in the street.

Now Jesus was profoundly bewildered,
Crying out to Saint Mary on high.
His tormentor yelled, "Papist! No wonder!"
Then he shoved him and spat in his eye.

Jesus toppled down in a mudhole,
All prepared to turn his spattered cheek.
But a heavenly vision rebuked him:
"Mud and shit are the marks of the meek.

"Our Lord grappled with thieves in the temple,
Spilled their tables just like a typhoon.
On your feet, little man, fight injustice;
Turn the tables on this young baboon."

So he picked up the sign that I gave him.
He never did learn what it said,
For he held it up to the young devil
And shattered it over his head.

All you Christians and sinners, be careful
When Jesus has you under his spell:
Though his chili is manna from heaven,
His temper is hotter than hell.

R afael Menchaca concluded the song with a loud flourish on his guitar. The party guests applauded. Though his ego knew no bounds, Mr. Menchaca hadn't intended to stop the dancing and make people listen to him. After all, it was a party. But any song he penned defied people *not* to listen, if only to make sure they weren't the target of his satire.

The hostess, an elegant woman with dark hair pulled back in a tight knot, came out of her tidy frame house with a cup of coffee for the musician. He took it and sipped, staring at the guests gathered in the open courtyard. Many were young people: bashful girls in bright calico and ribbons, their boyfriends decked out in wide-brimmed sombreros. A few middle-aged men leaned against the picket fence, smoking cigarettes. Some elderly crones sat around a table, gossiping and picking at the cabrito, tamales, queso and chocolates set before them. None of the guests maintained eye contact with Menchaca for very long: he had a dark, almost mocking gaze that made most people uncomfortable.

Near the front gate, a boy hung back in the shadows. Menchaca glared at him. The kid had been watching him too intently when he played, and the musician didn't like him. The boy stared back. Menchaca dismissed him with a snort.

He started another of his corridos, this one celebrating a Tejano Robin Hood who was shot by the Texas Rangers. The troubadour's songs often chronicled real events. Many of them were local ruckuses that took place on Military Plaza, where he sold chili con carne when he had nothing more pressing to do.

By then the dancing was over. A few of the young couples, inclined to gather their rosebuds, drifted off into the night. The old women took note.

The boy stayed until the end. He kept staring while Menchaca's fingers deftly manipulated the guitar frets.

Eventually the kerosene lantern on the porch flickered. Menchaca used that as an excuse to bid goodnight, amid protests: "Uno más!" He stood up, straightening his striped serape and red silk sash. Then he strapped his guitar to his back. He set out on a winding dirt lane heading downtown. The adobe cantinas and casinos of the West Side were in full swing, but he passed them by. He was ready to call it a night.

Then he noticed the boy following him at a distance. It suddenly occurred to Menchaca: this little hoodlum was after his guitar. That was what he had been looking at all night.

Menchaca took a detour down an unlighted, twisting alley to see if he could lose him. Incidents of thuggery were starting to occur on the West Side: young hooligans brandishing Bowie knives and robbing people outside cantinas. And his guitar was a fine instrument, easily worth ten dollars in a pawn shop. Rafael Menchaca knew he was stronger and smarter than this boy; but the kid might have friends waiting nearby.

The boy took the detour. He was getting closer.

Menchaca rounded a corner, then ducked into the doorway of a brick warehouse. Silently he unstrapped his guitar and set it aside. Then he waited.

The boy appeared cautiously in the shadows. Menchaca leapt out and knocked him down. Startled, the kid cried out. He struggled violently, but Menchaca had him pinned to the ground, kneeling on his back.

The boy's face was in the dust. "Let me go!"

"Shut up! Little shit punk." Menchaca cuffed him on the neck.

He let the boy squirm just enough to free one arm, then jerked the arm behind his back and twisted it. "Now you can talk to me. What's your name?"

"Enrique Herrera."

"Are you alone?"

"Yes."

"Why were you following me?"

The kid struggled again. "Get off, I can't breathe—"

"Shut up. Why are you following me?"

The kid panicked. "I just wanted to ask you if . . . your songs. . . ."

He trailed off into a hoarse coughing fit as he swallowed dust. Menchaca thought it was safe to let go of him. The kid rose slowly, brushing off his shirt and trousers. When he looked up again, Menchaca was smiling at him—not kindly—and holding a knife.

"Now let's talk."

The kid was terrified. He glanced first at the knife, then at the man's angry black eyes. "Yes, sir."

"What about my songs?"

"Sir?"

Menchaca grabbed his shirt and slammed him against the brick wall, holding the kid in place with his thick forearm. He shouted in the boy's face: "What's the matter? Don't you remember what shit lie you were saying? What about my songs?"

"I—I want to learn to play like you. I write songs."

Menchaca placed the knife against his throat. Their faces were inches apart. "It's not my guitar?"

"Sir?"

"You were after my guitar!"

"No, sir. I swear."

"Little shit."

He let him go. The kid wiped his mouth but didn't try to run.

"Where do you come from?"

The boy looked down. "Alamo Heights."

The man stared in disbelief. "Are you joking? Alamo Heights?"

"Yes, sir."

Menchaca was stunned for a moment. Then his eyes started to sparkle, and his head rolled back in peals of laughter. "Little boy! How did you wander so far from home?"

That made the kid mad. "I told you, I wanted to—"

"Yes, yes, I know. You told me. And your father is . . ."

"Antonio Herrera."

"Are you serious? The lawyer?"

"Yes, sir."

"And your mother—the daughter of Fermin De León?"

"Yes, sir."

"She drives that automobile? Like a crazy person?"

"Yes, sir."

Menchaca clasped the kid's shoulders and rocked him, still laughing. "Alamo Heights! If only I had known at the party! We were graced by royalty."

Enrique had worshipped this man from afar. Now he despised him.

"And you write songs?"asked the man.

"Yes, sir. Corridos."

"Corridos! Astonishing! What are your songs about?"

The kid was sullen. He didn't answer.

"Let me guess. Oppression in the Heights, hmm? The trials of life in the suburbs? Which shoes to wear with which trousers?"

"No, sir."

Menchaca saw that he was hurting the boy's feelings. He wrapped one arm around his neck and drew him near, paternally. "Now, now, don't look like that. I'm only fooling with you."

The boy nodded.

"I should congratulate you instead! You've escaped from Alamo Heights. So what made you come here? Are you slumming?"

"I want to be a mariachi."

Menchaca was startled. "A mariachi?"

"I want to be a mariachi, like you."

"Like me?"

"Yes, sir."

The man was greatly offended. His face darkened again, and he spat. "Shit! You want to be like me? Have you heard my songs?"

"Yes, sir."

"You don't know anything. My songs are about immigrants. Workers. Discrimination! I am the voice of the people! You know that?"

"Yes, sir. I know that."

"Do you?"

"Yes, sir. You wear it on your sleeve like a red flag."

Enrique was amazed that he said that. It had just slipped out: the De León in him. The remark also caught Menchaca off guard. And rather pleased him. He nodded. "So. You have your father's intelligence. And your mother's spirit."

The boy grimaced. "You know my parents?"

"No, no. But everyone on the West Side knows *of* them. The Tejano bourgeoisie."

"Enough! Please."

"All right. All right, Enrique Herrera. I should hear your songs."

Enrique reached for the guitar, but Menchaca blocked him. "No, not here. You've come all the way from the Heights. Ha! You're going to get a proper reception. My place."

The man strapped the guitar on his back and beckoned Enrique to follow.

"Not long ago I saw this brochure for Alamo Heights," Menchaca ranted as they crossed Military Plaza. "It said there's no railway tracks. No unsightly parts of town to drive through. And it's so high on the hill that the breezes there don't even pass over town first--so they're uncontaminated by impurities rising from the city. Ha! Those capitalists don't even want to smell the rest of us!" He laughed. Enrique joined him, wishing the man would change the subject.

Though he owned a house on the West Side, Rafael Menchaca kept a rented room on Camaron Street near the plaza. It was on the second floor of the Palace Livery Stable. Renting a room gave him the satisfaction of aligning himself against a landlord. He also liked to stay close to the center of San Antonio life.

With an exaggerated bow, Menchaca opened one of the wide double doors of the limestone stable. "Those ricos may think Alamo Heights is the pinnacle, my friend. But nothing compares to the Palace." He put his arm around Enrique and ushered him through.

The boy was thrilled. Inside the stable he inhaled the strong aromas of hay and leather tack and manure. Muffled shouts, stomps, laughter filtered down from above. This, he felt sure, was a place where people measured each other by their character and didn't tolerate posers.

The ground floor of the Palace was lit by a single electric bulb. They walked the length of the building, over packed earth and flattened straw, past horses settled in their stalls for the night and dark, empty carriages. At the far end Menchaca led Enrique up a narrow flight of wooden stairs.

The second floor was brighter and noisier, with sporadic guffaws and bursts of profanity from the cowhands boarding there for the night. Menchaca's room was at the end of the hallway overlooking the street. Its green walls were bare and the windows curtainless. The ceiling was mapped in water-stain islands. A cot, chair and bare table were the only furnishings. Enrique liked the spareness of the room. He was surprised to see a pot of coffee already brewing on a kerosene burner.

"Sit anywhere."

There weren't many choices. Enrique took the cot, leaving the chair for his host.

For the first time the boy got a look at his idol in the light. He guessed Rafael Menchaca was about forty-five, but he might have been older. His rough brown face was lined in deep ruts, like the West Side roads the troubadour wandered. His black goatee and penetrating eyes made him look threatening, even when he laughed. Despite his paunch, his body had the naturally hard, muscled look of an outdoor laborer.

Menchaca was unstrapping his guitar when a slender girl entered carrying a large straw basket. She was dressed in a bright floral skirt and wore a yellow rose in her long black hair, as if she were coming from a party. Her face had the finest, most delicate features Enrique had ever seen, but her hands looked strong and supple. She moved silently, her eyes demurely fixed on the floor. Enrique wondered if she was one of many paramours the troubadour kept, and if they were all so young.

"Ah, princesa," said Menchaca. "Did you have a good evening?"

She nodded. Then she reached for the pot and started pouring. Enrique tried not to stare as the girl brought him black coffee in a chipped cup. He murmured a shy "Gracias."

Menchaca set the straw basket in front of Enrique. "Look inside. Go ahead." His eyes were dancing with pride.

The basket was filled with little clay figures, all meticulously decorated and painted red and yellow and blue. There were bullfighters.

Monte players. Calaveras in sombreros, their skeleton faces grinning. Angry Aztec gods.

"Go on. Take them out."

Enrique carefully removed a statue of a mariachi, who looked a great deal like Menchaca.

The boy looked up at his hero. "You're an artist also?"

"Me? No. These big hands are clumsy, except on the guitar. Eva is the artist. She's been out selling her sculptures to all the tourists around the plaza."

Enrique looked at the girl. She smiled briefly, then glanced down.

He put the figure back in the basket. "These are good."

"Good? They are the best quality!" exclaimed Menchaca. "All the old men around the plaza say they've never seen figures like these."

"Yes. These are the best."

"And look at this." He handed Enrique a broadside sheet with the lyric of "Jesus at the Chili Stand." It was illustrated with calaveras depicting the characters and events in the tale. "See? She can draw just as well."

Enrique studied the sheet and nodded. "These should be in a book."

The girl stood against the wall, her hands behind her. Menchaca stared at her with great pride. "As soon as I think she's ready, Eva is going to school to study art. Her sisters can marry and have children if they want, but I have big plans for this girl. I've told her I'll cut the huevos off the first boy that even looks at her." He glanced at Enrique. "So. My daughter and I have shown you our talents. Let's see what *you* can do." He held out his guitar to Enrique.

The boy nodded. Menchaca's daughter. He tuned the strings one by one, stalling. "This is the first song I ever wrote."

Enrique had never played his song for anyone. He strummed the opening chords but faltered. The man's face terrified him.

He got up, walked to the other side of the cot, and sat with his back to his audience. Then he started again. The song was a sentimental ballad about lost love. He sang it with as much conviction as his nervousness would allow. But halfway through the chorus, he became aware of its inadequacy: the paltry word choices, the tired harmonies. The song was serious, but he was convinced that his listeners were about to burst with laughter. His confidence gone, he missed a few chord changes.

When he finished, he turned around to face the verdict. The girl was still looking down. But Rafael Menchaca's stern gaze withered him.

"That is perhaps the worst song I have ever heard."

Enrique swallowed audibly. He was afraid he wouldn't be able to stay the tears.

The girl suddenly looked up and hissed, "Shame on you!" Her vehement outburst surprised Enrique, cutting the sting of her father's words.

"Hush!" Menchaca ordered.

"It was a beautiful song!"

He turned to her. "Be quiet. The boy is very talented. I can see that. But this! Uh! This needs a great deal of fixing."

Enrique managed to smile a little.

Menchaca looked at him and spoke, softer this time, but urgently. "You play very well, and your melody is good. You have a talent for words, also. If that weren't true, I wouldn't waste my time on you. I'm the best; I know what I'm talking about. Your first song is terrible, not because it didn't please my ear, but because it didn't convince my heart. Tell me. Have you ever loved and lost?"

The boy shook his head.

"There. You've copied a hundred other writers, and most of them have copied one another. You must write songs about the things that stir your blood and ignite a fire in your belly! Understand?"

Enrique nodded.

"I wrote my first song when I was twenty and had a job at the flour mill. That was the only time I ever worked for an employer! The workers went on strike, and I wrote a corrido about how our families were starving while the ricos got fat in the Heights. Let me tell you—it was a terrible song. But it came from inside me. Understand? We sang it at the mill until the cops came and beat us up and threw us in jail. Then we sang it to the jailers! When we got out I wrote another song, this time a funny one. I portrayed the employer as a stubborn burro and the worker as a wise old billy goat. Ha! They sang that verso in cantinas all over the city, even along the border. I was famous! But I couldn't have written either of those corridos until my blood was boiling. You see, my friend: that's where songs come from."

Enrique stared at him seriously. Menchaca smiled. "As for you—you haven't found your subject yet. When you do, I'll teach you craft. How to make your songs better. You're very lucky. You've got the best teacher there is. When will you come for lessons?"

The boy shrugged. "I don't know. I must be careful. My parents are--"

"Your parents!" The man was scornful. "An artist doesn't live his life within limits set by his parents."

Enrique looked down, shamed in front of his new mentor--and the girl.

"And a man of the people doesn't stay in Alamo Heights. Every afternoon this week I'll be playing out there on the plaza. You have your own guitar?"

"Yes, sir."

"Bring it. You can join me. But next time, don't turn your back on your audience. You should take pride in your music!"

Enrique nodded. He knew he must be dreaming. He thought of all those times he had slipped out of his window late at night to hear this man sing in the plazas and cantinas. For many months his most cherished fantasy had been to perform someday with Rafael Menchaca, the Corrido King. He had expected to spend years in apprenticeship. And an hour earlier he had been elated just to walk the streets of the West Side at the man's side. But now—to perform with the King himself before the end of the week! He summoned all his boyish machismo to keep from breaking out in a big grin.

Awkwardly, he said, "For payment, perhaps I can—"

"Bah!" the man barked. "You talk like a bourgeoisie employer. You'll give me exactly what I demand–your best effort. And your loyalty. I'll share my time and my wisdom with you. But you must be careful to respect what is mine. And anything that I may not want to share." With that he casually drew his knife and started cleaning his nails.

75

Enrique quickly finished his coffee and thanked both of them again. On his way out, Eva took his hand and placed in it the figure of the mariachi.

"This one is for you. To keep."

He was standing close enough to smell her yellow rose. And to see the tiny beads of perspiration forming on the smooth skin of her neck. "You saw it was my favorite."

She closed his hand around it. Enrique glanced nervously at her father. It was probably his imagination, but he thought he saw the man wave his knife once in a rapid slashing motion.

The boy left hurriedly, clutching the figure as he rushed along the hall, nearly colliding with a drunken cowboy. He clambered down the wooden staircase. The horses stirred as he ran by. He burst out the wide double doors and into the dark street.

Then he let out a wild, high-pitched grito of pure joy. This was just the beginning! Now he had two reasons to come back to the West Side.

WILLINGHAM HOTEL COMPANY

Clifford Building
Commerce Street Bridge
San Antonio, Texas

September 30, 1907

Mrs. Antonio Herrera
1211 Townsend Avenue
City

Dear Madam:

May I be pardoned, a stranger, for intruding upon your attention.

I represent the Willingham Hotel Company of Philadelphia. I was privileged to hear your gallant and stirring remarks at the Root dinner of Saturday last, and I have since been informed that you are the custodian of that hallowed shrine of liberty, the Alamo.

Noble lady, I beg to put before you a proposal in which, I believe, you and I have identical interests. The Willingham Company is negotiating this week to purchase the property now occupied by the Hugo & Schmeltzer warehouse on Alamo Plaza. We intend to erect a modern, concrete, first-class hotel on the site. It will be perhaps the handsomest building of its kind in the Southwest.

However, before construction can proceed, it will be necessary for us to wreck the unsightly Hugo & Schmeltzer building and level the site. In the course of this demolition, it may prove necessary for our workmen to occasionally trespass upon the grounds of the Alamo. I am sending this missive to beg your permission for these intrusions, apologizing in advance, and to implore your cooperation in helping us remove that common nuisance, the Hugo & Schmeltzer warehouse. Soon our beloved Alamo will be unburdened of this highly objectionable structure!

Of course, our workmen shall be strictly instructed to use their utmost care and decorum on the Alamo grounds, removing their hats as they pass by those sacred portals. They shall clear away all debris as quickly as possible.

I trust that these plans meet with your approval, and that this will be the beginning of a long and mutually beneficial association.

And, as you say in these parts — howdy, neighbor!

Very sincerely yours,
Wilton A. Peck
Senior Development Coordinator

cc: Mr. C. C. Willingham

H owdy, neighbor?

What a detestable, apple-polishing, boot-licking, back-stabbing little weasel, thought Rose. In a flash of fury she crumpled Peck's letter.

By the time she got this message, she had already mobilized the Daughters of the Republic and contacted Mr. Hugo, the owner, about buying the warehouse building. She was waiting for his reply. Peck's letter impressed on her the urgency of the situation: "Howdy, neighbor! Pardon me while I knock down the building where your grandfather and the other rebels fell and build a concrete hotel on top of the Alamo." *Concrete*: the little vermin even boasted about it! She thought of the ruined wall around San José–the price of having come on the scene a day too late—and shuddered.

At dinner Wednesday evening, she told her husband about the plan she'd come up with. "The Daughters can't afford to buy the property outright," she explained. "But if Mr. Hugo will sell us an option, say, for six months, I'm sure we could raise the purchase price. What do you think?"

Antonio frowned. "That's a valuable lot."

"Of course it is. That's why we can't lose any time."

She waited for him to respond. He kept chewing. And chewing.

Dinner had become an ordeal at the Herrera house. To help Enrique acculturate, Antonio had decided that their cook, Eloisa, should prepare every American and Continental dish in the book. All were beyond her abilities. Tonight's effort was Beef Wellington.

She had succeeded only in extracting all traces of flavor, moisture and texture from the meat. And her pastry shell—though it might have made decent sopaipillas, given the chance—broke into crumbs en route from the tray to the plate.

What's more, the dinner table was much too long for the small family, with Mr. and Mrs. Herrera conversing at a distance from opposite ends. Between them, Enrique silently and dutifully worked his way through each of the bland courses intended to better prepare him as a citizen.

Antonio spoke only English at the table so that his son's vocabulary would improve. "Naturally, this will be in the papers," he finally said, coolly. "Won't that be interesting?"

His wife made no reply. This time she was the one chewing strenuously.

He took cruel advantage of her incapacity, continuing his sarcastic assault. "Just what every man wants. To open the *Journal* and see his wife's name blasted across the business page. Especially when he's just started to make some headway in society."

She rolled her eyes, swallowing with difficulty. "Oh! You and Edna Duvalier. That's all she was worried about, too. How it was going to look for the Daughters to be at odds with the Business Men's Club."

"The Business Men's Club?"

"Yes. Your partner Mr. Franck was quoted today: the Club thinks the new hotel is just *bully*. Horatio Franck, the original thinker! Wonder where he got that?"

"Mr. Franck was quoted?" That made her husband uneasy.

She nodded, struggling with another bite. Enrique mopped his brow with his napkin. The overhead fan did little to dispel the October heat.

Antonio's knife scraped his plate. He gave up. "Rose, I can't cut this."

"I'll speak to Eloisa. Excuse me."

She left the table and went to the kitchen. With the exception of her study, the kitchen was the only room in the big house where she really felt comfortable. Eloisa was scrubbing pans. Rose had no

intention of instructing the cook at the moment. Instead, she headed straight for the woodstove. She lifted a heavy lid and sniffed the
refritos in the frying pan. Then she grabbed a warm flour tortilla and
spooned the bean paste onto it.

"Those are for Santos," protested Eloisa.

"There's plenty for Santos. I am starving." She sat by the stove and
gulped the refritos and tortilla in enormous bites. While she ate, the
cook kept up a running monologue of gossip her sister had brought
from the West Side. Rose was not particularly fond of Eloisa, who
was given to idle prattle and dire superstitions. But she'd inherited
her from an aunt; she couldn't turn her out.

She stood up to get another tortilla. "You've got my head spin-
ning," she told the cook. "I can't keep up with all these people you
tell me about."

"Perhaps you should try," the woman warned portentously.

Her employer humored her. "Why do you say that?"

"My sister has seen Enrique across the river." Eloisa dried her
hands on her apron.

Rose put down her tortilla. "Where?"

"Several places. But that's not the worst part."

Rose sat. Her appetite was gone. "Tell me."

"He was seen with Rafael Menchaca." Eloisa rubbed the wart on
her chin, milking this bit of bad news as long as she could.

"Who is Rafael Menchaca?"

"Ai! He's a jailbird, a cutthroat, a lowlife son of Satan. And a musician! Believe me, he's bad company for a boy."

"Was she sure it was Enrique?"

"Of course! My sister knows your son."

"What was he doing with this man?"

"No one knows."

Rose felt weak. It was worse than she'd imagined. She wished now
it had been a girl that was drawing him away, even a girl of easy
virtue.

"Where can I find this Menchaca?" she asked.

"He has a chili stand on Military Plaza."

"He and two dozen others!"

"You'll know this criminal. He has a goatee. And he always wears a derby. Sometimes he plays his guitar there. Also, he's got mean, frightening eyes."

Rose brooded. She wasn't prepared for *this* news. And the last thing she wanted was for her husband to find out about this Menchaca business and blame her.

She stood up. "Don't tell anyone about this," she charged Eloisa. "And don't mention it to Mr. Herrera. Let me know if you hear any more."

She had gone to the kitchen for solace; instead, she had only gained a new worry. At least it had taken her mind off Wilton Peck's letter for the moment. She was too distraught to go back to the dining room and face the Beef Wellington, or her cranky husband and errant son. Quietly she slipped out the kitchen door and headed for the garage.

"¡Santos! Traiga el Peerless. En seguida."

"¿Mande?"

"El Peerless. Muy pronto, por favor."

She plucked a pear from one of Antonio's trees and munched on it until Santos brought the automobile. Then she sped out of the driveway. She didn't bother with a hat. The evening breeze felt good as it brushed against her cheeks and rustled her hair.

She hoped a drive would clear her head of Eloisa's news. Motoring had become her means of release. Over the course of a year, it had even changed her appearance. Driving the Peerless demanded free use of her limbs. Her sleeves opened. Her skirts climbed three inches.

The route down Broadway cut through newly-platted residential blocks. She rushed by grandiose manses of iron and granite, where San Antonio's most substantial citizens dwelled in secure isolation. The lawns still had the raw look of recent and aggressive landscaping. Gas pipes and eight-inch water mains jutted out of the ground like galvanized tubers pushing up from some dank netherworld.

Rose scowled. She detested these inhospitable fortresses. And the drive wasn't clearing her head. She couldn't stop fretting about her son and Rafael Menchaca. Surely Enrique wasn't mixed up in anything illicit. But what was he doing consorting with a notorious West Side jailbird? She knew she'd soon have to investigate the matter herself. Even if that meant going to Military Plaza to confront this underworld figure—who might be dangerous.

But she wasn't going to look for the man tonight. Without slowing the car she swung left at Houston Street. She ran the engine full throttle to Alamo Plaza and circled once, passing the Menger Hotel. Then she stopped short beneath a street lamp in front of the Alamo. She needed to pay her grandfather a visit.

Meanwhile, upstairs in the most elegant suite at the Menger, Alva Carson Keane glanced up as she heard the Peerless roar through the plaza. Then she went back to scribbling a letter in her expansive, confident handwriting. Though she would be late meeting her dinner companions at Scholz's Palm Garden, she was obsessed with finishing this letter. Something she had seen that day had distressed her. And—though she hardly realized it yet—held great promise for her. She put down her pen and read what she had written. It gave her goose bumps. Then she put the letter in an engraved envelope and instructed her serving girl to hand-deliver it to the *Journal*.

THE SAN ANTONIO JOURNAL

Thursday, October 3, 1907

Letters to the Editor

Dear Sir:

This week—after having been away from the enchanting City of San Antonio for nearly a year—I had the privilege of standing once again before the grandest monument in the United States—the Thermopylae of America—the Alamo!

How many of you in San Antonio today have really considered the Alamo and the wonderful lesson of self-sacrifice that it teaches? Think of how it speaks to every true Texan heart!

Yet how do we treat our Alamo? On one side we leave it hemmed in by a hideous warehouse, and on the other by a row of saloons.

The Alamo should stand out free and clear. All the unsightly obstructions that hide it must be torn away. Fellow Texans, shall we not rally once more to the defense of our dear old Alamo?

Alva Carson Keane
New York, New York
"Always a Texas Girl"

16

E arly Thursday morning Alva stood in front of a full-length
mirror in her hotel suite. She was alone.

"Y'all," she said tentatively.

She smiled her sweetest smile.

"Thank y'all for coming."

She frowned. It still wasn't right. Perhaps with more energy. . . .

"Howdy," she said loudly, "how're y'all doing?"

Oh God, that sounded awful. She turned away in disgust.

Alva was practicing for her autograph party that afternoon. More
than anything, she wanted to make a big hit in her native state. She'd
been away from it for a long time.

When Alva was ten, her daddy decided to send her to Miss Anna
Falconer Perrin's School for Girls in New York City. Alva was starting to neglect her lessons, spending all her time riding and shooting
and pestering the vaqueros to teach her how to rope. Oscar Carson
didn't care if his daughter grew up to be uncouth; but he did think
she needed to gain enough discipline and book learning to be able
to run the ranch someday. Besides, he felt a proper education was
what Alva's mother would have wanted for her.

"Remember where you came from, Alva," The Old Man told her
when he put her on the train in Laredo.

Alva hated boarding school. The matrons made her go to church
every Sunday. Her horseback riding was limited to one hour a week
in Central Park, sidesaddle. The other girls mimicked her accent,
and Miss Perrin, the principal, decried her tomboyish ways.

Once when she was thirteen, she was asked to read from *Ivanhoe* in class. Alva loved that story. She was putting all her heart—practically her whole body—into her reading when the teacher interrupted her and said:

"Remember, Miss Carson, a common girl sometimes speaks with too much enthusiasm, but a young lady never does."

The other pupils giggled. Alva threw ink at the hateful old cow. Two days later she was on a train back to Texas. The letter of expulsion charged that she had failed to develop a sense of Christian responsibility and was a bad influence on her peers. Alva spent a very happy year at Tres Piedras while her daddy pondered what to do with her.

Her next school was Chateau Diendonne, a convent near Paris. There, as a teenager, Alva started to see the world differently. She became interested in art and music and good cuisine. She worked hard to learn French and paid attention to fashion. For the first time Oscar Carson's daughter was embarrassed by her rough edges, and she made up her mind that the world would never see the "country" in her again.

She succeeded. By the time she returned to New York four years later, she had made herself over into a perfect cosmopolite. People stopped asking where she was from. Her Texas twang had almost vanished.

Now, at age twenty-six, she wanted it back. She was tired of blending in. And she had started to miss Tres Piedras. In her mind she romanticized her childhood on the ranch. At parties she told exaggerated tales about her cowpuncher days. By the time her novel was in print, Alva Carson Keane had acquired a new public image: the Texas cattle queen blazing a trail through the highest echelon of New York society.

Her publisher, Max Rosenthal, was delighted. "It's just what the public wants," he assured her. "The more colorful, the better. You should ride your horse through the Waldorf or shoot out the lights in Times Square or something."

Alva's Texas act worked splendidly for her in New York. But this trip marked her first chance to test it at home. That morning she had doubts whether she could really pull it off. She had never dreamed it would be so hard to come back.

Nervously, she picked up the telephone. Her first local audience would be the hotel staff. "Operator? Y'all are slower than molasses this morning. Could y'all send up my breakfast right away, please ma'am?"

17

Mrs. Herrera was expected at Madame Guenther's on Thursday. By then her plan to battle the Willingham Hotel Company was well underway. She had an appointment to meet with Mr. Hugo about the warehouse the next morning. She would go well armed. All week she'd been poring over musty histories in her study until deep into the night, pausing at her typewriter only long enough to reach for her coffee cup. The result of her obsessive effort was a detailed proposal bound in a handsome leather portfolio. It told the whole story of the Alamo and the DRT.

Of course, before the Alamo was safe from the Willinghams, she still had to come up with the money to buy an option. That was her goal for the day, after she made her social call.

Early that morning she drove to La Villita to visit the sculptor. The ancient housekeeper Toombs examined her card and scowled. "Yes," he determined, "she will want to see *you*." He admitted her without announcement.

In the studio the sculptor, in her trademark black frock, was refining her clay rendering of Prometheus, sans model.

"Please don't let me interrupt your work," Rose said.

"I won't," replied the older woman. "But I am glad you came."

Rose seated herself on a stool nearby. "I can't stay long. I'd like to watch you for a moment, though."

"Feel free. But you are blocking my light."

"Perdón." Rose shifted her stool.

It was a welcome change for her to have a conversation that required no small talk, and periodically no talk at all. Despite the German woman's coldness, Rose felt compelled to seek out her company. Most likely it was because of the woman's honesty. However blunt the artist might be, she would always give her a straight answer when she needed one.

"You will be interested to know," Madame Guenther told her, "that I have declined Mr. Peck's hotel commission."

The week had been so frenetic that Rose had already forgotten about that. She immediately started telling the sculptor about her plan for buying the Hugo & Schmeltzer. "I've got to find the money for an option before tomorrow. I'm on my way to see the owner of the Menger Hotel. Lord knows if anyone's going to help us, he should be the one. With the threat of a new hotel next door."

Madame Guenther took a sudden interest. "May I go with you?"

Rose was surprised. "Of course. I could use some support."

The sculptor stopped working and went to wash her hands in a basin. "I will be frank with you, Mrs. Herrera."

"I'm sure you will."

"I am not going just to support you—although I do support what you are doing. You see, people think that because I am an artist, I live apart from the world of commerce. Ivory towers and all that nonsense. But I have learned what I must do to get commissions and keep my art going. I humble myself: I would be grateful if you would introduce me at the Menger."

Rose nodded. Somehow she felt responsible for Madame Guenther's loss of the Willingham commission, although she knew the artist had made her own decision. "Yes, I know from my own experience how hard it is to raise money. And believe me, I'd much rather see the Menger buy your pieces than another wall-to-wall painting of cows. I'd be glad to introduce you."

Madame Guenther turned to face her visitor as she dried her hands and brushed specks of clay from her frock. "Perhaps you'll be embarrassed by the way I'm dressed? If your clubwomen should see us?"

"Oh, please! Your clothes won't make a bit of difference. Once people see me associating with you, that'll be enough to get me booted out of respectable society."

"Good, good. You must struggle to free yourself from the bonds of respectable society. Am I to ride in your automobile?"

"Unless you want to drive it."

"Certainly not. Come, then." The bulky artist could move quickly when she wanted. "Toombs, never mind the tea."

A quarter of an hour later they arrived in the lobby of the Menger, an oddly matched pair, one in festive plumage and the other in morbid black. They drew attention for their brisk pace and solid determination in the midst of idle tourists lounging and reading the *Journal*.

But they were disappointed when they reached the office. The hotel's owner was away in Paris. His sister from Galveston was managing in his absence. They were admitted to see her.

The woman was uninterested in the Daughters' plan, listening to Rose's fervent pitch with placid indifference. "Yes. Umm. I see."

Rose held out the leather portfolio that contained her proposal. "This explains what I have in mind--"

"Uh-huh. Well, I'm sure I won't have time to read all that. And besides, I'm not authorized to make any civic contributions while my brother is away. But you can talk to him when he gets back next month."

"Next month will be too late." Rose didn't try to hide her annoyance.

Madame Guenther produced her card. "Will you let him know I called?"

The woman took it, aloof. "Umm."

The two visitors stood up to go. "You may be interested to know," the woman volunteered, "that the society woman who wrote that letter in today's paper is staying here. She might be able to help you."

Rose turned. "What letter?"

"About fixing up the Alamo. What's her name?" She thumbed through the *Journal* on her desk. "Here. Alva Carson Keane."

Rose studied the letter intently.

Madame Guenther perked up. "A society woman?"

"She's always in the papers. Very ambitious."

"Is she a patron of the arts?"

Rose looked up, amused by her companion's lack of subtlety.

"I don't know,"said the woman. "But she's rich. She's the heir to some big ranch in South Texas."

"Tres Piedras,"mumbled Rose.

"Oh,"said Madame Guenther, disappointed. "A cattlewoman."

"She lives in New York,"said the woman. "She's in San Antonio to promote a book she wrote."

That sounded more promising to the artist. "And she's here this morning? Right now?"

"I suppose. The desk clerk can tell you."

They were off, Madame Guenther leading the way through the lobby. Rose tugged at her elbow. "Wait! I can't explain right now, but I don't want this woman involved."

The sculptor stopped and turned around. "You know her?"

Rose answered carefully. "No . . . we've never met. But she's a Carson. Believe me, if she's anything like her father—oh, don't get me started!"

Madame Guenther was irritated. "Started on what? Mrs. Herrera, you are not talking sense. This woman is in a position to help both of us."

"I don't care. There was bad blood between our families."

The artist paused. "Long ago?"

Rose nodded. "It still gives me cold shivers."

Madame Guenther sighed. "Mrs. Herrera. You need money, and so do I, and this woman has it. Can either of us afford to miss this chance?"

Rose frowned. Her German friend was right.

The artist proceeded to the reception desk. After she stated their purpose, the desk clerk called upstairs to announce them. They were invited up. "The Renaissance Suite,"he told them. "Second floor, facing the plaza."

Madame Guenther looked at her companion. "Well. Shall we make our hay while the sun is shining?"

Rose shook her head in dismay. "Santa María. . . ."

The artist charged ahead through the marble rotunda toward the staircase. "It will all be fine,"she tried to assure her accomplice.

"You don't know the Carsons,"replied Rose. "They try to take control of everything."

The older woman climbed the stairs with surprising ease. "Just stick to your guns. And be careful not to let your feelings fly."

"If anything flies, it'll be fur,"muttered Rose.

"Remember the Alamo, my friend. Your purpose in coming here today."The sculptor located the suite and knocked.

A serving girl opened the door.

The suite was commodious and airy in spite of its cheerless mauve tones. Vases of fresh flowers adorned every surface. All the windows facing the plaza were open. The French doors leading to the balcony stood ajar, and the October breeze was having its way with the jonquil curtains.

The young author was seated at a writing table, surrounded by piles of manuscript pages in her expansive scrawl. A yellow garland crowned her reddish-brown hair, which was shorter than most women's: an athlete's cut. Although she hadn't been out this morning, she was flawlessly groomed, as if she'd been expecting callers.

She stood to greet them. Rose took a deep breath and said, "Please don't get up."

"Oh, but I need to! Pardon the mess, I've been working since seven. I've got three weeks to write a Broadway script!" She moved toward them with the intensity of a twister.

Rose replied, "We shouldn't have—"

"We'll be brief," the artist interrupted.

"Nonsense! The day a Texan doesn't have time to discuss the Alamo, I want y'all to hang me for treason." Her "y'all" still sounded a little forced.

She ushered them to the reception alcove. The serving girl removed a cluttered breakfast tray from the coffee table. In its place Rose put the leather portfolio with her proposal. The two guests sat on the sofa, and their host took the chaise longue opposite them.

A busy woman, Alva Carson Keane went straight to the point. "Now what's all this hoopla about the Alamo chapel?"

"No, not the chapel. The property next door,"said Rose. "The old convent."

"Right. Where those horrible saloons are."

"No, the warehouse on the other side. It used to be—"

"Oh, of course. The long barracks."Alva blushed.

"Yes. My grandfather, Francisco De León, was killed there."She paused, tense. "My father was there, too. Fermin De León."

"Yes, I know. Ladies, I'll confess, I daydreamed through most of my history classes, but I do know all about the Alamo."

Rose had her doubts. "I'm sure you do."Then she spilled the gist of the Daughters' dilemma, briefing her host on the current crisis. "Mrs. Keane, the DRT has worked for over ten years to get that property into our hands,"she concluded. "You don't know how it kills me to think of a hotel there."

The younger woman listened with great interest. "Oh, but I do know. You're darned right. It's a desecration."

"I'm telling you, it's *going* to happen if I don't move quickly. I'm meeting with Mr. Hugo at ten tomorrow morning. I've *got* to get enough money to buy an option before then."

"How much have you raised so far?"

Rose sighed, embarrassed. "Mrs. Keane, you wouldn't believe. I've worked night and day. All I've got to show for it is eighty-five dollars and a bunch of worthless promises."

The Carson heiress regarded her with sympathy—and just a trace of noblesse oblige. "Rose, you may be the last true patriot in Texas."

Madame Guenther, trying to be helpful, grabbed the leather portfolio off the table and thrust it toward their host. "Here. Take a look at this plan my friend has made. Perhaps you two would make a good team."

Rose wished the sculptor would stay out of this. She wasn't trying to woo Alva Keane as a partner, just as a contributor. She said, "Pardon me for being so forward, but I have no time to lose. I need to raise some money right away."

The ranch heiress barely glanced at the contents of the proposal. She was already convinced. "They can't do it. We're just not going to let it happen."

Then she sprang from the chaise longue and began pacing her suite. She clutched the portfolio, pressing it tightly against her breast. Uneasy with her host towering over her, Rose stood up and started circling in the opposite direction.

All at once Alva smiled broadly, her face set in solid determination. "Gals, I'm with you. We're going to get that property! Even if we have to strap ourselves with rifles and take it by force."

Rose tingled with excitement. "So I can count on you to contribute?"

"Rose, you can count on me to float the option."

"You don't mean—you'd put up *all* the option money for me?"

"I'd do more than that. For Texas. Texas has been generous to me."

Actually, it was her father who had been generous to her, as Rose well knew. Texas had been generous to him.

"Oh!"Alva added, pacing again. "There's something else I can do, to hurry things along."

Warily, Rose replied, "Please don't try to do any more. As busy as you are."

"Nonsense. I'll get Daddy's lawyers here in San Antonio to handle the deal. Could I send them this proposal, Rose?"

"Well, I—"

"Actually, I can cancel tomorrow's engagements. I'll go with them myself to meet with this Hugo fellow."

Rose's De León spirit flared. "No! No, Mrs. Keane, I can't let you do that. I've been corresponding with Mr. Hugo for years. You see, he's used to me. And I have my own way of doing things."

Alva paused, surprised. "Oh. Of course, Rose. I didn't mean to horn in."

Rose realized she had been brusque. Still, she had worked too long and too hard to surrender this project to a novice. Suddenly she felt an odd need to get her proposal back.

The two women kept circling the room like prizefighters in a round of intense contemplation. Madame Guenther didn't know what to make of this. Feeling left out, she suggested, "Why don't the both of you go to meet with Mr. Hugo? Would that not give you more clout?"

Alva looked at Rose as if this possibility had never occurred to her. "Well, that's up to Rose."

Indeed it was. She felt all eyes on her. She didn't like this turn of events. But her host *was* supplying the money; she couldn't afford to seem petty at the moment. "Yes, I suppose Mr. Hugo wouldn't mind if you sat in with me. To observe our meeting."

"Good! I will, then. Rose, Mathilda, this is just the beginning,"continued Alva. "We'll go down in history, the three of us. The rescuers!" She shook the portfolio for emphasis. "No, that's too modest. The *saviors* of the Alamo! How about that?"

"I'll have to cheer you from the sidelines,"Madame Guenther informed her. "At my stage in life, I must choose my battles carefully."

"All right. The two of us, then. But Madame Guenther—I won't let you off this easily. I've always thought the Alamo should have a marble bust of Colonel Travis. Would you do that much for me?"

The sculptor was agog. "I am very busy, of course—"

Rose raised her eyebrows at the artist.

"—but yes, as soon as I have time, it would be my privilege."

"Good. And let's get some publicity going. Rose, is there anything in this proposal we can give to the papers?"

Rose hurried to her, a little peeved. "If you'll hand it here, I can—"

"I'll cable my husband to put something in the wire service tomorrow. We'll get nationwide coverage. The saviors of the Alamo!" By now she was shaking the portfolio wildly.

Rose reached toward her and blurted out, "Careful, please, my pages—"

And then her proposal slid out in a shower of white paper, falling around Alva's feet in disarray. The Carson heiress exclaimed, "Oh, how clumsy of me!"

Rose was quick. Before the younger woman had even bent a knee, she was on the floor, scooping up the papers and hugging them close to her bodice.

"Here,"said Alva. "Let me put them back in order."

"No, that's all right. I'll do it later." Rose took the leather portfolio from her and stuffed the pages into it.

As the two visitors got ready to go, Alva thought of one more thing. "Gals, let me leave y'all with something. "She autographed two copies of *Angelina, Sweetheart of the Chaparral* and gave one to each guest. "It's not Tolstoy, but it might entertain you."

They thanked her graciously.

"Really, you shouldn't,"added Madame Guenther. She detested popular romances.

The author told Rose, "Meet me in the lobby tomorrow at nine. I'll arrange for a taxi to take us to Hugo's."

"That's very kind of you, but I have my own automobile,"replied Rose. "I'll pick you up at nine-thirty. It won't take me long to get us there."

The young woman wasn't used to having her generosity refused. "Well, all right . . . if you're sure. . . ."

"I insist."

"Very well, then. Adiós, compadres!"

The two visitors left the suite. Relieved, Rose checked to make sure she had all her pages. As they went down the stairs to the rotunda, Madame Guenther said, "I owe you a great debt."

Rose was still a little shaken. "Actually, I'm the one who's indebted. You made me go see her, and I did get my money. I just hope I didn't get more than I bargained for. "But it was too late: already she knew she had gained Alva Carson Keane as a partner.

The artist studied her. "Now tell the truth. Was that really so difficult?"

"More than you can imagine. I almost—oh, never mind. Do you have to go back to work immediately?"

"Under the circumstances, Mrs. Herrera, I think a celebration is in order."

"Good. Come with me. I'll treat you to the best restaurant in town."

19

That morning Rose Herrera and Alva Carson Keane, the belated successors of Travis and Bowie, joined hands to defend the Alamo. The two women had been drawn together in an unlikely alliance by their common goal. What stood between them, keeping them from fully embracing, was something else they had in common: Tres Piedras Ranch.

It was a choice 8,000 acres of strong cattle country, once part of the De León land grant on the lower Rio Grande. And it had been in the De León family until 1885. That year Rose's father lost Tres Piedras—to Oscar Carson—at a tax sale in Laredo. Two months later Fermin De León was dead. In her mind Rose had never been able to separate the two events. That was why she could hardly bring herself to call on Oscar Carson's daughter, even though Alva had been a toddler at the time Tres Piedras was auctioned and probably knew little about Fermin De León.

But she *was* a Carson. Alva *Carson* Keane. She even flaunted the name.

For years Rose had tried to block out her memories of the night her father was killed. That single act of violence in front of the Vaudeville Theatre had divided her life into two periods. While Fermin De León lived—although he was profligate, and his fortunes steadily dwindled—his youngest daughter was always secure in her notion of family and of who she was. Then his death had given Rose her first ugly encounter with publicity. For weeks the murder of

Fermin De León had resurfaced in the papers. Each feature story in the tabloids, each new revelation about his rather seamy life and the De Leóns' decline, had pounded at his family like a tidal wave.

Unable to live down the dishonor, her mother, sisters and brother had all eventually relocated to El Paso. Only Rose had remained to carry on the De León legacy in San Antonio. She forced herself back into society. She was still a fighter, but a sense of shame had poisoned her self-esteem.

Alva, on the other hand, had no firsthand memories of the events that had divided the Carsons and the De Leóns. But she'd heard her father talk about Fermin De León, how he'd gambled away his inheritance and died in a drunken brawl. After meeting Rose Herrera that morning, she wanted to know more.

As soon as her guests left, she placed a telephone call. One of her old school chums and traveling companions, Josephine Pearce, was librarian of the new Carnegie Library in San Antonio. Though scatterbrained, Miss Pearce was a loyal friend and would retrieve the information she needed.

"Hello, Josie, it's Alva."

"Alva! My word, I've been trying to reach you. I've read *Angelina* three times, I think it's thrilling! The death scene had me in convulsions, it was so moving, and the adventures were all so laughable, your sense of humor—"

"Listen, dear, I need your help. You have all the Texas newspapers there?"

"Why Alva, we have quite a collection, thanks to your generosity."

"Good! Listen, Josie, I'd like to take a look at everything in the San Antonio papers about the death of Fermin De León, way back, I'm not sure of the year. Exactly what happened. Also about the sale of Tres Piedras Ranch in Laredo—about the same time, I think. Got that, hon? Whatever you have about either."

"Oh Alva, if you're planning to write about the De Leóns, Francisco's the one you want. He was the Alamo hero, and very well educated for a Mexican. Forgive my saying so, but his son Fermin was sort of a no-account, they say he gambled and—"

"No, Josie, this has nothing to do with my writing. I just need to know about Fermin."

"Well, certainly, Alva, I'll see what I have. I'll call you when I get it ready, and—"

"You're the best, Josie. Just drop it off at the Menger for me, would you?"

"Well . . . Alva. Our rules don't allow us to take newspapers out of the reserve room, unless you—"

"Josie, don't be silly, I *paid* for that reserve room after the Carnegie grant ran out. Besides, you and I used to get into much worse mischief in school. If anyone gives you a hard time, just call me. By the way, I'm dying to see you at the autograph party tomorrow."

"Oh, I can't wait! Tell me, Alva, the scene where Angelina is being held captive by the bandidos and Farnsworth rescues her and they end up . . . well, kissing, ha-ha-ha, of course it's preposterous, but did anything like that ever really—"

"Josie, dear, I'd love to talk more, but these awful appointments—listen, I'll tell you all about it at the party. Cheerio, sweetie."

"Ch . . . huh?"

When she got off the telephone, Alva tried to go back to work on her script. But she couldn't concentrate. Instead, she headed downstairs and outside the hotel. She strolled across the street to the Alamo, trying to get her bearings. It still embarrassed her that Rose had corrected her careless slip over where the Alamo convent used to be. She shook her head as she looked at the Hugo & Schmeltzer monstrosity. Once it was demolished, she hoped to erect a beautiful monument to the heroes of 1836.

Then she got another idea. Perhaps the monument could somehow honor the frontier cattlemen of Texas as well. She would even offer to pay for it herself. But what would people think about a monument at that site to great men other than the Texas rebels? Alva spent the rest of the morning debating how Texans would react if she paid tribute to her daddy on the hallowed Alamo grounds.

As promised, Rose treated the sculptor to the best restaurant in town, which wasn't listed in any tourist guide. In fact, it wasn't even in a building. From noon till dusk Military Plaza was the province of the chili vendors. Dozens of tables were set up along the perimeter, overflowing with all sorts of spicy concoctions that lured locals and tourists alike, the converts and the curious: chili con carne, tamales, frijoles, tortillas and dulces. The customers, ranging from bankers in business suits to bricklayers, ate casually and often messily at wooden tables lined with benches. Now and then they were approached by street hawkers offering caged birds and Mexican trinkets.

"Where do we start?" asked Madame Guenther. "Do you have a favorite?"

Rose was distracted. "Today I'm looking for one man in particular."

They were halfway around the crowded plaza when they found him. As Eloisa had said, he was the only chili vendor sporting a goatee and a derby hat. And he kept a guitar behind his table. Immediately Rose felt unsettled: it was the man's obscenely probing eyes, his out-and-out lack of modesty. The facial hair that framed his smile only made his appearance more fiendish. On instinct she crossed herself.

They approached his table. Rose noticed the girl that was helping him. She seemed far too unblemished and well-mannered to be mixed up with this man. Madame Guenther studied the little clay figures she was selling. "I would like to take a closer look at these. There might be some talent here."

"Some other time, please," said Rose. "Let's order and move on." She didn't want to linger near this man.

Madame Guenther chose first—chili con carne and frijoles, the staple item on the menu. Rose selected the tamales and a flour tortilla. She felt the man's gaze on her, close, shameless in its liberty, and—though she didn't look directly at him—mocking. She was overcome by an odd fear: it seemed unnatural for one person to exert so much influence over another simply by staring.

Most of the customers at the tables were men. The two women headed for a vacant park bench on the edge of the plaza where they could talk privately.

"Our chili vendor," said Madame Guenther, "there is something remarkable about him, don't you think? An uncommon quality?"

"He reminds me of a reptile."

"He stirs something inside me."

"Yes. Revulsion."

"No. He has the likeness of a Greek god. A pure specimen of the male ego."

Rose scoffed. "Ego—my God yes. But hardly pure."

"Do you know him?"

"I know of him. He's called Rafael Menchaca." She spoke the name like a disease.

"I would like to meet him."

"Why waste your time? You're always saying you have so little."

"Yes, you mock me. But someday you will know the feeling. I probably have no more than ten good years left, and I must devote them entirely to my art."

They ate for a moment in silence. Rose debated what to do. She couldn't confront this Menchaca at his chili booth for all the world to see. She would have to find out from Eloisa where he lived, then seek him out in private.

She turned to Madame Guenther and unburdened herself. "I think this man is corrupting my son."

"What do you mean?"

"Enrique has been running with him. I don't know what they do together. But now that I've seen this Menchaca, I'm convinced he's dangerous."

"Ridiculous!"

They both watched him. Eventually Menchaca left his chili stand in the care of an underling and took up his guitar. Other mariachis joined him. They began circling the plaza, performing satirical versos and political tragedias for anyone whom their leader deemed worthy of serenading. The girl followed them, selling illustrated broadsides of the lyrics for a penny apiece.

Madame Guenther was spellbound. "You must interpret these songs for me."

Rose nodded. "Once they're close enough for me to hear, I will. If they're not too profane."

"Ach! Don't give me some watered-down English version. I'm old enough to hear the real thing."

By now the mariachi band had gained a concertina and a violin. They were singing Menchaca's allegorical ballad about the burro and the billy goat.

"So what will you do?" asked Madame Guenther.

"What?"

"About your son. And this man."

Rose glared at the troubadour. "I intend to pay him a visit."

Dangerous or not, the man still had a hold on Madame Guenther's fancy. "When you go see him, I would consent to going with you. To lend you support."

"I might take you up on that. Be sure you bring your pistol."

"If he is as dangerous as you say, I would hardly want to provoke him."

"You don't need to provoke him. All you have to do is shoot him."

The mariachis were drawing nearer. Rose made up her mind that when he strolled by, she would look him in the eye and stare back. He would find that two could play his game—especially when his opponent was a De León. Madame Guenther was also determined to meet the man's gaze with her own. If he passed them by, she would boldly demand a serenade. If he spurned her, she might even lower herself and beg.

Suddenly her companion jumped up in a panic. She spilled the remains of her tamales and grabbed her leather portfolio. "My God. Quickly. We must go."

"What? Aren't you—"

"Please. Hurry. Don't ask questions."

Madame Guenther left her bowl of chili barely sampled. She was annoyed, but her friend seemed badly shaken, so she did as she was asked. Rose took her arm and rushed her out of the plaza. They were well across the street before she explained. "Look back. Carefully."

They both did so.

"You see the young guitarist? The boy?"

"Yes."

"That is my son."

It was in fact Enrique, fully outfitted in sombrero and embroidered vest, strumming his guitar and supplying harmonies behind Menchaca's lead.

"A musician?"said Madame Guenther. "You must be proud."

"No. No."

Rose stole one more quick glance at her son. "Let's go. Before he sees me."

They started off. Madame Guenther was puzzled. "should think you would want to hear him. I do."

"No."

"Is this what you call corrupting?"

Rose nodded.

"I don't understand. What's wrong with this? He is an artist."

Rose didn't answer. A mariachi! That was no artist. This was much worse than she could have ever imagined. Her son--descendant of conquistadors—crooning peasant songs on the plaza for tips! It had come to that. She prayed no one would recognize him.

For a moment it occurred to her: Enrique had inherited the De León spirit, just as she had. Only this time it had gone awry—passion without pride. In Madame Guenther's eyes it was fine for him to act beneath his station. But to Rose this went beyond defying convention. This was the De Leóns debased. She couldn't stand to live through any more humiliation.

Antonio must never find out about this. Rose realized she would have to pay a visit to Rafael Menchaca very soon. After seeing what he had done to Enrique, she was no longer afraid of the man. Her fury would make her strong enough to kill him if she had to. She took the sculptor's arm again and hurried her along.

As they headed up Commerce Street, Madame Guenther, her imagination fired, looked back and caught one more precious glimpse of the chili vendor with the hypnotic eyes. She, too, was determined to meet the Corrido King.

GUENTHER STUDIO
502 Villita Street
San Antonio, Texas

October 3, 1907

Hand Delivered by Silas Toombs

Mr. Rafael Menchaca
A Chili Stand
Military Plaza

My dear Sir:

    I am a sculptor. Today I visited your chili stand.
    Would you consent to sitting for a portrait in marble at my studio? You possess a countenance of extraordinary aesthetic integrity.
    Regrettably, your chili was too pungent for my palate.
    I would be most pleased if you would call at your earliest convenience.

Admiringly,
Mathilda Guenther

21

Dinner that night was unbearable. Rose was still too upset to even look at Enrique. She fought to keep from bursting out in tears of anger and dismay. Antonio was annoyed by her unresponsiveness. After a few difficult bites of overcooked pork loin, she excused herself and withdrew to her study. She should have spent the evening preparing for her meeting with Mr. Hugo. Instead she used it to rehearse the tongue-lashing she was going to give Rafael Menchaca.

Consequently, when she picked up Alva in the Peerless the next morning, she wasn't feeling as confident about the meeting as she would have liked.

"Rose, don't worry about a thing," the younger woman was saying as she climbed into the front seat. "Daddy's lawyers are already drawing up the option papers. My, what a gorgeous automobile!"

Rose beamed. "Wait till you see it run."

They left the Menger with a jolt. Alva shrieked in delight. "Daddy won't *have* one of these things at Tres Piedras. He tried driving one once in Laredo. For some reason it scared him to go in reverse. I guess it seemed unnatural to an old horseman. I made fun of him, and he got mad and hasn't driven since."

She guffawed at the recollection. Rose forced a smile. Since the previous day Oscar Carson and the loss of Tres Piedras Ranch had crossed her mind often. It was still hard for her to be allied with the Carson heiress.

Alva gushed. "I can't wait to get to Tres Piedras and tell Daddy what we're doing. By God, we'll put our mark on this state—even the nation! Keane and Herrera–patriots!"

107

Herrera and Keane, thought the senior patriot. Squinting, she increased the throttle.

"Oh—Rose. It occurred to me last night: I'm not officially a Daughter of the Republic. I live in New York, but—would you mind taking me into your San Antonio chapter?"

Rose was caught by surprise. "Well . . . are you sure, Alva? You know, we San Antonio Daughters are known as a bunch of hell-raisers and malcontents."

"I'll wager I can raise hell with the best of y'all."

Rose nodded. "I don't doubt it. I'd be pleased to have you." For an instant she visualized her father rising up in revolt. "As one of my helpers," she added.

The younger woman studied her for a moment. "I consulted a seer when I was in Bombay. I don't know how you feel about clairvoyants. But she told me that things never happen by chance. Rose, I believe there's a reason destiny brought us together. Do you ever have premonitions like that?"

"Yes. I do." Right now she had a vision of Fermin De León standing on the hood of the Peerless, railing against his daughter for joining forces with a usurper.

"I have this feeling you and I are going to wage the biggest battle Texas has seen since the revolution."

Rose looked at her partner in mock alarm. "Oh! I didn't think I was going to have to fight you, too."

"Oh, stop it. You know what I mean. Rose, you and I will be remembered as the second generation of Alamo defenders. We'll end up just like the heroes of the revolution."

"Yes. Dead."

"Probably. But not forgotten!"

Rose smiled. She reminded herself that the young woman wasn't to blame for the events of 1885. Suddenly she felt ashamed for having distrusted the DRT's new benefactor.

They were heading west on Commerce Street, one of the busiest and most cluttered avenues downtown. Rose zipped the Peerless around horse-drawn wagons and pushcarts, sounding the Gabriel horn. The women came up behind a man in a 1906 Compound tourer. Sluggishly propelled by a sixteen-horsepower engine, the lightweight Compound was delaying the women in the Peerless.

Alva gave her ally a knowing look. "Rose."

"No."

"Do it."

"It's too narrow here."

"I dare you."

"You shouldn't have said that."Rose swerved the Peerless. She overtook the Compound, squeezing between its fenders on one side and the hitching posts on the other. They barely cleared both. She blasted the horn as they passed by. The two women waved.

The man in the Compound recognized Rose from the Root banquet. Hoping to win her favor, he smiled broadly and waved without thinking. One of the odd features of the Compound was the deadman's switch that operated its power brakes. The weight of the driver's arm normally held it closed. But when the driver lifted that arm—for instance, to wave at two women in a Peerless that was overtaking him—the brakes were suddenly activated with great force. Wilton Peck screeched to an abrupt halt on Commerce Street, leaving skid marks. His engine sputtered and died.

Peck seethed. The Peerless was already far ahead. Without even looking up, he could sense people on the sidewalks pointing and laughing at him. There was no use even pretending he had stopped on purpose. *Never again,* he thought. After this San Antonio project was through and his promotion assured, never again would he deal with Texans of any sort.

Meanwhile, at the reception desk of the Menger Hotel, a beanpole librarian with frizzy hair inquired about her friend Mrs. Keane. Told that she was out, Josephine Pearce left a package for her. It was a large hat box from Joske Brothers tied with ribbons and bows. The disguise was clever: no one would ever suspect that it contained two yellowed newspapers that the dutiful librarian had pilfered from the Carnegie Reserve Room, in flagrant violation of library rules.

October 4, 1907

Alva, my Dear Sweet Friend,

These are the two articles I've located for you. The first is a Notice of Sale that appeared in the Laredo paper. It is the only mention I could find of the Tres Piedras sale. The second is the San Antonio Journal's headline story about the death of Fermin De León. There are many more articles on this shooting, and I will bring them to you as soon as I can assemble them and concoct another means of getting them out. My, what a crowd you drew at your autograph party yesterday! People say it was a sickening, disgraceful event. Most shootings are, I suppose.

Your faithful servant,
Josephine Pearce

NOTICE OF SALE OF PROPERTY

STATE OF TEXAS,
COUNTY OF WEBB.

COLLECTOR' S OFFICE. *Laredo, May 5th, 1885.*

WHEREAS, a certain party owning property in Webb County has failed to pay the amount assessed against him for property taxes, after having received due notice,

THEREFORE, I, B. R. Salmond, Tax Collector of Webb County, have levied upon, and will, on the 4th day of June, 1885, at 10:00 o'clock in the morning, sell at public outcry to the highest bidder for cash, the below described parcel of land, to satisfy the amount due and unpaid, before the door of the Webb County Courthouse, in the City of Laredo.

The amount due, with accrued cost, may be paid in cash at any time before the hour of sale.

B. R. SALMOND,
County Collector.

Notice issued May 5th, 1885.

DESCRIPTION OF PROPERTY LEVIED UPON:

That 8,037-acre tract in Webb County commonly known as the Tres Piedras Ranch, bounded on the west by the Rio Grande River, and on the north, east, and south by the property of Oscar Carson.

Amount of taxes due: $42.

THE SAN ANTONIO JOURNAL
Wednesday, July 15, 1885

FERMIN DE LEON KILLED
IN BARROOM TRAGEDY

Fermin De León, son of Alamo hero Francisco De León, expected to leave today for a trip to New Orleans. Instead, he has embarked on a longer voyage.

Last night at about 8:15, two bullets took the life of Mr. De León, fired from the pistol of Rowdy Smith, a drifter and a cowhand at the stockyards.

Mr. De León was attending a performance at the Vaudeville Theatre with his wife, Florencia, and their daughter, Rose. He left the theatre around 7:30 to take refreshment at the Jack Harris Saloon next door.

It was there that Mr. De León got into an altercation with Mr. Smith. Although the facts are disputed, it is believed that Mr. De León drew a knife, whereupon Mr. Smith produced a pistol and fired two shots at close range. Mr. De León died during the night at his home.

It is unclear just how the altercation started. However, some acquaintances of Mr. De León said that he had been moody and distraught ever since his ranch near Laredo was auctioned at a public tax sale last month. Mr. Smith is expected to be cleared of criminal charges following an inquest.

The local of the Journal solicited the following testimony from witnesses:

Major Fikes: Smith was profane and boisterous all evening, but I don't think he intended to insult De León. De León mistakenly thought he was being insulted and drew a knife.

Miss Bridges: I was drawing beers behind the bar when I heard Rowdy insult Fermin. I didn't see Fermin draw a knife.

A Mexican: De León drew a knife, but I didn't see him threaten Smith. Smith said, "What are you doing with that knife, you d—s—of a b—!"De León said, "You—my—, you—."Those were their exact words.

Fellow San Antonians, the killing of Fermin De León brings to the public mind the man as we knew him.

How many of you recall that he descended from one of our oldest and finest families? Although Fermin himself was not a pattern of a citizen to put up for our young men to follow, be it said to his credit that his vices, namely his profligacy and his hedonism, were visible and unhidden. Before we judge him too harshly, let us remember that he was orphaned at the tender age of six in the wake of his father's valiant death at the Alamo. Like a waif, tossed about on the crest of the fiercest wave, he was the child of adventure, and in his formative years his companions were reckless and fast-living men. Let us also remember that, to those among us whom he counted as friends, he could be uncommonly generous, and that his company was always pleasant and jovial. We shall miss him.

The two Alamo defenders sped away from Mr. Hugo's office, one bubbling, the other outraged.

"By God, we did it!" shouted Alva, throwing up her arms in triumph. "I never thought it would be that easy."

Rose's face tightened as she shoved the gearshift.

"Oh, cheer up, Rose! Five hundred dollars isn't highway robbery. Not for an option on a downtown lot. Besides, I'm the one paying for it."

Rose kept staring straight ahead, throwing the automobile into final drive. "I'm not worried about the price of the option. It's the duration."

That took some of the wind out of Alva's sails. "Yes. Well, we tried our darndest to get six months. Hugo wasn't going to budge, that was plain. But he is on our side. He didn't even want to see your proposal before he made up his mind."

That stung. It seemed that no one wanted to look at Rose Herrera's scholarly treatise. "How can you say he's on our side?"she replied. "He's giving us one month! To raise seventy-five thousand dollars!"

"Well, I really didn't expect him to take the property off the market for half a year. Not with Wilton Peck breathing down his neck and offering a lot of money. Hugo's no fool."

"*Seventy-five thousand dollars!* That's ridiculous."

Alva looked at the driver and placed a hand on her shoulder. "Rose, I know it's a lot, but we can do it! We have to! Once people find out what's at stake, they'll get behind us. I can just feel it."

Rose glanced at her for a moment. "You're still very young, Alva. You have no idea."

The other woman resented that. They drove in silence, both thinking hard. Finally Rose said, "There won't be time for a fundraising drive like I'd planned. The way I see it, our only chance is to go straight to Austin. Ask the legislature for an appropriation to cover the purchase price."

"I was thinking the same thing," said Alva. "Who do you know there?"

"Senator Pratt might help us."

"Hobo Pratt? I think Daddy knows him. Isn't he just an old windbag?"

"He is, but he's an influential old windbag. And he was a friend of my father's. He comes to San Antonio often."

They reached the esplanade outside the Menger. Rose kept the engine idling while they sat in the car.

"I have to leave for the ranch tomorrow," said Alva. "My timing is terrible! But Daddy's expecting me, and I've got to finish the draft of *Angelina*. Rose, I'm sorry to run out on you like this. Will you forgive me?"

"Never."

"I'll have to make it up to you, then."

"Just help me keep an eye on Wilton Peck."

"I don't even know what he looks like."

"Neither do I."

Alva was surprised. "You've never met him?"

"No. What I meant was, keep your ears open."

"I will. So when can you start lobbying Pratt?"

"As soon as I get home."

"That's about two minutes, the way you drive. I'll tell my publicist to let the *Journal* know what we're doing. We can stir up some support that way. And my husband's family owns the UAPA wire service. Keep me abreast while I'm gone, Rose. You know my address—Tres Piedras Ranch, Laredo?"

"Yes. I know it."

She stepped down onto the sidewalk. "I'd like to talk to you when I get back from Laredo, when we have more time. I'm an admirer of Mexican culture. I've got an idea for a new book. You could help me a lot with the particulars."

The driver of the Peerless studied her new ally. Her resolve to keep a prudent distance was wearing away. "I've known you just one day, and already you've been a tremendous help to me."

"We'll be heroes, Rose. Friends, too, I hope. Good luck!" The young woman offered her hand, and the driver accepted it with a smile.

Rose headed up Avenue C toward Alamo Heights. By then she was feeling a little more hopeful. At least the Alamo was safe from Wilton Peck and the Willinghams, if only for a month.

Secretly she was a little relieved that Alva would be out of pocket in Laredo for a few weeks. That way she knew the young woman wouldn't take over the project in her sudden rush of enthusiasm. All the same, Rose had to admit: doors flew open and the sun broke through when Alva Carson Keane pulled out her checkbook. And yes, she conceded, her energetic partner was a pleasure to work with. It had never occurred to her that she might actually *like* a Carson.

When she got home, Rose started to draft the letter to Senator Pratt requesting a meeting about the appropriation. Then the De León spirit took control of her. She grinned. She shouldn't do it, she told herself. Better to keep things quiet as long as possible. And it would be unkind of her to gloat. But she couldn't stop herself. She put the letter to Senator Pratt aside and began writing a different one instead. It was pure mischief, she realized, and by God she relished it.

SAN ANTONIO CHAPTER
Daughters of the Republic of Texas
"Texas, One and Indivisible"

Rose De León Herrera, President
1211 Townsend Avenue
San Antonio, Texas

October 4, 1907

Mr. Wilton A. Peck
Willingham Hotel Company
Clifford Building
City

Dear Sir:

Kindly forgive my delay in replying to yours of September 30.

Sir, I feel compelled to inform you that one of my organization's most devoted members, Mrs. Alva Keane, holds an option on the property you seek to acquire, namely, the lot adjacent to the Alamo chapel.

I must further inform you that the Daughters of the Republic of Texas have no intention of tearing down the Alamo. The building now occupied by the Hugo & Schmeltzer warehouse is the Alamo proper; it was the scene of the famous siege and massacre. Of course, only the stone walls are the originals. However, all the galleries, woodwork, sheds—everything modern—will be removed and the structure remodeled to reflect its character at the time of the famous battle.

We have not sufficient funds on hand to start this project immediately, but we expect the State and our citizenry to assist us materially in the coming months. Since your hotel company will benefit through its association with our historic city after you have secured an alternate site, we shall be pleased if you will help us handsomely. What may we expect from you in contribution?

Trusting that this is eminently satisfactory, and that I shall hear from you soon.

Very sincerely,
Rose De León Herrera

cc: Mrs. Alva Keane

Wilton Peck hurled Mrs. Herrera's letter across his desk. He stomped from one end of his office to the other, his face perilously red.

"Goddamned meddlesome bitches!"

But he knew it was his fault, not theirs: a grave miscalculation. For weeks he'd been courting Mr. Hugo in a slow, gentlemanly fashion, over scotch and casual conversation at the White Elephant Saloon. He thought that was the southern way. Now his prize had been snatched away with galling aplomb by two club ladies.

The humiliation! And what would Philadelphia think?

Philadelphia must not find out. That was all there was to it. He would simply have to find another location for the hotel.

But no site in San Antonio was as good as next door to the Alamo. And he had already assured the senior Mr. Willingham that the property was theirs. Another miscalculation.

Of course, he reminded himself, there was a good chance the women wouldn't be able to raise the purchase money in a month, and their option would expire. But he couldn't twiddle his thumbs for a month waiting to see.

In a way he had to admire Rose Herrera and Alva Keane. It was a real coup. He would have done the same, given the opportunity. He realized it might have been his own letter to Mrs. Herrera that had tipped them off and spurred them into their devious action.

"Jezebels!"

Well, he couldn't sit around and mope. It was already Saturday noon, and he had to think about containing the damage.

First, he would send a telegram to Mr. Willingham.

Then he would go see the real-estate lawyer he had met at the Root banquet—Horatio Franck. Maybe Franck would have some idea what he should do.

Finally, he would approach Alva Carson Keane directly and make her some sort of offer. Obviously she didn't need money, but—he would think of something that might appeal to her.

Peck slammed his desk shut and reached for his jacket. It was time to go to battle. *"What may we expect from you in contribution?"* that woman had the nerve to ask. Well, she was about to find out. The women had underestimated him. He had ways of seducing powerful people; plus, he had access to smoky back rooms and fraternal lodges where ladies couldn't go. Though stymied, Wilton Peck wasn't going to give up on the Hugo & Schmeltzer property without a Texas-style showdown.

THE WESTERN UNION TELEGRAPH COMPANY.
——— INCORPORATED ———

23,000 OFFICES IN AMERICA. CABLE SERVICE TO ALL THE WORLD.

San Antonio Texas Oct. 5th-1907.
Mr. C. C. Willingham,
    Willingham Hotel Company, Philadelphia Pennsylvania.
Full speed ahead everything falling into place beautifully however inquiring about alternate sites Alamo Plaza more congested and run-down than originally thought best wishes.

Wilton A. Peck.

1244pm

"Well. Let's have a look."

The corpulent lawyer pushed his spectacles up his nose with an air of supreme confidence, then started flipping through his file. "There's a vacant lot on Houston Street. It's not big enough for what you need. And a corner building on Military Plaza—you don't want that, it's too close to the West Side. Besides, it used to be a bordello. There's an old warehouse on Nueva—but that's too far from downtown."

Wilton Peck didn't try to hide his ill humor. He was tired and anxious, and his cowboy boots were hurting his feet. "You don't know of anything as good as Alamo Plaza."

Horatio Franck squinted and closed the file. "No. Not right now. But things can change in a week."

"Those goddamned. . . ."Peck caught himself. "No offense. I mean, your partner's wife. But—Jesus!"

The lawyer leaned back, and his swivel chair squeaked beneath the strain. "I don't like Herrera's wife either. She's from an old family that couldn't hold on to what it had. She's got axes to grind."

"And just between us—God damn the Daughters of the Republic, and God damn the Alamo."

"I shall hold *that* in strictest confidence, Mr. Peck. Or you'll be finished in this state."

"There's got to be something else on the market."

"If I were you, I'd wait. The DRT will never raise seventy-five grand. Certainly not in thirty days."

"I'm not so sure of that. Your fellow Texans are awfully tender-hearted about the Alamo."

Franck shook his head. "When push comes to shove, no businessman today is going to let misguided patriotism stand in the way of progress. Not even if the Alamo's involved. Don't quote me on that, but it's true."

"What about your legislature? That Herrera woman said the DRT expects the state to help them."

"Huh. The ladies will lobby, of course. But there are other ways of persuading our legislators, better than lobbying."

Peck was surly. "And how much will that cost me?"

The lawyer was careful. "I wouldn't know about that, Mr. Peck. But I'm sure the Willinghams can afford it."

Nothing could assuage Wilton Peck. "Damn it. I've got to have something to fall back on. I need to start building in thirty days. There are three other hotels in the works."

"Yes, I know that," Franck replied, annoyed to be told anything about real estate in his home town. "The St. Anthony, the Gunter and the Crockett, to be precise. But Willingham has a national reputation."

"Still, the Willingham has got to open before any of the competitors. I'm not going to just sit around. And I'm not going to give up on the Hugo & Schmeltzer, either."

Franck scoffed. "So you really plan to go begging to Oscar Carson's daughter?"

"I have to. Shit! You can't begin to know how much I've got riding on this."

The lawyer sat up. "I know lots of things, Mr. Peck. Especially about this state and how it works. For one thing, I know you're wasting your time talking to the Carsons once they've made up their minds."

Peck jumped up and grabbed his hat. "Well, thanks, counselor. You've been a lot of help," he grumbled.

A prominent vein across Franck's forehead protruded ominously when he got excited. "I've told you what's out there. What do you expect me to do? I didn't create your problem."

Peck thought for a moment. "I'm desperate, Mr. Franck. People say you know what comes on the market before anyone else in town. Do whatever you have to. Find me another site. If it's as good as the Hugo & Schmeltzer—better still, if you can think of some way to *get* me the Hugo & Schmeltzer—let's just say I'm prepared to cut you a very good deal on an interest in the Willingham Palace."

The lawyer's vein was throbbing. "Mr. Peck, it is my duty to advise you that it would be a violation of professional ethics for me to enter into a business transaction with a client."

"Of course. I understand."Peck put on his hat.

"On the other hand, if you care to make your offer to *Mrs.* Franck, I will urge her to entertain your proposal favorably."

For the first time that day, Peck felt there was hope.

"And I'll speak to my partner Herrera,"the lawyer continued, his vein subsiding. "We'll get his wife to back off. Now I want you to stop sweating and relax. It's Saturday. Go out to a whorehouse or something. Trust me to find us a site. We're on the same team."

Peck left the lawyer's office in much better spirits. But he wouldn't stop sweating, or relax, or go to a whorehouse, until he had made one last attempt to sway Alva Carson Keane.

WILLINGHAM HOTEL COMPANY

Clifford Building
Commerce Street Bridge
San Antonio, Texas

October 5, 1907

Mrs. Alva Carson Keane
Tres Piedras Ranch
Laredo, Texas

Dear Madam:

May I be pardoned, a stranger, for intruding upon your attention.

First, three cheers for your letter in the Journal of October 3. Or, as you say in Texas—yee-hah! I heartily agree with you. Let the Alamo stand out free and clear!

Second, I received Mrs. Herrera's interesting letter of October 4, a copy of which, I noticed, was also directed to you.

Please forgive my frankness if I say that the plan she proposes is not practical and can only result in disappointment to the noble women who are endeavoring to perpetuate the glorious memories of the Texas heroes.

I say this, Mrs. Keane, not in an unkindly spirit, but simply as the result of experience. What Mrs. Herrera proposes to do with the Hugo & Schmeltzer property, should the Daughters acquire it, would simply result in preserving indefinitely an eyesore which would be a source of humiliation and regret to the people of San Antonio for all time. Furthermore, your gallant organization will

have to draw support from businessmen, and no business-
man today is going to let misguided patriotism stand in
the way of progress.

Mrs. Keane, I know you are a reasonable and sophisti-
cated lady, as well as a patriotic one. Let me offer you a
vision of hope for the future of the DRT and all the peo-
ple of San Antonio.

The Willingham Hotel Company is willing to enter
into a unique partnership with the Daughters of the
Republic of Texas, under which we would work together
to transform the Hugo & Schmeltzer property from a
hideous monstrosity into a magnificent monument. At our
own expense, the Willingham Company will convert the
now unsightly place into a bower of beauty.

I would prefer to discuss the details of this proposal
with you face to face, like Texans. Can we arrange an
appointment at your earliest convenience?

Magnanimous lady, let us join forces to carry to a glo-
rious fruition this plan for indelibly perpetuating the
memories of the Alamo and its valiant heroes!

> *Very sincerely yours,*
> *Wilton A. Peck*
> *Senior Development Coordinator*
> *"Nearly a Naturalized Texan"*

T he lawyer lost no time. As soon as Wilton Peck was gone, he struggled to his feet and into his overcoat.

Horatio Franck hadn't made his fortune by practicing law. Instead, he used his real estate practice as a means of keeping up with the latest news. He never missed a chance to gain a toehold in San Antonio's up-and-coming business ventures. And the Willingham Palace by the Alamo promised to be the cream of the city's new hotel crop—as long as Rose Herrera and the Daughters were kept at bay.

He knew exactly where to find his partner, Antonio Herrera, on a Saturday afternoon. Dan Breen's Saloon, a comfortable den of dark mahogany and polished brass, was the public room most frequented by local businessmen. A no-nonsense Irish bar, it rarely drew the tourists and strutters, who flocked to the White Elephant; but its tariff was high enough to discourage the cowboys and Mexican toughs who gravitated toward the Buckhorn. Dan Breen's was the private domain of well-informed men who made the city revolve.

Though he drank little, Antonio Herrera spent every Saturday afternoon there, just to stay abreast. Perhaps he would strike up a conversation with a tract developer or a land agent from the Rio Grande Valley.

But this was a slow Saturday at Dan Breen's. Herrera sat alone at a table in the rear, lulled by the whir of a fan hanging from the pressed tin ceiling and feeling smugly self-confident just to be sitting there. He contemplated ordering a second lager. It was risky. Lager made him say too much and say it clumsily.

Better not, he thought. He was there on business. He decided to finish reading the *Journal* instead.

THE SAN ANTONIO JOURNAL
Saturday, October 5, 1907

Tales & Tattlers

There she goes again! Mrs. Alva Carson Keane, the irrepressible young authoress of *Angelina, Sweetheart of the Chaparral,* leaves today for Tres Piedras Ranch near Laredo, after a brief visit to our city. Kudos are in order: while she was here, this patriotic lady generously purchased an option on the property next to the Alamo, and she plans to turn the site into a beautiful monument. Aren't we proud of her! You can take the girl out of Texas—but home is where her heart is. Mrs. Keane was assisted in her undertaking by some local ladies, including Mrs. Antonio Herrera. Hasta la vista, Alva!

Antonio Herrera sighed. At least his wife's name was buried beneath Mrs. Keane's at the end of the society column, not emblazoned across the business page. He folded his newspaper and glanced up. In the beveled mirror he saw the reflection of Horatio Franck maneuvering his bulk through the etched-glass doors. Herrera snapped to attention and straightened his tie. Thank God, he thought, he hadn't ordered that second lager.

They were partners, of course, and that implied a parity. But Franck was a good ten years Herrera's senior and had been his employer for eight years before inviting him into a partnership. What's more, Franck had been the one who had rescued Herrera from West Side obscurity. And Franck wouldn't tolerate a loose tongue or a muddled mind.

The older man made his way to the back of the saloon and pulled up a chair without a word of greeting. He sat heavily, short of breath. His face was blotchy. He snapped his fingers at a waiter, demanding a scotch. Then he lost no time spilling his good news: they had a new client, Wilton Peck—

"A visionary. A true civic giant. He's going to drag this cowtown kicking and screaming into the twentieth century."

Herrera tensed. "The hotel man?"

His partner nodded brusquely. "I believe your wife has already had a run-in with him." A blunt man, Franck didn't bother to coat the word "wife" with any false affection.

Herrera tried to laugh it off. "Yes, well, Rose has a way with developers."

The senior partner wasn't amused. The vein on his forehead bulged. Although adding "Herrera" to the name of his law office had been a smart business move in a Hispanic town, he sometimes wondered whether *Mrs.* Herrera was more of a liability to him than her husband was an asset.

"Herrera, I don't want to interfere in your family life. God knows every man's home is his castle."

Herrera glanced down, his heart pounding. His own castle in Alamo Heights still wasn't paid for. This was no time to alienate a partner who brought in most of their clients.

"But Peck is already fit to be tied over what the Carson girl did, buying that option. I think she's a friend of your wife's. God knows why—didn't Old Man Carson end up with most of Fermin's land? Anyway, the DRT is right in the middle of this. I mean—Christ. There's any number of ladies' clubs your wife could join. Do you know what I mean?"

Herrera stared into his glass grimly. "Yes. I've been meaning to speak to her about this."

The scotch arrived. Franck downed it in one swallow. "I want to see this city prosper. I think you do, too."

"Of course."

"My feeling is, let the ladies *have* their parks and museums. By all means. It's good for the city, and it's good for business. But if they thought about it rationally, they wouldn't want to stand in the way of development. They'd be cutting their own throats."

Herrera looked up and nodded. "I think Rose will understand. She's a very intelligent woman."

Franck exhaled. His vein retracted. "Well, in that case, I don't need to say any more." And then, without excusing himself or bidding farewell, he tossed some coins on the table and left as abruptly as he had arrived.

Antonio Herrera didn't relish the thought of going home that evening. He brooded over the task at hand. For some years it had been one of the tacit understandings of his marriage that he and his wife wouldn't interfere in each other's activities outside their home. But Franck had a point. This Alamo business was getting out of control.

On the other hand, Rose *was* a very intelligent woman. And she was a De León. Anything he said would be more likely to inflame her than deter her.

Perhaps it could wait until Monday. He could give it more thought. And why spoil a Saturday evening at home?

But Rose and her friends moved quickly. He shouldn't wait.

Damn the whole complicated world! What the hell? He decided he might as well have that second lager.

26

Had Antonio Herrera better anticipated his wife's reaction, he wouldn't have broached the subject at dinner. Especially not on the evening of Eloisa's first attempt at veal paupiettes, with everyone's nerves already on edge. Nor would he have opened with the man-of-the-house approach. But that fourth lager at Dan Breen's had given him a sudden rush of virility.

"Rose, I've been thinking. You're getting a lot of press over this Alamo thing. It's about time for us to put an end to it."

She had to chew and swallow—easier stated than executed—and take a sip of water before she responded. "Well. I can't control what the papers say. And this 'Alamo thing' is far from over."

"That's what I mean. And it's going to get nasty. That's why I want you out of it altogether."

They were staring at each other guardedly. Enrique, on alert, followed their tug-of-war without looking up.

"You know who I am," she said. "The De Leóns don't run from trouble. Or from bullies."

"The De Leóns, yes. But the name in today's paper was Mrs. Herrera. You're my wife. And this is my house. So oblige me."

She was silent, inscrutable. That made him retreat. "I think I've been more generous than most men. I've never interfered with your club activities, have I? But this Alamo business has gone too far."

She was no longer looking at him. "Enrique. Finish the potatoes."

"They're black."

"Finish them anyway."

Antonio pushed ahead. "You like music. How about the Tuesday Musical Club?"

"I don't have time for another club," she said irritably.

"Rose, I'm not saying give up the DRT for good. Just until this blows over."

She couldn't believe what she was hearing. "*Give up?*"

"The Daughters. I want you to resign—"

"*Now?* With the Alamo at stake?"

"Just temporarily."

"That is out of the question."

He bristled. "I don't want to discuss it any more. The matter is closed."

She dabbed at her lips and glared at him. Then she bolted up, her chair scraping the polished wood floor and tottering behind her. "Excuse me." She walked briskly to her study.

Antonio Herrera glanced at his son, embarrassed. He pushed away from the table and followed his wife into her small chamber, slamming the door behind him. She stood framed against the window with her back to him.

Never, never had he felt such rage toward her! He spoke in Spanish. "I don't care—I don't care if your family owned this town for two hundred years. I built this house. I will not be humiliated in this house! In front of my son. I am the man of this house."

She wheeled around, her tone low but violent. "Then act like a man!"

His face was flushed. "Don't push me, Rose."

"Tell me one thing. Did Horatio Franck put you up to this?"

He stepped toward her, furious. "It's not your—"

"I want to know if he's behind this. Is he the one who—"

"Shut up! Mr. Franck is not behind anything, understand? But you're causing him one hell of a problem, the same as me. Did you ever think of that?"

"I despise that man. He's turning you into a toady."

He stopped short, more wounded than angry. "I see. So that's how you've come to think of me."

She backed down a little. "I've always respected you, Antonio. Truly, I have. I've respected your intellect. Your perseverance." She shook her fist at him. "But where is your spirit? Your sense of pride? Where did that—"

He grabbed her wrists and shoved her against the desk, looming over her. "You want to see my spirit, hmm? I'll show you spirit!"

"Let go of me!" Struggling, she finally broke away. She had forgotten how strong he was.

"I'll show you!" He raised his palm. She drew back against the bookshelves, shocked.

Slowly he lowered his arm. He had never threatened her before. He stepped back awkwardly and smoothed his moustache.

"You've been drinking," she said. "I can smell it on you. It's not like you to drink."

He spoke quietly and deliberately. "Why in the hell do you think I've been drinking, Rose?"

"I don't know. And I don't care—drink if you want. But I don't like the company you're keeping. They've changed you."

"*My* company?" He shook his head with an incredulous smile. "Good God, Rose. What about yours? That German artist? That lunatic? Do you think—"

"I will not hear another word against Madame Guenther—"

"If you care nothing for me, at least think of our son. Do you think he's proud to see his mother's name in the papers every day?"

"How dare you mention my name! You built your career on my family's name!"

"I built my career on my own hard work. Your family! What man today would be proud to call himself the son-in-law of Fermin De León?"

He shouldn't have said that. "Peon!" she hissed. "You came from nowhere. Nowhere!"

"Yes! Yes! I was nobody! Just another barefoot shit kid from the West Side. And what did you ever do to help me get on? Did you ever introduce me to any of the best people? If I'd waited for you to help me, I'd still be on my knees shining shoes. And you could have done so much for me in society!"

"Whose society? Who are these people you're posturing for? They're all boors! Upstarts!"

"You're living in the past, Rose. Give it up."

"Your society! I'll show you what I think of your society!" She grabbed her *Ladies' At-Home Directory* off the shelf and hurled it at his feet.

"Pick it up!" He took hold of her forearms. They scuffled. "Pick it up! Now!"

"There! You can keep your society!"

They knocked over her desk lamp. It fell against the window, cracking the pane.

"Look out!" He let go of her.

"Your stupid society! What do they know about this city? Did they make it what it is today?"

"You're talking nonsense."

"Do they care about its history? Its character? Have any of your 'best people' read Augustin Morfi?"

Father Morfi's *Historia de Texas* struck his ankle. He stumbled back, bumping his head on the telephone. The bell sounded. "Damn it!"

"How about Galvez?"

He caught *The Interior Provinces of New Spain* in the chest. "Stop this! Right now!"

He gripped her arms hard. Her fists struck at his breast, but he held her in check. Then she jerked back and broke free, tearing her gown and striking her elbow on the bookshelves.

In the dining room, Enrique and Eloisa stood staring at the closed door, dumbfounded. They heard the shouts and the shoes scraping the parquetry.

"Have they read Olmsted? Roemer?"

More crashes.

"Enough!"

Eloisa snapped to attention, realizing the boy shouldn't witness this. "Enrique! Out! ¡Adelante!"

She took hold of his shoulders and shoved him all the way across the dining room, through the parlor and into the vestibule.

"Go on! ¡Andale!"

He managed to grab his guitar off the sofa before she pushed him out of the house and slammed the front door.

"So then your parents shouted at each other. And threw things."

"My father shouted. My mother threw books."

"Only books?"

Enrique stared at the girl, disbelieving. "You don't know my parents."

Eva Menchaca stirred the simmering pot of frijoles with a long wooden spoon. The boy watched her closely in the faint lantern-light. "My mother threw *priceless* books."

"What other kind *would* people throw in Alamo Heights?"

He didn't want to be reminded. "Now you sound like Rafael."

They were sitting by the woodstove in her mother's kitchen, far on the West Side near the edge of the city. The house was merely a glorified jacal, fronted by a room of sturdy adobe with an iron-clad roof. But behind that, the walls were framed of twisted juniper and mesquite poles, covered with rough cowhides and flattened kerosene cans. The roof consisted of tightly woven reeds from the river banks. In this kitchen there was little decoration: only Eva's clay statue of St. Joseph, crimson-robed, with large eyes and hammer in hand.

She tested the frijoles. "Here." She held the spoon to his lips. He nodded.

"Too much cilantro?"

He shook his head.

"Too much jalapeño?"

He swallowed, thinking of Eloisa's bland veal paupiettes. "I like to eat fire."

"Good. It's too late to take it out."

The girl ladled the frijoles into a clay bowl and set it before him. She offered him some corn tortillas.

"This is good," he told her.

She was awkward with compliments. "It's not much. ¡Muchachos! ¡Muchachas!"

Her young siblings appeared silently, as if from the woodwork, waiting to be served. They all stared at Enrique with serious faces. He mussed the youngest boy's hair, and they all drew back and giggled.

"My parents used to shout and throw things all the time," Eva said as she filled several bowls. "Whenever my father drank too much. That was before he took his room at the Palace. I'm glad he did."

"Does he ever come back here?"

"Every few days. To see the children and argue with my mother." Then she smiled, realizing what Enrique was thinking. "Don't worry. He won't come here tonight. We're safe."

Enrique nodded, tossing the kids some tortillas. He hoped none of them would mention his visit when they saw Rafael. They took their bowls, still staring at him, and withdrew to the far corners of the dark kitchen, remaining clustered around a straw mattress.

Eva watched him eat before she served herself. Enrique liked the feel of this kitchen, the way it drew them all close around the big frijoles pot and the warmth of the stove. He glanced around, trying to locate all her siblings.

"I can't keep up with them. They're multiplying."

"We are ten, all together," Eva told him. "That includes my two older brothers in Nacogdoches. And you?"

"Only me."

"Just one?"

Enrique nodded and took a bite of a tortilla.

"Why?"

"I had a sister and a brother. They both died."

Eva looked at her feet. "Oh. I'm sorry."

"The sister—I don't remember her. And my brother—I was five, I believe. So I've been the only one for a long time."

Eva didn't know what to say. She stood up and poured the coffee.

Enrique realized he needed to change the subject. "I like this room."

She handed him a cup. "Why?"

He shrugged. "I don't know. It feels like a home."

Eva smiled at him. He felt silly for saying that.

Later that night, after the children had bedded down, the two of them walked along the deserted river. The sky was overcast. There were no street lights.

The girl and boy stayed close to each other. He took her hand, working his fingers through hers. They said very little as they strolled. They listened to the crickets and bullfrogs along the river bank. In the cottonwoods the warblers were branch-hopping and bickering.

They came to an opening in the reeds. He led her down the grassy slope of the river bank. His foot slipped

"Careful! Your guitar," she said.

He spread his denim jacket over the grass and helped her sit. "I brought you a present," he told her.

"You shouldn't do that."

"Why not? You gave me that statue."

She turned away and smiled, embarrassed. "I don't see any present."

"You can't see it." He adjusted his guitar and plucked a few strings. "It's in here. I wrote this for you. But look the other way, you'll make me nervous."

"I want to watch you."

"Then I'll have to look away."

He fixed his gaze on the water and sang to the lily pads, self-consciously, a tender ballad in E-minor. It compared Eva to a yellow rose. What his lyric lacked in originality was countered by its sincerity. And the feelings were new to him.

Apparently to her as well. Only once did he look in her direction, and he saw how deeply she was affected. It surprised him. He finished and put his guitar aside. Transported, she placed her hand on his arm. "It's so beautiful. Enrique. . . ."

She kept her hand there. He reached for it just as she was about to take it away. He leaned over, gently placing his other hand on her shoulder, and kissed her forehead several times. Then he backed off. He didn't think she was pleased. Neither of them said anything.

Finally he ventured an expectant look at her. She returned it.

He acted swiftly, pulling her close to him and planting eager, clumsy kisses all over her lips and neck, and grabbing strands of her long black hair. This time she responded, her breath hot on his collar. He stroked her back and her waist. But when his hand slid up to her bosom, she pushed him away.

"Enrique . . . no."

Frustrated, he moved back again and looked away. He was about to stand up—then realized he shouldn't. "If you'd like, I'll play you another—"

"No. Enrique. . . ." This time she came to him, startling him and knocking him on his back. "Enrique. . . ."

"Amante," he whispered softly, tasting her hair.

"Ahora . . . bien. . . ."

She had her arms around his neck, and her strength surprised him. They changed positions without realizing it. He groped at the buttons on her blouse, floundering in his haste, until she pushed his hands aside and unfastened them herself. He stopped, astonished, and stared at the small round breasts beneath him. He wasn't aware when his trousers came undone, or how her slender legs were bared. The next thing he realized, to his chagrin, was that he was off course.

"Perdón. . . ."

"Ohh. . . ."

She shifted and helped him, her eyes staring steadily into his. By now they were off his jacket and on the grass. Her legs were smooth against him. His shin was pressed hard against a rock. He barely noticed. What bewildered him was his absolute loss of control, something he had never known before, as if someone else had taken possession of him. She cried out. He groaned.

"¡Sí!"

"Shh!"

"Eva!"

The moon stole out from behind the clouds, and the crickets, the bullfrogs, the warblers all raised their voices at once in a resounding chorus. But their chatter was all for their own pleasure; they had lost the attention of their young audience.

Tres Piedras Ranch
October 14, 1907

My dear Mr. Peck:

Please forgive my delay in replying. I have been frightfully busy writing a Broadway play—with the attendant pressure of deadlines looming—and consequently have neglected all correspondence.

Unfortunately, with respect to your requested appointment, I shall not return to San Antonio until November. However—should you still desire to meet with me this month—you are welcome to come to Tres Piedras.

Mr. Peck, I hope you will forgive my candor—but I know that neither of us wishes to waste the other's time. If your "proposal" for a "partnership" with the DRT is actually a thinly disguised attempt to purchase my option on the Hugo & Schmeltzer property—and erect a hotel on the site—let me assure you that the Daughters will not consider any plans along those lines. I am of one mind with Mrs. Herrera on this—and it is our common goal to guard against commercialization of this sacred spot.

I trust that I have made my position clear. If I am mistaken and you have a different idea for working with the Daughters, by all means let me hear it—come be my guest at the ranch.

Sincerely,
Alva Carson Keane

P.S. If you do come, bring your riding clothes.

THE WESTERN UNION TELEGRAPH COMPANY.
——— INCORPORATED ———
23,000 OFFICES IN AMERICA. CABLE SERVICE TO ALL THE WORLD.

Laredo Texas Oct. 14th-1907.
Mrs. Rose Herrera,
    1211 Townsend Avenue, San Antonio Texas.
Smell rat Peck up to something keep close tabs on him.
                                                Alva.

W ilton Peck adjusted his tie and got ready to go downstairs for dinner—with tremendous resentment.

He resented being stuck in Laredo, Texas (actually, in a hinterland seven miles outside of Laredo).

He resented losing the three precious days it took to make this trip.

Most of all, he resented having to kowtow to a woman who was dangling the best real estate in San Antonio over his head and now seemed hell-bent on testing him. But he felt there was still a chance of swaying Mrs. Keane, if he played his cards right during this visit.

At least—he had consoled himself as he boarded the I. & G. N. train in San Antonio—a visit to the Oscar Carson estate would mean luxurious accommodations and good food.

He was wrong on both counts. As the horse-drawn wagon approached the main compound of Tres Piedras Ranch, after traversing what seemed like half a continent of thorny scrubland, the path finally ended in a clearing. He asked the Mexican driver, "Is that the bunkhouse?"

The man looked at him as if he were crazy.

"You know—where the cowboys stay?"

The driver spat tobacco. "That? That's the ranch headquarters. Señor Carson's house."

Obviously, Old Man Carson hadn't become one of the most successful cattlemen in Texas by pouring his money into anything frivolous. For him that meant anything other than ranch land. His two-story house at Tres Piedras was roomy but spartan: a weathered, barnlike heap of clapboard, with no color, ornament or personality. Around the house grew no flowers, no shrubs, no lawn to speak of; just a few scraggly mesquites and patches of dry prairie grass.

Peck's hostess was waiting on the long veranda when he arrived. She was sipping lemonade with her young husband, who was there on a brief vacation from New York. She waved to her guest with extravagant arcs of her arm. She might be his nemesis, but—Peck had to admit—Alva Carson Keane was all charm when she wanted to be. As he climbed up the porch steps, she received him warmly.

"Welcome to Tres Piedras! I was hoping you'd get here in time for the branding. I made Keane try it; he's been bellyaching about it ever since. But don't worry, we've got lots of things in store for you."

Peck was disarmed by the genuine enthusiasm in her voice. But he suddenly felt like a fool, dressed in his cowboy boots and the ill-fitting Stetson hat he'd purchased in San Antonio just for this trip. Mrs. Keane was dressed in a plain but well-tailored muslin gown that was not at all ranch-like. Her husband was wearing khakis.

"Peck—it's nice to have you here." Robert Keane put his newspaper down in a sagging wicker chair and shook Peck's hand firmly. He was slim and clean-cut. "Watch out for Alva, though," he said with a wink. "I'm here on vacation, and she's been running me ragged. She'll start on you next."

"Mr. Peck, come look at this." Alva motioned their guest to the end of the veranda. Her husband followed.

Wilton Peck was so startled by what he saw that one of his loud hiccups leapt out. Hanging from a mesquite tree was the large carcass of some recently slain wild mammal, suspended by ropes tied through slits in its hind legs. Two Mexican men were working it over, yanking the hide downward and exposing the dark red muscles and white membranes. A hound and a border collie kept close watch, fighting over the scraps the men tossed aside.

Peck nearly lost his lunch. He laughed a little. "What is it?"

"It's a deer," replied his hostess, surprised by the question. "Domingo killed it when he heard you were coming."

"Well . . . wasn't that thoughtful."

He glanced at Keane, who shrugged. "All for you, Peck. That's Texas hospitality for you. This . . . delectable beast."

"Stop it," his wife reprimanded him. "I'm sure Mr. Peck will like venison. *You* do. Besides, I won't insult Domingo."

Robert Keane put his arm around his wife's waist, watching the men work. "Why can't they ever miss and shoot one of your father's fatted calves by mistake?"

She broke away and led them back to the front door. "You'll meet Daddy later, Mr. Peck. He's out mending fence with the men." Then, with a mildly disapproving look at her husband, she added: "I'm sure *he'll* be hungry tonight, after a full day's work."

"Why? He's probably been chewing up the Mexicans for lunch."

She shot her husband a little smirk. "Dinner at eight, Mr. Peck, unless Daddy gets in late. I'll send Dolores to fetch you something to drink. If Keane gets tiresome, just have him take you upstairs to your room." With that, she disappeared for the rest of the afternoon to work on the script of *Angelina*.

"You play chess?" Keane asked him.

Wilton Peck nodded. Already he was miserable on the ranch.

"Good. 'Daddy' won't be around to catch us not working. This morning he knocked on our door at five o'clock to call us to breakfast. Five o'clock! And the way The Old Man guards his money—now *there's* a story. See these two screen doors?"

He pointed at the two separate doors leading from the veranda into the house. Peck nodded.

"Notice how the screen on the left door is in pretty bad shape. Those holes at the bottom are big enough to let in small animals: you know, mice, maybe a squirrel now and then, or a few rattlesnakes—nothing that would bother The Old Man."

Peck stared at the door. He wondered whether rattlesnakes could crawl up stairs.

"Now the screen on the right-hand door is much worse: completely rusted out. I'd say jackrabbits, raccoons, even javelinas could pass right through these holes without even slowing down, wouldn't you?"

Peck nodded again. He wasn't sure exactly what a javelina was, but he felt certain it could climb stairs.

"The door on the left is the main entrance to the house. That other door goes into a bedroom, what used to be Alva's mother's room. They never use that entrance any more. So one day The Old Man noticed that the bedroom entrance had the better screen—you know, the one that would only let in rattlesnakes and such. Now mind you, it would take about fifteen cents' worth of screen wire to fix both doors. But rather than spend the money, 'Daddy' had one of his Mexican serfs take both of those screen doors off their hinges and switch them. To save *fifteen cents!* Peck, what do you think of a man who would do that?"

Wilton Peck was wary of a potential trap. He chuckled. "Well, I'd say your father-in-law is a durn bit . . . uh . . ."

"Parsimonious. That's the word you're looking for." Robert Keane was staring intently at the visitor. He had already pegged the Philadelphian as a bootlicker. "And by the way, you can go easy on the 'durns' and all that Texas talk. Geez—Alva's started using those sorts of words all the time, for some reason. I'm from Long Island, and it drives me crazy."

Peck laughed nervously. He wondered if Alva was as miserly as her father, and if so, whether he might appeal to her with some kind of money offer after all.

"There's one good thing about The Old Man," Keane continued. "He takes everything entirely seriously, so you can have a lot of fun needling him, if you're so inclined. You've got to stand up to him, though, or he'll run over you. The same goes for Alva. Oh—I nearly forgot. I was going to beat you at chess."

The two men passed a couple of hours playing chess on the veranda. When it came time to wash up and dress for dinner, Keane led the visitor upstairs. The hall smelled of old leather tack and cedar. In the guest room the furnishings were rustic and functional. A Navajo rug over the rough plank floor gave the dark chamber its only color. On the dresser was a kerosene lamp and a wash basin. With great trepidation Peck tilted the basin and checked it for snakes. All he found was a dead centipede. The house had no electricity and

no toilet: according to Keane, The Old Man thought it was disgust-
ing for humans to relieve themselves inside their living quarters.

Standing at the rusted mirror, Wilton Peck checked his appearance
one last time. He looked as presentable as he could be expected to way
out here—and certainly good enough for dining on a wild mammal.

He sighed. At least he had managed to miss the branding.

Peck decided he'd been a good sport long enough. As he started
downstairs, he made a resolution: if he didn't get his promotion after
all this was over, he was going to take great pleasure in inviting the
senior Mr. Willingham to go jump in a lake—preferably one in
Texas—and die.

Wilton Peck walked into the den—which reminded him of a run-down hunting lodge—just after Robert Keane had picked an argument with his father-in-law over suffrage. Alva was watching, amused, from a large wing chair. She made the introductions.

"Some wine, Mr. Peck?" she asked.

Quickly he took stock of the situation. Carson wasn't drinking; but both the Keanes were. "Yes, thank you."

Oscar Carson occupied his bearskin-covered chair by the broad rock fireplace and the spittoon, beneath a mounted elkhead. As it turned out, The Old Man was not the towering giant Peck was expecting. Rather, the Carson patriarch was a short, portly man, bald and bespectacled. He was intimidating nonetheless, even while seated. His hands were hard and gnarled, and his chapped, sunburned cheek bulged with a wad of tobacco. His cold gray eyes seemed harshly judgmental. He barely acknowledged the visitor's presence.

The debate resumed. "A woman who does her duty at home," said the older man, "will have far more influence on the affairs of this nation than one who goes to the ballot box."

"I think suffrage is going to come whether *we* like it or not," replied Keane, refilling his wine glass. "Some states already have it. And I think they should."

"So you would have them meddling and discussing things they know nothing about? Thrown together at the ballot box with people from all walks of life?"

"I would give them every right that men have. If a vote means so much to a man, it must mean something to a woman. Or to your serfs, for that matter." The young man winked at Peck, as if inviting him to jump in.

But Wilton Peck was watching Alva. Her brown eyes twinkled in the gaslight. He was waiting for some hint of her views on the issue, praying she would air them before he was called on to join in the discussion. However, she was enjoying the match too much to interrupt it.

Carson reached for a poker and skewered a scorpion crawling on the floor beside him. "I think we have too much suffrage already. I don't think the ladies want it, and I don't think they need it."

"Let's find out," said the young man. "Alva? Do you want to be emancipated?"

Carson looked at her. "Daughter?"

She leaned back, smiling, a hint of mischief. "Mr. Peck is our guest. Let's give him a chance to speak first."

Peck chuckled. "Oh, I'm not a married man. I don't think I'm qualified to say whether women should vote."

"Take a stand, Peck," said Robert Keane, not concealing his disdain. "Alva won't speak until you do."

Wilton Peck was fully aware that the woman was sizing him up. "Well . . . frankly, the more I've read about this issue, the more confused I've become. But I believe, in time, it's going to be resolved by the best minds, one way or the other, if we just apply the principles of reason and . . . and. . . ."

Alva suddenly sat up and addressed her husband. "Of course I believe in women's rights. But so far, I've always had mine."

"Well, yes," agreed Peck. "Like I was about to say, I think women should vote. By all means."

Alva slowly sank back into the wing chair and looked at her guest. Her smile withered him.

The Old Man shook his head in stern dismay. "Well, this is an odd new generation, I must say. And your friend from the East must be as close to my age as he is to yours. I would have expected him to see things differently." From behind his spectacles Carson convicted the visitor of treason.

At dinner, Peck managed to get through the fried venison, despite its strong, gamy flavor, by smothering it with cream gravy. The only time he came close to excusing himself was when The Old Man inquired into the details of the deer's demise.

"Domingo shot it?"

Alva nodded, chewing. A spider dropped from the timbered ceiling to the tablecloth. She brushed it to the floor and stepped on it.

"Was it a clean shot?"

She frowned, shaking her head as she dabbed her lips. "Gut shot. That's not like Domingo to make a mess of things."

Peck felt the saliva welling in his mouth and reached for his wine. It steadied him.

Carson wasn't finished. "Did you give the Mexicans the liver?"

"Yes. I told them to take the diaphragm, too. At least what wasn't too bloodshot."

"Enough, you two!" said Robert Keane, much to Peck's relief.

"Keane's a finicky eater," the young woman explained to her guest. "I'm glad to see you're not like that, Mr. Peck."

He smiled but dared not open his mouth.

"When we were in India," she continued, "he wouldn't try any of the native food."

"The chicken was orange. And tough."

"How would *you* know it was tough?"

"I watched you chew."

"He was so scared of getting sick, I called him Hygiene Keane."

Wilton Peck chuckled, more than was obligatory.

"Dolores!" she called. "Mr. Peck needs some more venison."

Alva Carson Keane held court all evening, amusing them with stories of traveling with Josephine Pearce in Italy and riding an elephant in Bengal. Her husband tried unsuccessfully to draw his father-in-law into another argument. But Oscar Carson said little, except when he attempted to shift the topic to cattle prices or interest rates or rainfall. The Old Man had no use for the guest from Philadelphia.

Peck listened attentively and spoke when spoken to. He decided not to mention anything about the Hugo & Schmeltzer property until he could get Mrs. Keane alone. Maybe she would bring it up first. However, they stayed at table until late in the evening. Business would have to wait. Just before retiring, she gave him some hint of what the next day would bring.

"I assumed you'd want to see Daddy's ranch."

"Well . . . naturally," said Peck. He would just as soon eat nails. "But don't go to any bother. I saw a good bit of it today on the way in."

"Nonsense," said her husband, determined to stir up trouble. "Alva wants to take you to places where no self-respecting easterner would be foolhardy enough to venture."

Peck laughed. "That sounds exciting. But Alva—Mrs. Keane—I know you're very busy with your play."

"I am, but I need a break. I've been waiting until you got here to go riding. I'll have Dolores bring you one of my brother's riding jackets."

"Thank you, but as hot as it's been, I don't think—"

"You'll need it for the brush. Chaps, too. Domingo will have the horses ready at seven. I told him to bring the Colts along as well. Do you prefer a long or short barrel, Mr. Peck?"

He had no idea what she was talking about. "Uh . . . long is fine." It sounded more manly.

"All right. I'll use the thirty-eight, then. Good night, Mr. Peck."

After that he was left alone with Keane. "I didn't know horses had barrels," Peck admitted.

"She's talking about pistols." Robert Keane seemed to be enjoying this.

"Oh. Well . . . which kind are you using?"

"Me? Oh, I'm not going. I think I'll make a trip into town tomorrow, pick up a paper and find out what's been happening on Wall Street. I wouldn't go on one of Alva's expeditions. You're a braver man than I am, Peck. Better get some sleep. You'll need it."

"Aquí. This is it."

The three riders stopped in a clearing beside a rounded earthen knoll. They had been riding toward the hill—the only feature on the joyless landscape—for what seemed like days to Wilton Peck.

Alva was in the lead. She looked back from atop her bay. "Mr. Peck, this is the second of the piedras that the ranch is named for. None of them are rocks, actually. Some homesick Spaniard had a lot of imagination, don't you think?"

Mounted precariously on the horse behind hers, he nodded. Behind him, Domingo Cantú was bringing up the rear, carrying their provisions in his saddlebags.

Everything was still and stiflingly hot. Peck removed his white Stetson, now streaked in brown, and wiped his brow with his hand. He could feel the gritty dust smearing across his forehead. "How many of these did you say we're going to see?"

"Three. 'Tres' means three, Mr. Peck. The third one will be the most difficult ride. We'll have to follow an embankment along the Rio Grande."

Peck's horse, Racer, was part Arabian. Racer didn't like to follow behind other horses, and he tossed back his head in revolt every time his rider tugged on the reins—which, in this case, was constantly. Racer was also skittish and had started twice that morning, first at a wild hog and later at a rattlesnake.

The clearing where they had stopped gradually sloped downward into a dry ravine where a cluster of live oaks grew. "Let's stop here for lunch," said Alva. "This is one of those places on the ranch that I always come back to."

Peck couldn't see why. This shadeless, barren opening in the thornbush seemed better suited for an agonizing death than a repast.

She swung off her horse in a single, graceful motion. Her smart riding outfit still looked fairly fresh, and her energy hadn't diminished since they left the corral.

Peck hesitated. He pulled his left leg out of the stirrup. Then he remembered: other side. Several times he brought his right leg up the side of the horse, nervous and unsteady. Clinging to the saddlehorn, he rolled out of the saddle, dropping the reins. His left foot caught in the stirrup.

"Racer . . . hold still . . . down, boy. . . ."

Racer danced in a circle while Peck yanked, panicked, stepping into a prickly pear. Finally he freed himself.

Alva and Cantú glanced at each other, trying not to laugh. Cantú led their horses through a thicket of cat's-claw and huisache and tied them to separate mesquites.

Alva took a long swig from her canteen. Then she offered it to Peck, who was pulling the thorns from his leggings. He took it gratefully. Cantú returned with the saddlebags. Alva removed a yellow gingham cloth and spread it over the patches of grass and baked soil. The three of them sat on the ground. The hostess served.

"Let's see here — Dolores packed roast beef. I hope that suits you, Mr. Peck."

The sandwich was, in fact, the most pleasant thing Peck had experienced in two days. They talked little while they ate. Cantú withdrew to one side and sat on a log. Alva seemed preoccupied as she surveyed the landscape.

In the shade of an agarita bush, Peck was rejoicing in being back on solid ground. His shins stung and itched from the thorns. Scratching them only inflamed them more. He reclined on his elbows and stared up at the cloudless sky. A pair of buzzards soared above him in wide, slow circles. They wished him dead, he realized, and he was almost ready to oblige.

At first he thought the woman was putting him through all this out of meanness. But perhaps she honestly thought he *wanted* to see every goddamned acre of this goddamned ranch. He had played his part too well: the rip-roaring Texas convert. Maybe, however, that would pay off in the end.

After she had finished her sandwich, Alva reached into the saddlebags and pulled out a revolver. Then she stood up and started filling the chambers with cartridges. "Mr. Peck. You see where that embankment drops off down there? The third oak from the right?"

He sat up, brushing off a horsefly. "Above that bush?"

"Yes. Watch closely." She cocked the hammer and took aim. "Let's see, we might be a little far here . . . ."

She fired. Peck hiccupped, then covered with a laugh.

"Did I hit it?" she asked.

"You hit it," said Domingo Cantú, nonchalant. "The bark flew."

She turned to her guest. "Have you finished your lunch, Mr. Peck?"

He nodded.

"Good. Let's have a go."

Cantú took out a Colt .45, loaded it calmly, and handed it to Peck. He stood up, petrified.

"You did want the long barrel, didn't you?" asked Alva.

Peck nodded.

"You have to cock it first."

He did so, handling it as if it might explode.

"That's right. Now you see that tree—that's right—good. Lower it—steady now."

He pulled the trigger.

"Was he too high?" she asked.

"Too low, I think," said Cantú.

"I couldn't see where it hit. Try again, Mr. Peck."

He did so and hit the embankment.

"Let me see if I can do that." She fired and hit close to the same spot he did.

"You're good," said Peck with a nervous laugh.

"You know, we've been having so much fun," she said, "we keep forgetting to talk business. I may be wrong, Mr. Peck, but I suspect you've come here to try to buy my option on the Hugo & Schmeltzer."

He was caught off guard. "Well, I—no, I mean—you made that clear in your letter, that it wasn't for sale. But I wanted you to know that if—that just in case—"

"Let's try for that log." She fired and hit it.

"I just don't think there's any way you're going to get the state—I mean, just in case you don't get the money—"

"We'll cross that bridge when we get there, Mr. Peck. How about that prickly pear?" She fired and hit it. "Darn. I was aiming for the small leaf. I'm not used to this thirty-eight. You try."

He took aim and fired. This time he hit something. That gave him confidence. "Mrs. Keane, if your plans for raising the money don't work out, I want you to know that the Willinghams will meet the Daughters halfway on the purchase price. A partnership. We'll work with the DRT; you can even approve the design. And the Daughters will get a stake in the hotel—I'm sure you know what a gold mine that could be for your organization. You see, we *want* the new hotel to fit in with the Alamo. We *want* to be your partner."

She looked directly at him and thought for a moment. "Well, Mr. Peck, that's very generous. But the thing is, I'm sort of a maverick myself, and to tell the truth, I don't like working with a partner. Other than Mrs. Herrera. And besides, we have our own plans for the property. I've been thinking of a park—maybe a sculpture garden with statues of Travis and Bowie and Crockett. And a special section honoring Daddy and the other great cattlemen who made Texas what it is today."

She took one last shot at the oak tree, sending chips of bark flying.

"So," she told him, "if that's all you came to Laredo to tell me, I'm afraid you've wasted your time."

She removed the last cartridge and put her revolver back in the saddlebags, satisfied with her shooting. Then she looked up at him and smiled. "No hard feelings, I hope."

He laughed—but just barely. "No, of course not. I've had a wonderful visit here."

Peck fantasized how easy it would be to point the gun at the unarmed woman and pull the trigger. Of course, then he would have to shoot the Mexican too, and flee across the border to Tamaulipas— on Racer. No, it wasn't *quite* worth it.

"The horses should be rested by now," said Alva. "Let's go have a look at the third hill. ¡Vamos, hombres!"

THE WESTERN UNION TELEGRAPH COMPANY.
——— INCORPORATED ———
23,000 OFFICES IN AMERICA. CABLE SERVICE TO ALL THE WORLD.

Laredo Texas Oct. 21st-1907.
Mrs. Rose Herrera,
    1211 Townsend Avenue, San Antonio Texas.
Peck is snake might try to sway legislature must press Senator Pratt for commitment immediately only twelve days left under option.

                                        Alva.

1054am

S enator H. B. Pratt said he'd be waiting for Rose at the Mexican Court of the Menger Hotel. When she got there, she had no trouble spotting him on the outdoor dining terrace: she simply looked for a mountain of ruddy flesh in a big Stetson. He got up to greet her.

"Rosalita!" he boomed. "How long has it been since I've seen you, precious?"

She smiled. "Last month at the banquet for Secretary Root."

"Oh, yes, of course." He introduced his aide Whatley, a slight, freckle-faced young man. The senator helped her with her chair. Then he snapped his fingers at a waiter. They all sat.

Senator Pratt turned to Whatley. "Rosalita's pappy practically raised me. Outstanding gentleman, treated me just like a son. I'm not putting you on, either: Fermin De León made me everything I am today."

"I hope not *everything*, senator," quipped Rose.

He grinned appreciatively. "Don't call me senator, peach blossom. Call me Hobo, just like your pappy did."

"All right. Hobo." She hated calling him Hobo almost as much as she resented being called Rosalita. But she knew he was holding all the cards in this game.

The senator studied her for a moment. "So. I got your letter, Rosalita."

She tried not to appear nervous. "Yes. I think I mentioned in the letter—I've written a proposal that tells more about our plans." She handed him the leather portfolio. Her hands were shaking.

"I don't even need to see this, sugar," he replied. "I've already decided—"

A waiter in a white jacket approached their table. The senator paused while the man poured lemonade. A few drops fell on the portfolio.

"Watch out!" bellowed Senator Pratt. "For crying out loud, you clumsy . . . . The lady's put a lot of work into this, and you go and mess it up."

The waiter apologized timidly and wiped off the portfolio. Rose glanced down, embarrassed. She had forgotten that the senator, for all his gregarious banter, could be quite hot-tempered.

The waiter left them. Senator Pratt's grin returned just as quickly as it had vanished. "You see, I have to raise my voice that same way at the capitol to keep some of my colleagues in line."

She forced a slight smile. She was afraid he was stalling.

"Rosalita," the senator continued, "about your letter. Now I'll be completely straight with you. What you and these other fair ladies propose to do at the Alamo is absolutely inspiring. My first thought was: wouldn't your grandpappy be proud of you? Your poor old pappy, too, God rest his soul."

"So you'll help us?"

"I swear to you, right here and now. I'll do everything in my power to make sure those old farm boys in Austin vote the right way."

Rose felt her whole body go limp. She glowed, barely able to speak. "I knew I could count on you. Muchas, muchas gracias, senator."

"Hobo," he insisted.

"This hotel man has been watching the DRT like a vulture. And we've only got ten days left under the option," she pointed out.

He leaned close to her. "Now I don't want you to worry that little red head a single whit. You leave it to this ornery old horse to build a fire in those boys' britches and get them going on this right away."

"Gentlemen," she said, "if you have a minute, we could go next door and take a look at the Hugo & Schmeltzer building."

"Rosalita, I don't need to see that, either," Senator Pratt told her. "I'm like that centurion in the Bible, when he asked Jesus to heal his servant. You just speak the word, little lady, and it'll be done."

"Very well, then," she said.

"So tell me, how is that shyster Herrera?" he asked.

"My husband is doing very well, thank you."

"Still working for that pompous know-it-all, Horatio Franck?"

"Working *with*. They're partners now."

"Isn't that a shame? A fellow as nice as Antonio. He ought to be in the legislature."

She smiled. "Mr. Herrera prefers to work behind the scenes. I'm the one who would enjoy being a legislator."

Senator Pratt responded with a belly laugh. "I'm sure you'd make a good one, Rosalita. The only problem is, most of those old boys at the capitol would be too distracted by a pretty little redhead speaking on the floor."

"I don't remember any men swooning when I made my speech at the banquet."

His face clouded. He turned to Whatley. "Go find our incompetent waiter and tell him to bring Mrs. Herrera a bowl of that mango ice cream."

"I thank you kindly, but it will have to be another time," she said as she stood up. "I've still got a lot of letters to write this afternoon. Hobo, you have my deepest gratitude. I guess chivalry isn't dead in Texas. Buenos tardes, gentlemen."

Both men stood as she left. They watched until she had crossed the terrace and disappeared into the hotel before they slowly sat down. The senator's campaign smile faded. He lit a cigar, then turned to Whatley. "Young man, what do you have on your agenda this afternoon?"

"To find out all there is to know about the Willingham hotel and who's in charge of it, sir."

"Then perhaps you'd better get your skinny ass in gear instead of sitting here like a half-wit, drinking all my lemonade. Savvy?"

fter her meeting with Senator Pratt, Rose felt relaxed for the first time in several days. She sent a cable to Alva relaying the good news. Experience had taught her not to celebrate until the prize was firmly within her grasp. And she was still trying to raise funds privately, just in case the legislature didn't come through. But with Hobo Pratt on her side, the Alamo was as good as saved.

At last Francisco De León and his slain comrades could rest in peace. Wilton Peck would fade, a tiny blemish on the face of San Antonio's history, and Rose could return to an orderly life of research and writing. Her name would vanish from the *Journal*. That would please Antonio. He might even congratulate her on her Alamo victory—if he ever decided to start speaking to her again.

Since their bitter row the week before, a chilly silence had fallen over the Herrera house. At dinner Antonio hid behind his newspaper. Without a word he had moved out of the master bedroom to the guest room down the hall. The Herreras had given their son no explanation. Nor had he asked for one.

Perhaps the boy hadn't even noticed. Enrique was spending more time away from home. Some nights his mother fretted until dawn, when she heard his knees rattling the drainpipe as he scrambled up to the sun deck. In her dreams the Corrido King made regular appearances, tormenting her. One night his image made her bolt upright in bed and gasp for breath. It was time to put an end to Menchaca's menace, once and for all.

She would need support. Early the next morning, after Antonio had left for his law office and Enrique for St. Mary's, she sped away in the Peerless to La Villita. Ordinarily she didn't call on Madame Guenther unannounced. But this was an emergency. Menchaca was gnawing at her serenity with the persistence of a sewer rat.

She needn't have worried about interrupting the sculptor's work. That morning Mathilda Guenther was upstairs in her parlor, poring over a thick, ornate volume in disbelief. She grunted aloud as she turned to the final page. What she read made her cheeks turn crimson and her icy eyes burn.

In anguish Farnsworth drew the dying girl to his warm breast. Feverishly, beseechingly,—with tear-streaming eyes—he cried out in aching sobs to the shrouded heavens above: "My God, do not take her! Take me in her stead!"

Then the murky clouds opened like a vast curtain, and brilliant, white moonlight flooded the chaparral, illuminating the girl's lithe frame. All at once, her red lips parted, and her dark, deep, soulful eyes opened—a miracle within his manly grasp!

"Angelina! My sweetheart! my love! my life!" Frantically, impulsively, he pressed his hot-blooded lips ardently against hers as he cradled her tender little body in his strong arms.

"Farnsworth!" She spoke softly, but even now with the flaming passion so characteristic of her race,—that fierce Mexican strain that marked his wild prairie flower.

"Oh Angelina, my own, my darling!" His tears fell like raindrops on her heaving bosom, glistening in the moonlight.

"Farnsworth! Zamora—is—trying—to—kill—you!"

"That's all over, my beloved. Zamora and his bandidos are dead. You saved my life, my brave little heroine. You have done the noblest, purest thing a person can do,—lay-ing down your life for the one who loves you!"

"Then you love me? And not that Boston girl?"

"Oh, my Angelina! How could you not have known, my precious little pearl? I have always loved you. Only you."

She smiled at him once more, the smile of the angels; then, slowly, her radiant eyes closed, never to shine again, as she drifted into that peaceful slumber from which there is no awakening; and the mournful prairie wind wafted her courageous soul upward, upward,—to a resplendent world that admits no pain or sorrow, and that embraces all true-hearted lovers who reach its balmy shores, be they swarthy or fair.

With his usual scowl, the housekeeper Silas Toombs admitted Rose and led her through a dim passageway. She followed him up the stairs. It was the first time she had been invited to the second floor apartment. To her surprise, the parlor was cluttered with lace, ornamental wood panels and Victorian bric-a-brac—entirely out of keeping with an artist who swore by the virtues of spareness and simplicity.

Madame Guenther, dressed in her usual black frock, comfortably filled a rocking chair. Her feet were elevated on an embroidered stool decorated with bow-knots. "Mrs. Herrera. Come in. I'm afraid you have caught me loafing."

"Nonsense. Reading can only improve us, Madame Guenther."

"Oh yes? Look at what I am reading, and you will think again. Have you had a chance to digest our patron's romantic novel?"

Rose shook her head. "My Lord, no. Not with the Alamo on my mind." She had no intention of reading a story so obviously set at Tres Piedras Ranch, in which Alva thinly disguised herself as an exotic señorita and portrayed her playboy husband as a strapping Galahad.

"This is an astounding book. American writing of the floral variety, I believe you would say. I decided to read it for insight into my client's way of thinking. But all this talk of hot red lips and heaving bosoms made me sick. And the plot! Preposterous. The Yankee hero falls in love with Angelina Del Rio, but he is too cowardly to marry outside his race."

That piqued Rose's curiosity. "So what does he do?"

"Hunh! He never gets to do anything! Our friend Mrs. Keane kills off Angelina, so that the Yankee will be spared the trauma of making a decision. Very convenient for Farnsworth. And for the author. I should not have given away the ending—but believe me, there are no surprises in her story."

Rose nodded, distracted. "Maybe not, but I've got a surprise for you. I'm going back to Military Plaza this morning, to track down Rafael Menchaca."

The artist sat up and put the novel aside. "Our chili vendor?"

"I thought you might like to come with me."

"Of course. If you wish, I can go. Would you excuse me for a moment? I'll ask Toombs to show you the piece I'm doing for Mrs. Keane." Then, with none of her usual protestations about being too busy, the artist disappeared into her bedroom.

Toombs was dusting the wind-up clock in the hall. Rose speculated that the black man with the unflappable decorum was the one who had decorated the parlor. Though Madame Guenther didn't shower any more affection on her housekeeper than she did on her friends, perhaps that was her way of pleasing him.

He led Rose downstairs to the studio. There he unveiled the clay bust of Colonel Travis that Alva had commissioned for the Alamo. "It is one of Madame's finest," said the housekeeper.

"Yes. The eyes are very expressive. But terribly sad."

"They are mine," Toombs admitted. "The forehead and the cheekbones are Madame's own. The mouth, I think, is yours."

That amused her. "So she's going to make all of us immortal before she dies."

The man glanced at her. "Madame's only fear is that she won't have enough time to finish everything."

"Yes," said Rose. "She once told me she feels she has only ten good years left."

For the first time she saw the old man smile. "Oh, but don't you know? She's been saying that for ten years already."

For someone who guarded her time like money, Madame Guenther kept them waiting for an unreasonable length. When she finally bustled into the studio, she was dressed in a flowing gown of emerald satin, trimmed in panne velvet and rich bodice lace. She had released her frosty brown hair from its tight knot and brushed it until it shone. Topping it all was a dusty old picture hat sprouting ostrich plumes. The aroma of too much perfume filled the room.

Rose gasped. Even Toombs wasn't prepared for the transformation. He upset a wicker chair.

The artist dismissed their reaction with contempt as she adjusted her long white gloves. "What do I have here, a pair of gaping fools?"

"I was just wondering," stammered Rose, "if you brought your pistol."

"Ach! Certainly not. Do you believe we will encounter danger this early in the day?"

She replied, "Right now I could believe anything."

"Come," said the artist. "Let us not stand around until we turn into fossils."

They parked the Peerless beneath a mulberry tree on Camaron Street, directly across from the Palace Livery Stable. From there, thought Rose, they could make a quick getaway if Menchaca tried anything violent or lecherous. The two women sat in the automobile for a moment, sizing up the situation. A grizzled vaquero stood leering at them from the wide double doors of the stone facade.

"Yes, you were right. I should have brought my pistol," Madame Guenther admitted.

"That cowboy doesn't scare me," replied Rose. "But a man like Menchaca would just as soon slash my throat as not."

"Oh! You always exaggerate. But just in case you are right, show me how to drive this thing."

"¿Por qué? If that animal does me in, he won't let you live to tell about it. Come, let's go find him." They stepped down from the Peerless and walked arm-in-arm toward the door.

Inside the noisy livery they passed several blacksmiths in dirty overalls, mending harnesses and oiling the carriage wheels. The men stopped to gape at the two well-dressed ladies. A stable boy led them up the back stairs. At the end of the hall he stopped and pointed to the room. Rose tipped him a nickel. He left them alone.

Rafael Menchaca's door was halfway ajar. Rose summoned her courage and knocked loudly. No one answered.

She looked back at the artist. "Do we dare?"

"Absolutely. You go first."

Rose crossed herself, then pushed the door all the way open and stepped over the threshold. Madame Guenther followed cautiously behind her. The man wasn't there. The women spoke in the low tones of prowlers.

"Watch out—he might be hiding," Rose warned.

"Ach!" Madame Guenther was disappointed. "Perhaps he has already gone to his chili stand."

"It's too early for the likes of him to do any useful work," replied her companion. "And look, his guitar is still here. He can't be far away."

They snooped around the spartan room like errant children. The cot was unmade, and dirty clothes were strewn across the floor. Rose sniffed the air with distaste. Over the lone chair hung Menchaca's striped serape. His derby hat rested on the table, beside a cast-iron pan of cold refritos.

"His room has a certain rustic charm," said Madame Guenther.

"It's a pig-sty!" Rose scowled, nosing through a stack of broadsheets and tintypes of lewd women. She found the man's Bowie knife underneath.

The sculptor came upon the basket filled with little clay statues. "Look! These are the figures the girl was selling at his chili stand. Do you think she is his daughter?"

"Don't be naive! More likely his concubine. Does he look like a family man to you?"

The plank floor behind them creaked; instinctively Rose grabbed the Bowie knife. The two women turned to see Rafael Menchaca framed in the doorway. The Corrido King was clad only in a white bath towel wrapped around his waist. Beads of water dripped from his black locks, his goatee, the small patch of matted chest hair. His big feet left wet prints. Across his paunchy midriff ran faint traces of a long, thin scar.

Both women gasped. The man's angry eyes accused them. Rose immediately glanced down at the floor, her bravado shattered. Her companion stared shamelessly, open-mouthed.

"I . . . I am Mrs. Herrera."

"And I am Madame Guenther."

"And I am obviously in the raw. Would you mind?"

He held the door for them, glowering. The two women hurried past him and into the hallway. He slammed the door. Rose exclaimed, "Oh my God! I still have his knife." She stared at it in disbelief.

"We were wrong to snoop," fretted Madame Guenther. "Now he will have a bad impression of us."

That fanned her friend's fire. "Santa María! We didn't come here to score points. That fiend got the better of us just now. But he won't catch us off guard again."

A sunburned cowpoke with long, droopy moustaches shuffled out from one of the rooms. He whistled at the women. "Well, I'll be a durned fool, look what we have—"

"¡Cállese! Por favor." Rose raised the knife.

The man threw up his hands and grinned. "Hold your danged horses, I'm just passing through." He sauntered down the stairs.

She simmered. "Swine! And to think of my son coming to this despicable rathole."

Madame Guenther said, "I'm wondering if I should do more than a bust."

"What?"

"Our chili vendor. At first I was taken only by his facial features. But he has a rather interesting torso, don't you think?"

Rose was appalled. "That pelado? You must be loca. I think he's broken-down and ugly."

"His very person is inscribed with history. Did you see his scar?"

"How could I have missed it?"

"It gave me chills," said the sculptor. "I wonder how he got it. I would like to think: this is a man who started peasant revolts in Mexico."

Rose scoffed. "Yes, and probably in some peasant cantina, over some peasant barmaid. You don't know these people. Take my word, this man—"

Just then Rafael Menchaca opened the door. He was groomed and cologned and draped in his colorful serape. His disposition had improved as radically as his appearance. "Come in, come in, señoras. By all means."

The women entered. The room looked almost orderly now. The man had shoved his dirty clothes and dishes under the cot.

"To what do I owe the honor of this visit?" he asked. "You're both decked out for tea and crumpets. But all I can offer you is strong coffee and a cold tortilla."

Rose replied, "We won't take anything from you, Menchaca."

"Perdón, my mistake! Señora De León Herrera comes to my hacienda to threaten me with my own knife."

She still clutched the Bowie knife. The two women crossed the room and sat side by side on the cot. The man grinned. That made Rose uneasy. "I think you know why we're here," she said.

"I have my suspicions. But let me tell you right away—the Corrido King can't sit around posing for you ladies all day. I'm a busy man; I go from place to place."

"What the devil are you talking about?"

He took a letter from the table. "Señora De León Herrera—surely you know!" He flashed them a wicked smile as he quoted. "I possess a countenance of extraordinary aesthetic integrity. Isn't that right, Señora . . . Sculptor?"

The artist froze, embarrassed.

Rose was outraged by the man's flippancy. "Let me be direct with you, please. We're not interested in your countenance or any other part of your person. I happen to know that you've been seeing my son. I'm here to warn you, Menchaca: don't have any further contact with Enrique. Or I'll come back here with a knife bigger than this one and cut you in places not so well-padded as your belly. Have I made myself clear?"

He mulled over her threat. Then he spoke quietly, but with a threat of his own. "Señora. It's true what people say. You have the De León spirit. I like that. But remember—you're talking to a man now, not your houseboy. Be careful."

"You don't scare me, Menchaca. I'll do anything to protect my son from your influence."

The man grinned, mocking her. "Then I do scare you. It's my songs that scare you ricos in Alamo Heights."

"Oh really!"

"You and your rich compadres! Living miles away from the common people, so you don't have to smell our sweat—"

"Don't change the subject—"

"My corridos hit too close to your fancy homes. Hmm?"

"Oh—you babbling fool! Get off your soapbox a minute." Rose leapt up from the cot and waved the knife at him. "You love to think you're oppressed, don't you? Poor Menchaca! Leaving his bed unmade and his clothes on the floor and his dishes dirty, so he can suffer in filth and squalor like—"

"And who invited you to—"

"The door was open—"

"*Half* open. And how dare you make a mockery of my principles! I've been beaten up by policemen more times than you can imagine—"

"For good reason, I'm sure—"

"For speaking out! You see, señora, when you speak your mind, the newspapers quote you and make you famous. When I speak mine, those capitalist's henchmen throw me in a dark cell for disturbing the peace, or inciting a riot. So I have to try harder. I write songs, and no policeman can stop the people from singing my songs."

Rose was still pacing. "I didn't come here to—"

"Just recently I read about you in the papers. The señora trying to save the Alamo. The Alamo! The cradle of oppression! And you, the Tejano bourgeoisie, the agringada, leading the fight to save it—"

"Let me ask you something—Corrido King. Who built the Alamo mission? The Spaniards! Who occupied it? The Mexicans! And who wants to destroy it? Some company from Philadelphia! By God I'll fight to save it, just like my grandfather fought—"

"For the Americanos!"

"For justice—you have no idea. Then things went wrong. Well, I say *remember* the Alamo! Yes! Remember what happened to Fermin De León and Juan Seguin and all the rest who fought for Texas and then got treated like the enemy. They lost everything. That's our legacy. My God! Let the Alamo stand—as a reminder of that!" She was surprised by her own vehemence.

Madame Guenther tugged at her arm. "Enough! Mrs. Herrera. You two will only encourage each other."

She sat down, fuming. "You see? This man got me off track on purpose."

Menchaca wheeled around. "¿Cómo? You came here to talk about your son? All right, talk. I'm listening. Tell me what you know about Enrique."

"Huh." Rose straightened her elbow sleeves. "Menchaca, I've said all you need to know about my son."

"There! I thought so. Then I'll talk, and you can listen." He paced as he spoke, building up steam. "I can tell you a few things about Enrique. Your son doesn't have any idea who he is, because you've kept him locked away in some artificial world in the clouds. The Heights! And the boy feels strange there, because he stands out; but when he comes to the West Side, he stands out just as much, since he hasn't learned how to act when he's not with stupid schoolboys. So he hates himself. He doesn't fit anywhere. Yes, you've protected him well, Señora De León Herrera, but you've protected him from *life*, and now he's old enough to realize that. It kills you that he spends so much time with me. But remember, I didn't seek out Enrique. He came to me. Tell me, señora—do you know your son at all?"

He fixed his eyes on her, bracing himself to fend off her attack. Instead he saw tears streaming down her cheeks. She looked at the floor, embarrassed. His glare melted in surprise. He stared, uncertain. Then he squatted beside her and took her forearm, very gently, in his rough hand. With his other hand he slowly reached for the knife. This time his voice was low and soothing. "Here. Let me have that. Please. I'm not going to hurt you, señora. I'm not going to hurt your son."

She looked at him, confused. For the first time the intensity of his eyes didn't repel her. She was trembling. His unexpected tenderness flustered her much more than his anger. Unable to speak, she let go of the knife. He offered her his handkerchief in its place. She took it and looked away.

Madame Guenther stuttered, "Please—my fine troubadour—I am an admirer. It would give me great pleasure to hear . . . ."

Rose was shaken. "No, really, I left the car—we don't have time—"

"Of course, Señora Sculptor." He was staring at Rose without realizing it. He stood slowly and took up his guitar. Facing them, with one foot on his chair, he began a ballad: "*Me abandonas, me desprecias porque quieres. . . .*"

Watching the man's calloused fingers work the strings, his eyes closed and his face contorted, Rose lost all sense of time and place. For the moment she was standing outside Turner Halle, and it was Christmas half her life ago; in a warm embrace, loved and in love, she thought the pain of her father's disgrace was behind her for good, and all the joys of life were in store for her. His song passed through her like soft rays from a refracted light. After he was finished she still heard his voice.

Even Madame Guenther was moved. "So. Mr. Menchaca. Will you come to my studio?"

The man nodded, but he was looking at Rose. "One day. I will come."

She stared back at him, startled. "Menchaca—you do have a daughter, don't you?"

He smiled. "I have five daughters. The one you've seen at the chili stand is Eva, my artist."

Madame Guenther gave her companion a reproving look. Rose didn't notice. "Menchaca—it may be true that you know Enrique better than I thought. But please respect my wishes. Don't take him out on the plaza, to play for money. I'm asking you as one parent to another."

The man sighed. "Your son is a fine musician. But if you don't want him to sing in public, for whatever crazy reason, I won't let him do that. Not until he has your permission." Rose nodded, hardly aware that she had compromised.

The two women got up to leave. The man added: "Señora De León Herrera, you still have much room for improvement. But I think you've got a true heart underneath all those fine rags. Someday you'll be proud to see your son singing with me on the plaza."

She turned to face him once more. The old mischief was back in his eyes, challenging her. She squinted and replied, "Don't hold your breath, Menchaca. Unless you intend to do so till you expire." But her voice quaked; quickly she turned away.

Outside the stable Madame Guenther poured out her frustration. "Oh! I was so tongue-tied. I failed to get a promise from him, when he will come for a sitting. Do you think he will really come?"

They waited for a horse-drawn carriage to pass. Rose seemed many miles away. "Don't fret about it. I mean, we have no way of knowing."

They crossed the street. Rose set the spark and choke and cranked the Peerless. The two women drove off without saying any more.

Wenching wasn't one of Wilton Peck's regular pursuits, and he looked forward to his evening at the bawdy house on Produce Row like another trip to Tres Piedras Ranch. But this, like the Tres Piedras trip, was business. He hoped he got the address right. The telephone connection with Austin had been bad:

"We do need to talk, amigo—CRACKLE—your latest proposal, let's powwow around nine—ZZZZZ—who knows, maybe you'll be up for a little po—MMMMM—"

Peck wasn't sure whether the senator had said "a little poke" or "a little poker." Just in case, he had brushed up on his card hands. And, to be safe, he brought his own deck.

It was night; still, he wore dark spectacles to hide his identity. He walked past the unmarked frame bungalow a few times, making sure no one was watching before he turned up the walk. Quickly he leapt up the porch steps and ducked inside the screen door. In the hall he found a sullen Mexican girl, her blouse partially opened. Removing his spectacles, he announced himself to her as if she were a receptionist.

"Wilton Peck to see Senator Pratt. Por favor."

The girl didn't reply. Sensing his condescension, she turned away with contempt and motioned for him to follow.

Peck had made only one previous visit to a brothel, in Philadelphia, at the insistence of the junior Mr. Willingham. Something about the brass parlor fixtures had particularly nauseated him: as if those shiny surfaces were teeming with invisible life of the vilest sort. In the end he remembered being on his hands and knees in an alley, heaving violently, without having rutted.

But that was years ago. Now he was more worldly. And he was becoming more adept in these Texas situations. He seldom hiccupped any more. As his cowboy boots pounded the wooden floor all the way down the hall, he actually liked the intimidating clatter they made.

The girl ushered him into a small chamber, closing the door as she left. A lantern dangling from the ceiling barely lit the green felt game table. There sat Senator Pratt, puffing on a fat cigar. He spoke in a big gravelly boom: "Pecker! Good to see you again, son. Come sit yourself down."

"Evening, senator."

"I want you to meet my aide-in-chief, Miss Annie."

At the senator's side sat a hefty, aging slattern layered in silk petticoats and orange curls. She smiled, and her painted face fractured into a thousand red crevices. Peck wasn't sure how to address a lewd matron. He simply nodded to her as he took a chair and removed his own Stetson.

"Annie and I have known each other since kitty was a puss. So Pecker—how do you like my San Antonio office?"

The hotel man had prepared a line in advance. "Well, I think this is a fine place to negotiate, senator. You know—it's an office where you can give a little and get a little."

The senator guffawed and slapped the table. "Get a little! I like that one. I tell you, Annie, Pecker's not half bad, for a Yankee."

"You behave yourself, Hobo. You hear?" The old whore had a sweet, grandmotherly twang that surprised Peck.

"Aw, Pecker knows I'm just full of horseshit."

The redheaded hussy turned to the Philadelphian. "You just enjoy yourself here at Annie's place. Yankees are welcome here, same as coloreds and Mexicans."

"That's mighty reassuring, ma'am." It may have been his imagination, but Peck thought he heard himself starting to drawl—and even drop his final g's.

"Smoke?" she asked.

"Yes, thank you." Peck lit the cigar she gave him. "So you got my latest proposal, senator."

"Call me Hobo, son. And yes, I've thought about your offer. I just don't know, Pecker. I've never put my money into a hotel before. Don't reckon I ought to start now."

Peck narrowed his eyes and blew smoke. He was careful not to sound too desperate. "Whatever you think, Hobo. But the Willinghams don't offer this good a cut very often."

"The talk on the street is that the Willinghams don't have a place to put their fancy new hotel."

"Well, Hobo, I'm not at liberty to say much, but just between us— the Willinghams have leads on some prime property."

The senator laughed. "Pecker, don't shit a shitter. I think the Daughters of the Republic have got you boys by the balls and they're making you sweat."

"I'm not worried, Hobo. Do I look worried?" Peck puffed on his cigar.

Senator Pratt studied him. "You know, Pecker, you've got a poker face. I like that; I'm a gambling man myself. Tell you what. I'll give you a chance to get what you want from me, fair and square. How about a little card game?"

Peck dug the heels of his cowboy boots into the soiled red carpet. "Suits me."

"Annie can deal for us. Unless you don't trust her."

He didn't. "That's fine. But would y'all mind if we used my deck? It's always brought me good luck, and . . . ."

The senator shrugged. "Fine with me, Pecker."

That surprised Peck. He had expected the game to be rigged. The buxom woman shuffled the deck several times and dealt each of them five cards. The senator explained, "This game is my own invention, Pecker. I call it Hobo's Draw."

The hotel man nodded. Already he didn't like the sound of this.

"What's unusual about it is the ante. Instead of putting up chips or cash, we each wager stakes in something we own. Percent interests. Now, I did some figuring, and I reckon your new hotel will be worth about the same as my twenty-five sections around Laredo. So if you ante up one percent of the Willingham Palace, I'll have to match it with one percent of my ranch, and so on. Are you with me?"

The room was warm, but Wilton Peck suddenly felt chills shooting up and down his body. The senator was interested in the hotel, all right; he was just holding out for a bigger stake. The Willinghams would be outraged. But the Willinghams knew nothing about dealing with Texans, who were all as mad as hatters in one way or another. Peck nodded and puffed faster.

"Okay," said the senator. "Let's start at one percent."

Peck looked at his hand. A pair of sixes. Pitiful.

The senator deliberated gravely. "I'll raise you, Pecker. Two percent."

Two percent of the Willingham Palace was an enormous stake. Peck didn't respond.

The senator's face grew red with impatience. "Oh, come on, Pecker. Do I have to spell it out for you, boy? *You can't lose.* Now look here. If you win this hand, you've got half a section of good cattle country coming to you. And if I were to win this hand—well, you'd give up two percent of Mr. Willingham's hotel. But that means you'd also get my help in Austin. Just ask old Annie here, I've got the biggest tally-whacker in the whole Texas Senate. And if I were to win, I'd want to make damned sure Rosalita Herrera and the DRT didn't get their paws on the lot we'd need for our hotel. Have I made it all plain enough for you, Pecker?"

Peck wasn't about to lose face. He anted up, and the dealer shot him two new cards. That gave him a pair of sixes, a pair of eights, and a jack.

The senator grinned behind a puff of smoke. "Okay, Pecker. I'll raise you once more. Five percent."

Out of the question! Peck tried to read his opponent. He looked at the woman. She drew a deep breath and raised her painted eyebrows. His future flew before him: if he lost this game, he might as well toss his promotion out the window. Unless he could somehow convince the Willinghams that—

"Oh, for crying out loud, Pecker!" exploded Senator Pratt. "I believe those DRT ladies have more cojones than you. I've a good mind to let Rosalita and the Carson girl have that property after all."

That did it. Wilton Peck would risk throwing away his future before he'd be humiliated again by those two women. "All right, Hobo. Five percent."

He closed his eyes as he placed his cards on the table. *Five percent!* He pictured the senior Mr. Willingham, the promised corner office in Philadelphia, his name on the door in gold letters—goddamned slaphappy Texans! Please, oh please, he chanted to himself. . . . a pair of sixes, a pair of eights, a jack, a pair of . . . .

Then he heard the senator sigh. Slowly Wilton Peck opened his eyes.

Out burst a startling hiccup, his first since Tres Piedras. He bolted from the table and rushed into the corridor. As he burst out the back door, he heard the senator booming "I'll be goddamned!" and the slattern cackling. Then, in the dark alley behind the whorehouse, he dropped on all fours and heaved.

TEXAS STATE SENATE
Office of Senator H. B. Pratt

October 30, 1907

Mrs. Rose Herrera
1211 Townsend Avenue
San Antonio, Texas

My dearest Rosalita:

I owe you an enormous apology—for a terrible oversight on the part of Whatley, my aide.

Whatley has informed me that the deadline for putting new items on the Appropriation Committee's agenda passed last Friday. Therefore, the legislature cannot consider your request regarding the Hugo & Schmeltzer property until next session.

I am deeply sorry for Whatley's bungling of this important matter. Best of luck with your endeavors, however. Please do not hesitate to let me know if I can ever be of any assistance in the future.

Your friend,
Hobo Pratt

36

As was fitting, Hobo Pratt's letter of doom arrived on Halloween. The news took Rose completely by surprise. Only three days earlier, she had spoken with Senator Pratt by telephone, and he'd assured her everything was going as planned. Neighbors all around the Herrera house heard the endless stream of blasphemies and Spanish curses. They shook their heads and said, "Those Latins are at it again." After the torrent subsided, Rose's cook chided her severely. Then Eloisa insisted that they go at once to San Fernando Cathedral, to pray for her employer's absolution—and for the Holy Mother to grant a miracle and save the Alamo.

In the narthex of the cathedral was a shrine to the Alamo defenders, surrounded by a field of flickering votive candles. The old woman, her head devoutly covered with a black lace veil, knelt in the shadows and mumbled. Behind her Rose sulked, leaning against the cool, chalk-stone wall. A miracle, indeed! Praying for a hex on the Willinghams would make more sense, she thought. Unrepentant, she couldn't bring herself to enter the confessional that day. Though it was the eve of the festival honoring all the saints, she felt out of sorts with every one of them.

She looked at her watch. "Psst!"

The old woman shushed her vehemently and went on with her supplications for the salvation of Alamo mission. Only once before had Rose seen her cook pray so fervently: the night of the long vigil, fourteen years earlier, when the Herreras' infant daughter Felicia had succumbed to fever. That time the miracle hadn't been granted.

Rose didn't know why Hobo Pratt had double-crossed her. But she felt certain Wilton Peck was involved. She had no idea what to do now, with Alva's option expiring in three days. Her fundraising appeals had largely fallen on deaf ears. For a moment she thought about going to La Villita for counsel. But no, the sculptor would only nod in sympathy and say: "It is true; your situation is hopeless." She didn't want Madame Guenther's honesty that day. She wanted Eloisa's miracle.

She nudged the old woman. "You're going to wear out the ears of every saint. Then they'll never listen to you again."

"Shh! Un momento." Eloisa clutched her rosary tightly, as if she could bring about the miracle through sheer will. "What's your hurry? You can't do anything for the Alamo that the Blessed Virgin can't."

"The Blessed Virgin can't send a cable."

"¡Respeto!" Shuddering and crossing herself twice, Eloisa whispered three quick Ave Marías. Then she stood reverently, genuflected and followed her employer out onto the brightly sunlit plaza.

Rose and her cook were on their way to visit Fermin De León and little Felicia and Carlos Herrera. The annual ceremony for the dead was one that intrigued Mathilda Guenther, though she had repudiated her Catholic upbringing long ago. The topic had come up once in her studio, when Rose pressed the issue: "Faith or no faith, don't you ever sense the presence of the departed around you?"

The artist reflected. "Well . . . I believe there are invisible forces in the world."

"You and Isaac Newton! That's too vague for me. Don't you ever think about angels, and signs, and visions, and the hereafter?"

"Me? Huh. I hardly have time to think about next week."

Rose shook her head. "Madame Guenther, you would never make a Mexican." Nonetheless, the doubting artist had sent some clay figures she'd purchased from Eva Menchaca as tributes to Rose's dead.

Antonio wasn't going with them to the cemetery this year. He told his wife he was too busy. At first she fumed, thinking he was shunning an old tradition that now embarrassed him. Later she realized:

the ceremony was simply too hard for him. He always grew morosely silent at their children's plot. At least he remembered to send two toys to decorate the graves.

The Peerless sped past a parade of Mexican merrymakers in macabre masks. Rose wasn't ready to join the procession just yet. First she needed to notify her partner of their dilemma. She wondered why she was even bothering. Since their meeting with Mr. Hugo, Alva had all but disappeared from the Alamo controversy, caught up in the frenzy of finishing her Broadway script. Besides, there wasn't much she could do from Tres Piedras.

In Laredo the telegraph operator was busy that day. Rose wasn't the first person to send a frightening cable to Alva on Halloween. In a cluttered office eight floors above the din of New York's Fifth Avenue, her publisher, Max Rosenthal, had paced and fretted all morning over how to break his own bad news to her. Finally he decided: he must come out with the whole truth. Then he reconsidered. No, he would break the news delicately—and only partially, for the time being.

THE WESTERN UNION TELEGRAPH COMPANY.

——————— INCORPORATED ———————

23,000 OFFICES IN AMERICA. CABLE SERVICE TO ALL THE WORLD.

New York N.Y. Oct. 31st-1907.
Mrs. Alva Keane,
   Tres Piedras Ranch, Laredo Texas.
First draft good things moving quickly New Amsterdam splendidly refurbished Menckens more difficult than expected have found you collaborator please hurry back please.

Max.

1147am

San Antonio Tex. Oct. 31st-1907.
Mrs. Alva Keane,
    Tres Piedras Ranch, Laredo Texas.
Pratt sandbagged us legislature will not consider proposal
until next year situation dire.

Rose.

0136pm

A lva Carson Keane had never considered the possibility that she might fail to save the Alamo. Unacquainted with failure, she wasn't prepared to make friends with it now. All afternoon, as she brooded in the shadows of her bedroom at Tres Piedras, the telegram from San Antonio mocked her, preventing her from working on her script. By dusk, scraps of paper scrawled with revisions of Angelina's death scene had drifted from her desk to the pine-plank floor, unnoticed.

The young woman had worked herself into a fury. She was furious not only with Senator Pratt but with the universe itself, the whole cosmic conspiracy that had somehow fouled her plans. She was even angry with her partner for having failed to win the legislature. Alva realized that her father was right. The De Leóns were thinkers, not doers. She had entrusted the most important work of her life to a *scholar.*

And to make matters worse—what was this urgent message from Max Rosenthal? She had no idea what her publisher meant by a collaborator. But she wasn't pleased. Whatever was going on, she ought to get back to New York right away.

Still, she wasn't about to abandon the Alamo struggle at this point. Texas needed her. In three days Wilton Peck would knock at Mr. Hugo's door, purchase money in hand. The thought of losing a battle on her home turf was giving her stomach cramps: Alva Carson Keane, bested—in Texas—by a spineless corporate tool from Philadelphia who could barely stay on a horse.

She didn't hear her husband enter the bedroom. Robert Keane was dressed for a costume ball. His wife had wanted him to go as Diego, the dashing vaquero in *Angelina, Sweetheart of the Chaparral.* To her disappointment he had chosen the role of Farnsworth, the Yankee financier; his costume was remarkably like his workaday Wall Street suit.

"Angelina?" he cooed. "Sweetheart?"

She scowled without looking up.

"Wild prairie flower? My love, my life?"

He saw her Angelina Del Rio costume, a bright calico skirt and embroidered blouse, still hanging from her wardrobe. "Why aren't you dressed, my precious little pearl?"

She glanced at him, irritated. "Oh, stop talking like that. I've decided to stay in tonight. But you go on to town."

"By myself?"

"I don't care. You can take Daddy if you want."

"Oh, *that* would be a hoot."

Though the masquerade at Laredo would surely be a tepid affair, it was unlike her to miss a party. Keane approached his wife from behind. Placing his hands gently on her neck, he made an effort to massage her shoulders. "It's our last night together."

She tensed at his touch. "Don't, Keane. I'm not in good humor."

He took that as his walking orders. Actually, he was relieved. With untiring enthusiasm the two newlyweds had made salacious demands on each other throughout his stay. On the first night, he had removed the cowbell tied to their bed-frame, so that it wouldn't ring by accident during their tumbles and wake The Old Man. Spent and smarting, he had had enough. He strung the bell back in its place.

"I think I *will* go. I need a little air." Tepid affair or not, the Halloween ball would be better than spending his last night at Tres Piedras with his father-in-law. And it would give him a chance to flirt with the local señoritas.

His wife bade him no farewell. It annoyed her that he wasn't standing by her side through this crisis. She ground a black widow spider into the Navajo rug with her shoe.

There *had* to be a way out. She knew that Mr. Hugo wouldn't extend the option. She didn't want to go begging to him, anyway. The DRT could try to borrow the money. But what banker in his right mind would lend the Daughters $75,000, with Rose Herrera's paltry fund-raising record?

Alva was talking herself into a corner. Finally she gave in and accepted her sobering responsibility: she was going to have to buy the Hugo & Schmeltzer herself. The prospect made her queasy. Seventy-five thousand dollars was three times the sum she and Keane were spending to build their estate in New Rochelle. It would buy thousands of acres of ranch land.

And how would she pay for it? The ranch heiress held most of her wealth in stocks and real estate. After furnishing her New York apartment, she no longer had $75,000 at her disposal. Keane's family could scrape together the cash by Sunday. But no, the Alamo should be saved with Texas money.

That left only one source—the most obvious one, and the one she was dancing in circles trying to avoid. Oscar Carson would have no problem coming up with $75,000 in cash. The Old Man probably had more than that stuffed away in a mattress somewhere. But she was terrified to ask him for it. Her father had always provided generously, to be sure; but with the tacit stipulation that he decide how much, and when, and what for.

Oh, to hell with it all! The *Alamo* was at stake, for God's sake—along with her reputation, and her self-esteem. Daddy would understand.

Well . . . Daddy might understand.

For an hour she paced her bedroom, rehearsing her pitch to her father. She borrowed liberally from Angelina's entreaties to Farnsworth, particularly the scene where the Mexican heroine implored her lover to help save the ranch that meant more to her than life itself. Finally, armed with purple rhetoric of desperation and defiance, she forced herself out of her room. The pine planks seemed to cringe and groan beneath her feet as she descended the dark staircase.

38

"**D**addy?"

She found him in the den, poring over cattle sales slips at his roll-top desk. The only light came from a kerosene lamp. He kept its chimney spotlessly clean, so that he could turn the wick very low and use as little fuel as possible. He looked up over his spectacles.

"I'm sorry to interrupt you, Daddy. I won't take long."

He sensed her anxiety. "Come. Sit next to me."

"No, that's all right. Thank you." She was afraid that if she sat, her resolve would somehow spill out of her.

"Why aren't you on your way to the costume ball?"

"I'm not up to it. I'm in a bit of a quandary tonight. I hope you'll pardon my . . . my addled ramblings." One of Angelina Del Rio's phrases, to the rescue.

"Tell me your trouble, daughter." It was a courtly command—but a command nonetheless.

Without realizing it she had placed one hand on her hip and the other across her forehead: Angelina's posture when she begged Farnsworth to save the ranch. "I'm afraid our Alamo has fallen on desperate times. The legislature didn't give us the money. If I don't do something now, everything's lost!"

He nodded and clasped his gnarled hands together. "Well. I'm sorry about the Alamo. But you needn't take this burden upon yourself, Alva. It's not your personal responsibility. You've done the most anyone could do."

"No. There's something else—that is, if someone . . . if some patriot were to put up the money herself—himself—expecting to be fully repaid by the state, of course—that person could still save the Alamo. Oh Daddy, don't you think it would be the noblest thing a person could do?"

He shook his head. "Daughter, this 'person' would have to be a certified lunatic. Do you know anyone that foolish?"

"Yes. Yes I do."

He scoffed. "Who?"

"Who?"

"Yes. Who would put up that kind of money?"

"The person?"

"Yes! Who are you talking about?"

"It's me. It's . . . myself. I'd do it."

He studied her in silence, stroking his chin. Then, deftly, he shot a stream of tobacco juice into his spittoon.

Feeling weaker, his daughter took the wing chair. For the first time she noticed the holes in the shafts of his boots where his spurs rubbed. He wouldn't dream of buying a new pair. She scanned her memory for more of Angelina's words, anything likely to inspire them both; but her alter ego failed her. Angelina was about to lose the ranch. And that wasn't in her script.

"Alva, have you given this enough thought? Are you sure you want to do this?"

His words destroyed what little confidence she had left. "Yes. Of course, Daddy. I'm absolutely sure."

He didn't appear to be displeased—or pleased, as far as she could tell. "Well, it's your decision. I suppose you have the money, if that's how you choose to spend it."

"Well—no. I mean yes, I have it—but not right now, not in cash. I'll have to borrow . . . ." She was losing her way.

"I see. Daughter, do you want me to lend you the money?"

She nodded, mortified. "I'd give you a lien, of course—"

"Alva, your word is good enough for me. I know you'll repay me. What worries me is whether *you'll* be repaid. Of course, if the state won't help you, I suppose you could always sell the property and get most of your money back."

"No, Daddy. I'm going to deed that lot over to the DRT. This is something I'm doing for the people of Texas. It wouldn't make sense for me to hold that property as my own."

"I'd advise you to do just that, Alva. At least until you've been reimbursed."

All at once she felt daring, imbued with Angelina's reckless passion. "I'm going to do this, Daddy, it doesn't matter what happens. I don't care if the legislature repays me or not."

That was the wrong thing to say. The Old Man's cheeks turned crimson. "For God's sake, Alva! Listen to yourself talk!"

She clutched the sides of the chair, petrified.

"Tell me something. How many years did you spend here on this ranch?"

The young woman was quaking. "I don't know, Daddy. A number of years."

"That's right. And how many times have you gone riding out there on the range?"

"A lot."

"Uh-huh. And how many—how many *trees* do you suppose you saw on the range?"

"Thousands." Bewildered, she shrugged timidly.

"Correct. And what grows on those trees, Alva?"

She was too shaken to reply.

"Mesquite beans, acorns, thorns, leaves and mistletoe," he answered for her. "But not money. In all those years, daughter, when you were out there on the ranch with Badger, didn't you ever observe that *money doesn't grow on trees?*"

She pressed hard against the back of her chair, bracing against the blast. Her father hadn't spoken to her this severely since she was a child.

"Sometimes I worry about you, Alva. Our family has a lot of assets, yes. But we're not the Rockefellers or the Carnegies. Your brother understands that. Do you see Tom taking on $75,000 in debt to finance his own pleasures?"

She shook her head. Though she recalled few Bible stories, she felt sudden empathy for Cain.

"No, not unless he's using the money to buy more land, or invest in oil fields. But you and Robert—it's always new clothes, and new automobiles, and a new mansion. Extravagances right and left! The best restaurants and clubs. Trips to the Orient. That apartment at the Antonia Hotel."

She nearly corrected him out of habit—then stopped herself.

His anger had run its course. "I didn't intend to scold you, Alva. I just don't want my only daughter to spend her twilight years worrying about whether her money will run out."

She swallowed hard. "Daddy, you know I take all your advice to heart. And Robert and I are trying to cut back on expenses. But you're wrong about one thing. This isn't something I'm doing for my own pleasure. This is for Texas. If I miss this chance—there won't be another. There's only one Alamo."

He nodded. "Well. You're determined, I can tell. I won't be the one to stop you."

That didn't satisfy her. She leaned over and grasped his arm. "Daddy, I won't do this unless I have your approval."

He took off his spectacles and stared at her. In the blur of the lantern-light he saw a headstrong girl of fourteen, red-haired and freckled, who was unable to toe the line at Miss Perrin's School but who held five Mexican bandits at bay and rescued his steers. Then, to her surprise, he smiled. "Daughter, you know I have every confidence in you. Tom is as good a son as any man could ask for. But you'll always be my favorite."

She smiled back hesitantly. Slowly her sparkle returned.

The lamp sputtered. The cattle baron didn't move to raise the wick. He and his daughter sat for some time, contented, keeping their peace. They watched a tarantula cross the pine-plank floor. Far away on the chaparral, a coyote howled into the night.

"Robert's going back to New York tomorrow?"

She nodded.

"I suppose this trip has been an education for him. I don't think he'll make a rancher, though."

"No."

"Someday you'll have to ride herd, Alva. You can't always leave your duties to your brother."

"I know, Daddy."

The Old Man wasn't looking at her. While they spoke, he was writing out a check.

At that moment, in the kitchen of the Herrera house in Alamo Heights, the cook gasped and dropped the dinner plate she was drying. It shattered. She fell to her knees among the broken pieces, crossing herself and uttering a profusion of Ave Marías. Somehow her miracle had been granted.

What she didn't know was that it had been delivered on credit. Before long her employer would have to pay the price.

THE SAN ANTONIO JOURNAL
Friday, November 8, 1907

Tales & Tattlers

Hats off to one patriotic young heroine! Has ever an act of selfless generosity so captured the hearts of this city? Of course we are referring to Alva Carson Keane, that remarkable ranch heiress who purchased the property next to the Alamo chapel last week and deeded it over to the Daughters of the Republic of Texas. Had the alert Mrs. Keane not seen the threat of commercialism and acted quickly, the site would have been desecrated. Our loyal Alva, who wields a pistol and a pen with equal dexterity, has put her indelible mark on her home state—and how! Already headlines across the nation have hailed her as the savior of the Alamo. This evening Mrs. Keane returns to New York to work on the stage adaptation of her novel, which the Mencken brothers will bring out at the New Amsterdam Theatre in January. We're willing to wager that Broadway will love our Alva as much as San Antonio does!

39

T his," proclaimed Alva, "will be our next project."

Rose frowned. "What's your rush? You're too young, that's what's wrong with you. First we take care of the Alamo." Things had moved so quickly, she hadn't even had time to think about the process of stripping off the Hugo & Schmeltzer facade and restoring the Alamo convent.

"At least it's safe. But look at this place!"

The two women stood beside the Peerless, gazing at the ragged outline of Mission San José y San Miguel de Aguayo. The massive church, built of gold-colored stone, was roofless and overgrown with brittle vines. Mesquite branches reached out from the arched apertures, and prickly pear grew in the bell tower and along the uneven upper walls.

Rose took her partner's arm. "It is magnificent, isn't it?"

"Rose, you're loco. It's depressing!"

"You're a writer; just use your imagination."

"I'm trying. But with all that brush—it reminds me of the arroyo where Zamora and his bandidos held Angelina captive. Don't you think?" It was a test. Secretly Alva suspected that her partner had never read *Angelina, Sweetheart of the Chaparral*, and that peeved her.

"Come," said Rose, blushing, "let's have a closer look."

They crossed the barren compound. It was their first time alone together since the purchase of the Alamo property. All week Alva had been whisked from one gala tribute to another, as San Antonio's leading citizens paid homage to the savior of the Alamo. Most of them had neglected to include Rose.

"Don't forget, I want you to advise me on my next book," said Alva. "This one will start out in Laredo, a few years back, when the land was changing hands." She knew she was venturing into hostile territory. But she longed to get Tres Piedras out in the open.

Rose nodded. "I can recommend some reading."

The younger woman laughed. "Rose, you won't believe this—I haven't been in a library since I got out of school. Would you glance over my early drafts, to make sure I don't stray too far on the history?"

"Of course. But let me warn you, I'll be tough. I don't want to see that part of history distorted."

Alva resented the insinuation. They had reached the crumbling walls of Mission San José. The big stone arches framed triangular sections of clear blue sky.

"I'd like to see the inside," Alva said.

"There's nothing but brush," Rose replied. "But go ahead, take a look." She helped her companion climb up onto a pile of fallen rocks.

Alva peered through one of the arches. "Oh Jesus. We've got our work cut out for us."

"Those land sales—it wasn't just a matter of poor Mexican management, like people say."

Alva watched an armadillo rooting around an agarita bush. Her father had always told her that some people just weren't born managers: "No matter how much they're given to start with, Alva, they'll squander it all."

"There was intrigue," Rose continued. "All manner of dispossession." She surprised herself by using one of Menchaca's words.

Alva replied, "I'm sure I can learn quite a bit from Daddy. He should know."

The De León spark ignited. "Yes, he certainly should."

The younger woman turned around. For a moment neither of them breathed. Then they both burst out in a quick shower of uncomfortable laughter.

"I set you up for that," admitted Alva.

"Yes, I think we both saw it coming."

"¿Qué pasa? What took you so long?" Alva reached for her partner's hand as she stepped down from the rock pile. "Actually, I can't find out much from Daddy; he's so bullheaded about those things."

"Well," said Rose, "that was a long time ago. Some things are best forgotten." Slowly they started to walk the perimeter of the ruined church.

Alva had hoped to broach the subject of honoring her daddy with a monument on the Alamo grounds. But this seemed like the worst possible time for that. "Rose, I still don't understand how your family lost that place," she said instead. "Your father only owed forty-two dollars."

Rose took a deep breath. "¿Quién sabe? It's not something my parents discussed."

Her companion blushed. "I'm prying too much. You should have stopped me."

"No. No, really, I don't mind you asking. I wish I knew the answer. When my father went to Laredo that day, he took some railroad stock certificates, enough to pay the tax. He never told us what happened."

Rose stopped there. Years ago, she had asked Hobo Pratt about that sale. He had been the county attorney in Laredo at the time. The senator had somberly replied, "Now, Rosalita, old Fermin was a prince of a man, God rest his soul, but now and then he got a little crocked. And that morning he showed up in Laredo on a bender. If he had any stock certificates on him, I never knew anything about it." Rose had always doubted his version of the story.

Alva bit against her lower lip. She knew that Fermin De León had been a gambler and a spendthrift; he had probably lost the stock certificates in a blackjack game. "Well, I'll deal with all that in my book. I haven't settled on the plot yet. But I'm basing my heroine on you. Maribel. She's going to die for something important at the end. It can't be a lover; that's the way *Angelina* ends. And I don't think it should be a ranch; that's in *Angelina,* too. But I want her sacrifice to really drive the story. 'Maribel: The Girl Who—Who—what?"

Rose broke out in a grin and took the other woman's elbow. "Who saved the Alamo. It's obvious."

Alva laughed. "That would be a riot! No, but I've already based one book on my own exploits. I can't expect my readers to indulge me twice."

Rose looked away, wounded. *My own exploits.* Though the newspapers had given Alva all the credit for their triumph, she had expected her friend to share the glory with her, at least in private.

Immediately the younger woman realized what she had done. She fumbled to cover, placing her arm around her partner. "We really did it, didn't we, Rose? We saved the Alamo!"

Rose nodded, pushing ahead. "Yes. Well. We'd better go now. You don't want to miss your train."

In silence the women walked back to the Peerless. Rose cranked the engine. Alva was desperate to repair the damage. "What's the best time you've ever made from here to town?"

"Oh, I don't know. Maybe twenty minutes."

The young woman winked. "Let's shoot for eighteen today."

Rose smiled distantly and shook her head. "Another day. My radiator's been over-heating."

They had little to say to each other on their way to the I. & G. N. depot. Alva was scourging herself for her clumsy, thoughtless remark. In the driver's seat, Rose tried not to dwell on the slight. But it wouldn't go away. For more than ten years she had worked hard to do what Alva had accomplished with a single stroke of her pen. Now it seemed as if no one remembered the long struggle.

No! She reminded herself: it wasn't important who did what, or how. And Alva had been astonishingly generous. The only thing that mattered was that Wilton Peck and the Willinghams were vanquished.

Vanquished with Carson money. Reaped from land stolen from the De Leóns.

There was no denying. It hurt. But Rose still had something Alva didn't: the key to the Alamo. There was only one custodian. She convinced herself that she would rather be the Alamo's keeper than its savior. As soon as the young woman's train left for New York, Rose would go visit her grandfather. The building where Francisco De León and his rebel comrades made their last stand was safe in her care. Everything else would be all right. It didn't matter who got the credit. Really—it didn't.

40

Alva Keane knew something was wrong when Max Rosenthal met her train at Pennsylvania Station, instead of waiting to call at her flat after she'd rested and unpacked. And he was much too cheery. Full of nervous chatter, he grabbed two of her bags, rounded up some porters to get the others, and hurried her toward his Packard. Her publisher, of all people, hauling her luggage — and then tipping the porters before she could open her purse.

All the way up Broadway, he questioned her with artificial enthusiasm about Texas and the ranch. Each time she brought up *Angelina*, he got her talking about her Alamo campaign. She was the toast of New York, he said. The savior of the Alamo had made the front page of the *Sun*. Finally she gave up. She let him rattle on uninterrupted until they reached the Ansonia Hotel.

The furniture in her long drawing room was draped with dust covers; her husband was away on business in Argentina. Their maid rushed in. "Ma'am! I wasn't expecting you this early."

"Sophie, you remember Mr. Rosenthal?"

Then, before the embarrassed maid had whisked the cover off an armchair, Alva blurted out: "It's terrible, isn't it?"

Her publisher froze. "What?"

"The show. Max, tell me."

He laughed wanly. "Don't be ridiculous! Rehearsals just started, and they're already calling it the hit of the season. Look. There was a blurb in the *Times* today."

He handed her the newspaper. She sat in the armchair beneath an enormous portrait of her daddy. Sophie busied around quietly unveiling furniture and tidying the room. Rosenthal, scratching his beard and adjusting his eyeglasses, hovered over the author. From the canvas above, Oscar Carson glowered at him.

The reference in the theatrical notes was brief and general. It didn't use the word "hit." And there was one thing in it that alarmed her. "Max. What's this title? This *Angelina, Sweetheart!* nonsense?"

"Oh. You didn't know?"

She put the paper aside. "No. How would I have known? At the top of my script, I wrote *Angelina, Sweetheart of the Chaparral, A Tragic Romance in Three Acts.* As plain as day."

"I know, I know. But the Menckens wanted something with a little more flair. Don't worry; it's not important."

"Yes, it is important. To me. *Angelina, Sweetheart!* sounds silly. Tell them to change it back."

Max Rosenthal folded his arms and inhaled deeply to expand his chest. He needed to look substantial before he went on. "Alva. You remember that contract you signed with Paul Mencken? We talked about that one clause that gave the producers a fair amount of leeway."

"A *fair* amount? What's fair about changing my title?"

"Now don't fly off the handle. I think you'll like the changes they've made."

She sat back, folding her own arms. "Try me."

Nervous, the publisher took the settee—clear across the room from his author. "Well, mainly, they just thought it needed a little more humor."

"*Angelina* is not a comedy, Max."

"No, of course not. There's still plenty of serious stuff. And lots of action. They're even working on a tornado ballet."

"A tornado! This takes place along the border. Tornadoes happen in North Texas!"

"Who's going to know the difference? Besides, when you see what they're doing with the special effects—"

"Max—wait. Back up. Did you say ballet?"

He nodded.

"You're talking about—dancing? To music?"

He glanced down guiltily. "Alva, that's the next thing I was going to tell you. You'll be working with a partner."

"I always work alone, Max."

"The Menckens have brought in a songwriter. The show is going to be, well, sort of a . . . musical."

She sprang to her feet. "A musical!" She stormed to the end of the room. Sophie ducked out of her path.

"Now don't panic," said Rosenthal. "This songwriter is top drawer—"

"A musical! Max, what about the drama? The integrity? All the things we talked about?"

"Don't worry, it'll be a musical with drama and integrity."

"In a pig's eye! It'll be another Mencken brothers beauty pageant and magic show."

"Alva, we've got to trust their judgment. They know this business better than we do."

She sulked for a moment while she let this news sink in. "Well. I hope to God there won't be any singing and dancing during Angelina's death scene."

Max Rosenthal sighed very slowly and stared at his shoes. "Alva, I saw the latest changes yesterday—and Angelina doesn't die in the end." He checked her reaction before adding: "The audience thinks she's dead, but then she springs back to life."

Sophie looked up cautiously from her dusting. But Alva was too numbed to do any more yelling. She sat at a mahogany table and cradled her head in her hands. "I was very proud of that story, Max. So tell me straight. What's left of my work? Does Angelina still save Farnsworth from the bandidos?"

"Oh yes, of course. She saves him. Only its going to be Indians instead of bandidos."

Her rage ignited again; she struck the table with her fist. "Indians! Where the hell did they come from?"

"That was B. J.'s idea. He had some feather headdresses left over from a show that closed in Boston. Please don't get B. J. riled about this. He's very proud of that idea."

"Don't get B. J. riled! What about—"

"Now look here, Alva." He stood up. "I'm sorry, but I have to be blunt. As a novelist, you're used to doing things your way, but in the theatre—"

"Don't lecture me, Max. You're not my daddy. If you *were* Daddy, you would have looked after my interests."

"Jesus Christ! What do you expect? You're a first-timer on Broadway; you can't expect to—"

"I can expect not to have my work butchered—"

"If you'll just give them a chance—"

"By some Tin Pan Alley hack—"

"Wait till you see the–"

"And producers whose idea of integrity is a—"

"Real working locomotive. On stage."

That stopped her short. "What?"

"It's Paul's darling. His special effects team is building a working steam locomotive. For the finale."

"Max, when I want to see a working locomotive, I go to Pennsylvania Station. When I go to the theater, I—"

"Alva, what you want and what the public wants are two different things. This isn't the Metropolitan Opera, it's a Mencken brothers show. Now listen. I'll take you to rehearsal this afternoon. You can see for yourself. And I'd wager quite a bit that you'll like it."

She stood up. "You already have wagered quite a bit, Max. Because if I don't like it, I'm shopping my next book around. We haven't signed a contract yet. And Putnam's and Scribner's have both approached me."

He knew she was probably bluffing. But he wasn't taking any chances. He swallowed his own anger. "All right. Let's get some lunch, have a glass of wine, calm down. Then we'll head to Forty-Second Street and see what you think."

He offered his arm. Alva brushed by him without taking it. Sophie opened the door, then quickly moved out of the way as the author stomped out.

41

Outside the New Amsterdam Theatre, the twin posters flanking the canopy heralded *Naughty But Nice*, the Menckens' fall revue that was in the last weeks of its run. But inside the ornate lobby, workmen were already preparing for the gala opening of *Angelina, Sweetheart!* The classical friezes of Siegfried and Titania were about to be covered over with painted panels depicting cactus in bloom on the Texas chaparral. The vaulted arches of the promenade would be strung with farolitos and imported Mexican piñatas.

Max Rosenthal led the author through the foyer to the rear of the orchestra level. On stage a couple of actors wandered amidst a bevy of dancing girls. Immediately Alva saw that the casting was all wrong. The actor playing Farnsworth, the leading man, was past forty and had a skin rash. Diego, the dashing ranch foreman, was played by an Irish tenor who lisped; a sombrero and black moustache wouldn't fix *that*. And the dancing girls—if there *had* to be dancing girls—looked like starving street waifs, pale and peaked in the footlights.

The director, Evan Drake, was choreographing the title song. Above the towering proscenium, allegorical figures of Poetry, Truth and Love smiled down on the cast. But on stage Chaos reigned. One of the girls couldn't get the steps right, and Drake stopped the number repeatedly while the dance captain demonstrated once again.

B. J. Mencken, a short, scrappy man with a pug nose and a raspy voice, walked up and down the side aisles of the auditorium in long strides. He watched the stage from different vantage points, firing off his comments like bullets.

"You're doing better, Sally," he yelled from a side aisle. "She's getting a hell of a lot better. Isn't she?"

A couple of dancing girls nodded wearily. Another looked away and rolled her eyes. The rehearsal pianist flexed his fingers.

"It's too complicated," whined Sally. "I don't think this dance is very good, anyway."

Alva and Rosenthal made their way down a dark aisle to the tenth row, where the young songwriter, Fred Irving, sat gnawing on his thumbnail. He looked pasty and frazzled. Rosenthal whispered quick introductions.

"Thank God you're here," Irving told the author. "I need to ask you about some of the Spanish words."

Alva was barely able to muster a polite smile. Diplomatically, Rosenthal took the seat between the two collaborators. Then he turned to Alva and explained the problem on stage. "B. J. hired this chorus girl; he's having a fling with her," he whispered. "She looks like a million bucks, but she can't dance her way out of a paper bag."

"They've already had to get rid of the best choreography because of her," Irving added. "B. J. will do anything to keep her from looking like a fool."

Rosenthal nodded. "The director thought about moving her to the singing chorus—"

"But she sings off pitch," said Irving.

"Right. Now Paul thinks she's not a bad comedian. He was wondering if you could write a new character role for her. It doesn't have to be big; just one good laugh in each act would do. That way we could keep her out of—"

"I most certainly will not." Alva was livid, and her voice carried a little too far.

Rosenthal sat back and shrugged. "Okay. Suit yourself. But if you don't, Paul will find some other writer who will. And God knows what you'll end up with."

She refused to look at her publisher. "*Angelina* is a carefully constructed story. Or at least it was. I spent years thinking it up. I can't just add another character out of the blue."

"Why not? This is a musical."

"It wasn't supposed to be." Her tone was so cool that Rosenthal dropped the subject.

Sally still couldn't follow the dance captain. "You're going too fast," she snapped.

B. J. Mencken had appeared in front of the orchestra pit. He stood between Drake and the lanky errand boy, Abbott. "Maybe you could just have her march back and forth carrying an American flag or something," suggested the producer. "You know, just walking in time to the music."

"She can't even *walk* in time," mumbled Irving.

"What does a flag have to do with this scene?" asked the director.

"What the hell does it matter?" the producer shot back. "As long as it looks good. Audiences like patriotic stuff."

"Okay, we need to move on," said Drake. "Let's start from the chorus this time. Skip the verse."

Alva announced loudly, "I'd like to hear the verse."

B. J. Mencken whirled around. "Who the hell's she? Who let her in here?"

"She's the author, B. J.," said Rosenthal. "This is Mrs. Keane."

"Yeah? Well, what's she doing here?"

Irving leaned over to the woman and whispered, "Later. I'll play the songs for you later."

"I haven't heard the verse," she said, even louder. "I want to hear it."

The director's patience was shot. "I can't work like this. Would somebody please refresh my memory: who's running this show?"

"Skip the verse." It was a deep voice from on high: God, perhaps, or B. J.'s brother Paul Mencken.

"Thank you," said Drake, exasperated. "Go ahead, Norman."

The pianist struck up two bars of a boom-chick fill, which, to Alva, sounded more like Gilbert and Sullivan than anything

Mexican. Conrad Hellinger, the leading man, snapped to attention and crooned:

> Oh, Angelina, sweetheart,
> Come here and hold me close,
> And say you'll never tell me
> Adios, adios!
> You're sweet as sasparilla.
> You're round as a tortilla.
> My little hot tamale,
> Let's saddle up and hit the trail!

Alva leapt out of her seat. "No! Stop right there!"

The pianist and leading man came to an abrupt halt, peering out at the dark auditorium. The dancing girls sighed. B. J. Mencken and the director turned around, floored.

"You, Farnsworth—your pronunciation's off," the author called out. "It's not tor-TILL-a. You say tor-TEE-yah. And it's ta-MALL-ly, not ta-MALE."

Cringing, Irving whispered: "We'll fix it later."

"It's a song, missy," snapped B. J. Mencken. "A song's got to rhyme. And tor-TEE-yah don't rhyme."

"That's right. Neither does ta-MALL-ly," Drake pointed out.

"Then you'll have to change it," said the woman.

"Who's calling the shots here? That's what I want to know," huffed the director.

"This is my play," she said, "and it'll be brought out the way I wrote it. Or not at all."

Rosenthal tugged at her sleeve. "Alva."

"Well, I'm the author, Max."

B. J. Mencken scowled at them. "Rosenthal. What's with this dame?"

"She just got in from Texas, B. J.," the publisher said apologetically. "She'll be fine once she's rested."

Alva looked down at him. "Don't patronize me, Max. If you wanted to speak on my behalf, you should have done so when I was away. Before things got in this mess." She waved her hand at the stage.

"Just look at this . . . this travesty!"

"Jesus!" The director turned to his cast and crew. "Girls, take five. You too, O'Keefe. Abbott, run get us coffee. Norman, take Conrad backstage, make him learn the melody."

"I haven't heard the rest of the song," protested Alva.

"Everyone else—down front." It was Paul Mencken, booming from the first mezzanine, his voice echoing off the gilded dome. Fred Irving rose and marched forward dutifully. Max Rosenthal nudged his author to follow.

Five minutes stretched into ten, then fifteen, then twenty, as the bickering in the front row escalated.

"You changed everything in my story," said Alva, "but I didn't know you were rewriting the Spanish language, too."

"Now Mrs. Keane, how many people are really going to know the difference?" asked Paul Mencken. His cold politeness masked a steely resolve, more menacing than his brother's noisy explosions.

"Please, I can fix it," promised Irving. "How about 'melancholy'? 'My little hot tamale, don't you look so melancholy.'"

"What's 'melancholy' mean?" asked B. J. Mencken.

"Sad," sniffed his brother. "B. J. never made it past the fourth grade."

"Piss off, Paul. I don't like two-dollar words in songs. If you mean 'sad,' Irving, say 'sad.'"

"That's a fine rhyme, B. J.," growled Paul. "Why don't you leave the writing to the writers?" He turned to Irving. "Now 'jolly' would work."

The songwriter shrugged. "Sure, Mr. Mencken. 'My little hot tamale, dah-dah-dah-dah, always jolly.'"

"Angelina's *not* always jolly," argued Alva. "The problem is, none of you understand the characters. For crying out loud, this girl's about to lose her ranch—"

"Then *you* come up with a rhyme, missy," said B. J. Mencken.

She replied, "I *have* a name. It's Alva Carson Keane. And I'm not used to people talking to me this way."

"Trolley . . . holly . . . folly . . ." murmured Irving.

Evan Drake said, "I thought the song was fine the way Fred wrote it. Before *she* came in. 'Saddle up and hit the trail' is active, and I've come up with this little horsey thing for the girls to do. If you change the line, it ruins the dance."

"Volley . . . Dolly . . . collie . . ." continued Irving.

"Let's get back at it," said B. J. Mencken. "I'm not paying these dancing beauties fifteen dollars a week to stand around."

"That's another thing," said the author. "Most of those girls haven't even filled out yet. Are they the best you could find?"

The producer blew up. "Missy, you leave the hiring and firing to me. You'd better read your contract. I can even fire the writers if—"

"I'll fight you every inch of the way, in court if I have to," she warned. "And I've got the money to do it—"

"Don't worry about the Spanish, Mrs. Keane," interrupted Paul, with a tight, cold smile. "Audiences won't be listening to the lyrics that close. Not when they've got a tornado and a train and all those costumes to look at. We're spending over twenty thousand dollars on this show. Why do you want to fight about everything?"

"I won't have her interrupting rehearsals," the director pouted. "No one can give the actors notes except me. That's in my contract."

She flared. "You little twit, I could lick you with one hand—"

"Easy, Alva," cautioned Rosenthal.

"Don't shush me, Max."

"Keep this up, missy, and you won't be showing your mug at rehearsals any more," threatened B. J. Mencken.

"I've had enough of your insolence, bud," she said. "And you just try to keep me out of this theater. I'm the author!"

"I'm going back upstairs," said Paul Mencken.

Alva started after him. "Wait, I'm not through—"

"Yes you are," snapped his brother.

"Abbott!" yelled Drake. "Bring the girls back in. Hurry!"

It had all the trappings of a family dinner: a secure oak-paneled room shrouded with heavy green drapes, a father and son huddled at one end of a long table, the wizened patriarch puffing on his pipe. At the other end their servant waited patiently for his orders. But this wasn't a dining room: it was a corporate board room in Philadelphia; the father and son were the Willinghams, senior and junior. They had summoned their servant Wilton Peck from San Antonio for a reckoning.

The son did the talking. "Correct me if I'm wrong, Wilt. By my calculations, five plus one equals six. One percent to a lawyer, who has yet to come through for us. And *five* percent to a senator, for killing a bill that might have died on its own. You've given away six percent of the Willingham Palace. And we still don't even have a site! Just how many more Texans were you planning to placate in this manner?"

The condemned man wondered whether it was even worth answering. "Those were the only two, Charlie."

The Willinghams weren't the first ones to lean on Peck since Alva Carson Keane bought the Hugo & Schmeltzer. He hadn't even recovered from his own shock before Hobo Pratt was in his office, shoving him against the wall and shouting at him as if he were to blame. And now this. "With all respect, Charlie, you don't know those people. It's a different world down there."

The father, an amorphous lump of bile and venom, took the pipe-stem from his lips just long enough to wheeze: "Tell him about Dallas."

"Wilt, Father and I think it's time to cut our losses and pull the plug on San Antonio. We're looking at Dallas instead."

Peck smiled weakly. Those three torturous months in San Antonio had been for naught, he thought. "Just say the word, gentlemen, and I'll be off to Dallas."

The father and son glanced at each other. The elder Willingham lowered his pipe again. "Tell him about Hart."

Junior smiled. "Hart is a young man we hired a couple of months ago, Wilt. Bright, personable, aggressive fellow. Father's thinking he might give Hart a shot at Dallas. Bring you back here for a while."

What did he mean? Demotion? The axe? The defendant made one last plea for leniency. "Charlie, Mr. Willingham, I know this San Antonio project has been riddled with problems. But believe you me, there's a gold mine there. Just give me till March to break ground. Please. You won't regret it. Just till March."

For an instant Wilton Peck saw the absurdity of his request: he loathed Texas, and he was begging to be sent back. But his whole future was riding on San Antonio.

"Out of the question," sniffed the younger Willingham, looking to the neckless lump for confirmation.

The father tapped his pipe on the table. "January."

A stay of execution. Peck nearly collapsed. "Thank you, sir."

The son didn't hide his disappointment. "Father, you're much too charitable."

"The end of January, and then he's out," coughed the lump. "You're one lucky fellow, Peck. Don't let us down again."

November brought fair, cooler days; and with each one Enrique Herrera grew more sure of himself. At the livery stable he played his new songs for Rafael Menchaca, who sipped coffee while he barked advice: "Contrast, muchacho! Your chorus sounds too much like your verse"; or "Don't use 'corazón' so often—it makes the word cheap." If Eva happened to stop by while Enrique was there, they would greet each other politely, like strangers. Enrique didn't think her father suspected anything so far. He tried not to think about the day when his mentor would learn how his favorite daughter had been spending her nights, and with whom.

Enrique lived mainly for his music; but when he wasn't working with his guitar, his world was Eva. The young lovers met secretly every chance they got. Hand-in-hand they explored the twisting paths of the old city as if for the first time. Beneath the wild plum trees along the river, they fell together in frantic embraces, then lay contented among the reeds, listening to the warblers.

After a while Enrique got to be so cocky that he began playing corridos in the parlor at home, for anyone to overhear. At first only Eloisa noticed. The cook looked at him suspiciously and thought: "This is what comes of running with that pelado. Before long this boy will have fathered ten bastards and will be stealing goats."

Then one night after dinner, Antonio Herrera looked up from his *Journal* long enough to realize what he was hearing. He went to the parlor. "What is this?" he asked casually.

Immediately the boy grew sullen. "Sir?"

"This song?"

"It's a corrido. A song of the people."

"I know what a corrido is. Where did you learn it?"

Enrique shrugged. "I just heard it."

Rose appeared behind her husband. "What's wrong?"

He ignored her. "I hear these songs coming from your room all the time," he told Enrique.

The boy was primed for a confrontation. "Is there a rule against playing corridos in Alamo Heights?" he asked.

"One more insolent remark and there will be," his father threatened. "Are these the only songs you play nowadays?"

The boy said nothing.

"Answer me."

"No, sir."

"Folk songs are all right in their place. But you need to concentrate on the classics. Where have you been going that you hear these corridos, across the river?"

Enrique sulked. "I heard it on the plaza."

"Then maybe you're spending too much time on the plaza."

The boy turned away.

Rose stepped forward. "Antonio, it's my fault. I should have told you. Enrique has a new teacher, named Menchaca. He thinks it's good for young musicians to learn folk songs."

Enrique looked at his mother in such alarm that she nearly burst out laughing. His father frowned. "Enrique's old enough to start thinking about his future. When I was sixteen, I was—"

Suddenly the boy stood up, grabbed his guitar and fled the parlor. They heard his footsteps pounding the staircase.

"Enrique!" shouted his father, starting to follow.

His wife tugged at his arm. "Antonio. Don't."

His eyes flashed in anger. "You let him walk over you. And you're right about one thing: this problem *is* your fault. You let him take up that guitar and get these ideas."

She glanced down miserably. More than a month after their row, he was still waiting for her to beg his forgiveness. "I'm going to speak to him," she murmured. She hurried into the vestibule and up the stairs.

Enrique was in his room, brooding and strumming his guitar very softly. She shut the door behind her. "All right," she told him. "I know you've been hiding some things. It's time for us to talk."

He stopped playing and turned away.

She sat on his bed. "I saw you singing on the plaza last month. Were you planning to keep your secrets forever?"

He shook his head.

"It's true what I told your father. I've been to see Rafael Menchaca. I've decided to let him keep teaching you."

He wondered if she had found out about Eva, too. He knew what she would think about him seeing a West Side girl. "Mother?"

"¿Sí?"

He turned away. "Nada."

"Go ahead. Tell me what's on your mind. I want you to tell me everything."

"Mother, I'm going to be. . . ."

She braced herself. "Yes?"

"Mother, I'm going to be a musician."

No. Don't tell me that, she thought. Tell me you vandalized St. Mary's, you got arrested, you got a girl with child, but don't tell me you're going to be . . . "A musician? Interesting."

"I want to be a good writer, like Rafael. Because that is who I am."

"Your father and I want you to continue your education," she said.

"I plan to continue it. I want to study music."

"And then do what?"

He shrugged. "Become a music professor. Maybe a mariachi. I don't know."

She forced a smile. "Enrique, your father may seem hard-headed, the way he insists you should study law. But in his heart he only wants what's best for you."

"My father made his own life from nothing. Someday I think he'll accept what I do with mine. But can you, Mother? Are you still afraid I'll turn out to be like your father instead of your grandfather?"

Her face clouded. "You hush! ¿Comprende?"

But she was stung by his question. She thought of that day on the plaza, and what Madame Guenther had told her: "He is an artist. You must be proud." She had refused to listen. Now she was beginning to understand: the conventions that confined the boy were not so much Antonio's as her own. Her husband merely wanted their son to earn a decent living. She was determined to see him live up to her ideal of a De León.

Finally she told him, "I was wrong to blame your father. I'm the one who asked Menchaca not to let you play on the plaza again."

He stared at her, more perplexed than angry. "¿Por qué?"

She shook her head. She felt that if his young ego ever experienced the thrill of getting paid for his music, he might be hooked. A music professor was one thing, but . . . *a mariachi!* Good God.

Then her thoughts drifted once more to the room at the Palace Livery Stable and to the man hunched over his guitar in intense concentration. "Enrique, I may have made a mistake. I may be wrong about a lot of things. Oh, let's not talk about it any more. Play me one of your songs. Por favor."

The boy nodded, satisfied. Apparently his mother didn't know about Eva. She couldn't have held it in this long if she did.

While he played, she gazed at his fingers dancing across the frets in sure leaps. But the moment she closed her eyes, it was his mentor she saw: the way he'd looked at her when he took her arm in his hand. Her mission to Military Plaza had been a disaster. Now, even at the safe distance of the Heights, she couldn't rid herself of the image of the Corrido King. It hovered around her all that night and didn't dissipate until the next morning, when she picked up the *Journal.*

THE SAN ANTONIO JOURNAL
Thursday, November 14, 1907

Tales & Tattlers

Ibsen, move over: New York's thespians are all abuzz about the Mencken brothers' forthcoming folly, *Angelina, Sweetheart!*, penned by the savior of the Alamo herself, Alva Carson Keane. Though she is busy giving notes on the production, the irrepressible Mrs. Keane, whose unselfish act of patriotism has elevated her to a peerless position in the hearts of Texans, is never too busy to talk to reporters about her first love, the Alamo. She says it is the DRT's desire to raze the unsightly Hugo & Schmeltzer Building to the ground and convert this property into a beautiful park, filled with swaying palms and tropical verdure. This park will honor not only the Alamo heroes, but also the great pioneer cattlemen of our state. Is there any other person in Texas who could bring this formidable task to fruition, having bravely weathered the many difficulties that have beset her thus far? Brava, bravissimo, fair savior!

45

*F*ollies, thought Rose Herrera. Not "folly." At least one hoped.
It wasn't that *Angelina, Sweetheart!* really interested her.
But for a moment she needed to think about something unim-
portant to keep from exploding. Once again she scrutinized the third
and fourth sentences of the blurb, praying this was a misquote. She
had to sit down to digest this turn of events.

At the time they formed their hasty alliance, Rose and Alva never
discussed what they would do with the Hugo & Schmeltzer property
once they got it. There hadn't been time. Rose had always assumed
that her partner understood: the stone walls of the warehouse,
beneath the hideous wooden facade, were those of the original convent of Alamo mission.

Why, why, why had she made that assumption? From their first
meeting, she'd known that Alva's history was faulty. The woman hadn't
been inside a library in years.

Rose realized the irony of her predicament: she had rescued the
Alamo convent from certain demolition by the Willingham Hotel
Company—*only to have it threatened with destruction by her partner
in preservation.* The convent razed to the ground! To make way for a
park honoring frontier land thieves like Oscar Carson? Over her
dead body! She hadn't struggled for fourteen years only to end up
with a park.

And what gave Alva Carson Keane the right to speak for the DRT
anyway? Rose bristled. The young philanthropist had deeded the
property to the Daughters; the Hugo & Schmeltzer wasn't hers to do

with as she pleased. Besides, the DRT should no longer feel beholden to her. The state had already reimbursed her for the $75,000 she spent—a fact never mentioned by the same newspapers that had dubbed her the savior of the Alamo.

But enough of that. Alva had come to the rescue, after all; Rose felt a little ashamed of herself for letting her resentment run wild. The first thing she needed to do was correct any wrong ideas that the *Journal* interview might have created. The best way to handle this would be to cable her partner about the "misprint" and give her a chance to correct it herself.

But the author was obviously caught up in the hubbub of *Angelina, Sweetheart!* It might take days or even weeks for her to respond. By then the San Antonio Daughters might have become unnecessarily agitated. Rose changed her mind: she would write a corrective letter to the *Journal* herself.

THE SAN ANTONIO JOURNAL
Friday, November 15, 1907

Letters to the Editor

Dear Sir:

Would you kindly grant me space to address an item in yesterday's paper that might have caused concern among our citizenry?

Having just acquired the Hugo & Schmeltzer warehouse next to the Alamo chapel, the Daughters of the Republic of Texas have no intention of razing that building, as your paper erroneously stated; for beneath the modern galleries and woodwork stand the old stone walls of the Alamo convent. The property was not purchased for the purpose of creating a park, but for rehabilitating the convent upon plans to be adopted by the DRT. Furthermore, since the site is sacred to the memory of our heroes of 1836, it would be inappropriate to use it to honor those Texans who came to our state in more recent years.

Fellow San Antonians, now that the recent threat of commercialism has passed, let us all join together in this restoration effort. One day we shall stand united before that mission long venerated by Spaniards, Mexicans, Indians and Americans alike, and proudly say to our grandchildren: "Behold your heritage, our Alamo!"

Rose De León Herrera
City

46

E dna Duvalier spotted Mrs. Herrera's letter at breakfast. She arched her eyebrows at a sharp angle, nearly choking on a bite of underripe grapefruit. Pushing her plate aside, she started plotting a revolution. Then she took to her telephone. She wouldn't rest that day until she had fired up every Daughter of the Republic in San Antonio.

"Disgraceful!" she told Josephine Pearce, the Carnegie librarian. "That letter is a slap in the face to Alva Keane."

"I haven't seen it, Mrs. Duvalier. I seldom read the papers, they're always full of such terrible things—"

"Read it, for God's sake. This is an insult!"

"Oh! I didn't mean to insult you, I just—"

"Not to *me*, Josephine. An insult to Alva! Rose Herrera calls her 'erroneous.' And that's not even the worst of it."

"Erroneous! My goodness gracious, I don't believe that."

"Are you saying I'm a liar?"

"Am I—oh, certainly not! I just meant—"

"Let me ask you one thing. If some of the Daughters decide to take Rose Herrera to task for this, will you stand with us?"

"Well, Mrs. Duvalier, I'm with you in spirit, of course, but I have to think of my position—"

"Josephine, this is war. I'm drawing a line in the dust. Now go get a *Journal*. Read that letter. And call every Daughter you know. We've got to stand by Alva!"

Edna Duvalier almost believed her own hysterical propaganda. For many years her jealousy of Rose Herrera had festered. Their differences went back to 1893, the year the other woman founded the San Antonio Chapter of the Daughters of the Republic of Texas. At the first meeting, Rose mentioned that she hoped to start a research library at the Alamo someday. Mrs. Duvalier, who thought it would be more fitting for ladies to beautify the grounds, scoffed, "We don't put libraries over our heroes' graves. We plant flowers."

To which a younger, less politic Rose Herrera replied: "It's a shame that so many people who ought to know better think the rebels were buried at the Alamo. Ladies, if we don't have a library where people can learn their history, even our own members will start believing these myths."

From that day the two women had been at odds on every issue. Most recently they had clashed while they were escorting Mrs. Root in the Peerless. Now Edna Duvalier saw her chance to get even. If she could get enough support, she wouldn't stop until Rose Herrera was deposed as the San Antonio Chapter's president.

Her telephone calls drew mixed reactions from the other Daughters. Even some of those who thought Rose had acted insensitively trusted her version of history. And at least half of them thought she was absolutely right in setting the record straight. One of those was Lorena Lovett, a diminutive schoolteacher. "Edna, you're out of line," she declared bluntly.

"Am I? Rose is getting so power hungry, I'm afraid she might try to make off with the Alamo relics."

"Oh bosh! Rose is the one who collected those relics in the first place."

"Bosh yourself! I suppose you believe this nonsense she wrote about the old stone walls? There's nothing original beneath the Hugo & Schmeltzer. That old convent fell to pieces years ago. You know she's bluffing."

"No, I don't know that. But I know that Rose has led our chapter for fourteen years, and—"

"Fourteen years is too many. It's time for new blood."

"And you're out to draw it, Edna. If you think the Daughters are going to dump Rose, think again."

Mrs. Duvalier hung up on Miss Lovett without saying goodbye. Out of line, indeed! But the schoolteacher was right about one thing: it was going to be an uphill battle getting the San Antonio Chapter to overthrow the granddaughter of Francisco De León.

Unless . . . .

Edna Duvalier came up with a better idea. Perhaps she wouldn't have to overthrow Rose Herrera. Her plan might not work, but it was worth a try. That evening she carefully composed an inflammatory letter of her own.

233 Terrell Road
San Antonio, Texas
November 15, 1907

Mrs. Alva Carson Keane
Ansonia Hotel
2109 Broadway
New York City

My Dear Friend:

All San Antonio is aglow with excitement, as our favorite Daughter is about to take a bow in the footlights and become the toast of Broadway!

I only wish that things were going as well within the DRT. I deeply regret to inform you that your noble work in rescuing the Alamo has been brutally sabotaged by the selfish desires of our local chapter president, Rose Herrera. Without provocation, she has taken to the warpath, publicly attacking your ingenious idea for creating a beautiful park—and with such vicious invective that, frankly, I am embarrassed for all the Daughters. I considered enclosing a clipping of her scandalous letter to the editor, but I feared it would only distress you. In essence, my dear sister, she has labeled you a liar, a traitor, and a fool. Even more shocking, she has effectively called your distinguished father an interloper and has disparaged his status as a Texan. One can only guess what sort of falsehoods she is circulating privately.

Since Mrs. Herrera has so solidly cemented herself in her post as president, I have reluctantly arrived at the unavoidable conclusion: the time has come to form a second DRT chapter in San Antonio. Many of our local Daughters are in agreement on this. With your kind permission, we would be most honored to name this new group the Carson Chapter, after our beloved savior of the Alamo and her remarkable father, and to designate you as our honorary president.

I realize that you are very busy right now, but, as you undoubtedly understand, this matter is quite urgent. It would be my pleasure to assist you in carrying out your plans for an Alamo park and, if you so desire, to give voice to your views during your absence from San Antonio.

Your faithful servant,
Edna Duvalier

New York N. Y. Nov. 20th-1907.
Mrs. Edna Duvalier,
    233 Terrell Road, San Antonio Texas.
Bewildered by what Rose has done hope there is some
explanation do what you think best about forming Carson
Chapter things frantic here see you at state convention in
January.

Alva Carson Keane.

0954am

47

And then came a great outcry, as Edna Duvalier's seeds of discord quickly took root. At stake was the Alamo convent. Rose Herrera's friends banded together to defend what they claimed were the original walls. With Alva Keane away in New York, Edna Duvalier took up the campaign for a park with equal zeal. In the heat of passion, the Carson Chapter of the DRT was conceived and born overnight. A week later the San Antonio Daughters were sharply divided into two hostile camps. Best friends were suddenly calling each other traitors. Old ties were severed.

Like a brushfire, the Alamo controversy spread far beyond San Antonio. Within a few weeks it had split the DRT into warring factions across Texas. In every chapter, from Houston to Austin, from Galveston to Goliad, the Daughters railed against one another. By Christmas the split was close to fifty-fifty. Rose could still claim more of the foot soldiers; but she was outnumbered on the powerful executive committee.

Was it really such a problem, some people asked, for San Antonio to have two DRT chapters? It was. Under the DRT's charter, the San Antonio chapter president was designated the custodian of the Alamo, charged with overseeing the Daughters' most important site. For many years Rose Herrera had been the undisputed custodian. But at the annual convention the following month, Daughters from all over the state would vote to decide which San Antonio chapter was legitimate. The leader of the winning group would walk away with the keys to the Alamo. Then, depending on who held tho͡se keys, the warehouse would either be restored or razed.

That Christmas, while both factions got ready for the battle ahead, Antonio and Rose tacitly called a truce in their own war long enough to attend the Business Men's Ball. As they were driving home in the Peerless, Antonio, warmed by a full measure of rum punch, turned to his wife and said, "Tell me your Christmas wishes, querida."

She was staring ahead into the darkness. "Just one. I wish you would come to the DRT convention next month."

That surprised him. "Why?"

To bring us back together, she thought. "To advise me on procedure. If things get tough, maybe I can clobber Edna Duvalier on some point of order."

His response was a cool silence.

"You wouldn't have to say anything," she pointed out. "Just sit beside me. Antonio, I have no one else to turn to."

He glanced at her. Then he shifted to final drive, grinding the gears. "This Alamo thing is your battle," he replied. "Haven't I made it clear that I want no part of it?"

She turned away. They headed for Alamo Heights without speaking again. The Alamo defender thought: "One wall, at least, is safe from being destroyed."

Publicly Rose denounced the break-away Carson Daughters. In private she grieved. It hurt her deeply that Alva had given her blessings, even lent her name, to the upstart chapter. That night she imagined Alva in her brightly lit apartment overlooking Broadway, enjoying the holiday cheer as snowflakes dusted the sidewalks of New York. She wondered whether her partner shared the pain of their estrangement.

Actually, the Carson heiress wasn't thinking much about Rose or the Alamo that week. Nor was she enjoying any holiday cheer. Throughout her unhappy Yuletide another battle was being fought.

THE NEW YORK TIMES
Sunday, December 29, 1907

Bits of Playhouse Gossip

Taste in the Theatre and the Question of Responsibility—
New Plays and Adaptations
New York Will Soon See.

Atornado swept through the New Amsterdam Theatre last week—and it wasn't the one the Mencken brothers were trying to simulate on stage. Producer B. J. Mencken banned Texas author Alva Carson Keane from rehearsals of the forthcoming *Angelina, Sweetheart!* after she got into one too many squalls with the director, the songwriter, the scenic artist, the costume designer, and, it seems, just about everyone else involved in the turbulent production. Mrs. Keane immediately retaliated by becoming one of the principal backers of the troubled show—thereby forcing the Menckens to let her resume giving notes. *Angelina, Sweetheart!* was originally budgeted at $20,000, but that figure has officially climbed to $50,000—and those in the know claim that closer to $60,000 has actually been expended. More than half that amount is said to have come from the author herself. Meanwhile, Broadway's newest "angel," rumored to be displeased with the show's dancing ensemble, has spearheaded a talent search for twelve of the most beautiful chorus girls ever to appear on stage. Once she finds them, she has bankrolled the Menckens to pay them fifty dollars per week (scale is fifteen!). Asked whether Mrs. Keane had abandoned her original artistic intentions in favor of a beauty pageant, her publisher, Max Rosenthal, would only say, "Alva has always been committed to a spectacular production, and the public won't be disappointed."

48

By January the Alamo battle was no longer confined to the broken ranks of the Daughters of the Republic of Texas. The old walls beneath the Hugo & Schmeltzer had become the most hotly debated issue in the state. Suddenly every Texan had an opinion about what the Daughters should do with the building. Those who claimed to know the Alamo story backwards and forwards were finding that their neighbors clung to a different version. In San Antonio fistfights broke out at the Buckhorn Saloon. Less pugnacious citizens flocked to the Carnegie Library to pore over brittle documents that would prove them right.

Despite the bitter words that flew back and forth between the two sides, Rose found it hard to hate Alva personally. Her former partner had never intended to set off a war. However, Rose was reluctant to send a conciliatory letter to New York, for fear that Alva might unwarily forward it to Edna Duvalier, who would publicize it as an attempted surrender. But she wondered if she might meet privately with Alva at the DRT convention and reason with her.

Nothing fueled the Alamo fire as much as the Business Men's petition. Two weeks before the DRT state convention, Horatio Franck drew up a letter to present to Governor Thomas M. Campbell, demanding that the warehouse be razed in the dual interests of aesthetics and commerce. And since the governor had the power to approve the DRT's final plans for the property, he was closely monitoring public opinion.

Rose reacted to the petition by calling a town meeting at Casino Hall. She knew what she had to do. If she could prove that the walls were original, the convent was safe. She knew that Alva would never sanction the destruction of any portion of the original mission. However, proof was hard to come by. Rose knew about those walls from her father, who had been there in 1836; but he couldn't help her now. There were no drawings dating back that far. And the earliest maps and descriptions were inconclusive, only adding to the confusion.

The turnout for the meeting was enormous: Daughters, businessmen, politicians and historians packed the hall. Rose sat in front. After Mayor Callaghan quieted the crowd, she read her prepared statement: "The San Antonio Chapter of the DRT trusts that no citizen who values the good name of our city will sign any petition circulated by self-seekers who would destroy the Alamo." Then she announced what she hoped would be her trump card: "Ladies and gentlemen, today we are honored to have with us one of our oldest citizens, Mrs. Amelia Carter. She remembers the Alamo convent before it was remodeled as a warehouse. Mrs. Carter, would you please tell us about those walls?"

The elderly woman rose with difficulty, leaning on her cane. She spoke in a frail voice. "I came to San Antonio in 1846, when Texas was still a republic. No—Texas became a state in . . ."

"1845," Rose prompted quietly.

"Yes," the old woman said. "I came to San Antonio in 1845, when Texas was—no. Well, I must have come here—was it?—yes, in 1844. And I used to play in the Alamo when I was a girl. Not in the Alamo—well, yes, the Alamo, but not in the chapel. It was in the convent—no, they called it the long barracks . . . ."

"They were the same thing," Rose reminded the assembly.

"Yes. The chapel and the long barracks were the same, and they were both part of the Alamo. And the building they're talking about tearing down was the convent, not the chapel."

The elderly woman took her seat again. Rose blushed in embarrassment. "Thank you very much, Mrs. Carter, for being with us today."

Edna Duvalier whispered to Horatio Franck, "That old biddy couldn't remember her name if Rose Herrera didn't prompt her."

Franck nodded, smiling. "Some proof."

Lorena Lovett, the schoolteacher, stood up to defend Rose. "There are lots of other people who remember the convent before it was a warehouse," she said. "All the old-timers know that building is hallowed in blood."

"Blood!" scoffed Horatio Franck. "It's never been hallowed in anything except Mr. Hugo's good, bad and indifferent whiskey."

The Carson supporters and businessmen laughed. Miss Lovett was irate. "And the members of the Business Men's Club have as much taste and sentiment as a bunch of old boar hogs—"

"My son is a member!" barked Edna Duvalier, as she sprang to her feet.

Mayor Callaghan pounded the table. "Please. Mrs. Herrera still has the floor."

"Gracias," she said. "We also have drawings and eyewitness descriptions of Mission San Antonio de Valero showing that the walls—"

"Who cares about Mission San Antonio de Valero?" Josephine Pearce interrupted. "We're here to talk about the Alamo." Mrs. Duvalier nudged the librarian as several people tittered.

"Drawings," continued Rose, amused, "of Mission San Antonio de Valero, popularly called *El Alamo*—"

"So what will these drawings prove?" asked Horatio Franck. "I happen to know that there are some older maps and plats, which no one has—"

"Amazing!" Rose exclaimed. "So after only one week of research, Mr. Franck has discovered some older maps, which I've somehow overlooked for the past fourteen years. Well, if he has, I welcome him with open arms as an honorary Daughter of the Republic for his remarkable scholarship."

That produced a round of cheers and applause from Lorena Lovett and the other Herrera supporters. The mayor rapped the table again. "Quiet. Judge Beasley has an opinion."

The judge stood up in the back of the room and raised his Baptist-preacher oratory above the hubbub. "Ladies and gentlemen, would you really raze those sacred walls? Why, the physical embodiment of aesthetics and history is of far more value than the growth of the city's wealth. If we permit that old institution to be desecrated, we advertise to the world a greater degradation than that of the Greeks when their national glory began to—"

"Is this an opinion or a campaign speech?" asked Horatio Franck. The crowd roared. After that the meeting disintegrated into a free-for-all. Franck, his mission accomplished, slipped out of the room unnoticed. He hailed a carriage and headed back to the offices of Franck & Herrera. There he burst in on his partner without knocking. "Herrera, I've signed you up to speak to the Business Men's Club next week."

For three months Antonio Herrera had longed for a chance to redeem himself in public, after his wife's debacle at the Root banquet. He beamed. "The club?"

"January thirty-first. I'm on the program that day. I hate to turn this over to a novice, but I have to go to a closing."

His partner said, "I'd like to talk to them about the new development in Summit Place and the—"

"No. This is about the Alamo petition. Urge all the men to sign it. I'll write the speech for you, to make sure it all comes out right. And get a new suit, you'll need to make a good impression." With that Franck turned to go.

Antonio Herrera had swallowed his pride and endured much worse insults from his partner. The remark that finally pushed him over the edge seemed minor in comparison: *Get a new suit.* For years he had prided himself on his taste in clothes. "Horatio," he said quietly.

The older man turned around. "What? I'm in a hurry."

"I'm afraid the thirty-first isn't good for me." He hesitated.

Franck scowled. "I'm not following you."

"I'll be in Austin that weekend. With Rose, at the DRT convention."

Franck stared at his partner with the glazed look of a man just bludgeoned. The protruding vein on his forehead popped up and pulsated like a fire alarm. Then, shaking his head in disbelief, he walked out and went to his own office.

Immediately Antonio Herrera regretted what he'd done. It was Rose's fault. Damn it! Instead of molding his wife in his own image, he was starting to act more like a De León. Moments earlier it had given him a tremendous charge to step out on a limb; now he felt it cracking beneath him. In his mind he saw the senior partner already removing "Herrera" from the front door.

But in the next room, Horatio Franck wasn't thinking about his partner. He had just placed a telephone call. Cupping his hand over the mouthpiece, he spoke in a low voice. "Mr. Peck?"

"Hunh."

"Thank God, I'm glad you're here in San Antonio."

"Well, I'm glad *someone's* glad."

"What's the news? The project's still on?"

"Barely. I have one week left to get it off the ground."

"Don't worry. Remember what I told you last fall? To leave everything to me?"

"Yes. That plan worked out just bully, didn't it?"

"Let me finish. I've found us a new lot, and it's—well, you won't believe where it's located."

"I'm on pins and needles."

"All right, if you're going to be a jackass—"

"Just tell me where it is."

Franck paused. "I'd rather not say over the telephone."

"Oh, for Christ's sake—"

"I'm not taking any chances this time. Meet me at midnight in front of the Menger."

"Midnight!"

"Yes, midnight! I don't want anyone to find out we're looking at it. Especially not Rose Herrera. Comprende?"

"Midnight."

"Wear dark clothes."

"Shit. This had better be worth it."

"Trust your lawyer, Mr. Peck. It will be."

T he town meeting did nothing to convince anyone of anything. Afterwards Rose drove to La Villita in defeat. Swept up
in the Alamo battle, she had fallen out of touch with
Mathilda Guenther. Meanwhile the sculptor had found a new
patron in Alva Carson Keane. Not only had the ranch heiress
ordered the bust of Colonel Travis for the DRT, she had also used
her influence to win Madame Guenther two new commissions for
public monuments. Rose wondered, in light of these events, whether
she and the German woman were still friends.

She found the artist at work. The studio was chilly, but Madame
Guenther's cough seemed to have disappeared. In fact her face radi-
ated a healthy glow. In front of her sat Rafael Menchaca, stripped to
the waist and not looking particularly pleased to pose. Rose hadn't
seen him since that day at the livery stable.

Menchaca brightened when he saw their visitor. "Ah, look! The
revolucionaria of Alamo Heights. Buenos días, señora."

"Stop smiling," the artist barked at him. "Come in, Mrs. Herrera."

"Gracias," she replied. "I came to see what you've been working
on." She drew near the artist, averting her eyes from Menchaca.
"Really, Madame Guenther!" she scoffed. "Models must be in short
supply these days."

Madame Guenther leaned back, holding her clay-caked hands at
her side so that Rose could inspect the bust. "If I find a purchaser, it
will be cut in marble. I shall call this piece 'El Hombre.'"

"Uh!" scoffed the model. "What a cliché! You should call it 'The Corrido King' so people will know who it is."

"People will know who it is," the artist replied indignantly, "because it will look like you."

"It doesn't look anything like me. Señora De León Herrera, look how she's distorting my features! She's made the face too rough and the nose too big." He turned to glare at the women.

"Profile, Mr. Menchaca," commanded the artist. "Imagine, Mrs. Herrera, me going in new directions at my age. This is the first time ever my subject is naturalistic rather than heroic."

Menchaca blew up. "Not heroic! You hear how I am insulted, señora? What am I, a coward?"

"Oh shut up and hold still!" shouted Madame Guenther. "You are so tiresome, you make me sick."

Rose didn't like the sculpture. The artist had succeeded too well in capturing the musician's unnerving gaze. She fumbled for words. "It's very . . . lifelike."

The sculptor told her, "One day I am going to model your portrait."

She grinned like an excited schoolgirl. "Really? When?"

"As soon as I can get you to sit in one place for eight hours."

Rose laughed. "I'll be stooped and wrinkled by then."

The model was still nursing his grievances. "She's made the chest sunken—"

"Oh, stop criticizing!" snapped the artist. "What do you know about art? I am one of the greatest living sculptors. You should be thankful; this portrait will make you immortal."

The man was offended. "My corridos will do that! I don't need my face carved in some block of marble, sitting in some capitalist's house in Alamo Heights." With that he stood up and reached for his shirt.

"Where are you going?" thundered the artist.

He didn't look at her. "I can't sit around all day gossiping with ladies."

"I am not through!"

"No, but I am. I sat for you last night, I've sat all morning. It's hard on my back."

"Burro! I give up." Madame Guenther hurled a lump of clay at the wall. Rose smiled to herself.

As he prepared to go, the man addressed her. "Señora, for the record, I hope you win your battle against that robber baron's daughter."

That surprised her. "Menchaca! The last time we talked, I was—how did you put it?—a rico. The Tejano bourgeoisie, trying to save the cradle of oppression—"

"Yes, none of that has changed. What's different is that now you're the underdog. Besides, I have an old score to settle myself. I once wrote a corrido about a vaquero I knew who stood up to Oscar Carson and made a fool of him. Everyone thought my song was very funny—except Señor Carson. So several of his thugs paid a visit to me here in San Antonio and tried to make sure I wouldn't write a sequel."

He looked down at his bare midriff and traced the long scar with his fingers. Rose blushed.

"So you see, señora," he continued, as he put on his shirt, "you may be a rico, but to take on the Carsons and their money—ai! That takes a strong heart. Or a weak mind. And I think you might be on to somthing, about letting the Alamo stand to remind us of those who were dispossessed. It's humiliating for me to admit: I could almost support you in your struggle to save that convent."

"Just what I need, Menchaca. Your support."

The man grinned. He draped himself in his serape and reached for his derby.

Rose added, "One other thing has changed. About my son performing in public. I give my permission now."

This time Menchaca was surprised. "Señora?"

"Yes. If Enrique wants to sing with you on the plaza, let him."

He thought for a moment. "That is a very bold thing to say. Are you so confident your son is that good?"

She narrowed her eyes. "Go away, Menchaca."

He tipped his hat at both of them and left, breaking into one of his sarcastic songs. When he was gone, Rose shook her head and hissed, "Pelado! How did you ever get him to come here and pose? Promise him a barrel of tequila?"

Madame Guenther studied her intently for a moment. "In fact, my friend, this man has spent a lot of time here since we last talked."

Rose tried to suppress her suspicions by changing the subject. "I hadn't heard from you in such a long time, I was worried—"

"I have been otherwise occupied, Mrs. Herrera." The artist ventured a tentative smirk.

Rose needed to sit for this. "Madame Guenther—forgive me for prying, but—when he said he had posed here last night. . . ."

When she glanced up, the sculptor was nodding.

"Do you mean, you and this man . . . and *you.* . . ."

"Ach!" It was a jovial rebuke. "You are still young. You think that because my face is lined and my proportions ample, I can no longer capture a man's fancy."

Rose tried to protest, but her voice failed her.

"You remember what I said earlier?" Madame Guenther went on. "How strange to be going in new directions at my age! It all began the first time he came here. I told him about my experiments with communal living in East Texas. We talked of philosophy, art, politics, even free love. And then I—are you very much appalled?"

"No, I don't think so. Just . . . perplexed." Her heart was pounding. She leaned closer. "Madame Guenther. . . ."

"Umm?"

She sat back and looked away. "No. Nothing."

"Mrs. Herrera, you must believe me: all my life has been a struggle against the animal passions that keep us from reaching a higher plane. But oh! This man has lived so much more than I have. And he has made me feel that perhaps I have more than ten good years left." She grinned sheepishly.

Rose blushed. Madame Guenther reached for her hand. "My friend, I know it will not last. Nor should it. I cannot let myself be encumbered; I have too much to accomplish still. Rafael is honest, and that is enough. And he has written two songs for me. But I know he has given his heart to another."

Rose nodded. "I don't mean to be cruel, Madame Guenther, but I think you're wise to look at this with a clear head. A man like Menchaca doesn't form attachments like we do. And he must have a dozen concubines on the West Side."

The artist frowned. "Mrs. Herrera, why must you close your eyes to the truth? When I am with Rafael, he speaks so much of the time about you."

Rose trembled. "No! I don't believe that."

"Mrs. Herrera, I am telling the truth. This man has been hurt before, so he hides his feelings, and he quarrels when he really wants to speak love. But believe me, he does have feelings. Very strong ones."

Rose toyed with the lace on her sleeve, trying to pull away. "No," she whispered.

The artist gripped her arm tightly. "And I think you have feelings for him, too. Mrs. Herrera, I am older. It is my duty to advise you: it would be easier to make peace with the truth now, and not fight it so hard."

Madame Guenther let go. It took some time for Rose to compose herself. As soon as she did, she made some hasty excuses and got ready to leave.

The artist looked sad. "I can see I have offended you. It was wrong of me to say what I did."

"Nonsense," replied Rose, forcing a smile. "We're friends; we should never keep anything from each other."

"Now I fear you will not come back to visit me."

"Don't be ridiculous."

But the artist was right. This time her candor had divided them. Rose couldn't wait to get outside the studio that day and crank the Peerless. Her hands were shaking when she sped off, and she missed one of the gears. As she headed for Alamo Heights, she wondered whether she could ever return to the house in La Villita and face the artist who knew more about her than she was prepared to admit to herself.

In the still of a moonless winter night, three men (two of them bulbous, one reedlike) glanced around at the same time to make sure no one was watching. Then they climbed carefully between the strands of a barbed wire fence. The last man didn't clear the opening. He hooked the seat of his trousers. His arms flailed wildly.

"God damn it, boys! Y'all lend a hand."

The lawyer frowned. "Shh! There's a watchman around the corner."

Horatio Franck and Wilton Peck tried to pull their accomplice through the fence. With a violent tug Hobo Pratt freed himself, ripping his trousers. Franck scowled in disgust. He and the senator had been competitors on several real estate deals, and they loathed each other.

"Shit!" said Senator Pratt. "Y'all took me away from a good night's sleep—"

"Quit your bellyaching," said Franck. "We all made sacrifices. Now, gentlemen, take a good look around. Tell me what you think." He started stepping off the property in long, confident strides.

The other two men stood there perplexed. All they saw was a rubbish heap. They were standing in the vacant lot behind the Hugo & Schmeltzer warehouse and the Alamo chapel—the same spot where Rose Herrera had first met Mathilda Guenther a few months earlier. From this angle the warehouse looked abysmal. The wood siding of the building was rotten, and the iron-clad sheds around the perimeter sagged. Abandoned stacks of utility poles and coils of wire were almost hidden by the weeds.

233

The hotel man couldn't believe what he saw. "This is *it*, Mr. Franck? You brought us out here in the middle of the night to look at the back of the Hugo & Schmeltzer?"

"Why, it's a piss-hole!" bellowed Senator Pratt.

"Shh!" The lawyer stopped to rest.

Peck said, "Besides, the DRT owns this property. Do you think I'm going to mess with those bitches again?"

"That's where you're mistaken," replied the lawyer, out of breath. He came back over to where they were standing. "The DRT's property line runs just a few feet behind the warehouse. This lot is a separate parcel. I've talked with the people who own it, the Gallaghers. Gentlemen, if we're very quick, and very quiet, we can buy this property before the ladies hear about it."

"But why, for Pete's sake?" exploded the senator. "It's a goddamned sewer!"

"Jesus!" muttered Frank. "Can't you *imagine* anything?"

Hobo Pratt towered over him. "You old bag of wind, I *imagine* I'm going to give you a good thrashing if—"

"It's no good," declared Wilton Peck. "There's no access to Alamo Plaza from here." He shook his head in dismay.

The lawyer's vein was throbbing. "If you gentlemen would read the papers now and then, you'd know what's going on in the DRT."

Peck snorted. "I've read about it, but so what? I don't care what those harpies do with that warehouse, it's still going to be an eyesore. I can't hide a hotel behind it."

"And I'm saying you won't have to. Alva Keane wants to tear down the Hugo & Schmeltzer and put a park there. Now, Mr. Peck, imagine this. You too, senator—if you can. First step: the warehouse is razed. Second step: we create a shady park, with lanes and fountains and flowers, all the way from Alamo Plaza to where we're standing. Don't you see? It won't matter that the hotel's set back from the plaza. We'll have a park for a hotel entrance, and that's even better."

Had Wilton Peck believed in miracles, he would have marveled that he'd been given two second chances: first a reprieve from the Willinghams, and now another Alamo site. Instead he kicked the dirt. "The DRT hasn't voted whether to build the park yet," he pointed out. "That's a big 'if.' What if they decide to leave the warehouse standing? This lot would be worthless."

"That's why you should go to the DRT convention," said the lawyer. "To lobby for Alva Keane."

"Christ!" the hotel man exploded. "I can't buy this lot for the company just on the chance that there might be a park here someday."

"Do you have a better idea?" snapped the lawyer. "You said yourself: you only have till the end of this week to get things moving. This is our last chance, man. Act on it."

In the weeks since his return from Philadelphia, Peck's efforts to find an alternate site had been snuffed out one after another. Now he saw one last flickering ray of hope. And he had nothing left to lose. "All right, Mr. Franck. Go ahead and draw up the contract tomorrow. I'll get in touch with Alva Keane." He felt his burden lightened, if only a little. "So, when shall we three meet again?"

Franck chuckled smugly, his vein retracting. "In thunder, lightning, or in rain, Mr. Peck."

"What in the Sam Hill . . ." muttered Hobo Pratt.

WILLINGHAM HOTEL COMPANY
Clifford Building
Commerce Street Bridge
San Antonio, Texas

January 23, 1908

Mrs. Alva Carson Keane
Ansonia Hotel
2109 Broadway
New York City

My dear Madam:

Since my delightful holiday at Tres Piedras Ranch last October, I have tried to stay abreast of your many amazing accomplishments, most recently your valiant campaign to transform the hideous Hugo & Schmeltzer property into a park and a monument honoring the frontier cattlemen of Texas. In that endeavor, I am with you in heart and soul.

Madam, I am pleased to inform you that we are now neighbors. This morning the Willingham Hotel Company acquired the Gallagher property just behind the Hugo & Schmeltzer building for the new Willingham Palace. As a token of our esteem for the Daughters, it is my honor to inform you that my company would be willing to assume the entire expense of demolishing the Hugo & Schmeltzer building and landscaping the grounds as a park, in accordance with your inspired proposal.

I kindly request that you inform your fellow Daughters of this offer, which, I dare say, could relieve the fair ladies of the embarrassment of having to solicit funds to complete this noble work. Pardon my boldness in suggesting that if this information is made known to the Daughters at large, perhaps a greater number of them will come to realize that the glorious dream of creating a park is within their reach, and they will therefore stand firm with you in your magnificent struggle against the selfishness of Mrs. Herrera.

Very sincerely yours,
Wilton A. Peck
Senior Development Coordinator

For two days Antonio Herrera procrastinated, waiting for the right moment to approach his wife. It was nearly midnight when he came to her bedroom. She was packing her things for the convention. At first she hardly glanced at him in the door.

"Oh. Antonio."

"I need to talk with you."

She nodded as she compared the merits of two elegant gowns. "Come in." Rose wondered what had gotten into her husband. It wasn't like him to be the first to apologize.

He retreated. "What are you doing?"

"Trying to decide what I should wear the first morning. This red gown. Or this redder one. But I know you don't want to talk about the convention."

He sat in her reading chair. "Rose, I think I've done a very foolish thing."

She waited cautiously.

"I had words with Mr. Franck yesterday."

That took her by surprise. She stopped what she was doing and turned to him. "What about?"

"It doesn't matter. Rose, I'm ready to part ways with him. I want to go out on my own."

At first she wasn't able to reply. Her husband's face clouded. He leaned forward intently. "I know what you're thinking, it's a rash thing to—"

"Shh. No." It was something she'd given up hoping for. She moved toward him without realizing it. They shared a long silence. "Antonio, you don't know how many years I've waited to hear that."

Slowly she extended her hand. He met it with his own and pressed his lips to her fingers. "I'm scared," he whispered.

She nodded. He slid his palm up her wrist. Then he reached for her other arm and guided her into the chair with him.

"It might be hard for us," he said. "I don't have many of my own clients, and Mr. Franck has the office lease—"

She placed her hand over his mouth. "I don't care, Antonio. We can quit the Heights. Sell the Peerless. Do whatever it takes. I'm so proud of you."

With one finger she traced his moustache. Then she rested her head on his shoulder for a long time while he cradled her in his arms. When she looked up again, he was gazing at the four-poster. He smiled at her. "Rose. These sheets. . . ."

"What?"

His eyes twinkled, a younger man's look. "¿Qué color es?"

"Blanco." She blushed. For a moment the memory of the brazen orchid bed of their youth flashed in her mind.

Then, in a low voice she thought had long ago died in him, he whispered: "Esta noche—for me—would you pretend they're orchid?"

That night, to her astonishment, they resumed their life as man and woman. As he came to her, eager and on fire, she held fast to his neck, then to the thick black hair on the back of his head; startled to be swept away by a deluge that had caught her unaware, she cried out as she slipped beneath the surface and then was pulled up, safe. Long after he had drifted off, his arm still lay across her, rising and falling with the even rhythm of her breathing. She clasped it, secure in the shelter, but wondering whether she would ever know this kind of rescue again.

THE NEW YORK TIMES
Wednesday, January 29, 1908

Theatre Review

Angelina, Sweetheart!

"Angelina, Sweetheart!"—the new musical show that was seen for the first time at the New Amsterdam Theatre last night—is in all likelihood the most costly entertainment of its kind ever produced. There the superlatives cease. It is not the worst comic opera ever written; nor is its plot the most ludicrous ever conceived, or its score the least musical. However, one would have to go back several seasons to find worthier contenders for these dubious distinctions.

The average musical play today is in many respects more like the circus than the theatre. In this case, a good deal of money has been spent upon costumes and scenery, and one effect, an operational steam locomotive, is particularly pleasing to the eye. However, the chaotic tornado ballet rather resembles bargain day at Macy's. Moreover, the much-advertised beauty show failed to materialize, and more than one person was heard to inquire whether the fifty-dollar-a-week showgirls had been lost while en route to New York.

The three-act book by Alva Carson Keane is labeled a comic opera, which again demonstrates that it is easier to write a label than to produce the article it describes. The story centers about a young señorita, winsomely portrayed by Maggie McPherson in a dark wig, and her absurd ploys to save her tenderfoot lover from crafty Mexicans, marauding Indians, and Texas weather. The affair quickly degenerates into the wildest tomfoolery imaginable. As a novelist, Mrs. Keane has been praised for her authentic detail. However, one leaves the theatre after this folly wondering: how much does this Texas expatriate really remember about her life back home on the range?

The three-day train ride from New York to Austin gave Alva plenty of solitary hours in her private Pullman car to dwell on her failure. Only hours earlier she had fled the opening night party, traumatized by the scathing notices. *How much does this Texas expatriate really remember about her life back home on the range?* Expatriate, for Christ's sake! And the *Times* review had been the kindest. Her husband had been no comfort; he'd managed to enjoy the party, guzzling the Menckens' champagne and flirting with the fifty-dollar-a-week showgirls. Max Rosenthal had driven her to Pennsylvania Station, trying to convince her that she'd get another chance to write for the theater someday. But she knew better. She'd made enemies of everyone from the Mencken brothers on down. During those horrible weeks of rehearsals, her only sympathizer had been Abbott, the errand boy, who had worked as a cowboy in Wyoming and knew that the things the Menckens were putting on stage didn't ring true. His encouragement was sweet, but she couldn't build a career in the theater on the friendship of errand boys.

Just before her train left, Rosenthal advised her: "The best thing you can do is get going on your next novel." She'd finally settled on a title: *Maribel, The Girl Who Saved Mission San José.* But now she was blocked. She had no idea what Maribel was going to do, or how, or why.

Her problem was Rose Herrera. The author was planning to model Maribel after her Alamo partner, and now Rose had turned against her and insulted her daddy. Alva was more perplexed than angry. Why was Rose being so hateful? Had she planned to do this all along, as some sort of perverted revenge for Tres Piedras? Whatever the reason, Alva saw no use in trying to mend fence at this stage, not unless the other woman made the first move.

She hoped she wouldn't have to confront Rose face to face at the DRT convention. Unlike her ex-partner, Alva didn't like to fight her battles in public. She knew she could count on Edna Duvalier to do that.

Alva hadn't decided how friendly she should appear when she encountered that little corporate weasel, Wilton Peck—although she had accepted his offer to pay for the Alamo park. That seemed harmless enough, as long as she had final say. Furthermore, it was a smart business decision, and that would impress her daddy.

But whatever happened in Austin, Alva was certain of one thing: her battered ego couldn't withstand two crippling blows in the same week. Though she might be the laughingstock of Broadway, she was still revered in Texas. Even more important, she couldn't lose face now that she had publicly announced her plan to honor her daddy on the Alamo grounds. No matter what it took, she had to leave the DRT convention the custodian of the Alamo.

Chances are the first day of the convention wouldn't have ended so dramatically had a copperhead not bit Birdie McElroy. The Daughters' state president was a stout, seventy-five-year-old curmudgeon from Fredericksburg. No one knew where she stood on the Alamo issue. But she was fair and tough; neither faction could railroad her.

Then the viper struck. One morning a week shy of the convention, Mrs. McElroy cooked a batch of cornbread and a mess of greens to take to her ailing sister. She wrapped the meal in a basket and started out on foot. Along the way she plucked some mistletoe from a mesquite tree to feed her sister's milk goat. She didn't notice the branch that moved. Calmly, Mrs. McElroy killed the snake with a rock. Next she slit her wrist twice with a paring knife, making a small X, and sucked out as much of the poison as she could. Finally she put the snake in her basket. That way, she figured, if she died along the way, people would know what had happened. She didn't die; but by the first afternoon of the convention, she was still too weak to stand at the podium for more than a few minutes.

That gave the Herrera Daughters an unexpected boon. Once Birdie McElroy surrendered the podium, the gavel was supposed to pass to the DRT's first vice-president: Lorena Lovett of San Antonio, one of Rose's staunchest champions. And the Herrera Daughters needed the advantage, now that Wilton Peck was back on the scene, circling like a buzzard.

The convention took place in the senate chamber of the state capitol in Austin. Up and down the center aisle ran an invisible but obvious dividing line: Alva Keane's supporters stayed on the right, the Herrera Daughters on the left. A few uncommitted delegates crisscrossed the room, but no one else stepped over that line. On the platform in front sat Birdie McElroy, flanked by the members of the DRT executive committee.

The only man on the convention floor was Antonio Herrera. On his desk lay a dog-eared copy of *Robert's Rules of Order*. Nervously he reached for his wife's hand. He noticed her Mexican undergarments peeking out beneath the hem of her gown. "You're still wearing lace," he whispered.

She squeezed his fingers so hard that he jumped. "Shh. Study the *Rules*, Antonio." She looked around the chamber for Alva. There was no sign of her. It didn't matter. Ever since Alva had accepted Wilton Peck's offer to pay for the park, Rose had lost her desire to try to negotiate a truce. It astounded her that her former ally could have joined forces with the Willinghams.

The DRT's parliamentarian, Josephine Pearce, took her place on the platform. Rose glanced up at the newspapermen in the gallery. She cringed any time Miss Pearce got that near to reporters. The scatterbrained parliamentarian spoke a great deal at conventions, and the papers were happy to quote her, usually all too accurately. The previous year an Austin journalist had made merry with one of Miss Pearce's most inane statements: "I move that we pin badges on all the new Daughters, no matter what sex."

And this year the DRT convention promised to be the best show in town. Overhead the senate gallery was packed with journalists, politicians, non-delegate Daughters and curiosity-seekers. Among them were Wilton Peck and Hobo Pratt, their Stetsons in hand and their cowboy boots polished. Peck had redeemed himself with the Willinghams by purchasing the Gallagher property—and by assuring them that the warehouse blocking their lot would be razed. He hadn't told them about the impending final battle for the Alamo.

But Peck felt fairly confident. He'd done his homework, digging up some dirt on the tiny schoolteacher slated to preside in Birdie

McElroy's place. "This Lorena Lovett is a troublemaker," he whispered to the senator. "The school board in San Antonio put her on probation. First she showed up a month late for classes, claimed she'd been studying in Mexico. In *Veracruz*—who studies in Veracruz? Then she missed several teachers' meetings, and when they asked her about it, she said, 'I attend those meetings when I have nothing more urgent to do.' Can you imagine how unpredictable she'd be at the podium?"

Hobo Pratt was impressed. "Pecker! Maybe old Birdie ought to know about this."

"I'm one step ahead of you, Hobo. I had breakfast with Mrs. McElroy this morning." He winked.

The senator smiled and shook his head. "I'll be damned, Pecker, if you're not a sly fox." He extended a pouch of tobacco. "Chew?" The hotel man nodded and helped himself.

Below them Birdie McElroy clumped heavily across the platform to the podium, shooing off any would-be helpers. She rapped the convention to order. The hall quieted. Then she introduced Governor Thomas M. Campbell, who gave the opening remarks. Without directly mentioning the indelicate matter of the Alamo squabble, he pleaded with the ladies not to let passion and personal ambition cloud their judgment. The delegates applauded him politely, wishing he would hurry and sit down.

When he did, Mrs. McElroy made an announcement: Alva Keane had been delayed, and she wouldn't be able to attend the first session. However, the bust that she'd commissioned for the Alamo would be on display at the Driskill Hotel that evening. That stirred a murmur of approval.

Then Mrs. McElroy said, "Most of you ladies know that I won't be able to preside this year. To take my place, I'd now like to call a long-time Daughter and a fine parliamentarian from San Antonio—"

"Give them hell, Lorena," whispered Rose to herself.

"Mrs. Edna Duvalier."

Wilton Peck smiled at Senator Pratt and spat. Down below a collective gasp went up from both sides of the convention floor, as seventy-odd Daughters of the Republic sat open-mouthed like nestlings waiting to be fed.

54

Within two minutes most of the delegates were on their feet: waving furiously, some practically leaping, all shouting at the platform and at each other.

"Point of order!" Rose Herrera yelled above the roar.

Edna Duvalier rapped the gavel, to no avail.

"Point of order!" repeated Rose. "The vice-presidents must preside in numerical sequence. It's in our constitution. And Miss Lovett is the first."

The chamber quieted a little as the woman at the podium arched her heavy eyebrows at Rose. "Has the member making so much noise been recognized by anyone?"

The Keane faction broke out in new cheers. Rose's supporters shouted rebukes.

Once the noise subsided, she replied, "You've refused to recognize me or anyone else from our side."

Mrs. Duvalier asked testily, "What is it the member wants?"

"Yes," echoed Josephine Pearce, "what is it the member wants?"

The room was still. "I want this assembly to choose who presides," said Rose.

Mrs. Duvalier snapped, "That question is closed. Mrs. McElroy called me to the chair, and there is no appeal from the ruling while I'm presiding." She brought down the gavel with a startling smack.

Pandemonium broke out again. Daughters from both sides of the floor clamored at once.

"I insist on my appeal!" shouted Rose.

"You are out of order," declared Mrs. Duvalier. "You've spoken more than two times on this subject. I've been very patient with you. Now sit down."

She looked at her husband. *Am I out of order?* her expression asked. He nodded.

She took her swivel chair. Antonio leaned toward her and pointed to *Robert's.* "Look—this is what you need to do," he whispered. She clasped his hand and studied the rule.

As soon as Mrs. Duvalier opened the floor to new business, she recognized a Keane Daughter, who went straight for the prize. "Since Alva Carson Keane has been hailed across the nation as the savior of the Alamo, I move that we recognize the Carson Chapter and appoint her custodian of the Alamo property."

At once the Herrera Daughters lifted their voices in an angry chorus of "Treason!" The Keane Daughters yelled "Quiet!" in response.

"Order!" Mrs. Duvalier banged the gavel repeatedly.

When the cries faded, another Keane Daughter rose to speak. But before she was recognized, one of Rose's supporters leapt up and said, "I move that we amend the motion by substituting the name of Rose Herrera—"

"Who recognized you?" thundered Mrs. Duvalier.

"You won't let us speak," the Daughter retorted.

Mrs. Duvalier nodded at Miss Pearce. The parliamentarian read from *Robert's:* "Where two or more rise at the same time, the chairman must decide who is entitled to the floor."

The Herrera Daughters mumbled indignantly. Antonio nudged his wife and pointed to the rúles. She stood and read in response, "As the interests of the assembly are best subserved by allowing the floor to alternate between the friends and enemies of a measure, the chairman—"

"Who asked you?" interrupted Mrs. Duvalier. "The chair wants no direction from you."

Antonio nudged and pointed again.

"Question of personal privilege," claimed Rose.

Mrs. Duvalier scowled. *"What?"*

"I raise a question of personal privilege to appeal the ruling of the chair."

"You can't do that. There's already a motion before the assembly."

"It doesn't matter. A question of privilege takes precedence." Rose glanced at her husband. He nodded in confirmation.

Mrs. Duvalier turned to Miss Pearce. "Look that up."

A murmur ran through the hall. Rose smiled conspiratorially at Antonio. "Gracias," she whispered.

While Miss Pearce nervously scanned the *Rules*, Edna Duvalier glared at the Herreras. "Perhaps the member who has raised the question of privilege would like to introduce the gentleman who's coaching her. Who asked him to interfere in our affairs?"

Rose flared. "Gentlemen have always been welcomed by the DRT," she shouted. "Gentlemen fought the battle at the Alamo, gentlemen fought the battle of San Jacinto, and if we need them, ten thousand gentlemen from across the state will fight to save the Alamo convent!"

That prompted an enormous round of excited applause from her group. Mrs. Duvalier sniffed, "Perhaps the gentleman would like to come forward to advise all of us on parliamentary matters."

"Heavens no!" replied Rose, one hand on his shoulder. "My husband is here for our side to use. You should have brought your own." Again she drew cheers and laughter from her faction.

Finally Miss Pearce found a passage in *Robert's*. "Here it is. Article Two, Section Nine. Privileged questions are undebatable, excepting when relating to—"

"That's the wrong place," bellowed Birdie McElroy impatiently. "Mrs. Herrera raised a question of personal privilege, not a privileged question."

Daughters from both sides broke out in titters. Miss Pearce's face turned red. Frantically she flipped through *Robert's*. Edna Duvalier left the podium to help her.

That was a serious mistake. Rose glanced up and noticed Lorena Lovett waving at her from the platform, trying to catch her attention. *The gavel*, mouthed the schoolteacher.

What? she mouthed back.

Miss Lovett grinned and pointed excitedly to the unguarded gavel on the podium. All at once Rose realized what her ally was about to do. She shook her head vehemently. But Miss Lovett was no longer looking at her. Before anyone knew what was happening, the tiny woman darted across the platform to the podium and grabbed the gavel. The delegates looked up in shock. Then, once again, the assembly cried out in a cacophony of cheers (left) and fury (right).

Wilton Peck hiccupped and swallowed tobacco juice. "What the hell—"

"Stop her!" boomed Hobo Pratt.

Mrs. Duvalier rushed back to the podium. Towering over the schoolteacher by more than a foot, she grappled with Miss Lovett, digging her nails into her opponent's wrist and trying to wrench the gavel away. Miss Lovett broke free and climbed up on a chair. She held the gavel high overhead. Mrs. Duvalier stood on tiptoes, reaching for it.

"Disgraceful!" hollered Birdie McElroy from her chair. "I won't allow this!" But her voice was lost in the tumult.

Mrs. Duvalier yanked hard on the schoolteacher's single long braid, eventually forcing the twisting figure down from her chair. Roused by the skirmish, Miss Lovett swung the gavel wildly. It struck Mrs. Duvalier in the knee.

"Oh!" Mrs. Duvalier drew up her injured leg and hopped about the platform. "Grab her! She's stark raving mad!"

The other women on the platform watched in horror. "Stop this!" cried Birdie McElroy, too weak to intervene herself.

A few Keane delegates tried to rush Miss Lovett from the floor. She fended them off by swinging the gavel like a mace.

"Watch out—she's dangerous!" warned Mrs. Duvalier.

They retreated. Miss Lovett brought the gavel down sharply on the podium. "Now, ladies, the *real* meeting can come to order."

The noise in the chamber became deafening. So many Daughters started shouting at once that the DRT secretary gave up trying to take notes.

Then Edna Duvalier raised her arm and extended it over the

assembly like Moses parting the Red Sea. She pointed toward the door in the rear. No one heard what she said. But the Keane Daughters understood the command. Suddenly they stood up and started filing out of the chamber in droves. Insults and wads of paper flew back and forth across the room.

From her chair Birdie McElroy said, "I declare this session adjourned." No one noticed. She got up and tortuously made her way off the platform.

"Well, I'll be damned," said Hobo Pratt. "What next?"

Wilton Peck shook his head grimly, his plan gone sour. "Let's get over to the hotel and find out." The two of them slipped out of the gallery.

Once the Keane faction was vanquished, a Herrera Daughter yelled: "I move that we re-elect Rose Herrera custodian of the Alamo—"

Applause.

"Dissolve the Carson Chapter—"

Louder applause.

"Censure Edna Duvalier—"

Wild cheers.

"And then go eat!"

Pandemonium. Before it was even seconded the motion was carried by a chorus of acclamation.

Rose grinned and waved her clenched fist, relishing this surprise victory as much as any of her supporters. But she knew better than to think the battle was won. The next day would be the real test. Alva Carson Keane had just arrived in town.

55

In what could only be described as a monumental lapse of judgment, the DRT secretary had booked all the convention delegates in the same downtown hotel, the Driskill. That made for a very uncomfortable evening. In the lobby the Herrera and Keane Daughters circled each other warily. As they filed in and out, members of both factions stopped to admire Mathilda Guenther's bust of Colonel Travis. Edna Duvalier hovered close by. She told two uncommitted delegates from Galveston that Alva Keane was planning to commission another piece for the Alamo, perhaps a painting—but the women moved on.

Across the lobby Antonio Herrera glanced over his shoulder. Then he led his wife out of view behind one of the columns. In a quick sweep, he drew her into his arms, nearly knocking her breath out, and kissed her full on the mouth. Once she recovered, she took hold of his neck and paid him back in kind. Then, with her hands still linked around him, she said, "Tonight I'm going to take you out on the town."

"I've got a better idea," he whispered. "Let's have dinner sent to our room."

She gave him a quick peck, then released him. "I'll meet you upstairs." She started off.

"Where are you going?"

She frowned back at him and headed toward the powder room.

From the doorway of the hotel bar, Wilton Peck watched until Rose had cleared the lobby. Then he scurried across the room to Edna Duvalier. "What did you find out?" he asked tensely.

Mrs. Duvalier smiled at another uncommitted delegate, making a fuss over her sheer marquisette, before she turned to Peck. "Stop fretting. Birdie McElroy adjourned the session. Anything those fools did after that doesn't count."

He frowned. "We still need five votes to—"

"Will you hush!" Mrs. Duvalier smiled and greeted a reporter. Then she glared at Peck. "Circulate. Don't hide in that bar. Show the ladies the drawings of the park. Act confident. And smile; you look like the grim reaper."

Meanwhile, in a function room upstairs, members of the DRT executive committee were meeting with Governor Campbell. Alva Carson Keane was among them. Only minutes earlier she had learned of the insurrection in the senate chamber that afternoon, and that the Herrera Daughters were already claiming victory. At first she had kept her distance, trying to remain aloof from the squabbling. Then bitterness crept in, mingled with frustration. Now she was on the verge of tears.

Birdie McElroy was saying, "For Pete's sake, if we're just going to fight among ourselves, we might as well ask the legislature to decide who should take charge of the Alamo."

Alva blurted out, "Governor Campbell, I'd be willing to buy the property back from the state and pay for the park myself. That might end all this bickering."

"I can guarantee it wouldn't," Lorena Lovett told him.

The governor handled this very gingerly. "That's very generous, Mrs. Keane. But now that you've deeded that property to the state, I'm afraid you'd need the legislature's approval to take it back."

Alva turned away, fuming. So this was how the DRT and the state showed their gratitude. It was *her* money that had saved the Alamo, by God! And now Rose had gone behind her back, scheming to thrust her out of the picture altogether.

After the meeting broke up, Alva charged down the stairs and through the crowded lobby like a locomotive about to jump its rails. As she passed Edna Duvalier she spewed, "Everywhere else in the country they're calling me the savior of the Alamo, but here in Texas I feel like I don't exist. I've a good mind to resign from the DRT and go back to New York." Without waiting for a response, she plowed ahead to the powder room.

Edna Duvalier didn't believe that threat for a minute. But she saw its potential. She didn't waste any time. There was a lot of work ahead of her that night.

And so it happened that the two estranged partners finally met face to face, not on the convention floor at the state capitol, but in the powder room of the Driskill Hotel. Rose was on her way out when Alva burst in. There was no avoiding it. Both stopped, breathless. They stared.

Finally Rose said, "Kindly let me pass."

Alva smirked. "What's the magic word?"

Rose gathered herself and squinted. "Custodian?"

All at once Alva felt the full weight of her failure: the spiteful reviews of *Angelina, Sweetheart!* mocking her; the humiliation of the Alamo battle, which she had tried to remain above, dragging her down. She brushed past Rose and threw open the partition door to one of the privies. Rose followed her inside and slammed the door. Huddled over the toilet, they stood with their long gowns touching and their faces inches apart.

"Go ahead," whispered Rose. "Say your piece."

Alva smiled briefly in dismay. She spoke quietly, not to be overheard. "The funny part is, I liked you enough to start writing a novel about you. You had me trusting you."

Trembling, Rose pulled the toilet chain. The water swooshed in a noisy downflow, covering her voice. "You had me trusting you, too. Then you went over my head. Why didn't you tell me what you had in mind?"

Alva turned icy. "I paid for that property. I could have kept it for myself and used it however I wanted."

"Yes, you paid for it. With money your father scavenged off De León land!"

The younger woman was shocked. Then she nodded. They finally had Tres Piedras out in the open. "I thought so. That's what this is really about."

She broke off when they heard the door of the powder room open. They waited for the intruder to pass by. Angrily Alva jerked the toilet chain, releasing a second volley. "You want the whole state to suffer because your father couldn't manage that ranch and lost it? Don't count on it, Rose. I'll fight you tooth and nail."

"How? With your daddy's money? Or Wilton Peck's?"

Alva gasped in disbelief. "No one talks to me that way!"

Rose yanked the chain so hard she almost broke it. The water roared. "No, you and your daddy will never rob the De Leóns again!" she spat in a harsh whisper. "You can't *buy* custody, Miss Savior of the Alamo. You have to earn it!"

Alva glowered at her enemy. "I will. And after I do, I hope to God I never have to deal with you again." Then she threw open the privy door and marched out.

Rose stayed behind in the water closet, exhaling in quick, shallow breaths. At last the bridges were burned. Menchaca would have been proud of her.

But to her surprise she felt worse than ever. She hadn't gained ground; if anything, she seemed more vulnerable than ever before. She'd been too direct, flinging every poison arrow she'd been storing up all those years at Alva Keane. Now the other woman could fire them back at her any time she wanted. Rose sank and buried her face in her hands.

By the time she returned to her hotel room, her expression was stony. Her husband reached out to her. She drew back. "No, Antonio."

"¿Qué pasa?"

She shook her head. "Nada." It was barely a whisper.

Tenderly he held her, caressing her back in light, slow strokes. She let his body absorb the spasms that were still shooting through her. Finally, in terse bits and pieces, she told him about her confrontation downstairs.

"Don't let her get the better of you," he counseled. "You're still custodian."

But nothing he said or did that night was any comfort to her. Already she felt defeated. Menchaca was right: she was crazy to go up against the Carsons' money. On the second day of the convention, she would have to stand by and watch as that money conquered her family once again.

And once more Edna Duvalier had chosen the right tactic. Her rumors that night about Alva Keane's bounty, with the shocking kicker that the DRT's new benefactor might resign, was just what was needed to push enough uncommitted delegates into the Keane camp. Even a couple of wavering Herrera supporters came over. The next morning it was clear who was in control.

The first motion was to rescind all action taken the day before. It carried.

The second motion was to recognize the Carson Chapter and name Alva Carson Keane custodian of the Alamo. Despite an outcry from the Herrera side, the ayes had it.

Alva looked at her feet. She had hoped to rejoice in her victory. Instead she felt soiled, as if she'd debased herself in that nasty spat at the Driskill. All she could think about was how good it would feel to escape from everything, to be loping on Badger across the brushy chaparral at Tres Piedras. She was tempted to protest, a few minutes later, when one of her supporters proposed a motion formally excommunicating the San Antonio Chapter. That motion carried.

One final bit of business was dispensed with, almost as an afterthought: the DRT formally accepted the Willingham Hotel Company's offer to raze the Hugo & Schmeltzer. A delegate sitting close to Rose heard her whisper to the ceiling: "Abuelo, I'm so sorry." Then the convention was adjourned.

Wilton Peck didn't get a chance to speak to Alva until she was already outside. He finally caught up with her on the wide granite steps of the capitol. He called her name.

She turned and smiled indifferently. "Oh, hello, Mr. Peck. Josephine Pearce is the one you'll need to speak with."

"I beg your pardon, ma'am?"

"I have to go back to New York tomorrow. Miss Pearce will be the acting custodian in San Antonio while I'm away."

"We'll start wrecking the building in a week or two," he promised. He made a feeble effort to rekindle some rapport. "You're not going to Tres Piedras?"

She shook her head impatiently.

"Too bad," he told her. "I was hoping to visit the ranch again. Racer must be missing me." He forced a little laugh.

Alva smiled to hide her irritation. "Who?"

He felt foolish. "Racer. The horse."

"Oh. Yes. Pardon me, this week has been so hectic. Do keep me posted, Mr. Peck." Then she was whisked away by an entourage of supporters and hangers-on.

Peck stood tall in the entrance of the capitol, looking almost at home in his broad-brimmed Stetson and black boots, a plug of tobacco filling one sunburned cheek. He watched the women hurry across the lawn to Congress Avenue. They weren't looking at him, but he waved and smiled all the same. It was he, not Alva Keane, who was the real victor that day. Never again would he have to battle the Daughters of the Republic of Texas over some goddamned holy ground. Now the Alamo was his, for all practical purposes; and the coveted corner office in Philadelphia would soon follow.

A pastel winter sunset was in the making, and the forms of the two young people cast a single elongated shadow across the driveway. Enrique Herrera stood behind the girl in the open doorway of the garage. He held her shoulders close against his denim jacket, his arms around her waist. Gently he nuzzled her neck as she shivered in the cool air. "Una vez," he whispered.

"No, Enrique."

"Por favor, mi querida."

"I won't do it."

In mock despair he bit some petals off the carnation in her hair. She smiled and broke away. "Stop it!"

"You're scared," he taunted.

She was; she had never been in an automobile. "What if your parents find out?"

"My parents are still in Austin. And Eloisa has gone to her sister's."

"I wish your mother were here," said Eva.

"Why?"

"She could take us riding."

"We don't need my mother. I told you, I can drive it."

Eva laughed. "You think I'd ride with you?"

"Why not?"

"I'm in the habit of staying alive."

He scowled. "¡Qué descaro! I've driven it before."

"I don't believe you."

"No? Well. I've watched my mother drive. I know what to do. Just trust me."

Suddenly Enrique placed both his hands on her waist and hoisted her up to the seat. She pushed against him, laughing and screaming. "Enrique! No!"

"Shh! The neighbors."

He set the spark and cranked the Peerless. Then he jumped up on the seat beside her. Very cautiously he engaged the gears. The powerful automobile shot out from under him. He braked hard.

Eva gasped, clutching his shoulder. "Enrique! Let me out."

"No, I can drive it!" he assured her. "Here . . . I remember now."

Enrique backed the car out of the garage and inched it down the driveway. He made a wide turn onto Broadway, heading downtown.

"Where are we going?" Eva asked.

"To your mother's house."

"No! That's too far." She sat close at his side, gripping his arm like a vice. He tried to plant a kiss on her cheek; he got her hair instead. "Don't," she murmured.

"You're scared."

"I am not."

"Then why are you trying to take my arm off?"

She released it with a petulant look, withdrawing to the far side of the cab. He laughed and tried to coax her back. "Mi amor," he cooed. "Ven aquí, guapa."

"Enrique, watch the road."

"I told you, I can drive."

She didn't reply. He smiled.

Though the Peerless jerked and swerved under Enrique's unsure hand, they made it all the way downtown without attracting attention. But neither of them had stopped to think that one of San Antonio's most admired motorcars would be easily recognized. When they reached Military Plaza, Eva was the first to see the familiar striped serape and derby hat.

"My God. Enrique!"

"What?"

"Look!"

Rafael Menchaca was strolling down Commerce Street with a large woman in an odd black frock. Their backs were to the Peerless.

"Enrique—turn around. Quick!"

The street was crowded. "I can't," he said.

"Do something! You've never seen my father when he's angry."

Actually, he had; Enrique thought of his first encounter with the musician in the dark alley. He hoped they could turn right on Camaron Street and disappear unnoticed. But as the automobile got closer, Menchaca and Madame Guenther heard the motor and looked around. Madame Guenther seemed pleasantly surprised. At first Menchaca grinned and waved. Then his smile suddenly vanished. He stood blocking their path.

"Enrique. . . . ¡Socorro!" was all the girl could say.

The boy braked too hard, and the engine died with a sudden jolt. Menchaca's big hand reached for the steering wheel, then for Enrique's collar, yanking him down from the seat in a single motion. Without warning the boy felt the full force of his mentor's fist against his face. The next thing he knew, he was lying on his back in the street. He heard Eva scream. Then he saw her and her father and the strange woman all staring down at him.

"Shame on you! Shame!" the woman was telling Menchaca.

Enrique's head was throbbing. He closed his eyes for a moment. When he opened them, Menchaca was holding his knife. The boy didn't move.

"I will not tolerate senseless violence," the woman said in her German accent.

Menchaca taunted Enrique. "You want a scar like mine, huh? So you can look like the tough punk you want to be?"

"Stop it!" shrieked Eva.

"Shut up!" he commanded.

To Enrique's amazement, the German woman drew a pistol. "You just get rid of that knife. Right now."

Menchaca seemed to notice that people were watching. He put his knife away. Then he glanced down at Enrique. "Get up," he muttered with contempt.

Slowly Enrique struggled to his feet and brushed himself off. He still felt dizzy. He wiped his sleeve across his nose and saw blood. Eva was sobbing quietly. "Don't cry, querida," he murmured.

Menchaca grabbed the lapel of the boy's jacket. "You don't learn very fast. You want me to take another swing? Huh?"

The woman jerked his arm. "Leave him alone. He's just a boy."

"Stay out of this." The man released Enrique. Then he turned to Eva. "Go home."

She stopped sobbing and looked at him with hatred.

"I said go home."

She glanced at Enrique. The boy nodded. She took off running down Commerce Street toward the West Side.

Her father glowered at Madame Guenther. "You say he's just a boy? I know he's a boy! What do you think he wants from my daughter?"

The artist threw up her hands in exasperation. "What are these feelings you profess to know in your songs? '¿Corazón?' '¿Mi amor?'"

"Yes, and my knife could cure him of those feelings. This punk has no respect for my daughter."

"I have respect!" Enrique said angrily. "What do you know about it?"

Menchaca ignored him. "My Eva has talent," he told Madame Guenther. "You've said so yourself. I won't have some hot-blooded schoolboy turning her head. I want her to concentrate on her art, just like you."

"No," the woman said quietly. "You do not want her to be just like me."

"What does this hoodlum care if she's an artist?" continued Menchaca, picking up steam. "This little rico in training! He thinks he has the right to come to the West Side and take whatever he wants. Haven't I treated this boy like my own son? And then he goes sneaking around behind my back. Judas! I should have known. These people from the Heights are all the same."

Enrique shook his head in disbelief. "All this time I thought I knew you. My God—you're a madman."

"Go back where you belong!" thundered Menchaca. "Go back to the Heights and stay there. We don't want you here." He shook his fist at the boy.

Enrique didn't step back. "I'm not afraid of you any more," he said. "I hate you."

"Good!" hissed Menchaca. "I want my enemies to hate me as much as I hate them."

"Oh, stop this cockfight!" said the artist. "You two will destroy each other, and for no reason." She reached out her hand to Enrique. But he started walking away. She turned and assailed Menchaca. "You stupid burro! And after I have admired your ideals so much, you do this! Commoner!"

Enrique left while the man and woman were still quarreling. He wiped the blood off his face; there were tears mixed with it. His cheek was swelling. As he cranked the Peerless and climbed in, he decided he was going to take one last bit of his former teacher's advice. This time, he thought, he would go back to Alamo Heights and stay there.

58

The Herreras got home from Austin late on the Monday after the convention. Immediately Rose shut herself in her study. Surrounded by years' worth of DRT memorabilia, the disgraced Daughter allowed herself half an hour to weep in private. Then she dried her eyes and went to work. Her last hope was to prove once and for all that the warehouse walls were original—before they came down. Even if the Carson Daughters were hell-bent on demolition, Rose knew she could get Governor Campbell to intervene once she had enough evidence.

Time was her worst enemy. She decided to delay in surrendering her keys to the Alamo. It was a desperate stalling tactic, but she hoped the Carson Daughters wouldn't think to ask for them right away. In the meantime she might uncover the proof she needed. She spent most of that night reviewing Father Morfi's *Historia de Texas* and some of her father's letters.

She first saw her son's black eye at breakfast the next morning, after her husband had left for his office. She walked around the dining table, hovering over him while she examined his face.

"It's nothing," murmured Enrique. "I fell."

"Ssss! You don't get an eye like that from a fall."

He looked down. "All right. I got in a fight at St. Mary's."

"Enrique. Don't exchange one lie for another."

Just then the telephone rang, drawing her into her study. At first she heard only static. "Hello? ¿Quién es?"

There was no response. Then a metallic voice said, "Uh-huh. You still have those keys, don't you?"

"Speak up, please." Another crackle shot over the line.

"Don't think you'll get away with anything." That brittle timbre could only come from Edna Duvalier. "I'm warning you, the Carson Chapter has hired Horatio Franck. We can hit you with an injunction."

"Oh, don't be ridiculous!" Rose replied.

"We need those keys by noon today," commanded Mrs. Duvalier. Then she hung up.

Rose slapped the receiver on its hook, missing it on the first try. When she stepped back into the dining room, Enrique had already left for school. She sighed. She felt her son was slipping away from her once more. And she hadn't heard him playing his guitar the night before, which was very unusual. She wondered what was going on.

That afternoon her telephone rang again. This time it was Lorena Lovett, who was terribly upset. "Rose, we have to get down to the Alamo right away."

"What's wrong?"

"I just heard they're trying to break down the door."

"Who? What are you talking about?"

"I'm not sure. I'm calling from school. I'm on my way."

"All right. But don't do anything till I get there."

Although Rose made the trip to Alamo Plaza in record time that afternoon, she wasn't able to enjoy her feat. All the way downtown she fretted. Lorena Lovett was her most militant supporter, and she was grateful for her loyalty. But the schoolteacher was also wildly unpredictable. Their best chance was to avoid an all-out confrontation with the Carson Daughters until she could finish her research. But Miss Lovett, who had wielded the gavel to inflict injuries at the convention, wasn't one to let things lie.

When she got to the Alamo, Rose saw Edna Duvalier and Josephine Pearce standing outside the chapel. With them was a man trying to remove the heavy padlock on the door. She abandoned the Peerless halfway in the street, too flustered to park it. She saw Lorena Lovett approaching the Alamo on foot from Crockett Street. As they both drew near, Miss Pearce frantically urged the man, "Oh, hurry! Here they come."

"What is going on here?" demanded Rose. She saw that the man had a box of tools.

"Stay out of this, Rose," warned Mrs. Duvalier.

"This is an illegal break-in!" Miss Lovett shouted.

"Oh, go on!" Mrs. Duvalier told her. "Your friend here wouldn't give us the keys. She left us no choice but to hire a locksmith."

"I'm calling the police," said Miss Lovett as she started off.

Rose wanted to stop her ally, but she knew the two of them needed to put up a united front. "Let's talk about this like civilized people," she told Mrs. Duvalier. "No one has the authority to change these locks. I don't, and neither do you." She placed her hand on the locksmith's crowbar. He looked at her in surprise and stopped what he was doing.

"Keep working!" ordered Mrs. Duvalier. "I hired you."

"Don't, please," Rose said softly.

They all stood there a moment in a silent stalemate. Then Miss Lovett returned with Officer Poppy McBride, who was walking his beat around the plaza. "All right, ladies. What's the trouble about?"

Miss Lovett blurted out, "See? They're trying to break and enter!"

"Outrageous!" boomed Mrs. Duvalier.

Josephine Pearce became hysterical. "Yes, outrageous, officer! Why, I've never been in any kind of trouble with the law—oh, what would my mother think! You should hear what these old cats have been saying about us—"

"Shh! Now, calm down, everyone," the officer said gently. He looked at the locksmith. "You. Who gave you permission to mess with this lock?"

The man was petrified. "I don't want no part of this, officer. These ladies just hired me to do this, and I thought they were—"

"All right, all right. Now which one of you ladies told this man—"

"Rose Herrera has refused to surrender the keys," Mrs. Duvalier broke in.

Rose had to think fast. "Officer McBride, I'd be willing to turn over the keys to the newly elected custodian."

"She's in New York!" hissed Mrs. Duvalier.

"Poppy, I'm not authorized to give the keys to anyone but Alva Keane," Rose explained. "I would be in breach of my duty if I did." It was a flimsy excuse, but she was backed into a corner.

Miss Pearce was on the verge of tears. "But I'm the custodian while Alva's away."

"Well, I don't know anything about that," the officer replied, scratching his head. "But I do know that Mrs. Herrera has always been the one in charge of the Alamo. I'm afraid you other ladies will have to wait and get this straightened out among yourselves."

Mrs. Duvalier arched her eyebrows. "Officer, are you saying that you're going to deny us our legal right to—"

"Easy now," said Poppy McBride. "I don't know anything about anyone's legal rights. I'm just saying that all of you will have to leave the plaza now, before I run you in for disturbing the peace."

Josephine Pearce burst into tears. The locksmith quickly put away his tools and fled. The women dispersed in different directions while the policeman stood guard in front of the chapel doors.

"Just wait till the governor gets wind of this," yelled Mrs. Duvalier.

"Yes," sobbed Miss Pearce. "Just wait."

Rose Herrera and Lorena Lovett walked away from them without replying.

"You're breaking the law!" Mrs. Duvalier shouted.

Miss Lovett wheeled around. "Possession, my dear sisters, is nine-tenths of the law. And the other one-tenth is Officer McBride!"

"Shh!" whispered Rose.

"You'll see!" warned Mrs. Duvalier. "The law is on our side."

"So sue us!" Miss Lovett cried out, as Rose tried to hurry her toward the Peerless.

IN THE DISTRICT COURT OF BEXAR COUNTY, TEXAS

DAUGHTERS OF THE REPUBLIC OF TEXAS,

Plaintiff,

v.

ROSE DE LEON HERRERA and
LORENA LOVETT,

Defendants.

SUMMONS

To the above-named Defendants:

Greetings. You have been sued.

Filed February 5, 1908.

59

"It's no use. You can't win, Rose." Antonio Herrera shook his head as he studied the petition at dinner.

"I didn't think so," Rose admitted. "But what about when they bolted the convention? Didn't the Carson group give up their rights to the property?"

"That's a separate issue. What matters here is that Alva Keane authorized Josephine Pearce to act as her agent. She has the right to do that."

Rose called to the kitchen. "Eloisa! Más tortillas, por favor." She had neglected to plan their menus that week. Eloisa had used the opportunity to prepare her favorite dish, a tender chicken in rich mole sauce. The family ate heartily that night.

"On the other hand," Antonio ventured carefully, "if you choose to fight this lawsuit, it could buy you more time for your research."

She knew what he was thinking, though. If she fought the Carson Daughters in court, it would be all over the papers. And Antonio was just starting his solo real estate practice; he was afraid that kind of publicity could cripple him. "No," she said quietly. "I'll have Santos deliver the keys to Josephine Pearce tomorrow. We'll get the suit dismissed."

He seemed relieved. "Rose, you've put up the best fight I've ever seen. I'm proud of you."

She nodded.

"My advice is: keep doing what you've been doing," he told her. "There's no need to resort to the courts. You can still win with your research. I know you'll find the proof you need."

In the days that followed she hardly took a break. Eloisa clucked her disapproval each time she brought her employer another pot of coffee. Rose pored over every local history book on her shelves, then spent hours in the Carnegie Library analyzing any document that might be of use.

What little sleep she got was fervid and restless. One night her grandfather appeared in her dreams. He stared at her from the foot of her bed, peeling an apple.

"Abuelo," she asked, very matter-of-factly, "what am I going to do now?"

He bit into a slice of the apple. "Try Juan Ramírez," he finally replied.

"Who?"

"Juan Ramírez."

"Who is he?"

Her grandfather didn't answer.

Then her scholar's skepticism crept in. "If he's someone you knew, he'd be dead by now," she said impatiently.

He ate another slice of the apple and vanished.

"Wait! Come back!" She must have called out loud for him, because Antonio stirred and grunted.

Wide awake, she sat up and switched on the lamp by their bed. Her husband murmured, "Qué —"

"Shh. Nothing." She scribbled the name on her note pad: *Juan Ramírez.* Then she slipped on a robe and hurried down the dark staircase to her study. She felt a little foolish, following instructions from her dead grandfather in a dream. Still, the name "Juan Ramírez" hadn't come out of thin air; she was sure she'd run across it long ago. She opened a cabinet and pulled out her father's child-hood journals. Several hours later she finally found the entry she vaguely remembered:

> *February 15, 1840. Today I went with Juan Ramírez and his father, Augustin, to the Alamo to show them where the battle took place. Juan and I ran up and slid down the embankment in the Chapel many and many a time. Then*

*we looked at the Convent, and I showed them the place
where my father and so many of the other Texans fell . . . .*

She closed the journal. That was it! Juan Ramírez would be an
old man by now, if he were even still alive. But he could say for sure
whether the walls her father showed him in 1840 were the same ones
that still stood beneath the Hugo & Schmeltzer.

She found someone by that name listed in her city directory.
There was an address, but no telephone number; she'd have to visit
him in person. At daybreak, her spirits high, she called Lorena Lovett
by telephone to share the good news. Then she headed downtown in
the Peerless to search for the old man. On her way she took a detour
toward the Alamo to offer her grandfather an apple in thanksgiving.

She had just rounded the corner of Houston Street when she saw
the derrick of a giant crane towering above the downtown stores.
"Now what are they building there?" she wondered aloud. Then she
cursed her own stupidity. Even before the crane came into full view,
she knew. Suspended from the boom was a wrecking ball, poised to
level the Hugo & Schmeltzer.

That wasn't all. As she got nearer she saw a steam shovel, wagons,
wheelbarrows, pickaxes. An army of workmen had the property surrounded. They were already tearing off scrap metal and disconnect-
ing the utility lines.

She didn't notice that the Peerless had veered off course until a
park bench stopped it with a sudden smack. The motor coughed and
died. Rose got out without even bothering to check the fender for
scratches. Dazed, she wandered among the workmen, still clutching
the apple. Operating the steam shovel was a large-bellied Mexican
man. She recognized him: he'd overseen the desecration of the wall
at Mission San José. He braked and stepped down.

"Get back," he warned her over the noise of the machine. "No
one's allowed here." Then he noticed the Peerless and saw who she
was. "Oh! The automobile lady. Still can't keep that thing in the
road?"

She felt numb. "What are. . . ."

He grinned. "See this old warehouse? Well. By tomorrow evening you won't." Then he remembered. "You're Mrs. Herrera, right?"

She nodded.

He whistled. "Well—very sorry, señora. Call me a pícaro if you want, but it's my job."

She said no more. Calling this man a pícaro wouldn't stop things. Nor could Juan Ramírez, for that matter. One old man's affidavit would be pitiful ammunition against a wrecking ball, a demolition crew, and the combined wealth of the Carsons and the Willinghams.

Then, from a distance came a shout: "Armando!"

The workman glanced toward a slim figure who was motioning to him. "Un momento, Mr. Peck." He turned to Rose. "Will you excuse me, señora?"

"Tomorrow . . ." she whispered after he left.

She squeezed the apple and hurled it with all her strength against the steam shovel. It struck with a thud and burst into uneven fragments, bouncing over the mesquite paving blocks and scattering across the plaza.

6 0

S he was never able to account for the rest of that day. She remembered staring out of her bedroom window at the leafless post oak trees until the light faded from the bleak February sky. She must have tried to nap once, for she recalled wanting to dream and maybe speak to her grandfather again. But in her brief doze the only voice that had come to her, oddly enough, was Alva Keane's: *Gals, we're going to get that property! Even if we have to strap ourselves with rifles and take it by force.* She woke and laughed bitterly at the irony.

Did she ever pick up her telephone? For some reason, it seemed, she hadn't thought to contact her supporters. The scene at the Hugo & Schmeltzer had left her paralyzed.

When Antonio got home, he held her and whispered, "It's all right, querida. Go ahead, cry." She didn't. That should have worried him. Instead he marveled at how well she was bearing up.

After dinner Eloisa appeared in her study with coffee, urging her to pray for a miracle. But Rose knew she didn't believe hard enough. She never tried.

She couldn't remember at what point the De León in her took hold and she started thinking: *the middle of the night would be the best time*. At midnight, still fully dressed, she trudged up the stairs, laboring as if her gown were made of lead, and stopped at her bedroom door.

She looked at her husband for a very long time. Antonio's brow was furrowed even while he slept.

Opening his own office hadn't been enough to fully revive his spirit. Since they'd returned from the DRT convention, he had seemed even more obsessed with what people thought. And she understood why.

Antonio had gotten his first bad scar when he was ten, working as an errand boy. Once as he was delivering a Colt six-shooter across town, he overheard a man with a strange accent ask: "Surely you don't let them carry firearms here?" The boy thought "them" meant children, until he heard the man's companion reply, "We can't stop them; they think they're just as good as us." Antonio had always believed that if he worked hard enough, he could clear all those sorts of obstacles from Enrique's path.

His wife knew that wasn't so. Their son would have to learn more than etiquette to succeed. He needed to know how to stand firm, to resist if necessary, to enter society on his own terms. And his father wasn't the one who could teach him that. She knew she had to do this for Enrique as well as for her grandfather.

Quietly she closed the bedroom door. Then she crept down the hall to Enrique's room. He was sound asleep. She nudged his shoulder, covering his mouth with her fingers.

"Shh. Don't say anything."

He peered at her, alarmed.

She took her hand away from his mouth. "Get dressed," she whispered. "We're going to find some men and take the Alamo."

The boy said nothing but grinned, ready.

She waited for him downstairs in the kitchen. "We'll start with Menchaca," she told Enrique.

"Why him?"

"Who else?" His mother thought he'd be pleased, but instead he seemed troubled. She said no more.

Together they slipped past Eloisa's room and felt their way across the back lawn to the garage. Inside Enrique switched on an electric bulb.

"No!" hissed his mother. "Santos."

They saw the coachman's slight frame draped ridiculously across several bales of hay. Enrique tickled the man's ribs with his boot.

Santos raised one arm, mumbling. Then he turned over with a long snore.

"Stop it!" Rose chided.

"Don't worry. Can't you smell the tequila?"

"Leave him alone. Vamos."

Moments later the Peerless was speeding down the dark, deserted streets of Alamo Heights, its solitary headlamps shining far ahead into the night. As they flew past the manses where San Antonio's elite slept securely, Rose wondered: can I ever come back to the suburbs, after what I'm about to do?

61

Enrique emerged from the doors of the livery and ran back to where the Peerless was parked in the shadows. "He's not here," he reported.

Rose sighed. The first snag in her plan: bad luck. "Did you ask?"

The boy nodded. "No one's seen him. His room was empty."

His mother glanced across the street at the shaggy vaqueros warming their hands over a mesquite fire. Frustrated, she slapped her palm against the steering wheel.

"It's all right," the boy tried to reassure her. "We can take the Alamo. Just the two of us."

She shook her head. "It's a big building. It'll take several men to hold it."

They both thought for a moment. Then Enrique said hesitantly: "He has a house on the West Side—"

"No," said Rose. "I know where to find him. Get in."

He did. They raced toward La Villita.

It took a full five minutes of persistent knocking to rouse the housekeeper. Silas Toombs finally appeared in an exceedingly ill humor, decrying the ungodly hour, the lack of respect for protocol, and the decline of contemporary standards in general.

Rose cut him off. "I'm very sorry, but it's urgent. Mr. Menchaca, please."

She met with the Corrido King out on the gallery. His hair was mussed; his big feet were bare and his shirt unbuttoned. Otherwise he seemed alert, and not especially surprised to see her. He listened to her with tense, grim nods. Madame Guenther silently appeared behind him in the unlit foyer.

Menchaca scratched his paunch, just above the long scar. "How many men will you need?" he asked.

Rose figured out loud. "I'm going to guard the room on the southwest corner myself. We'll need one at the chapel door, probably two to watch the main entrance on the plaza. One upstairs. And two along the north wall. That's six altogether."

Just then Menchaca noticed Enrique, hanging back in the shadows by the Peerless. He scowled.

Madame Guenther poked him in the ribs from behind. "Don't be a burro!" she said in a harsh whisper. "Go on!"

He hesitated for a moment. Then he motioned to the boy. "Ven aquí, muchacho," he said quietly and gruffly.

Cautiously, Enrique climbed the steps to the porch. His mother watched, baffled by his behavior, but too preoccupied with her own concerns to give it much thought.

"So," Menchaca continued, "I need to find four men."

"Five," corrected Rose. "You and five others."

"What about Enrique?"

She shook her head. "I don't want Enrique in there."

"I won't leave you," the boy told his mother.

"Hush," she replied. But she knew he meant it.

The sculptor poked Menchaca again. Tentatively, he placed one arm around Enrique's shoulders. "We'll need guns," he said.

"No!" exclaimed Rose. "No guns."

The man snorted. "How can you hold the Alamo without guns?"

"No guns," she repeated. "I mean it, Menchaca."

He shook his head with contempt. "You'll get us all killed."

It was possible. She looked at her feet. "Maybe I've gone crazy. I just don't know what else to do."

Madame Guenther reached for her hand. "Rose. I would like to stand by you in the Alamo. Where you fall, I will fall also."

She was caught off guard and nearly laughed. "Holy Mary! I have no intention of falling. Besides, you've said yourself: this isn't your battle."

Madame Guenther gripped her arm and replied, with great difficulty: "But you are my best friend."

Touched, Rose smiled at her. "Then do what I need most. Stay on the outside, please. Speak for me. And let me know what's happening."

Madame Guenther looked at the mariachi, then at Rose. She sighed. "As you wish."

Menchaca was eager to get going. "I'll find you five men, señora," he promised as he started down the steps.

"Reputable men," she pleaded.

"What do you want? A bunch of lawyers?" he scoffed. She blushed. He realized he'd said the wrong thing. "I'll meet you in Alamo Plaza. One hour."

Rose nodded. "Be careful, Menchaca. Don't do anything risky."

He glanced back at her, grinning in disbelief.

6 2

She stopped the Peerless in front of the Menger Hotel. It was half past one. No one was out. In the lamplight the wrecking crane cast long, eerie shadows across the plaza.

Enrique was restless. "I'll go watch for them."

"No," she whispered. "Stay close. They'll find us."

Already she regretted having gotten her son mixed up in this. She'd only brought him along for security as she drove through the deserted streets. Now she realized he could get hurt. At the very least she expected them all to be arrested. She wondered whether Enrique could go back to St. Mary's Academy with a criminal record.

It struck her how Menchaca would mock her middle-class anxieties: "Bah! A revolucionaria doesn't grovel before some rico schoolmaster." She smiled.

Her son was watching for movement on the plaza. She reached over and smoothed his hair. "Enrique, I'd rather you didn't go in there with us."

He didn't reply. She knew it was useless.

A bellhop wandered out of the Menger Hotel. She watched him nervously in her mirror. He stood on the portico, smoking a cigarette and eyeing the Peerless. Eventually he strolled back inside. Rose sighed in relief.

She had no plan, really, other than to barricade herself in the old convent. It might buy time and stir up publicity. Or it might just be a fiasco. Of course she and the men couldn't hold the building very long. In a few days they would be starved out, gassed out, or laughed out; or maybe the city council would simply allow Wilton Peck to bring down the walls on top of them.

At a quarter after two, a horse-drawn wagon pulled up across the plaza. Rose held her breath. Several shadowy figures alighted. The driver came toward them. In the dim light she could barely make out his derby hat.

He spoke to Enrique first. "Go circle the building," he said, pointing to the Hugo & Schmeltzer. "Find out where the watchman is."

Enrique slid out of the Peerless. He took off at a half-trot.

Menchaca whistled at him. "Slow down, muchacho! You look like you're up to no good."

Then he climbed into the automobile and waited with Rose. She didn't look at him. "I must be loco," she said.

He didn't contradict her. They watched her son disappear into the shadows behind the Alamo chapel.

Rose pictured her husband asleep in the Heights. He'd come to her aid at the DRT convention. He'd even been willing to stand by her if she'd wanted to fight the lawsuit. Now she was repaying his loyalty by becoming a desperado. "I'm not sure if I can go through with it," she murmured.

She glanced at Menchaca, expecting a sharp rebuke. Instead his eyes seemed sympathetic. "It's not too late to back out."

"If I did, you'd call me a coward."

"No. But I'd go ahead with it anyway. For you."

She looked down, flustered. "No. . . ."

He reached for her hand. "Mi amor."

She tensed. He ran the length of her fingers with his calloused thumb.

She glanced behind her nervously. No sooner had she turned around than his lips were pressed hard against hers. She didn't move. She felt herself sinking into the cushioned seat, his torso heavy on her bosom. The goatee bristled against her face, then her neck, then her bodice. She arched her back and reached for his shoulder. When she finally opened her eyes, he was staring at her, bewildered. She let go. He drew away.

She pulled herself up. He scratched his face and mumbled

awkwardly, "There are some cement sacks we can use. In case they try to break down the doors."

Her heart was pounding. She thought: I'll be several days, perhaps, inside the Alamo with this man.

He must have been thinking the same thing. "You're right about Enrique."

"What?"

"He shouldn't go in there with us."

She could barely whisper. "He won't leave me. I know him."

Menchaca looked out across the plaza. Then he changed the subject. "What we need is a howitzer," he sighed.

The prudent thing, she realized, would be to post Menchaca along the north wall, far away from her room on the southwest corner. She leaned over and placed her hand on his chest. He covered it with his own. "Will you stay near my room?" she asked. "At the south entrance?"

He nodded and glanced away. They saw Enrique hurrying around the corner of Crockett Street. Menchaca released her hand. They both stepped down from the Peerless.

"The watchman's over on the east side," the boy reported. "But he's coming this way."

His mother looked at Menchaca. Her face tightened. "All right, men. Let's do it. Before I change my mind."

6 3

Rafael Menchaca took her hand and led her across the street. The men he'd assembled were a rough-looking crew. They gave her cold chills. He pulled back the canvas covering the wagon bed. "Look!" he declared proudly.

She shrank back. The wagon was an arsenal. He pointed out a .30-30, a .30-06, an Army Krag, a 7-mm. Mauser, a .22 automatic, two Colt .45s, and a double-barreled shotgun.

"Menchaca! Please leave these things here," she begged.

He grunted in disappointment.

"At least for now," she compromised. "Let's have a look inside first."

He motioned to the men. They all made their way across the shadowy plaza toward the Alamo, Rose in the lead. But when they got to the chapel door, she stopped short and cursed under her breath. She had completely forgotten about one thing.

"I no longer have the key," she told Menchaca, embarrassed.

He was amused. "Señora, remind me not to let you plan my next revolution."

He sent one of the men back to the wagon to get a crowbar. They all waited anxiously while the man pried at the padlock.

"I suppose this is my first illegal act," fretted Rose.

"Don't worry; your next ones will come easier," Menchaca assured her.

She glanced up at him tensely.

Finally the lock broke free and fell to the sidewalk with a startling clatter. They all glanced around to see if anyone had heard. Then Rose shoved open the chapel door. She paused.

"¿Cómo?" whispered Enrique.

She held up her hand. "Footsteps."

They all listened. The plaza was still.

She asked, "Where's the watchman?"

"¡Adelante!" urged Menchaca. They poured inside, pushing ahead into the dark sanctuary.

She had to feel her way until her eyes adjusted. The others followed close behind her, through the sacristy and into the Hugo & Schmeltzer building. Single file they navigated the long stone corridor at a steady clip. No one spoke.

Suddenly a whiskey crate crashed to the floor. She screamed, clutching her breast.

"¡Cuidado!" Menchaca hissed at the men.

They hurried through the long warehouse, past boxes of tinned foods and sacks of flour. She stationed the men at the various posts along the way. Finally only she and Menchaca were left. They stopped at the south door. He opened the porthole and looked outside.

"Menchaca," she whispered nervously. "About what happened in the motorcar. We can't—I mean, I can't—"

"Shh." Gently he placed his fingers across her lips. His eyes were sad. "Don't spoil it."

She touched his face. "Stay here where I can see you," she told him.

Then she proceeded to the southwest corner and pushed open the heavy door to her grandfather's chamber. The air was dank and musty. She brushed a cobweb from her face. Fumbling for her rosary, she murmured, "Dios te salve, María, llena eres de gracia—oh God, what am I doing?" When she turned around, Rafael Menchaca was right behind her. She gasped.

"The men say they won't stay," he reported, "unless they can go get the guns."

She stamped her foot and swore. But he was already on his way out. She watched angrily as the men, even Enrique, filed out in high spirits. One of them grabbed a whiskey bottle from a crate. They laughed.

"Quiet!" she ordered.

Then she heard other voices, close outside: excited, speaking English; not whispering, and not laughing.

"Wait!" she cried.

But one of the men was already opening the main door to the plaza. The corridor brightened. The voices were louder.

"Watch out!" she cried.

It was over in moments. She only caught glimpses: figures passing through a narrow column of light from outside, police uniforms, scuffling feet, crates overturning, a billy club smacking the back of a man's head. A derby flew off as he fell.

"Rafael!" she screamed.

A policeman turned the beam of his torch on her. She froze.

Then she lunged forward in a panic and threw all her weight against the door of her room. It slammed shut. She slid the bolt in place. An instant later a billy club rapped on the other side.

"Open up! Police!"

She stepped back, staring at the door. She couldn't move.

The pounding continued. "Open this door or we'll break it down!"

That made her mad. "Go ahead and try!" she cried. Surprised by the fear in her voice, she said no more.

Finally the rapping and shouting stopped. The footsteps retreated. She rushed to the door and pressed her ear against it. There were no more voices.

"Rafael!" she screamed again.

No one answered. All she heard was the steady drip of a distant water pipe.

The window. . . . She clawed at the latches on the shutters and yanked them open. Faint voices drifted across the plaza. She couldn't tell where they were coming from.

"Enrique!"

The street was dark and empty. Good God! What had they done to her son? She longed to open the door. But she didn't dare.

Suddenly her fear gave way to a sob of frustration and anger. She slammed the shutters and latched them again. If only those bull-headed idiots hadn't tried to go back for the guns! Now she was left to hold the Alamo without them. There was nothing to do but wait.

64

"**B**y virtue of the authority vested in me as sheriff of Bexar County, Texas—"

She kept the shutters fastened. The voice droned on.

"I command you to appear in a suit wherein the Carson Chapter of the Daughters of the Republic of Texas is the plaintiff, and Rose De León Herrera is the defendant—"

She had no watch. But she could see daylight through the space between the shutters.

"And I hereby serve this injunction ordering you not to interfere with the custodianship of—"

Finally Rose flung open the shutters. An iron grating was the only thing between Sheriff Tobin's face and hers. Behind him on the plaza a small crowd had already gathered. A police line kept the onlookers back. The sheriff's frame blocked most of her view.

"Rose Herrera—you come out of there! Do you hear me?"

"I demand to see the governor," she told him. Past the point of fear, the lone woman was all defiance: she expected no leniency and had nothing left to lose.

He started reading the injunction again. "By virtue of the authority vested in me—"

"Oh, save your breath!" She covered her ears with her hands. "I won't come out till I'm good and ready."

The sheriff turned to the spectators, trying to make light of the situation. "She'll come out as soon as she's good and hungry."

"My grandfather and my father didn't!" she reminded him.

That drew cheers from a few people in the crowd. The sheriff's face reddened. He announced: "Anybody who gets close to this window or tries to bring her any food will spend tonight in jail. Along with *her*." He marched off, leaving a deputy posted to enforce his order.

At last the woman in the Alamo convent could see the crowd outside. Lorena Lovett and Madame Guenther stood in silent support. Josephine Pearce looked away in consternation. Edna Duvalier scowled and addressed the man beside her.

"My feeling is: if she wants to go down beneath the wrecking ball, good riddance," she said.

Wilton Peck shook his head. "Be careful. We're sitting on a volcano, if you know what I mean."

"Speak plain English and I will," she snapped.

"Yes, speak plainly," echoed Josephine Pearce. Rose Herrera's latest offensive in the Alamo war had shortened all their tempers to a nub.

"I'm talking about public opinion," Peck said testily. "Rose Herrera could become a celebrity if we don't handle this right."

Mrs. Duvalier rolled her eyes. "Oh, for crying out loud!"

"Cry all you want," Peck huffed. "But I'm going to make sure that woman doesn't climb into bed with these reporters. Is that plain enough for you, Miss Pearce?"

The spindly librarian was beside herself with nervous strain. "I don't think there should be any talk of that kind among ladies." Then she burst into tears.

From behind the window bars Rose looked in vain for other familiar faces. All at once she felt overcome by a terrible load of guilt. She longed to see her husband, hoping against the odds for some sign of his assurance. But he wasn't there. She didn't see Enrique or Rafael. She was certain they were either in jail or in a hospital, bruised and beaten. And it was her fault.

No. It was Wilton Peck's fault. He had set off the chain of events that had finally pushed her into this corner. She turned to glare at the hotel man. But he was gone.

The two conspirators found their third accomplice at the Imperial Bath Company on Houston Street. Hobo Pratt was getting a massage. "Is it over?" he asked from the table.

"She's still in there," Peck said grimly.

"And why in the hell isn't she out?"

The vein on Horatio Franck's forehead popped up. "Why indeed, senator? Why don't you just waltz right down there yourself and try asking her in your most charming voice to step out? See how far *you* get, you gaping baboon!"

Hobo Pratt was disgusted. "God damn, what a pair of weak sisters." He motioned to the masseuse to stop. Then he sat up on the table and arranged a towel around his waist.

"She's been served with the injunction," the lawyer said. "She won't last long."

"Injunction, my ass!" the senator replied. "Just break down the goddamned door. Drag her out if you have to!"

The hotel man took charge. "We're not going to force her out. I won't have any bad press for the hotel. And just to be safe, I'm going to send a telegram to Alva Keane, so she doesn't get cold feet and call a halt to the demolition. Now stop your bellyaching; that woman will be out soon enough."

The senator shook his head. "Goddamned corporate flunkies. Lawyers. Hell, can't you find a sharpshooter to take her out?"

The other two men didn't dignify that suggestion with a response.

"All we can do is wait," Franck declared.

Peck nodded in agreement. "Starve her out."

Hobo Pratt sighed. "What a pair of pussies." He stood up and walked around the room. Suddenly he placed both hands on the massage table and pushed it over. The crash echoed off the wall tiles. "God damn it, boys!"

THE WESTERN UNION TELEGRAPH COMPANY.
———— INCORPORATED ————
23,000 OFFICES IN AMERICA. CABLE SERVICE TO ALL THE WORLD.

San Antonio Texas Feb. 11th-1908.
Mrs. Alva Carson Keane,
      Ansonia Hotel, 2109 Broadway, New York N.Y.
No cause for alarm demolition will proceed once lunatic dispatched best wishes.
              Wilton A. Peck.

0137pm

66

By afternoon the crowd outside the Alamo had grown. Rose Herrera's supporters kept a faithful vigil. Reporters swarmed. Meanwhile, the steam shovel and the wrecking crane stood idle. Sheriff Tobin didn't know what to do.

Rose was surprised to see Madame Guenther and Silas Toombs setting up a table at the front of the police line. On it was a large block of clay. Madame Guenther waved for her to stand at the window.

No, Rose tried to mouth. *Not like this.*

The artist disregarded her protests, motioning for her to turn profile. With a laugh Rose gave in and complied. She remained at the window while Madame Guenther sculpted her portrait. It was far from an ideal sitting. The sculptor often had to resort to opera glasses for a better view of her subject. When that failed, she had to trust a photograph and her memory.

Late in the day Sheriff Tobin bowed to public pressure, announcing that Mrs. Herrera could have a canteen of water. Wilton Peck pulled him aside. "Is that wise, sheriff? We don't want to prolong this."

The sheriff indicated the crowd. "A lot of these folks are on her side," he pointed out. "And I'm up for re-election."

"But, sheriff—"

"Don't argue with me. She gets the water."

The hotel man fumed. "Let me take it to her, then," he suggested. "I may be able to make some headway."

And so Wilton Peck crossed the police line and approached the window for his first meeting ever with Rose Herrera. He cloaked his hatred in sarcasm. "My dear madam, pardon me for intruding on your privacy. I am—"

"I know who you are," she said. "What do you want?"

He narrowed his eyes. "I want to give you some water, señora." He held up the canteen.

She started to unlatch the iron mesh that separated them. Then she thought: if she opened it and reached for the canteen, he could grab her arms; he could hold her until the deputy got there; a few men could probably pull her through the window.

"Leave it on the ledge," she told him.

He didn't move. There before him was a bedraggled woman whose auburn bouffant dome was sinking, whose face was streaked with soot and whose gown was soiled with cement dust—and this loathsome agitator was the only thing that was standing between him and his promotion back home.

"No," he finally said, very deliberately. "I won't leave it on the ledge. You might spill it."

He was smirking in triumph as he unscrewed the cap from the canteen. She swallowed hard—but there was nothing to swallow. She was sure he was going to empty the water on the ground. But he didn't. Instead he extended the spout through the iron bars. Very slowly he tilted the canteen upwards.

At once she understood. She dropped to her knees and opened her mouth, frantically trying to gulp the stream of water as it cascaded down from the window and splashed over her face.

"That's right, drink," whispered the hotel man. "Lap it up on all fours like the bitch you are."

When Peck stepped back across the police line, the local for the *Journal* pushed his way toward him. "What did she say?" he asked. "Is she coming out?"

Peck thought for a moment as he stared at the young newspaperman.

"People are calling this the second siege of the Alamo," the reporter persisted. "Do you think she'd really die in there?"

Wilton Peck smiled paternally as he clasped the man's shoulder. "It's crowded here. Let me buy you a drink at the Menger. I'll tell you a few things most of your readers don't know about Rose Herrera."

6 7

Rose decided that she probably could have held the Alamo indefinitely if only she'd brought a supply of coffee. Early that day the headaches had begun. Had the De León spirit not possessed her the night before, she might have entered the convent better prepared for a siege. As it was, she had no food, no water, no warm clothes, no reinforcements, and no strategy. Her confidence faded with the daylight. By sunset she felt dull, exhausted, and entirely foolish.

The crowd dispersed at nightfall. Outside a lone deputy kept watch beneath the street lamp. Downtown San Antonio was silent and still. As the temperature dropped, Rose fastened the shutters, rubbing her shoulders. In the darkness she groped for a burlap sack to use as a shawl.

With nothing to distract her, she couldn't stop thinking about how hungry she was. Against one wall was a sack of dried corn kernels: livestock feed. She found that if she let the corn soak in her mouth long enough, she could chew it. But after a couple of kernels she panicked: what if she got choked and had no water? She stopped trying to eat.

Then she needed a privy. The closest thing she could find was an empty paint can—and she felt lucky to have *that*.

Finally she arranged some dusty sacks in a corner, shaking off the mice droppings. The floor was hard and damp, and the burlap made her hands and face itch. But at least her bed would be warm.

She wondered what would become of her after this was over.

Would she go to prison? Antonio would disown her if she did. Perhaps she'd spend the rest of her days walking the streets of San Antonio, picking through garbage: the final decline of the De Leóns. Wilton Peck would laugh as she begged for scraps from the kitchen of the Willingham Palace. She closed her eyes and tried to think about something else.

She thought about how hungry she was. And thirsty.

She thought about Alva. Their confrontation at the Driskill Hotel had done nothing to unburden Rose. It was unfair: both of their fathers had acted dishonorably in the sale of Tres Piedras—Carson by conquering ruthlessly and De León by paving the way for his own downfall. Yet Rose alone was left to contend with the shame. Still, she had come so close to making her peace before she and Alva parted ways unexpectedly. She wondered what Alva was thinking now.

She thought about her son. Then her husband.

Finally she thought about Menchaca in the Peerless. Madame Guenther was right: it was foolish to fight one's feelings. She no longer felt ashamed, for she knew it wasn't simply desire of the flesh that had drawn her to him. Rafael was so devoted to her that he'd been willing to risk everything, even go into the Alamo alone; Antonio hadn't even made an appearance on the plaza. But there were some bonds she wasn't strong enough to break. She wept to think that her amour with Rafael, though barely illicit, might have already reached its culmination. Rafael had seemed to realize that even before she did.

It would be a long night. When she finally slept, in uncomfortable fits and starts, she dreamed of thousands of flaming swords hovering around the convent walls. They all shot straight up into the night sky in one giant pillar and exploded into millions of shimmering stars, leaving only the three De Leóns—Francisco, Fermin and Rose—to hold the old mission below.

68

Hobo Pratt seldom thought about the past. To the extent he subscribed to any philosophy at all, he believed in fate. Any of his past deeds that might have bothered his conscience at the time had turned out to be inevitable events in some unknowable plan to propel him to where he was meant to go. But now, with Rosalita Herrera standing between him and what was rightfully his, he wondered if he was paying for something he'd done one morning in the summer of 1885.

He'd been a young man then. Only a week earlier, he and his most jocular companion, Fermin De León, had gotten drunk together at the Two Brothers Saloon in San Antonio. Though De León was almost old enough to be his father, the two men were drawn together by their passion for cantinas and casinos and good times. The older man had given his protégé the nickname Hobo a few years back, when he had gotten so soused that he mistook a boxcar for his hotel room and woke up in Eagle Pass. De León had joked with Pratt about the tax sale that was coming up in Laredo. He could scrape together forty-two dollars easily.

But when the county attorney saw his compadre bounding up Flores Avenue that morning, grim-faced and disheveled, he knew it was all over. He sighed and looked at B. R. Salmond, the tax collector. "Shit."

De León should have arrived in Laredo the night before. Hobo Pratt had hoped to broker a private deal that would pacify both Fermin and his neighbor Oscar Carson. But Pratt learned from the stationmaster that the I. & G. N. train from San Antonio had broken down. The locomotive had blown the throttle valve. The passengers were stranded somewhere on the brushy flats between Encinal and Cactus and would probably stay there all night.

It was fate, Pratt decided. The train was always on schedule; this could be no coincidence. He didn't even try to postpone the sale. Oscar Carson was already leaning on him to make sure the bids didn't get too competitive. Pratt hoped they could get the auction over with quickly.

From the look on Fermin De León's face that morning, it was likely he didn't have the forty-two dollars. Even if he'd started to Laredo with it, Pratt guessed that his friend had lost it on a bad hand in monte the night before. If so, that was also fate.

A small group of cowboys and businessmen had assembled below the courthouse steps. Among them was Oscar Carson, dressed just like one of his trail hands. De León's arrival made everyone stop talking. Working his way through the group, he sprinted up the steps to where Pratt and Salmond were standing.

De León tried to act casual. "Top of the day, gentlemen. I've come to render unto Caesar."

No one spoke. A cowboy spat tobacco juice loudly. Hobo Pratt admired his compadre's ability to keep his sense of humor at a time like this.

"Here." De León produced two railroad stock certificates. "Mr. Salmond, your bandidos in the tax office have assessed the outrageous sum of forty-two dollars against Tres Piedras. But to show I have no hard feelings, I'm endorsing these certificates over to the county coffers."

The two men glanced at the stock certificates. Salmond snorted. "Just hold your horses, Fermin. Don't go endorsing anything yet."

The tax collector took Pratt aside. "Now, young fellow, you're finally going to earn that drinking and whoring money the county pays you by giving me some legal advice. What do you think I should do?"

The attorney wasn't prepared for this turn of events. Fate must be testing his mettle, he realized. He glanced down at Fermin, then the group below. Carson was watching him with steely gray eyes. Pratt had never liked The Old Man, who took everything too seriously and didn't have an ounce of sport in him. But the cattle baron had promised to help bankroll his senate race.

Pratt knew what he had to do. "The notice of sale says the amount due may be paid in *cash* at any time before the hour of sale," he pointed out to the tax collector in a low whisper. "By law, Fermin can only redeem his land for cash."

Salmond frowned. "That's being awfully picky. I think the law gives us a little leeway in these situations."

Pratt knew the tax collector was probably right. "But we sure wouldn't want a judge to set aside this sale," he argued. "We'd look like a pair of goddamned fools."

Salmond hesitated. "I don't know. I've half a mind to accept that sorry bastard's stock certificates."

The attorney's temper rose. "Look here, the notice says 'paid in cash,' as plain as day. If you didn't mean that, why in the hell did you put it in there?"

The tax collector sighed. "Shit. I guess you're right." He turned and addressed De León. "I'm afraid you have to pay in cash, señor."

Fermin De León was caught off guard. He tried to laugh, but it sounded forced. "Bureaucrats! These are premium stocks."

Salmond stood firm. "Either pay in cash, or step down and let this sale proceed."

"All right, all right." De León turned to face the crowd, still trying to make a joke of it. "Here, muchachos, I've got a deal for you. Which one of you lucky sons of bitches is going to walk away with these hundred-dollar certificates for only fifty dollars cash?"

No one moved. They all looked uncomfortable. Pratt heard one cowboy say to another, "Thought *I* was broke—he don't even have forty-two dollars to his name." The other grinned without spilling his tobacco wad.

The debtor's smile faltered as he started down the steps. "You, sir? What, don't tell me you're holding out for forty-five!" But his easy banter wasn't fooling anyone.

Suddenly Salmond blurted out: "For God's sake, Fermin! You go through this every time. If you don't have the money now, you won't have it next week, or next month." Then he read the formalities and started the auction.

The first bid came from Oscar Carson: "Forty-two dollars."

"Cash, I trust," mumbled the tax collector.

A few men chuckled uncomfortably. Carson never cracked a smile. There were no other bids. The cowboys in the group worked for Carson.

"Forty-two dollars!" shouted De León. "Forty-two dollars for eight thousand choice acres on the Rio Grande. Do you think that'll hold up in court, Hobo?"

The county attorney froze.

"God damn it, Fermin," snapped Salmond. "Make a bid yourself or shut your trap."

The debtor didn't say anything else. Tres Piedras was the last of his family's land. He seemed too exhausted to comprehend the finality of the sale.

Forty-two dollars—cash.

Going, going.

Gone.

The group started to disperse. Pratt passed by his drinking partner. "I did everything I could," he said in a low voice. "Sorry, amigo."

Fermin De León spat and walked away.

A few minutes later, Pratt, Salmond and Carson were relieving themselves in the thicket behind the courthouse. The tax collector was saying, "You know, that family used to own half the damn valley. He's gone and pissed it all away."

"Pitiful, wouldn't you say?" Oscar Carson remarked gruffly.

"I'd say so, Mr. Carson," agreed Hobo Pratt. "I reckon now he's just another greaser on the bum."

Then he noticed De León passing by on the other side of a picket fence. He was almost sure he'd overheard.

That was the last time Hobo Pratt ever saw Fermin De León. On those rare occasions when he felt guilty, he reminded himself: Fermin had always wanted him to succeed. Fermin, when he still had some clout, had used his influence to get his protégé elected county attorney. If Fermin had known what was at stake for his friend that day, he surely would have understood.

Pratt felt absolved. Rosalita's act of defiance couldn't be his punishment. No; fate was simply testing his mettle again. He knew everything would work out for him, just as it did that day in Laredo. He rolled over and sank into his bed. Soon he was snoring.

69

Hobo Pratt wasn't the only one thinking about the summer of 1885 that night. Rose Herrera woke long before dawn, cramped and sore. She couldn't go back to sleep. Counting sheep seemed ridiculous. Instead, she tried picturing in her mind pleasant scenes from her youth. But what kept coming back to her was a broadside she'd seen once on Main Plaza: "A sumptuous extravaganza! A mammoth entertainment of laughter and beauty."

Fermin De León had promised his youngest she could have anything she wanted for her fifteenth birthday—never expecting she would ask for a night out at the Vaudeville Theatre.

Her mother protested half-heartedly. "No one goes to the Vaudeville but thugs and cretins. It's no place for a child."

"Fine. Rosie's not a child any more."

Rose suspected that her mother secretly wanted to see the Vaudeville herself. "Get her a new white dress instead," said Florencia De León.

"I promised her we'd take her," said her father.

And they would—because Rose, his most rebellious child, was also his favorite. So De León bought three tickets for the early show at the Vaudeville. *And* he bought Rose a new white dress. He could still get credit in San Antonio. He felt confident he could pay off his debts once he returned from the casinos of New Orleans.

When the De Leóns arrived at the Vaudeville that evening, Rose *was* the only member of the audience escorted by her parents, and the only one wearing white lace. But that didn't bother her. None of her schoolmates at Ursuline had ever seen a show at the Vaudeville. And her new white dress was a present from her papa.

They found their aisle seats in the balcony. Fermin De León glanced over his program absently while his wife and daughter ogled the chandelier. Some latecomers brushed against his knees. He bolted up. "What?" he shouted.

Rose was startled. "Papa?"

He looked at his daughter. Then he winked and smiled. "You just sit back and enjoy yourself, Rosie. You're in with high rollers tonight."

The band struck up a brassy incidental intended to quiet the audience. De León shifted impatiently.

The curtain rose on a slapstick: two fellows clowning in big vaudeville suits, one elevated on stilts. Rose kept looking over at her father. He was mumbling something. Her mother touched her shoulder to reassure her.

But halfway through the next act—the East India dancing girls, swaying to strains of exotic music—he stood up abruptly and left. Rose wanted to follow. Her mother wouldn't let her. The girl didn't see any more of the show after that. She only watched the door.

It was during the cannibal specialty act that the usher came to summon Florencia De León. "Come," she whispered to her daughter. The look on her face so terrified Rose that the girl asked no questions.

Outside on Main Plaza, beneath the gaslights and the austere face of San Fernando Cathedral, a crowd was stirring in front of the Jack Harris Saloon. Rose heard a barmaid assailing a man. Her mother took her arm. She seemed to float, lightheaded. The voices around her sounded distant.

"Easy. Easy now."

"There—that's his daughter."

"Don't let the girl see."

"He's calling for her."

"Let her through."

Someone led her to the bench where her father was laid out. She dropped to her knees and took his hand. Her mother knelt at his other side. But Fermín De León looked at his daughter.

"Rosie. . . ."

He smiled. He was trying to tell her something, but the words couldn't surface. She pressed closer to his face. All she heard was a faint gurgling.

"Oh sweet Jesus—look at his eyes."

"Shut up, will you?"

"Back off, give him some air."

"For Christ's sake, someone take the girl away."

When Rose stood up, the bodice of her new white dress was blotted in red.

Her mother motioned for a policeman. "Please, could you take my daughter home?"

The girl still hadn't lost her composure. "I want to stay."

The policeman looked at Rose, then her mother. "Well, I—well, certainly, ma'am." He took the girl's elbow and started leading her away. She kept looking back.

"Please, I want to stay," she said.

"You have to mind your mother, now."

"I want to stay with him."

"Easy. They'll be bringing him home directly."

"I want to find out what happened."

"Let me take you home, ma'am. You can read about it in the papers tomorrow."

70

"*Let me take you home, ma'am.*" In her half-sleep she heard the policeman's voice, steady and gentle, leading her away.

"Mrs. Herrera?"

She wasn't dreaming. She opened her eyes.

"Psst! Mrs. Herrera."

It *was* the policeman's voice. She threw back the burlap sacks and struggled to her feet. Her limbs were stiff. The mildew made her sneeze.

"Poppy?" She felt her way through the dark chamber and unfastened the window shutters. Outside stood Officer McBride.

"What time is it?" she asked.

"Quarter past five. Sun'll be up before long."

She wiped her eyes. The morning air was cold. The empty plaza was still shrouded in shadows.

"How're you doing in there?" he asked her.

She smiled weakly. "I'm still kicking."

He leaned close to the iron grating. His long moustaches made him look sad. "Mrs. Herrera. Let me take you home, ma'am."

It occurred to her that Poppy McBride had been present at two of her life's darkest events. The first was that night in front of the Vaudeville. Then, eleven years later, he'd been outside Casino Hall when the horse kicked Carlos, her two-year-old. Again the policeman had taken her home, after the doctor had shaken his head and closed her son's eyes.

He peered at her earnestly. "No one's out here, ma'am. Come with me."

She smiled sadly. "Not this time, Poppy. I'm sorry."

He glanced around furtively. Then he pushed a flask of water and half a sandwich through the window bars.

THE SAN ANTONIO JOURNAL
Wednesday, February 12, 1908

MRS. HERRERA THREATENS SHERIFF, DEFIES COURT

Insanity Apparently to Blame for Woman's Bizarre Behavior.

Defying an injunction to quit the Hugo & Schmeltzer premises, Mrs. Rose De León Herrera, wife of local attorney Antonio Herrera, continues to hold the warehouse in violation of both law and reason.

"I'll stay here forever if I must," the wild-eyed woman threatened yesterday, as the bizarre and pathetic spectacle continued.

"You'll come out as soon as you get good and hungry," replied the sheriff, and onlookers roared with laughter. The sheriff pointed out, "Mrs. Herrera is at liberty to leave the building any time she sees fit to end this stunt. She will not be prosecuted; she is to be pitied."

Indeed, the tragically deluded woman, formerly a respected historian and civic leader, seems to relish the primitive conditions to which she has subjected herself. Yesterday she even knelt and lapped water like a dog. Despite her rather alarming appearance, she demands an audience with Governor Campbell.

Mr. Wilton Peck, local representative of the Philadelphia hotel company that has generously offered to undertake the expense of parking the unsightly warehouse grounds, had these comments: "I pray that this unfortunate woman will do no harm to herself. My only concern is to look after her welfare and remove her from the building uninjured, so that she may enjoy a long rest." His company has further offered to pay for her rehabilitation at Dr. Moody's Sanitarium for Nervous and Mental Diseases once she vacates the building.

Mrs. Edna Duvalier, vice-president of the local chapter of the DRT, added: "Our chapter president, Mrs. Alva Carson Keane, has been recognized as the rightful custodian of the property. It is galling to all law-abiding Daughters of the Republic that one who is no longer connected with our organization is persevering in this embarrassing and illegal behavior. Mrs. Herrera does not deserve the kindness that Mr. Peck and Sheriff Tobin have shown her; she has been on the warpath for several years and will stop at nothing."

When asked whether the Daughters were concerned about the unfavorable attention Mrs. Herrera has drawn to the Alamo, Mrs. Duvalier pointed out vehemently, "Mrs. Herrera is not in the Alamo. She is in the Hugo & Schmeltzer warehouse—although in her present state of mind, I doubt whether she has even the vaguest idea where she is."

71

By the second day Rose Herrera's siege had become a fiesta, a Fourth of July picnic in February. Once the *Journal* hit the streets, dozens of people flocked to the Hugo & Schmeltzer building, hoping to get a glimpse of the crazy lady inside. They waited for the sheriff to make his next move. In the meantime, curio hawkers circulated, offering Mexican trinkets and sweets. Mariachis entertained the crowd. At noon a few chili vendors moved their stands from Military Plaza to the Alamo.

Though Rose had no glass in her room, she could imagine how she looked after thirty-odd hours inside the old convent. She tried to pin her unruly bouffant and smooth her wrinkled gown. But she couldn't spare any water to wash her face. That day she mostly kept back in the shadows.

Poppy's sandwich had been enough to stave off her hunger. Her biggest problem the second day was cabin fever. She paced. She had too much time to think, and she thought too much about Antonio, and about Rafael Menchaca. As the hours wore on, she realized she couldn't hold up to another day of this. She tried to figure out a way to end the standoff without surrendering.

That afternoon the sheriff's deputy, lulled by the music and the holiday atmosphere, grew lax. One of the curio hawkers kept her eye on him. When he stepped away from the building to buy a tamale, she darted up to the window with her basket of clay figures. She placed two on the ledge: a matador and a bull.

"Para qué?" asked Rose.

305

Before the girl could explain, the deputy saw her. "You! Get away from there!" he shouted.

The girl fled and disappeared into the crowd. The deputy ran toward the window. Quickly Rose reached through the iron grating and pulled the two statues inside.

"Give those to me," demanded the deputy.

"They're not for you," she replied.

"The sheriff said you can't have anything."

"He said I can't have any food," she corrected. "What do you think I'm going to do with these, eat them?"

The deputy swore and stepped away.

Rose knew the girl was Menchaca's daughter. But the figures had none of the precision and artistry of the ones she'd seen before. They were more like miniature piñatas, bulky and crude. Then it dawned on her: these weren't to keep. She shook the matador. Something moved inside. She dropped it on the stone floor and smiled when it shattered. Out rolled an orange. She cracked the bull against the wall and found two more.

Late that afternoon Wilton Peck returned to the plaza, smugly satisfied. After the *Journal* article, he was confident the public was solidly on his side. He asked Sheriff Tobin: "Don't you think we could start wrecking the north end of the building tomorrow? It wouldn't put that loony in any danger."

The sheriff nodded. "I don't see why not."

He was going to say more, but just then a group of mariachis, which included Enrique Herrera and Rafael Menchaca, started playing nearby. Peck and the sheriff stepped aside, annoyed. Had either of them understood Spanish, or had they noticed the woman in the Alamo smiling in delight, they would have fallen over each other in their haste to silence the seditious anthem.

ROSE OF THE ALAMO

Words and Music by Enrique Herrera

You obreros who toil in the factories,
You peónes who till the land:
Put your tools down and come to the plaza
To lend a brave comrade a hand.
She's hungry and tired, but determined.
Won't you bolster her final stand?
Rose, Rose of the Alamo,
Though some of her Daughters forsake her,
Rose, Rose of the Alamo,
Nothing can ever break her.

Don't give up on your struggle, fair lady.
Juan Ramírez is here in the yard.
Madame Guenther has sent for assistance.
Miss Lovett is standing guard.
And that proud Philadelphia peacock
Is about to get feathered and tarred.
Rose, Rose of the Alamo,
Noble and lion-hearted,
Rose, Rose of the Alamo,
Finish this battle you started.

72

It was after sunset on the second day before she saw Antonio on the plaza. Just about everyone else had gone. He was talking to the deputy, who gave him permission to approach her window. His eyes were red and swollen. She wondered if he'd been crying, or drinking, or just unable to sleep.

Neither of them knew how to start. Finally she said, "I watched for you all day. Yesterday, too. I didn't know if you'd come."

"I went to see the judge this afternoon," he told her. "If you give this up tomorrow, he promised not to hold you in contempt of court." He seemed more sad than bitter.

She tried to smile. "You didn't have to get involved. I never asked you to help me, counselor."

"You did once before. I was proud to stand by your side at the convention."

She felt tears coming. "Antonio. . . ."

"What I can't understand is, I thought you and I were a team again. I was happy to be your partner . . . ." His voice cracked. He couldn't finish.

She had expected cold fury from him; she hadn't counted on breaking his heart. She wiped her cheeks. "Stand by me now, Antonio."

He shook his head. "We had an understanding. You were going to fight this battle within the limits of the law."

"The law!" For a moment her temper flared. "My father lost everything he had under the law."

"That may be true. But my whole life revolves around the law, Rose. I can't follow where you're going."

"Antonio," she whispered, "what about us?"

He seemed resolved, as if he had already thought about that. "When you come home, we'll run our household the same as before. We'll raise our son. We'll go out in public. But don't demand anything else from me. I don't know how to be your partner any more. Not after this."

"I still love you," she told him.

His eyes were damp. The deputy came over. "The sheriff says that everyone has to clear the plaza now," he announced.

Antonio took a deep breath. "Remember what the judge offered."

"It's too late . . ." she whispered.

He nodded. "I know. Goodbye, Rose. Good luck."

Antonio turned and walked away. She watched him in the lamp light until he got in the rockaway across the plaza. Santos shook the reins, and the coach took off for Alamo Heights. She kept watching until it disappeared into the night. Quickly she closed the window shutters and fastened the latches.

THE WESTERN UNION TELEGRAPH COMPANY.
——————— INCORPORATED ———————
23,000 OFFICES IN AMERICA. CABLE SERVICE TO ALL THE WORLD.

San Antonio Texas Feb. 12th-1908.
Mrs. Alva Carson Keane,
            Ansonia Hotel, 2109 Broadway, New York N.Y.
Rose fading fast my patron will you not help our friend?

                                    Mathilda Guenther.

0354pm

All through Wednesday a cold, persistent drizzle had fallen over New York. It chiseled away at the previous week's muddy snow, which turned to ice again as night set in. From the long windows of her study, Alva Carson Keane watched two men trying to dig their delivery wagon out of a snowbank along Broadway.

That morning Alva and Robert Keane had stood with Max Rosenthal in Times Square to watch the start of the New York-to-Paris automobile race. Its course would cover 20,000 miles through Alaska and Siberia. Alva had stared solemnly at the six motorcars on the line. In each driver, behind the goggles and motoring scarves, she'd seen Rose Herrera. Finally she had excused herself and gone back to the Ansonia Hotel.

The young author was in the thick of writing *Maribel, The Girl Who Saved Mission San José*. But it was hard for her to focus. Every few hours Edna Duvalier sent her another telegram, keeping the savior of the Alamo abreast of all the details throughout the siege. Alva hadn't responded. Time was running out.

Earlier she'd been ready to send her DRT colleague and the hotel man cables of reassurance and drop Madame Guenther's telegram in the dustbin. But after seeing the automobiles that morning, her will was starting to crumble. She'd never liked Wilton Peck. As a matter of fact, she detested the shifty-eyed, pandering little toad.

Nor was she particularly fond of Edna Duvalier. Recently she'd learned that her most vocal supporter in Texas had exaggerated many claims to serve her own purposes.

But the whole Alamo mess had spun out of control. Alva doubted whether she still had the power to get the Carson Daughters in San Antonio to relent. And she couldn't very well intervene from New York.

Not that she should, actually. She still thought her idea for an Alamo park and a monument to the frontier cattlemen was an inspired one.

On the other hand, had she known how strongly Rose felt about those walls, she never would have announced her plan to tear them down. And what if it turned out that the walls were original after all? She had never given that possibility any serious thought. But now she was worried. She had to admit that Rose had the better knowledge of Alamo history. If Alva Carson Keane were someday blamed for demolishing part of the old mission, Texans would rise up against her, changing her sobriquet to the Destroyer of the Alamo.

But she'd made up her mind and spoken it publicly. She couldn't back down now. What would her daddy think if she caved in? What's more, her former partner had betrayed her and insulted her family, calling the Carsons robbers and scavengers. Rose deserved whatever humiliation she was in for.

Alva went back to her writing desk. She was about to draft a telegram to Edna Duvalier when she glanced at her notes for the final chapter of *Maribel:* the delicate Mexican flower bravely holding Mission San José, defying the corrupt developers even unto death, while the wrecking ball sent the stone walls crashing down around her. The image gave the author chills. The end of the story was in her hands, at least in her novel.

And perhaps in San Antonio as well. . . .

Suddenly she threw her pen down on her desk. Damn it all! She knew whose side she really wanted to be on. She thought about those rides in the Peerless, the lively conversations, the laughs they'd shared, the obstacles they'd faced together. Alva had never liked to have enemies or hold grudges.

She also realized who was likely to emerge as the heroine of this incident. Alva herself had become a legend in Laredo merely by keeping five Mexican cattle rustlers at bay; now Rose was successfully fending off the law, the Willingham Hotel Company, and the most powerful business interests in Texas. Oddly enough, Alva wished she were in the Alamo with Rose. Of course, it was much too late for that. The most honorable thing she could do at this stage would be to try to convince the Carson Daughters to call off the wrecking crew. The only problem was finding a way to surrender without losing face.

Then she got an idea. She grinned, excited. Alva wasn't going to surrender. Instead, she was going to attempt a daring rescue. If it worked, she could still come out of this episode a heroine along with Rose.

She found her husband puffing on his pipe in the drawing room, reading the *Wall Street Journal*. "Keane. I need you to do something for me. I'm going to write an article for the wire service. I want it on the front page in every city across the country tomorrow morning."

He raised his eyebrows. "Tomorrow?"

"Yes. In the early edition."

He sighed. What she was asking him to do was to go out in the freezing rain, take a taxicab through the slush to his office way down on Broad Street, find a security guard to let him in, find a maintenance man to turn up the heat, track down a copy editor, and spend the rest of this miserable night making sure every UAPA newspaper in America printed his wife's article before daybreak.

But he owed it to her. They both knew that. Recently she had learned about two of his dalliances: one involving a señorita at the Laredo Halloween masquerade, the other a fifty-dollar-a-week showgirl after the opening of *Angelina, Sweetheart!*

"Yes, Alva," he said.

"Make sure my byline is in fourteen-point type. And boldfaced."

Then she went back to her study. Fervently she started scribbling away at the article. She paused, smiling to herself.

"Rose, I think I'll give you . . . "

A fierce blast of wet wind swept down Seventy-Third Street, rattling her window.

"A chill wind wailing," she decided. "Yes! And rats."

That night in Alamo Heights, Eloisa awoke with a start and sat up in her bed. At first the cook panicked, certain there was a prowler in the kitchen. Then she realized it was only another miracle. She sighed, murmuring thanks to the Holy Mother, and went back to sleep.

* * * United American Press Association News Service * * *
* * * For Immediate Release * * *
* * *Thursday, February 13, 1908 * * *

FAIR TEXAS HEROINE HOLDING ALAMO AGAINST ALL ODDS

BY ALVA CARSON KEANE

In utter darkness, without food or water for over forty-eight hours, Rose De León Herrera continues her solitary siege of the Alamo—while the wrecking ball, that black, pitiless sphere of destruction, looms overhead, poised to crush this delicate Mexican flower in her lovely prime.

Early Tuesday morning she barricaded herself in the room where her grandfather fell beneath the tyrant's sword—to prevent that building from being razed. With the flaming passion so characteristic of her ancestors, she declared that she would go down beneath the wrecking ball before she would surrender.

Faint from hunger—exhausted for want of sleep and begrimed from exposure—she is completely cut off from the world outside. She has no place to lie down, and nothing to keep her warm but the clothes she wore into the Alamo. The electricity has been cut, but still she holds the fort from the cold, dark room, while rats scamper over her feet and the chill wind wails mournfully through the rafters above her.

How much longer can the brave little heroine endure these harsh conditions? Already her strength is slipping away like sand through an hour-glass. Unless Governor Campbell intervenes on her behalf, her friends fear that by tomorrow evening her courageous soul may be wafted upward to that resplendent world that admits no pain or sorrow—leaving only rubble and dust to mark the site of her last, valiant struggle on this terrestrial ball.

THE WESTERN UNION TELEGRAPH COMPANY.
——— I N C O R P O R A T E D ———
23,000 OFFICES IN AMERICA. CABLE SERVICE TO ALL THE WORLD.

Washington D.C. Feb. 13th-1908.
Mrs. Rose Herrera,
     1211 Townsend Avenue, San Antonio Texas.
Stick to what you think right all Washington is with you
your patriotism will be remembered long after your cow-
ardly opponents are forgotten.
Clara Root.

0832am

74

Alva's plan turned out to be more brilliant than even she had realized. Thanks to the wire service, Wednesday's Texas madwoman was reborn as Thursday's American heroine. Mrs. Root's telegram was only one among hundreds. Some were addressed to Rose, but many others flooded Governor Campbell's office. There were telephone calls, too, as an outraged public demanded that the governor take immediate action to protect the "delicate Mexican flower" who was fearlessly holding the Alamo.

Rose, of course, knew nothing of all this. She awoke early the third morning to the sound of heavy equipment. She crossed herself, wondering how long she should wait before she came out. For a moment she toyed with the idea of actually going down beneath the wrecking ball. But if she waited that long, she reasoned, the whole building would already be leveled, and she would have perished for nothing, except to make Wilton Peck and Edna Duvalier happy.

But before long the sound stopped. She went to the window. She couldn't see the wrecking crane. All she heard was a man's muffled, angry voice.

Outside Wilton Peck kicked the ground. "God damn it! You promised we could start today," he told the sheriff.

"The governor's office says wait," replied Sheriff Tobin. "Hell, I can't fight the public and Austin, too."

All that morning Rose anxiously wondered what was going on. At noon Sheriff Tobin brought her some water, even a sandwich.

"What's happening?" she asked him. "What's this for?"

"Shut up and eat it," he grumbled. "And fix your hair."

She saw her friend Lorena Lovett holding a placard: "Hold on, Rose, help on the way." Everyone was excited about something. The mariachis sang "Rose of the Alamo" several times. Rose waved to her DRT sisters, to Enrique, to Madame Guenther. But despite their support, she felt very much alone. She knew Antonio wouldn't be back.

It was late in the day before Sheriff Tobin approached the window again. "You have visitors," he said after he spat.

By then the crowd filled the plaza, extending as far as the Menger Hotel. In front of the Alamo chapel Senator Pratt was hovering near a group from Austin, trying hard to be photographed. No doubt he was taking credit for handling the crisis. Nearby Lorena Lovett was leading an elderly man by the arm.

"Tell them I'll be glad to receive them," Rose instructed the sheriff.

"You'd better be damned glad," he growled. "And fix your hair."

A few minutes later, after making herself as presentable as she could, she slid the bolt back and threw open the door. Sheriff Tobin was standing on the other side. He looked grim. At first she thought he was going to arrest her. But as he stepped aside, she saw the group pouring into the corridor behind him.

"Only Governor Campbell, if you please," she said with a sharp look at Hobo Pratt. "And Don Ramírez, if he would be so kind."

The others retreated. The governor bowed, gallant and good-humored. "Madam, I remember you from last fall. The banquet for Secretary Root."

She walked up to him and extended her hand. "Sir, how long were you going to let me wait before you rescued me?"

"Actually, I thought I was here to surrender," he admitted.

She smiled at him, satisfied. "Then come with me, please. Let me give you the Alamo."

And so the standoff ended. While the rest of the group waited outside, Rose walked the length of the Hugo & Schmeltzer with Juan Ramírez at one side and Governor Campbell on the other. She pointed out the places where the rebels fell.

Ramírez squinted in the darkness. Eventually he said, "The roof used to be flat. Mexican style."

"And the walls, señor?" she pressed.

"Yes, these are the walls that were here when I was young," replied the old man. "Fermin showed me many times."

The governor peered at him. "Don Ramírez, are you absolutely certain these are the same walls?"

Rose held her breath. Ramírez didn't respond immediately. He seemed to be trying to remember something. Then, carefully, he proceeded to a place along the west wall. He stooped and wiped the dust off several stones near the floor before he found what he was looking for. "Aquí."

The governor and Rose drew near him. At first they didn't see anything. Then, after Ramírez pointed again, they noticed some letters carved in the stone, very faint. They made out two names: "Fermin" and "Juan."

The old man stood up. "I'll never forget the whipping my papa gave us when he saw what we'd done."

The governor smiled. "That's good enough for me. But to make things official, I'll appoint a committee to study the masonry," he promised. "No one's going to tear down any part of the Alamo that was built in the Spanish days."

Rose sent up a quick prayer of thanks. They concluded their tour in her chamber on the southwest corner. "There was no way out," she remarked. "My grandfather, all of them—they knew they didn't stand a chance."

They contemplated the room in silence. Finally Governor Campbell said, "Those men may have started out as fortune-hunters. But you have to admit they were brave in the end."

"They took a risk," was her vague reply.

Governor Campbell held the door for her. As they headed down the corridor, Juan Ramírez told her, "Your father used to say: of all his children, you were the most like Francisco."

She nodded.

"Fermin was brave, too," he added. "His luck turned bad. He shouldn't have ended up like that."

Quickly she glanced away, brushing the back of her hand across her cheek. Then she took the old man's arm. The governor was close behind them. She shielded her eyes from the evening sun as they stepped out onto the plaza.

AUTHOR'S NOTE

This story was inspired by actual events that occurred between 1903 and 1908. Adina De Zavala, an ardent San Antonio preservationist, and Clara Driscoll, a wealthy socialite and writer, joined forces to rescue the Alamo convent from commercial developers, then had a public falling-out over how to use the property once it was in their hands. Their bitter feud ignited a statewide controversy. De Zavala's defiant, solitary standoff at the Alamo in February 1908 made the front page of the *New York Times* three days in a row. In the end, the original convent walls were saved from complete destruction through the perseverance of De Zavala and many other Daughters of the Republic of Texas (however, the second story was torn down in 1913). De Zavala's lifelong efforts to preserve the old Spanish mission finally bore fruit in 1968, thirteen years after her death, when the DRT opened the restored convent as a museum.